THE FRONTIERS SAGA

PART 2: ROGUE CASTES

EPISODE 9

I AM JUSTICE

RYK BROWN

The Frontiers Saga Part 2: Rogue Castes
Episode #9: I Am Justice

CHAPTER ONE

Nathan stood at the podium, looking out at the cheering crowds gathered in the memorial square at the center of Rakuen's capital city. Thousands had come to witness this historic moment. The moment when Rakuen and Neramese put their past conflicts behind them, allied with the Karuzari, and became part of the galactic human community, once again.

The old traditions and attitudes of their founders had kept them all but isolated for far too long. The jump drive had brought increased wealth and prosperity to both worlds, and recent events had convinced most people that the time for change was upon them. Unfortunately, the refusal of their elders to embrace such change had nearly torn their world apart.

Those who had opposed the change had been swept aside by a single act of violence, proving that the will of the people of Rakuen could not be stopped; not by foolish, old men who feared change. Now, the people of *both* worlds had come together to celebrate their new alliance and to hail the man who not only made it possible, but had saved their entire system from certain destruction at the hands of the Dusahn.

The cheers began to subside, replaced by a chant that grew in intensity with each cycle. *Na-Tan, Na-Tan, Na-tan...* The infectious chant rapidly grew in volume as more joined in. Taking advantage of the moment, Ito Yokimah stepped forward and took Nathan's left hand, raising it triumphantly in the air with his own, prompting an instant doubling of volume in the crowd. The chant swelled into a deafening roar as the crowd celebrated their new hero.

Nathan held both hands in the air, even after Ito stepped back out of the spotlight. After a few seconds, he lowered his hands, placing them on the podium before him. He nodded his appreciation to the crowd, over and over again, as he waited for their cheers to die down. Finally, he spoke; his words echoing through the loudspeakers surrounding the square.

"I am but a single soul. Alone, I am powerless, but when joined with thousands, with tens of thousands, with *hundreds* of thousands, *we* are an *unstoppable* force!"

The crowd erupted again, causing him to pause.

"A force for justice! A force for equality! A force for *freedom*!"

Again, Nathan paused, allowing the thousands gathered before him to express their emotions.

"Today, the accords that created *decades* of mistrust, and prevented Neramese and Rakuen from achieving their *true* potential, have been swept aside by the leaders of *both worlds*!" Nathan continued. "*Today*, you are no longer just Rakuens or Nerameseans, all of you are also *Rogens*! Proud and strong! And it is my honor to welcome you *all* into the Karuzari Alliance!"

The crowd erupted into a mixture of cheers and chants of *Na-Tan, Na-Tan.*

"History will mark this day as the beginning of the end of Dusahn tyranny," Nathan continued, nearly yelling into the microphones to be heard over the roar of the crowd. "The people of the Pentaurus sector, the Bellius sector, the Rogen sector, and all sectors between and around them, will herald this day! As our victories mount, the worlds of these sectors will join our alliance! And our numbers will no longer be in the hundreds of thousands! Not even in the millions! The souls joined together for the cause of freedom from oppression will number in the *trillions*!"

The cheers swelled even louder, to the point of challenging nature's thunder itself. Nathan stood proudly, his hands held high, again. After a moment of cheers, he reached out for the hands of Ito Yokimah, Rakuen's interim minister, and Minister Cornell of Neramese. The three of them raised their hands together, celebrating the historic moment along with their people.

Nathan wondered what exactly the history books would say about this day. Would they see it as he had played it? As the beginning of a new era? Or would they discover the truth about how this moment actually came to be?

* * *

Doctor Symyri had been kind enough to send a pair of medical techs to help move Miri's stasis pod from the Seiiki's hangar bay to his medical center deep within Sanctuary. As promised, the arrival inspection process had been far quicker than their first visit, possibly due to the influence of the good doctor.

Unfortunately, the actual medical facility had been considerably further than the doctor's business offices had been. Without the use of the transport tube shuttles, it would have taken them hours to reach their destination.

The transport tube system was extremely complex. Fully automated, it allowed those who could afford it rapid transit between any two sections within the asteroid colony. After an eight-minute, high-speed shuttle ride, they had reached their destination and were walking the corridors toward Doctor Symyri's medical center.

The route clearly marked, Jessica led the entourage through the maze of corridors. The local medical techs handled Miri's stasis pod, and Lieutenant Rezhik and his men provided escort, with Doctor Chen and Doctor Sato following.

The entrance to the medical center was fairly nondescript. It didn't even look like a hospital. Double doors parted automatically as Jessica approached, and a young man in medical attire, data pad in hand, was waiting for them.

"The Scott-Thornton party?" the man asked, already knowing the answer when he spotted two of his medical techs escorting the stasis pod.

"Yes," Jessica replied.

"Room four," the man said, his response directed more toward the medical techs managing the stasis pod than to the rest of them.

Lieutenant Rezhik glanced at the signs above the doors, immediately spotting the aforementioned room and heading toward it.

"I'm sorry, but only medical personnel and family are allowed in the examination rooms," the young man insisted.

Lieutenant Rezhik glared at him. "Where she goes, we go," he stated emphatically.

The young man's expression changed instantly, unsure of how to respond. "Uh..." He looked to Jessica, whom he assumed was their leader.

"Security," Jessica told him.

"I assure you, this facility is more than secure."

"We just waltzed right in," Jessica pointed out.

"Only because we were expecting you," the young man defended. "And those two are our medical technicians, with appropriate access badges."

"Then, give us appropriate access badges, as well," Jessica suggested.

The young man was flabbergasted. "I'm afraid it's not that simple. There are background checks, procedures... It takes days..."

Jessica stepped over next to the nervous young man, putting her arm around his shoulders. "The lady in that stasis pod is Captain Scott's sister. You know who Captain Scott is, don't you?"

"Of course," the young man assured her. "Na-Tan."

"Correct," Jessica replied. "And *Na-Tan* has entrusted his *sole* surviving family member to *myself* and *these four men*, and believe me when I tell you that we are quite serious about that responsibility." Jessica looked into the young man's eyes. "*Deadly* serious."

The man swallowed hard, his eyes darting back and forth. "Can they at least change into clean attire before the examination process?"

"I don't know," Jessica replied. "Whattaya got?"

"Uh...I'm sure we can find them something," the young man promised. "But, I'll have to clear it with my supervisor first."

"Might I suggest you go directly to Doctor Symyri?" Jessica urged.

"Of course," the young man replied, eager to extract himself from the situation.

"He's just trying to keep the exam room as sterile as possible," Doctor Chen assured Jessica as soon as the young man departed.

"I'm sure he is," Jessica replied, seemingly unconcerned. "Vasya, Brill, check the perimeter.

This floor, the one above, and the one below. Junior should be back with clean duds for us by the time you return."

"What do we do if someone objects to us poking around?" Corporal Vasya asked.

"Give them your best Ghatazhak death stare," Jessica suggested. She looked at the corporal's boyish face. "Maybe Brill should give them the look," she added with a slight grin.

"Funny," the corporal replied as he and the specialist moved past her.

"Perhaps one of us should accompany them," one of the medical techs suggested. "In case they have any questions."

"Good idea," Jessica agreed. "We can handle the stasis pod ourselves, right, doc?" she asked Doctor Chen.

"Stasis pods are designed to run automatically for hundreds of years, if need be. So, yes, I think we'll be okay for a few minutes."

"Give them the grand tour, then," Jessica instructed the medical tech.

* * *

"You handled that quite well," General Telles congratulated Nathan as he escorted him from the stage to the Reaper waiting nearby. The crowds were still cheering as he and the general disappeared into the Reaper's passenger bay.

"Take us back to the ship," Nathan ordered the pilot as he activated the door controls.

"Aye, sir," the pilot replied.

"It would have been a lot easier if you had waited until *after* the signing to tell me who *really* killed Minister Sebaron."

"He was an obstacle to our cause and to the

security of his own people," General Telles replied calmly as he took his seat.

"I'm sure he was," Nathan agreed, fastening his seatbelt. "But that was for his people to decide, not your blade."

"His people *had* decided," General Telles countered. "The minister refused to listen. My blade only hastened the inevitable with far less loss of life."

"Perhaps," Nathan admitted as the shuttle rose off the ground. "But his resignation could have been achieved without taking his life, given time."

"*Time* is a commodity in short supply," General Telles insisted. "The Dusahn *will* attack again, and soon. They have no alternative. To ignore the Rogen system invites failure. Minister Sebaron was a fool to believe that Rakuen could defend itself against the Dusahn. You and I both know this, Captain. Every minute he remained in power brought his world one step closer to destruction. Even his *people* knew this."

"Which is precisely *why* we should have sought a less violent resolution," Nathan argued.

"Were circumstances more favorable, I might agree with you. Unfortunately, the good minister brought his doom upon himself when he illegally seized Karuzari assets. Illegally by the laws of his *own world*, I might add. Laws that he was *sworn* to uphold. The man was without honor, and without wisdom. I feel no guilt over the taking of his miserable life."

Nathan looked at Telles, one eyebrow raised.

"Frankly, Captain, it worries me that you are so bothered by my actions. Can you honestly tell me it was a mistake to assassinate Minister Sebaron?"

"I never said it was a mistake," Nathan pointed

out. The shuttle jumped from the lower atmosphere of Rakuen to a few kilometers away from the Aurora's position orbiting the Rogen sun, halfway between the orbits of Rakuen and Neramese. "I just wish there had been another way."

"Are you saying that, had you been present at the time, you would *not* have authorized the assassination?" General Telles asked directly.

"No, I'm sure I would have," Nathan sighed. "And that's what bothers me."

"I'm afraid I do not understand," the general admitted.

"That it *doesn't* bother me," Nathan explained, "when I feel like it should."

"Leaders must decide who lives and dies on a daily basis during times of war," the general reminded him. "If it makes you feel any better, the fact that you still question the morality of assassination, even in the face of overwhelming evidence that such an act is necessary for the greater good of all, should put your mind somewhat at ease."

Nathan looked at the general. "It doesn't," he replied, leaning back in his seat and closing his eyes for a moment.

* * *

"This facility is *definitely* more advanced than anything we have back on Earth," Doctor Chen announced as she wandered the room, examining the various devices.

"More advanced than anything from Nifelm *or* Corinair, as well," Doctor Sato added. "And it's only the examination room."

Doctor Chen stopped at a large, multi-jointed arm with some sort of a scanner head attached to the end of it. "I have no idea what this is," she admitted.

"Some type of scanning device?" Jessica suggested.

Doctor Sato touched a view screen on the console in the corner of the room, causing it to come to life. "Oh, my," she exclaimed. "I think it's a molecular scanner."

"What's that?" Jessica wondered.

"It's like our medical scanner on the Aurora, only instead of giving you images of tissues and structures inside the body, it gives you images at the molecular level," Doctor Chen explained. "We've been experimenting with something similar on Earth but have yet to perfect the technology."

"It's probably more similar to your medical scanner than you think," the medical tech explained. "It scans at the molecular level and then uses that data to build images of any structure within the body, allowing you to see them with as much detail as if you were holding them in your hand. More, in fact, since it can see *inside* those structures, right down to the molecular level."

"We could really use one of these on the Aurora," Doctor Chen admitted.

"There are portable versions," the medical tech assured her. "They are commonly used on the battlefield or by emergency responders. There are even handheld versions, although they are nowhere near as powerful or accurate as the clinical models."

"You know how to use this?" Doctor Sato asked the young man.

"I know how to *operate* it, yes. However, I am not qualified to offer a definitive diagnosis based on its scans. That would be up to the doctor," the tech insisted.

"Don't worry, I wasn't going to ask you to," Doctor Sato assured him.

"Mister Selly is far too modest," Doctor Symyri said as he entered the exam room. "He is one of my best medical technicians." The doctor paused, looking at Doctor Sato. "You must be Doctor Sato," he gushed, moving to shake her hand.

"I am," Doctor Sato replied, appearing a bit uneasy.

"I am Doctor Nikolori Symyri," he said, bowing respectfully as he took her hand. "It is an honor to meet you, Doctor Sato. I am a great admirer of your work and that of the late Doctor Megel. Such a tragic loss. My deepest condolences."

"Thank you," Doctor Sato replied.

"And you must be the infamous Doctor Chen," Doctor Symyri said, turning his attention to Melei with equal fervor. "The one doctor in all the galaxy whom the legendary Captain Scott trusts." Doctor Symyri reached out to shake Melei's hand as he bowed respectfully. "I am equally honored. I hope he will soon have that same trust in me."

"I am honored, as well," Doctor Chen replied.

Doctor Symyri looked around. "Where is the good captain?"

"He was unable to return with us," Jessica explained. "We have been tasked with the patient's protection."

"I see," the doctor replied. "It would be better if he were here."

"Responsibilities of his position, I'm afraid," Jessica replied.

"You have an impressive facility," Doctor Chen interrupted. "It appears that you have diagnostic methods unfamiliar to us."

"Being located on Sanctuary has given me an unparalleled advantage. So many people come through this world, selling so many goods and information. It is a veritable gold mine of technology, science, and culture that, I suspect, is without equal anywhere in the galaxy. Were I based in the average hospital, or in the medical department of a starship, my expertise would be significantly diminished." Doctor Symyri paused for a moment, appearing horrified. "Oh, dear, I hope that didn't seem as egotistical and insulting as it sounded."

"Not at all," Doctor Chen assured him. "I understood your intended meaning."

Doctor Symyri sighed with relief. "Oh, thank God. It is always such a delicate moment, meeting people whose culture and mannerisms are unfamiliar. It can be so easy to say the wrong thing." The doctor leaned closer to Doctor Chen for a moment. "*Wars* have started for less, you know."

"I assure you, we are not overly sensitive."

"Good, good, good," the doctor replied. "Now, the first order of business is to review *your* findings. I assume you have brought them with you?"

"Of course," Doctor Chen replied, handing her data pad to Doctor Symyri.

"Yes, yes, yes," the elder doctor muttered as he examined the medical information displayed on Doctor Chen's data pad. "I see, I see," he said as he scrolled through the pages.

"I'm afraid our scans are not as sophisticated as yours," Doctor Chen apologized. "We have yet to perfect molecular scanning technology."

"Of course, of course," Doctor Symyri replied. He glanced up from the data pad for a moment, looking at Doctor Chen. "A tip for your people...it's all in the rendering software. The molecular scanning head is a simple device, from an engineering standpoint. But the medical AI is a beast of a program. I never would have been able to perfect this system were it not for the help of the Lisorens. Greatest coders in all the galaxy, they are." He returned to the data pad, sighing as he read on. "I was afraid of this."

"Afraid of what?" Doctor Sato wondered.

"These are the most recent scans?"

"Taken twenty-four hours ago," Doctor Chen replied. "What is the problem?"

"The corinite component that I mentioned before, they are affecting the majority of the tissues in her body."

"What?" Doctor Chen replied in disbelief. "We didn't detect any spread."

"Here, and here," Doctor Symyri explained. "The slight shift in electrolytes, the increased number of mutated cells..."

"What mutated cells?" Doctor Chen defended. "We detected no mutated cells, only traumatized ones."

"You have to know what to look for," Doctor Symyri explained. "Which you could only know after *years* of experience with a molecular scanner."

"What are you saying?" Jessica demanded to know.

"The patient must be moved to one of *our* medical stasis units, *immediately*. Corinite radiation is not slowed by RMS pods. The body's reduced metabolic state does impede its spread to some degree, but it does not stop it. This is another reason that I insisted you come," Doctor Symyri added, looking at Doctor Sato. "It may be difficult to find enough unaffected tissue to successfully clone her most severely damaged organs. Furthermore, the spread of the corinite radiation may cause problems when she is brought *out* of RMS. She may not survive long enough to transfer her to one of our medical stasis pods."

"You're saying she could die?" Jessica asked, looking for confirmation.

"I am," Doctor Symyri admitted. "But if we do not move her, she will undoubtedly die, and soon."

"How soon?" Jessica asked.

"I'm guessing weeks," Doctor Chen said.

"Possibly less," Doctor Symyri warned. "We must move quickly."

Doctor Chen sighed, looking at Jessica, then back at Doctor Symyri. "Any chance we can confirm your suspicions using your molecular scanner?"

"To some extent, yes, but your RMS pod will cause some inaccuracies, I'm afraid."

"So, you can't verify his opinion," Jessica said, looking at Doctor Chen.

"No, I suppose I cannot."

Jessica looked at Doctor Chen, becoming concerned. "Can you clone her?" she asked Michi. "Like you cloned Nathan?"

"It is possible," Michi replied, "but we don't have a scan of her memories and personality. She'd be a clean slate."

"But you *can* clone her damaged organs for replantation," Jessica surmised.

"Yes," Michi assured her, "even if they *are* already radiated. I can correct any deformities that are found. But the procedures require either a live, stable patient or a corpse. She would need to *survive* the resuscitation process."

Jessica sighed, looking to Doctor Chen again.

"You cannot ask me to make this decision, Jess," Melei objected. "This is for Nathan to decide."

"Agreed, but I *am* asking for your advice, just like Nathan would if he were here."

Corporal Vasya and Specialist Brill appeared at the observation window, tapping on the glass to get Lieutenant Rezhik's attention.

"Pardon me a moment," the lieutenant told Jessica.

Doctor Chen took a slow, deep breath. "*If* Doctor Symyri's interpretation of *our* rudimentary scans is correct..."

"*Are* they?"

"I assure you, they are," Doctor Symyri insisted.

"Assume for the moment they are," Doctor Chen told her. "If we try to save her, she might die. If we do nothing, she will most certainly die. The only thing in question is, *when*?"

"What happens if we wait?" Jessica wondered.

"Wait for what?" Doctor Symyri asked.

"For a better option," Jessica replied.

"There is no better option, I'm afraid," Doctor Symyri insisted.

"Even if there were, it is doubtful she would survive long enough," Doctor Chen added. "Even if Doctor Symyri's assumptions are incorrect."

"They are not *assumptions*," Doctor Symyri defended.

"Sensitivities, Doctor?" Melei challenged.

"Quite right, my apologies," Doctor Symyri replied, dipping his head in acknowledgment of her point.

"Then, you think we should wake her and move her to one of *his* medical pods," Jessica surmised.

"My recommendation would be that you get

Nathan back here as quickly as possible, so *he* can make that decision."

"Very well," Jessica replied, tapping her comm-set. "Josh, Jess. You copy?"

"*A little brok...n, but ...copy,*" Josh replied over her comm-set.

"Take the Seiki back to the Aurora and fetch Nathan, ASAP."

"*I thou... he ...too busy......come?*"

"Don't give him a choice. Understood?"

"*But we......got here!*"

"Josh," Jessica warned.

"*On o... way,*" he replied, recognizing her tone.

"How long will it take for him to get here?" Doctor Symyri wondered.

"At least eighteen hours," Jessica replied. "She will survive *that* long, won't she?"

"I certainly hope so," Doctor Symyri replied.

"A moment?" Lieutenant Rezhik asked Jessica, having just returned to the room.

Jessica followed the lieutenant out of the examination room and into the observation chamber, where Vasya and Brill were waiting.

"Nice duds," Corporal Vasya said, commenting on the medical uniforms that Jessica and the lieutenant were both wearing.

"What's up?" Jessica asked the corporal.

"This place is a joke," Vasya reported.

"What do you mean?"

"I mean, the security is practically nonexistent. It's a glass house, with open windows."

Jessica looked at Brill, who nodded his agreement. "Cameras? Card locks?"

"They have them, yes, but they don't have any

response teams. They just call it in to Sanctuary Security," Vasya explained.

"What kind of response time?"

"A few minutes, at best, unless someone just *happens* to be in the area."

"The card locks take all of five seconds to bypass," Specialist Brill added.

"What about those?" Jessica wondered, pointing at the small emitters in the upper corners of the room. "Aren't they stunners?"

"Yeah, but they have to get an *activation code* from Sanctuary Security Command to use them," Corporal Vasya replied. "Like I said, a joke."

"How many men would it take to make this facility secure?"

"Well, there are only two entry points, so at least four, and probably another two roaming," Vasya suggested.

"And another two as backup," the lieutenant added.

"And at least two shifts," Brill chimed in.

Jessica sighed. "Can we hack the stunners?"

"Probably," Specialist Brill replied. "But I'd sure hate to find out in a crisis that security has override capabilities."

"We could do it with fewer men," the lieutenant said, "*if* we were allowed to carry our weapons."

"At least our sidearms," Brill added.

"Screw that," Vasya argued, "I want full combat gear."

Jessica let out an annoyed chuckle. "That's not going to happen." She sighed, thinking, and then looked at the lieutenant. "Can you do it with twelve?"

"If we get to carry," Lieutenant Rezhik replied. "One on each door, two with the principal, a roamer and a backup; two shifts. And the off-shift needs to be no more than a minute away."

"Very well," Jessica replied, tapping her comm-set again. "Josh, Jess. Bring eight more Ghatazhak. Armed."

"*Did you......armed?*" Josh asked.

"Yup. Full combat gear. And have them bring gear for the five of us, as well."

"*They're ......impound it......arrival,*" Josh warned.

"Let me worry about that," Jessica told him.

"*Under...od.*"

Corporal Vasya smiled. "This ought to be good. Mind if I tag along and observe your *negotiating* tactics?"

"I work better alone," Jessica told him. "Besides, you guys need to stay here and keep this place secure."

"What do we do if someone tries to crash this place in the meantime?" Vasya wondered.

"You're a Ghatazhak, Kit," Jessica replied. "Beat the snot out of them."

* * *

"I don't know," Nathan admitted, sipping his tea. "As Connor Tuplo, I met a *lot* of unsavory characters."

"Any of them seem like would-be dictators?" Cameron wondered.

"That's a little strong, isn't it?"

"You said he was looking to start his own empire, didn't you?"

"Yeah, I suppose. I just figured he was a common pirate with delusions of grandeur. You'd be surprised how many of those I've met over the last five years."

"Are you going to send Jessica back to interrogate the guy?" Cameron wondered, setting her tea on the dining table in the captain's mess.

"I don't think I have much choice," Nathan admitted with a chuckle. "If I don't give her permission, she'll probably go anyway, or kick my ass and *then* go."

Cameron took a deep breath, letting it out slowly. "You nearly got yourself killed, Nathan."

"Doesn't sound to me like it was any safer here."

"Not much, no," Cameron agreed.

"I wasn't really in *that* much danger, you know," Nathan insisted.

"How do you figure?"

"The Ghatazhak," Nathan replied. "If I didn't know better, I'd say they're even tougher now than they were before, if that's even possible."

"They're *different*, that's for sure," Cameron agreed. "They're a bit less rigid, and a bit more like the Corinari were."

"I think Jessica has been a bad influence on them," Nathan joked.

"She's changed, as well."

"She has. She's a lot tougher than she was. She's still unpredictable, but she's more in control than I remember."

Cameron paused a moment. "You know, I would have gone had I been asked."

"Gone where?" Nathan wondered.

"To rescue you from the Jung."

"Oh, that. You were injured, Cam. They couldn't wait."

"I took command of the Aurora *before* they rescued you, Nathan. I wasn't *that* badly hurt. Part of me is angry that they didn't ask."

"Yeah, Vlad feels the same way," Nathan replied.

"I just thought you should know."

"I *do* know, Cam. Believe me, I do. Don't be mad at Jess for not telling you. She was trying to protect you and Vlad. She honestly didn't believe they were going to pull it off. She didn't want to take you guys down with her."

"The point is, it should have been *our* choice."

"Had she asked you, we wouldn't have the Aurora now, and the Dusahn would have complete control over the Pentaurus sector, with no one to oppose them."

"She couldn't have known that at the time," Cameron argued. "She was acting on instinct."

"And her instincts were right."

"That doesn't mean she was right at the time."

"It kind of does, Cam," Nathan argued. "Just accept that her decision was not a selfish one, and leave it at that, okay?"

"Of course," Cameron replied. "I just wanted you to know."

"I never doubted it," Nathan insisted.

"You know, I was unsure about you when you first set foot on this ship again."

"I know. I would've been unsure about me, too." Nathan cocked his head to one side. "How about now?"

"The jury is still out," Cameron joked, picking up her tea again. After sipping it, she asked, "So, what's next?"

"Next, we meet with the military leaders of Rakuen, as well as the industrial leaders of both Rakuen *and* Neramese, to determine what resources they have, if any, to aid in their defense."

"Like what?"

"I don't know," Nathan admitted. "But a bunch of jump missile launchers on the surface is only going to slow the Dusahn down. Stationary targets are easy to pick off."

"We could put them on some of our flatbed pod haulers," Cameron suggested. "Jump them around; make them difficult to target."

"The Dusahn are too good at pursuing jump ships, and the pod haulers don't have any defenses."

"Maybe we could put them on the gunships?"

"You couldn't fit more than a few of them on a Cobra gunship," Nathan pointed out. "And if the Dusahn attack in force, we'll be too busy slugging it out with their main ships to play missile frigate. If anything, it would be our job to lure their big ships into kill zones."

"Could we mount a few on a Gunyoki?" Cameron wondered. "There are five hundred of them, you know. Even if you only got one on each ship..."

"There's no way to mount a jump missile on a Gunyoki without interfering with their gungines."

"Gungines?"

"Josh's name for their engine nacelles, because they have a big plasma cannon on the front of them."

"Cute."

"I'd suggest using Reapers, but with that much weight under their extended wings, their CG would be off, and they wouldn't be able to maneuver very well."

"We need combat ships," Nathan told her. "The question is where to get them."

* * *

"Being deep in Sanctuary's core, open space is rather limited," the steward explained as he led Marcus, Neli, Kyle, and Melanie through the entry foyer into the main living space.

"Limited?" Marcus chuckled. "This room, alone, is large enough to hold our entire ship."

"No, it's not," Neli corrected.

"Near enough."

"The galley is to the right and is fully stocked. The dining space is to the left and is capable of seating up to fourteen." The steward continued inside, pausing to turn around to face them as he continued his presentation. "You have corridors on either side leading to your staterooms, eight on each side, for a total of sixteen. Each stateroom has its own attached bathroom and can be configured to sleep one or two. Several of the rooms can be combined to form larger staterooms by retracting the common wall, and, if necessary, additional rooms can be added at either end, bringing the number of staterooms up to sixteen per side, for a total of thirty-two...depending on availability, of course."

"I'm pretty sure we'll be fine with sixteen, even with the extra people coming," Neli explained.

"If not, please do not hesitate to let us know," the steward insisted.

"What's out there?" Kyle wondered, pointing to the large, sliding glass doors on the other side of the main living space.

"That is your outdoor terrace," the steward explained. "As I said, space on this part of Sanctuary is limited, so there is no real courtyard. However, I personally prefer the simulation, as it provides a greater variety of environments for you to enjoy."

"Environments?" Melanie asked, confused.

"Allow me to demonstrate," the steward suggested, leading them through the massive, glass doors and out onto the terrace. "Set environment to the forests of Boroden," he requested aloud. A moment later, the pale blue sky beyond the railing changed to a thick, overgrown forest of deep greens, dark browns, and rusty reds, with hints of turquoise light trickling through from above. Creatures of all kinds could be heard in the distance, and the smell and humidity of a dense forest immediately hit them.

"Wow!" Kyle exclaimed.

"It's beautiful!" Melanie added. She turned to the steward. "Is it real?"

"No, my dear, but it *feels* real enough." The steward noticed Kyle trying to reach out and touch the screens against which the projections were being made. "The screens are just out of reach, at five meters. The projections are three-dimensional. Along with the sounds, smells, and environmental changes, the simulation is quite convincing. Even the animals that wander by seem real and will run away if you startle them."

"What else can it do?" Kyle wondered.

"Change environment to the beaches of Ipsil Gada," the steward requested. A moment later, the forest was transformed into a vast stretch of sparkling white sands against a brilliant blue ocean, complete with crashing waves and seabirds squawking in the distance. The humidity of the forest was gone, replaced by an afternoon ocean breeze.

"This is amazing!" Kyle exclaimed.

"Each room has its own environmental simulator terrace, albeit on a smaller scale," the steward explained.

"How much is all this costing the captain?" Marcus asked.

"Nothing," the steward assured him. "Such accommodations are provided for all families of those being treated in the Symyri Medical Center. The doctor believes that a patient's family plays a major role in successful treatment. They must be happy and stress-free, or at least as much as can be expected, while their loved one is undergoing medical treatment."

"But *sixteen rooms*?" Neli wondered. "Who has that big of a family?"

"Granted, it does not happen often," the steward admitted.

"I don't believe it," Marcus grumbled.

"Marcus," Neli scolded.

"I assure you, these accommodations are included in whatever compensation the doctor and Captain Scott have already agreed upon," the steward assured Marcus. "There will be no additional charges."

"Even if we ask for sixteen more rooms?" Marcus asked.

"*That* I am not sure of," the steward admitted. "However, we would disclose any additional charges for the added rooms, prior to your acceptance of them."

"Fair enough," Marcus said, scratching his head in disbelief at their luxurious accommodations.

"Would you like me to demonstrate the accommodations in the staterooms, sir?"

"I think we can figure it out," Marcus replied.

"As you wish. Will there be anything else?" the steward asked.

Marcus looked at Neli, who shook her head. "Uh, I guess not," Marcus replied. "Are we supposed to tip you?" he wondered.

"We are not allowed to accept gratuities," the steward replied, "but I thank you for the consideration." He turned to Kyle and Melanie. "I do hope that your mother recovers," he told them, "and if there is anything you need, please do not hesitate to ask for me. My name is Olan."

"Thank you, Olan," Melanie said.

"Yeah, thanks," Kyle added.

Marcus followed Olan to the door, then peeled off to the left into the galley, immediately opening the door to the large refrigerator. "Holy crap! Score!" he exclaimed. He turned back toward the others, a grin on his face. "Who's hungry?"

* * *

Nathan, Cameron, and General Telles studied the images that Deliza and Lieutenant Commander Shinoda had brought them.

"Right there," Deliza said, pausing the video for a moment. "Look at the ground. No dust. That means no thruster wash. The Dusahn shuttles aren't using lift thrusters. They're using anti-gravity fields, just like the ones on the Contra ships you brought back. Even their fighters are using them. *Maybe* even their gunships. We've seen them on the surface. We just haven't seen them actually land yet."

"You think the Dusahn got the anti-gravity technology from the Contras?" General Telles asked.

"No way of telling," Deliza admitted. "Anti-gravity lift systems were already in widespread use before the bio-digital plague, so it stands to reason that many of the fleeing colonists brought the technology with them. Even the Aurora uses anti-gravity lift beds to move heavy cargo around."

"Yes, but it can't lift something more than half a meter off the deck," Nathan pointed out.

"There's really no way to tell *where* the Dusahn got the technology," Lieutenant Commander Shinoda stated. "To be honest, I'm not sure it matters much."

"There is *one* way to tell," Nathan corrected. "We could steal one of their shuttles."

"Why take the risk?" Cameron wondered.

"Deliza, if we brought you one of the Dusahn

shuttles, could you figure out a way to disrupt their anti-gravity lift systems?" Nathan asked.

"Probably."

"That *could* provide a tactical advantage," the general admitted.

"If nothing else, it would give us *another* anti-gravity lift system to study, before we start trying to retrofit our own ships with the technology," Deliza said.

"You want to fit *our* ships with anti-gravity lift systems?" Cameron asked.

"Of course," Deliza replied, surprised that Cameron was questioning the idea. "The propellant savings alone would be worth the effort."

"It would also allow our ships and shuttles to carry more weight," Nathan realized. "Reapers carrying twice the ordnance, fighters carrying twice as many missiles, and the Gunyoki...they can barely make it from the surface to orbit on a full load of propellant. Because of that, they currently offer us no tactical advantage in atmospheric operations. Imagine their ground support capabilities; with those missile pods and their plasma turrets...they'd be frightening."

"I'm not disagreeing," Cameron pointed out, "I'm just surprised you are already thinking of refits. I thought it would take much more time."

"I'm not suggesting we do it tomorrow," Deliza admitted. "We haven't even completely disassembled one of them yet, let alone scanned their components for replication. But once we have, I see no reason to delay refit."

"I'd suggest you talk to Commander Verbeek, first," Nathan suggested. "I suspect he's going to have a few concerns that need to be addressed."

"Of course," Deliza agreed.

"Anything else to report?" Nathan asked the lieutenant commander.

"Yes, Captain," Lieutenant Commander Shinoda replied. "During the siege of the Ranni plant, we picked up a conversation between one of the Rakuen generals and one of their ministers. They were talking about ships called Orochis. They were used during the war between Rakuen and Neramese. Apparently, they've been mothballed since then. They were talking about pressing them back into service and fitting them with jump drives, using the Ranni plant to make the drives. The general felt it was more important to fit out the Gunyoki, first."

"I remember those ships," Deliza commented. "When we first set up operations on Rakuen, there was talk of turning them into jump cargo ships, but it never happened."

"Any idea why?" Cameron wondered.

"I'm afraid not."

"Why is this the first we're hearing about these ships?" Nathan wondered.

"Probably because they're not where you'd expect to find mothballed space warships," the lieutenant commander replied. "They're on the surface."

"So, they're hidden," Cameron surmised.

"Nope, in plain sight."

"Then, how did we miss them?" Nathan wondered.

"We didn't," the lieutenant commander replied. "We thought they were seagoing vessels. They're floating in a sheltered harbor, along with a bunch of other mothballed ships."

"Their spaceships float?" Nathan said, surprised.

"Their world *is* predominantly water," General Telles reminded him. "It makes perfect sense, both logistically *and* economically."

"How big are they?" Cameron asked.

"We don't have exact measurements just yet, but they appear to be about the size of a Dusahn gunship, with a bit more width and overall mass." The lieutenant commander pressed a button on the remote, causing an aerial image of the Orochi ships to appear on the view screen in the command briefing room. "So far, we've discovered five of them in a protected harbor, off Onaro Seykora, and another seven at the Jinnatay Harbor in the southern seas. However, our research indicates there were at least twenty of them in service during the war, so..."

"What are those pads on the sides?" Nathan asked, studying the aerial photos.

"We did some research on the Orochi ships," the lieutenant commander explained. "They were designed as Gunyoki carriers. Their mission profile was to ferry fourteen Gunyoki fighters to high orbit over Neramese, where the Gunyoki would attack targets on the surface. They had considerable defensive weapons, as well as pulse energy cannons that could reach the surface of Neramese; although, they were not very accurate. For the most part, their weapons were only used for defense, while the Gunyoki carried out their attacks. They were equipped with very short-range FTL drives, allowing them to reach Neramese in less than ten minutes."

"I was under the assumption that the Gunyoki were basically defensive craft," Cameron commented.

"Originally, they were," Lieutenant Commander Shinoda agreed. "The Orochi ships enabled the Gunyoki to carry out offensive operations. It is believed that the Orochi were largely responsible for the Rakuen's victory over Neramese. Those 'pads' you asked about were the platforms on which the original Gunyoki fighters rode. They were lowered into the hull during FTL operations, probably to make it easier to establish and maintain the mass-canceling fields the old FTL drives used."

"How did the flight crews get in and out of their fighters?" Nathan wondered.

"On the surface," the lieutenant commander replied, "before and after the mission. The entire ship only had a crew of twenty-eight."

"How the hell did they get that thing back and forth between the surface and orbit?" Nathan wondered.

"The bulk of the ship is comprised of propulsion and propellant storage. Their lift drives are *very* powerful and *very* efficient, even by today's standards."

Cameron noticed the look in Nathan's eyes as he studied the images. "What are you thinking?"

Nathan's gaze shifted toward Cameron. "Eleven ships, fourteen pads, a quad jump-missile launcher on each pad..." Nathan smiled. "That's six hundred and sixteen jump missiles. Fit those ships with jump drives, and they'd be a lot harder to pick off than surface-based launchers."

"We don't even have fifty-six jump missiles left on board *this ship*," Cameron reminded him.

"Maybe not, but we've got the industrial infrastructure of *two* highly motivated worlds at our disposal," Nathan pointed out.

"If the Orochi were the reason the Nerameseans were defeated, they will not react favorably to their resurrection," General Telles warned.

"*Especially* if they are carrying fifty-six jump missiles each," Cameron added.

"Mix the crews," Nathan replied. "Half from Rakuen, and half from Neramese. Half of them commanded by a Rakuen, the other half by a Neramesean. Make the XO from the opposite world as the CO and have a dual-key missile launch system."

"That might work," Cameron commented.

"Agreed," the general added.

"There *could* be one little wrinkle," Deliza warned. "When Neramese surrendered, they did so only under the condition that Rakuen destroyed the Orochi fleet."

"Are you telling me Neramese doesn't *know* that the Orochi still exist?" Nathan asked.

"I don't think so," Deliza replied.

Nathan let out a sigh. "Well, this should be interesting."

CHAPTER TWO

As Jessica entered Sanctuary Security's main administration center, she immediately took notice of multiple security cameras, as well as several strategically placed, miniature stunner turrets. While the cameras were obvious and prevalent throughout the asteroid station, the turrets here were recessed and easy to miss by the untrained eye. It was obvious that this lobby was meant to promote a sense of confidence. Here, of all places, one was safe, even without the threat of stunner turrets looming from the ceiling in every corner.

However, the officers working the front desk, as well as at the numerous desks further back, were all wearing sidearms. Even those not in uniform had obvious bulges under their suit jackets. The Sanctuary Security Force took pride in their strength, training, and numbers—a point that amused her. It was easy to feel superior when you were the only ones carrying guns, and all your world's visitors were pre-screened.

Jessica stepped up to the counter, not one full meter from a barrel-chested, bearded officer on the other side. She waited a moment, expecting the officer to offer greeting or, at least, acknowledge her presence. When he did not, she cleared her throat. The officer glanced at her out of the corner of his eye and then continued with his task without uttering a word in response.

"Excuse me," Jessica said, making no effort to hide her annoyance. "I need to speak to the person in charge."

"In charge of what?" the officer grumbled without looking up.

"In charge of you," Jessica replied, her tone dripping with sarcasm.

"That would be my wife," the officer replied in similar tone, "and she's not here."

"Good thing," Jessica snapped back. "Otherwise, I'd have to tell her what an ass her husband is."

"She already knows," the officer replied, almost laughing.

"I'd *like* to speak to the person in charge of station security," Jessica announced, changing tactics, "*if* it's not too much trouble."

"No trouble for me," the officer replied. "Might be for the commander, though."

"You people always so nice?" Jessica asked playfully, trying to keep the banter light and non-adversarial.

"Caught me on a bad day, lady." The officer finally looked up, giving Jessica his full attention. "I'm normally a sweetheart of a guy."

"Yeah, I'm sure you're a real teddy bear."

"A what?"

"Nothing," Jessica replied, not wanting to take the time to explain. "May I *please* speak to the person in charge of station security?"

"Better," the officer replied. "And you are?"

"Lieutenant Commander Jessica Nash, chief tactical officer and head of security for the Aurora, under the command of Captain Nathan Scott."

The officer looked her over, trying to hide his reaction to her response. "I'll see if the commander has time for you. *Please*, take a seat."

"Thank you," Jessica replied, nearly choking on the words. She moved over to the seating area, scanning the room as she took her seat. There were a total of fifteen uniformed officers and at least six others in civilian attire, four of whom she was certain were carrying weapons. In addition, there were four offices across the back, all with closed doors. They were close enough together that they likely led to small offices, none of which would have more than a few people in them at any one time. She also noted that corridors led off to the left and right of the room, at both the front and back corners.

A few minutes later, the officer returned, stepping over to the security gate at the end of the counter. "Lieutenant Commander," he said, inviting her over.

Jessica rose and walked over to the officer at the gate.

"Place your feet within the red circles, and hold your arms up, hands higher than your head," the officer instructed.

Jessica complied. A moment later, a flat, red beam of light moved up from the floor, passing over her body from feet to fingertips, and back down again. The officer watched the display on the wall as the scan completed then pressed a button, causing the gate to swing open.

"You may enter," the officer announced.

Jessica stepped through the gate, which automatically closed behind her as she followed the officer across the room, toward one of the offices along the back wall. She could feel the eyes of the other officers at their desks as she passed, unsure of whether they were curious about who she worked for or because of the skintight outfit she was wearing. She assumed it was the latter, which was usually the case. It was one of the easiest ways to get the drop on a male adversary; causing them to think with their little brain instead of their big one.

Unfortunately, the moment she stepped into the commander's office, she realized her outfit might not have its usual effect.

"Lieutenant Commander Nash, this is Commander Elise Manderon, chief of Sanctuary Security Force," the officer introduced.

"An honor to meet you, sir," Jessica replied, paying the respect due her rank and position.

"The pleasure is mine, Lieutenant Commander," Commander Manderon insisted. "These are two of my officers, Lieutenant Jordu and Captain Stegarat."

"Lieutenant, Captain," Jessica greeted, reaching out to shake each of their hands while she mentally sized them up. The lieutenant was a bit younger, had a firm handshake, and appeared to be physically fit. The captain, on the other hand, although firm of handshake and confident in his expression, had clearly been riding a desk for some time, now. The ring on his finger probably meant he was a family man, and thus had retired from frontline duty long ago. Experience would likely be on his side, but not physical prowess.

A quick glance at the commander told the same story. She, too, wore a wedding ring and had become a bit rotund behind her desk. She appeared confident, as expected, but it was the confidence one had from outranking everyone around her rather than being the toughest, most deadly person in the room.

"Please, be seated," the commander invited, gesturing toward the empty chair next to Captain Stegarat. "I don't normally grant an audience with someone just because they ask for it," the commander continued as everyone took their seats. "However, the efforts of the Aurora and her crew, on the behalf of humanity, are well known, *even* on Sanctuary."

"I appreciate your seeing me, sir," Jessica replied.

"What can I do for you, Lieutenant Commander?"

"My men and I have been tasked to provide security for Captain Scott's sister while she undergoes critical treatment in Doctor Symyri's medical facility," Jessica explained.

"Yes, Doctor Symyri's personal assistant has made me aware of this patient. I believe she has been registered as Dorremonte, first name of Alyssa, for security purposes."

"I wasn't aware that the doctor's staff shared this information with Sanctuary Security," Jessica said, one eyebrow raised. "Just how many people under your command are aware of her true identity?"

"Only a select handful," the commander assured her. "Myself, the captain and the lieutenant, and three other watch commanders. As Doctor Symyri treats a number of, shall we say, *renowned* individuals, many of whom constitute increased risk to this station, he is required to notify us when doing so."

"Understandable, I suppose," Jessica said, obviously not happy with the idea.

"You stated that you and *your men* have been assigned the task of providing security for Captain Scott's sister," the commander commented.

"That is correct."

"Who exactly are...*these men*?" the commander inquired.

"They are *my* men," Jessica replied, "under *my* command."

"And what type of training do they have?" the commander pressed.

"Their training is more than adequate," Jessica

assured the commander. "In fact, their training is vastly superior to my own."

"And yet, *you* command *them.*"

"I do."

"And what is it that you require from me, Lieutenant Commander?" the commander asked, suspicion tainting her words.

"Security at Doctor Symyri's facility is woefully inadequate. Captain Scott has many enemies. Furthermore, this station is regularly visited by persons of questionable background...persons who might see the captain's sister's presence as an opportunity."

"Hence the need for you and your men," the commander surmised.

"Precisely."

"You do realize that Sanctuary Security is *designed* to protect *everyone* from those very people you speak of?"

"I do."

"No person is allowed to bring a weapon into Sanctuary," the commander continued. "We have cameras in every corridor and every compartment, and automated stunner turrets capable of reaching ninety percent of the station's interior spaces, all of which are controlled from this facility, I might add. Now, while the presence of you and your men may make Captain Scott feel more at ease, I assure you that his sister is safer *here* than anywhere else in the galaxy."

"No disrespect intended, Commander, but I think you're underestimating the rest of the galaxy. My men have already hacked the stunner systems in Doctor Symyri's facility and taken control for themselves.

They have also demonstrated that the good doctor's card-lock system is easily hacked, as well."

"That's impossible," the commander insisted. "We would have been alerted if control over any part of our system had been lost."

"Not if properly hacked, you wouldn't," Jessica replied.

"I must warn you, Lieutenant Commander, tampering with station security systems constitutes a crime for which I could arrest you on the spot. After all, you did just confess."

Jessica stared confidently at the commander, saying nothing.

"What is it you came here for, Lieutenant Commander?" the commander wondered. "Was it just to confess to a crime, or was there something else you were hoping to accomplish?"

"I was hoping to get permission for my men and myself to carry weapons in the performance of our duties," Jessica stated.

Perhaps it was the nature of the request, or possibly the matter-of-fact way in which the lieutenant commander presented it. Either way, the commander couldn't help but laugh. "Even if I had the power to do so—which I don't, by the way—why would I arm a bunch of men I know nothing about?"

"Because your responsibility is the security of not only this station, but of everyone aboard it," Jessica explained.

"I am well aware of my responsibilities, Lieutenant Commander," the commander scowled as she pressed the small button under the edge of her desk.

Jessica noticed the odd movement of the commander's hand but did not react.

"Furthermore, I take your insinuation to mean

that we are incapable of protecting ourselves and our visitors...apparently from the likes of *you* and your men."

The door suddenly burst open, and the first of four men charged into the room. Jessica shifted to her right, toward the first man, widening her stance slightly and putting her weight on the front pads of her feet as she reached out with her left hand, grabbing the first officer's gun hand. She pulled it hard as she spun in a semi-squatting position and drove her left knee into the first officer's gut, folding him over so she could then drive her right elbow into the base of his skull.

The officer's weapon discharged, stunning both Lieutenant Jordu and Captain Stegarat. Jessica released the now-unconscious officer, spinning all the way around to her left, driving her left foot into the face of the second officer as she grabbed his stunner from his hand. The officer fell backwards into the third officer, giving Jessica the time she needed to reset and bring her weapon to bear on them.

Two shots rang out, striking the third and fourth officers, rendering them unconscious and dropping them into a pile atop the second officer.

Jessica sensed the commander coming toward her from behind and dropped down on one hand, kicking one leg out, catching the commander in the chest and sending her tumbling back into her chair.

Now on the floor, Jessica used the pile of unconscious officers as cover and opened fire with her stunner. One by one, she dropped the other officers charging toward the commander's office, until finally she had cleared the room.

Jessica jumped to her feet, leaping over the pile of

officers and charging out into the middle of the room in preparation for the additional officers she knew would rush in at any moment. But instead of getting into a safe firing position, she dropped her weapon and stood in the middle of the room, her hands high above her head, in a position of surrender.

As expected, more officers responded. Every one of them had stunners in hand, ready to fire, but the shot that rendered Jessica unconscious came from behind.

Jessica fell to the floor and was immediately put in restraints.

"Put that bitch in holding," Commander Manderon barked, standing at the doorway to her office, stunner in hand.

* * *

Vol Kaguchi had never been on the Aurora's command deck and was surprised to see that it was smaller than he had imagined. It was a short walk from the top of the main ramp to the bridge; past the elevators, the security and intelligence office, then a left and a right, and past the captain's quarters.

His escort stopped at the outer port entrance to the bridge. "End of the tunnel, then an about-face to your right. The guard will direct you, sir."

"Thank you," Vol replied, entering the short tunnel. He made his way past the emergency lockers in the tunnel and through the inner hatch at the far end.

The interior of the Aurora's bridge was a wondrous sight; a shining example of form, function, and efficiency. Its ceilings were irregular, with electronic conduit and ventilation ducting running in all directions. Both sides of its back half were covered with displays clustered around workstations, and its back wall had a large, wraparound console with three communications officers behind it. In the middle of the back half was a massive, stand-up tactical station with multiple clear screens on which all manner of information was displayed.

But it was the front half of the bridge that really took his breath away. It was a few steps lower than the back half and was surrounded by a semispherical view screen that looked like a window to space. Were it not for the various data windows seemingly floating on the massive view screen itself, Vol might have believed that it was indeed a window. “Wow,” he muttered to himself.

“You said it.”

Vol looked at the guard, his mouth still agape.

“It has that effect the first few times you see it,” the guard agreed. “The captain is expecting you, sir,” he added, pointing aft.

Vol made an about-face to his right, as instructed, and walked the few steps to the captain’s ready room, passing the communications station along the way. The hatch was open, so he stepped inside. “You wanted to see me, Captain?”

“Mister Kaguchi,” Nathan greeted, rising from his seat and coming around his desk to shake the Gunyoki’s hand. “It is good to see you again.”

“It is good to see you, as well, Captain. Forgive me in saying so but, *technically*, it is *Master* Kaguchi,” Vol corrected.

“Of course. My apologies, Master Kaguchi,” Nathan replied, gesturing for his guest to sit.

“To what do I owe this honor?” Vol wondered as he sat.

“During my short time with him, Master Koku spoke highly of you. As I found him to be an incredibly brave and honorable man, I have the utmost faith in his opinion. Because of this, I would like to ask if you would be willing to serve as wing commander of the Gunyoki."

Vol looked surprised. "You wish *me* to be Gunyoki Shenzai?"

"*Shenzai no rido kai,*" Nathan replied, his Rakuen accent near perfect. "*Anoto gai yorokondi irunaro ye.*"

"I am impressed, Captain. I did not realize you spoke Raku."

"I started studying it a few weeks ago."

"And your accent is nearly perfect, already. Again, impressive," Vol praised.

"I'm a quick study," Nathan replied. "So, will you accept the position?"

"Where will I be based?" Vol wondered.

"On Rakuen. Now that your people have signed the charter, the Gunyoki will be based at the race platform, after repairs and modifications have been made."

"Modifications?" Vol wondered.

"Beefing up its defenses, changing some of the spectator areas into support facilities, remodeling the team bays to accommodate a greater number of fighters at one time, among others."

"I see." Vol thought for a moment. "I assume I can select my own staff?"

"Of course," Nathan assured him.

"And what would our primary tasking be?" Vol wondered.

"The defense of the Rogen system will always be the Gunyoki's primary task," Nathan promised. "In addition, we will likely call on some of your forces to aid us in our campaign against the Dusahn, but we will never ask you to leave your world inadequately defended in the process."

"I would be honored to accept the assignment," Vol told him. "However, I do not think the race platform is capable of supporting the Gunyoki in the numbers necessary to defend the system."

"Which is why our R and D people are investigating the possibility of fitting the Gunyoki with anti-gravity lift systems that would allow them to respond to an attack from the surface, nearly as effectively as from the race platform," Nathan explained.

"Interesting. Have you considered how such a device might affect the Gunyoki's unique handling characteristics?"

Nathan smiled, remembering those unique characteristics. "Like I said, we are *investigating* the idea, among other methods of improving the Rogen system's ability to defend itself."

"Such as?"

Nathan paused a moment, unsure of how to broach the subject. He had no idea if Vol was aware of the existence of the Orochi, and if so, how he might react to the news. "We are looking for alternatives to placing jump missile launchers on the surface of Rakuen and Neramese."

"You are concerned about the political ramifications of putting such weapons on Neramese?"

"Both worlds, actually," Nathan admitted. "However, I am more concerned with the ease with which the Dusahn could destroy those defenses, as well as the collateral damage that might occur. It would be better all around, both strategically *and* politically, if we could put those launchers on jump-equipped ships, making them more difficult to target."

"It seems that your flatbed pod haulers would be most suitable for that purpose," Vol suggested.

"Yes, they would be," Nathan agreed. "But we only have six of them, and we use them quite a bit, as it is."

Vol thought for a moment. "Have you considered the Orochi?"

"The *Orochi*?" Nathan replied, pretending to be unfamiliar with them.

"When Neramese first attacked Rakuen, we had no offensive capabilities. Our Gunyoki had been designed to protect *our* world, not to attack another. After several years of defending ourselves against the Nerameseans, our leaders decided to build carrier ships, to transport our Gunyoki to Neramese, in order to take the war to *their* world instead of ours. The Orochi carrier ships are what won the war for Rakuen. I believe Rakuen still has twenty of them in storage, in case they are needed for defense."

"Actually, I am aware of the Orochi," Nathan admitted. "I apologize for the deception, but I was not certain if *you* knew that the Orochi still existed."

"A logical precaution on your part," Vol agreed, appearing unoffended. "It was a contentious issue during the peace negotiations. Rakuen agreed not to advertise that twenty Orochi were kept in reserve, not even to our own people. Tension and distrust had existed between our worlds for more than a century, Captain. Well before the wars began. While Rakuen was unwilling to leave herself defenseless, we also did not wish the Nerameseans to live in constant fear of the Orochi."

"Understandable," Nathan agreed. "Do you mind if I ask, was the war *really* about water?"

Vol sighed. "You and I both come from worlds

where water is abundant. And you also have the advantage of having seen just how much water is truly available in space. When the Rogen system was first settled, it was by two ships. The Neramai and the Rakai. The colonists from both ships were predominantly Asian, with the majority being from the Earth nations of Japan and Korea. The leaders of the Neramai colonists feared that the lack of arable land on the third world in the Rogen system would restrict growth, while the leaders of the Rakai colonists had similar concerns over the lack of water on the fourth world. It was decided that each would settle independently, and that what remained of our colony ships would be combined to provide transport and trade between our two worlds. Alas, both groups were correct in their fears, but the problems of each were overcome through trade. Rakuen's water was shipped to Neramese to irrigate their crops, which in turn helped feed everyone. But eventually, both worlds became greedy, and when a compromise could not be found, each cut the other off. Rakuen's food supply dwindled, as did Neramese's water supply, and therefore its food supply. Rakuen found other solutions. We moved our cities from the land to the oceans, freeing up soil for crops. Then, we moved dirt from mountainous terrain to our floating agricultural platforms and began turning sea plants into food sources, creating massive sea farms to increase our fishing harvests. We had been correct in choosing a water world; the Neramai had chosen poorly, and they despised us for their mistake. The result was war; one which *they* began, I might add."

Nathan sighed. "It is easy to identify which side fired the first shot, but history shows that in *most* cases, both parties involved in a conflict shared equal blame."

"I'm sure you are correct," Vol agreed. "However, the people of Rakuen will always remember the day that Neramese first attacked our world. Still, we were able to forgive them and find peace."

"As long as they remained defenseless," Nathan pointed out.

"I do not seek disagreement with you, Captain. I am a warrior, not a statesman. My duty is to protect the *Rogen system*, as best I can. Not just Rakuen, but the *entire* system, Neramese included. Those were the terms of the peace agreement between our worlds, and that is why Neramese eventually capitulated and allowed us to keep twenty Orochi carriers."

"Then, Neramese will be neither surprised nor upset when we pull the Orochi out of retirement and press them into service," Nathan surmised.

"Their *leaders* will not, but the *people* of Neramese may not be pleased. However, I suspect that once you explain how the Orochi will greatly improve our own ability to defend both worlds, the Nerameseans will accept their existence. Despite our past history, personally, I find the Nerameseans to be pleasant, reasonable people."

"You don't know how happy I am to hear that," Nathan admitted with relief.

"I assume the Orochi will be commanded by both Rakuens *and* Nerameseans?" Vol asked.

"Commanded and crewed, fifty-fifty," Nathan assured him.

"As they should be," Vol agreed. After a moment, he spoke again. "May I ask a question?"

"Of course," Nathan replied.

"Am I to be given a rank within your Alliance?"

"Of course, *Commander.*"

Vol smiled. "Commander Kaguchi. It has a nice ring to it, does it not?"

Nathan also smiled. "It surely does."

* * *

There were few things more painful than the hangover from a full-on stunner blast. Even worse was the humiliation of being manhandled by a bunch of security guards whom she could have easily subdued. The fact that she had *let* herself get captured didn't help.

Jessica didn't bother looking up when she heard the door at the far end of the detention block open, nor as the footsteps marked the approach of visitors.

"I'm told that our stunners are a bit more painful than others," the commander said.

"I've experienced worse," Jessica muttered, still not looking up. When a strange fizzling sound followed, she raised her head slightly, just in time to see Commander Manderon walking through the active force field. "One-way, huh?" she mumbled, one eyebrow raised. "We're going to want that tech," she added, closing her eyes again.

"Everything on Sanctuary is for sale," the commander replied, as if repeating some long-held mantra. "For the right price."

Jessica continued nursing her stunner hangover.

"Interesting negotiating tactic," the commander continued. "Did you really think beating up my office staff was going to get you what you want?"

"I was trying to make a point," Jessica told her, sounding slightly annoyed.

"What, that you're stupid?" the commander laughed.

"Fuck you."

The commander signaled the two guards still standing outside the restraint force field. The two men stepped through the force field, taking Jessica by her arms and raising her to her feet.

"That was a mistake," Jessica muttered. In the blink of an eye, she swept the left foot of the guard to her right out from under him, pulling him forward and to the left. At the same time, she pivoted left, pulling her left arm from the grasp of the guard to her left, who was now taking the full weight of the other guard as he stumbled into him. Her left elbow came around, striking the second guard in the face as she made a complete rotation, after which her right hand struck downward into the back of the first guard's head.

With her left hand, Jessica yanked the nameplate from the second guard's uniform as she dove forward into a tumble. As she came over, she dragged the small, metal nameplate along the rough, rocky floor of her cell, quickly grinding its edge. She came up from her tumble in the face of the commander. The commander took a swing at her, which Jessica easily avoided as she twisted around and caught the commander in a choke hold, the sharpened edge of the stolen nameplate held firmly against the commander's external jugular vein.

The two guards scrambled to their feet, ready to attack, but froze when they saw their commander's life threatened.

"Half a kilogram of pressure and you'll bleed out in seconds," Jessica whispered. "You get my point now?"

"I got your point the first time," the commander insisted. "Are you finished with the theatrics now?"

Jessica released the commander, tossing her makeshift weapon to the floor as she stepped back. "At least your men weren't stupid enough to enter the cell with sidearms," she said. "I'll give them that."

The commander nodded to her men, indicating for them to depart. The force field disengaged, and the men departed.

"You're not going to activate it again?" Jessica wondered.

"What would be the point?" the commander admitted. "You'd find a way out no matter what."

"True."

"But that's not part of your plan, is it."

"You're smarter than you look," Jessica quipped, returning to her bunk and sitting down, her head still feeling like it was in a vise.

"Are you always this difficult?" the commander wondered.

"It's been a rough week," Jessica replied. "I'm usually a much more pleasant person."

The commander laughed. "I suspect you're generally hell on wheels, twenty-four seven."

"Twenty-four seven?" Jessica laughed. "I haven't heard that in a while."

"Unlike most of the colonized worlds, Sanctuary still follows Earth's old calendar and timekeeping standards," the commander explained. "Zulu time, in fact. Is not your ship on Zulu time?"

"Yeah, but we call it Earth Mean Time or Ship Time."

"So, I'm assuming the point you've been trying to make is that there are people who might visit this station, who are capable of circumventing our security measures, and causing harm to those your men are assigned to protect."

"Precisely."

"And by not allowing your men to carrying weapons, we are in fact putting everyone at risk," the commander continued.

"Two for two."

"Well, it seems to me you've just demonstrated that you are quite capable of protecting yourself *against* men with weapons, even when *you* have none."

"If they come, they will not be carrying stunners," Jessica told her.

"No one gets weapons into Sanctuary without our permission."

"Weapons are for sale in your marketplace," Jessica pointed out.

"Those models have been deactivated and have been cleared for use as demonstrators only," the commander insisted.

"And they couldn't be *re*-activated?"

"Not a chance," the commander assured her. "Their power conduits and firing mechanisms have been removed, and the spaces filled with perma-bond. It would be impossible."

"Nothing is impossible," Jessica insisted.

"Agreed. But...highly *improbable.*"

"And that is what I'm worried about," Jessica said, looking up again. "As good as the Ghatazhak are, they are *not* invincible, and we cannot afford to lose any more of them."

"And if we allow you to carry weapons, what assurances do we have that you will not use them against *us*?"

"We have no quarrel with you," Jessica assured her.

"Not yet."

"Hopefully, not ever." Jessica took a deep breath, letting it out slowly. "Look, Commander, all we want to do is keep our captain's sister and her children safe for the duration of their stay on Sanctuary."

"And how long will that be?"

"At this point, I have no way of knowing," Jessica admitted.

"I see," the commander sighed. She paced the width of the cell for a minute before continuing. "We have heard stories of the Ghatazhak," she began. "Horrible stories. Acts of violence and terror that sour the expressions of good people."

"The stories you have heard are not of the *true* Ghatazhak," Jessica corrected. "They are of the *Ybaran Legions*. Brutal men dressed in Ghatazhak armor, trained to fight like Ghatazhak, but without the intelligence or education that make the Ghatazhak the remarkable warriors they are."

Commander Manderon looked at Jessica. "It is true that abilities such as theirs require considerable commitment and training, as well as an unwavering sense of right and wrong, but..."

"I know," Jessica said, cutting her off. "They do things at times that even the most hardened soldier cannot comprehend. That is what *makes* them Ghatazhak, the fact that they are *able* to do what *must* be done, regardless of how distasteful they may find it. Those are the men you want on your side."

"If they are allowed to carry weapons, others will make similar requests," the commander said. "It will lead us *back* to the chaos that plagued us in our early days."

"Then make them members of your security force," Jessica suggested.

"Excuse me?" the commander said, not sure that she heard Jessica correctly.

"Not officially. Just put them in uniform so everyone *thinks* they are Sanctuary Security."

"My people worked hard to earn their uniforms," the commander told her.

"Not as hard as the Ghatazhak have worked to earn theirs, I assure you," Jessica replied.

"Perhaps, but..."

"If they come," Jessica interrupted, "you will wish you *had* armed the Ghatazhak...*believe me.*"

"Based on what you're saying, I *should* recommend that Captain Scott's sister *not* be given treatment on this station," the commander warned. "However, the legend of Captain Scott, and his exploits, is quite popular among the people of Sanctuary. Refusal would not go over well, and Congress knows this." Commander Manderon began pacing again, thinking. "Just how many men are we talking about?"

"Twenty, maybe, thirty at the most," Jessica replied. "And we will need full control over the security systems in both the medical center and our quarters."

"Twenty, no more, and they are to be in TRT uniforms at all times," the commander insisted.

"TRT?"

"Tactical Response Team."

"And they can carry their own weapons?"

"No, they must carry TRT weapons. *And* they must wear trackers and be on *our* comms at all times."

"Agreed."

"And if one of my officers gives them an order, they are to comply."

"As long as that order does not jeopardize the ones they are protecting," Jessica insisted.

"Agreed."

"Then, we have a deal?" Jessica asked, standing.

"Pending congressional approval, yes," the commander replied.

"How long will that take?" Jessica wondered.

"An hour," the commander replied. "Two, at the most."

"Good enough."

"And next time, Lieutenant Commander...please, no theatrics."

Jessica patted the commander on the shoulder as she walked past her, toward the exit, smiling. "Hell on wheels, remember?"

* * *

Abby and Deliza stood on the observation platform overlooking pier one-fourteen south. The pier contained several large buildings surrounded by access roads and a few smaller buildings.

"*This*?" Abby wondered. "*This* is one-fourteen south?"

"Yes," Deliza replied. "I know it doesn't look like much, but it's more than enough space, and it's easy to isolate, thus making it more secure."

"What about its defense?"

"General Telles suggested that no defenses be placed near this pier, so as not to draw attention."

"What if we're attacked?" Abby asked.

"My plant is only eight piers over, so we can defend *this* pier from there," Deliza explained. "There are also several underwater transit tubes, one of which is designed for cargo, which feed this pier, so we can move people and supplies to and from here without detection."

"So, we're hiding in plain sight, then," Abby surmised.

"That's the idea," Deliza replied. "The transit tubes will also make it quick and easy to evacuate, in case of attack."

"What about the piers on either side?" Abby asked.

"Both are populated primarily by automated warehouses, so staffing is minimal."

"Then *some* people will be at risk." Abby didn't sound happy.

"If we put the facility in an isolated location, it would be difficult to support and defend, not to mention it would look suspicious to the Dusahn," Deliza explained. "This pier is the best balance of safety and functionality we could find. Besides, Yokimah owns it, so we don't have to pay to use it."

"I wasn't aware that Ito Yokimah was into real estate," Abby commented.

"Ito Yokimah is into anything that will make him money," Deliza replied. "Personally, I think he bought most of the south-side piers when I purchased one-twenty-two south, just to prevent me from expanding...or to make a profit from me when I did."

"I guess the joke is on him, then," Abby said.

Deliza smiled.

"When can we move in?" Abby asked.

"It will take a few days to beef up the power systems for the entire pier, but we can begin setting up in the meantime."

"So, we're going to have to shuttle down for work, I suppose," Abby commented.

"Yanni and I are getting a place in the city," Deliza told her. "Vinto District. A ten-minute transit ride to the plant. Maybe you should do the same?"

"I hate the idea of moving the kids again," Abby

said, "and Erik is actually enjoying the work he is doing for Lieutenant Commander Shinoda."

"The children are likely to be even happier on Rakuen," Deliza pointed out, "and couldn't your husband do his work from Rakuen just as easily as from the Mystic Empress?"

"I suppose he could," Abby agreed, sighing. She looked out at the ocean beyond the piers. "I think my children *would* like it here. But, now that Rakuen has joined the Karuzari Alliance, it *does* make it a target."

"No more so than *any* ship in the fleet, *including* the Mystic," Deliza said. "And if Rakuen *is* attacked, you and your family would be among the first to be evacuated."

"I suppose." Abby looked out at the ocean again, noticing several odd-looking ships approaching the next pier over. "What are those?"

Deliza looked at the ships and smiled. "*Those* are Orochi carriers...our first project."

* * *

Vladimir and Dalen followed Marcus through the maze of vendor booths, racks of parts, and tables full of various tools and equipment.

"This place is like a giant flea market, but of technology," Vladimir said, pausing to examine a strange-looking piece of equipment.

"I bet we could find some JT8s here," Dalen suggested.

"What are JT8s?"

"Pieces of garbage," Marcus muttered, stopping to look back at Vladimir and Dalen. "You two need to keep up."

"How are we going to find anything if we plow

through without stopping to look at stuff?" Vladimir wondered.

"This is all crap," Marcus insisted. "The good stuff is *always* at the center."

"JT8s are not garbage," Dalen argued.

"You don't know what you're talking about, kid."

"Is someone going to tell me what JT8s are?" Vladimir wondered.

"What, you prefer the two-twenties we have on there now?" Dalen asked, laughing.

"The two-twenties don't blow out as often," Marcus insisted.

"That's cuz they got too much resistance, so they never get up to full power," Dalen argued. "Which means the stream accelerators never run at full power."

"We don't need them to run at full power," Marcus replied.

"Oh, *now* I know what you're talking about," Vladimir realized. "Those little flow regulators."

"Of course, we need them to run at full power," Dalen argued. "Why the hell wouldn't you want them to run at full power? They're engines. That's what they're supposed to do."

"No, he's right," Vladimir told Dalen as they continued following Marcus through the crowded market. "Full power is not good if you have to constantly make repairs. Better to run at less than full power and run reliably."

"Don't agree with me," Marcus grumbled. "It makes me nervous." Marcus suddenly stopped. "This is where the good stuff is," he announced, spreading his arms wide.

Vladimir and Dalen both stood with their mouths agape. Before them was the central square of the tech market on Sanctuary. While the space they had been walking through was a single level, the central square—which was actually round—was four levels high, two of which were below them. And these vendors were unlike those they had seen thus far. These vendors were selling new tech, not broken-down, used stuff like everyone else. Before them lay the cutting edges of technology, from as many as seven different sectors of space.

"*Bozhe moi,*" Vladimir exclaimed.

"Screw the JT8s," Dalen added.

Vladimir looked at Marcus. "How did you ever pull yourself away from this place?"

Marcus laughed. "It wasn't always like *this,*" he pointed out as he led them around to the right. "It's grown tenfold, at least, since the last time I was here. Probably because of the jump drive."

"Just how far has the jump drive spread?" Vladimir wondered.

"Best I can tell, across nine sectors, not including Sol and Pentaurus," Marcus replied.

"This is going to take a while," Vladimir realized.

"Just remember one thing," Marcus warned. "Never pay asking. Hell, don't even pay *half* what they ask. Otherwise, you'll become a mark for every other vendor in the market."

"Please," Vladimir replied. "I once watched my mother argue over the price of an apple for twenty minutes, just to save half a credit. I know how to haggle."

"Yeah, we'll see," Marcus grumbled.

* * *

"One more thing," Cameron said. "Commander Kaguchi is requesting use of the fleet's boxcars."

"Don't the Rakuen have their own haulers?" Nathan wondered.

"They do, but most of them are busy moving materials from the belt to Rakuen and Neramese, to feed the fabricators," Cameron explained.

Nathan leaned back in his chair, turning to study the view screen on his ready room wall as he called up the mission schedules for the Karuzari fleet. "They're busy rearranging pods on the Inman and the Manamu," Nathan observed. "Did the commander say *why* he needed them?"

"He said they are not getting materials up to them in a timely fashion."

"What about those spectator haulers?" Nathan wondered. "Those things were pretty big. Maybe he can strip the seats out of a few and use them to haul cargo?"

"He's already done that," Cameron replied. "We've got all four boxcars working on the Inman and the Manamu. Maybe we can cut that number in half and assign two of them to Commander Kaguchi for a while?"

"I suppose so," Nathan agreed, "but only long enough to get him stocked up for a few days. We need to finish converting those ships into carriers if we're ever going to take the fight to the Dusahn."

Cameron studied the view screen a moment. "What if we used a few of the repair tugs to rearrange the cargo pods on those ships?"

"They're not designed to move that much mass," Nathan pointed out. "As soon as they fired up their mains, their crane arms would snap."

"What if they don't use their mains?" Cameron suggested. "We could park a flatbed pod hauler right next to each ship. Then, the repair tugs could just put the cargo pods on the flatbed until they were ready to restack them. They could do it all with docking thrusters. It would take a little longer, but not *much* longer."

"And it would free up all four boxcars," Nathan realized. "Good idea."

"I'll tell flight ops."

The intercom beeped. "*Captain, Comms.*"

Nathan pressed the button on the intercom panel on his desk. "Go ahead."

"*The Seiiki is calling for you, sir. They just jumped in and are on approach.*"

"Patch them through," Nathan instructed.

"*Aye, sir.*"

"*Captain?*" Loki called over the intercom.

"Yes, Loki."

"*Lieutenant Commander Nash ordered us back to fetch you, sir,*" Loki explained. "*Doctor Chen needs you to come to Sanctuary to make a decision in regards to your sister's treatment.*"

"Not really a good time, Loki."

"*The lieutenant commander instructed us not to take no for an answer...sir. She also instructed us to pick up eight more Ghatazhak, with full combat gear.*"

"Uh-oh," Cameron muttered.

Nathan sighed.

"Go, Nathan," Cameron urged. "I can handle things."

"How long until touchdown?" Nathan asked over the intercom.

"*Two and a half minutes, sir,*" Loki replied.

"I'll meet you on the flight deck," Nathan replied.

"*Understood. Seiiki out.*"

"Maybe we should set up a dedicated jump comm-drone between Sanctuary and the Rogen system,"

Cameron suggested as they both rose from their seats. “At least until Miri is well again.”

“Probably a good idea,” Nathan agreed. “But we’ll need to clear it with Sanctuary Security first, or they’ll shoot it down the moment it jumps in.”

“I’ll get it ready while you’re away,” Cameron assured him.

CHAPTER THREE

"What took you so long?" Vladimir asked Jessica as she sat down next to him at the bar. After looking her over a moment, he added, "What *happened* to you?"

"I got in an argument with a really nasty-ass stunner," she groaned, signaling the barkeep. "Something strong."

"By the looks of you, I'm guessing you lost."

"That bad, huh?" Jessica tossed back the drink offered to her. "I said *strong*, pal. Try again," she said crossly, pushing the shot glass back across the bar. "What was so important that I had to come all the way down here?" Jessica asked.

"I met a man," Vladimir explained.

"*Really*?" Jessica took the next shot and tossed it back. "Better," she told the barkeep and then turned to Vladimir. "Was it love at first sight?"

"He says he can get us in touch with a man who has many Sugali fighters for sale."

"How many?" Jessica asked, not yet impressed.

"More than one hundred, if I understood him correctly. His Angla was not so good."

Jessica was intrigued. "Surely, he doesn't have them *here*."

"He didn't say, but probably not," Vladimir agreed.

"Did he say how much?"

"No, but he said he could get us a very good deal, *if* we were willing to cooperate."

"I can't say I like the sound of that," Jessica commented, signaling the bartender for another shot. "Nathan should be here in about six hours.

Maybe we can strike a deal with this friend of yours then."

"We cannot wait that long," Vladimir warned. "He is leaving in less than two hours."

Jessica took the refilled shot glass and drank its contents in a single motion. "Where's this guy at?"

Vladimir looked to his right. "In the corner, with the two bodyguards."

"Figures." Jessica rose from her seat and headed toward the man in the corner. "Let's go have a chat." Jessica made her way through the dimly lit bar, with Vladimir a step behind. She walked up to the table in the corner but said nothing, instead just sizing up the two bodyguards sitting on either side of the older gentleman.

"Commander!" the old man greeted, his arms open wide. "You have come so to drink with me, yes? And you bring the beautiful woman, also!"

"Mister Orloff, this is Lieutenant Commander Nash, chief of security for the Aurora," Vladimir said.

The old man rose to his feet, albeit with some difficulty, reaching out across the table to take Jessica's hand. "Sosius Orloff, at service to you," he said, kissing her hand as he introduced himself. "My friends to call me Sosi. You should do same."

"You got it, Sosi."

"And you have first name?"

Jessica smiled. "Lieutenant Commander."

Sosi also smiled.

"The commander, here, tells me you know someone with a few Sugali fighters to sell. Is that true?"

"Sosi does not speak things not true. Such is waste of time. Time is most important to Sosi. When time is gone, it is gone forever, not to be regained. It is thing we have little of, yet we take for granted."

"Yet you just wasted a full minute of mine with your little speech," Jessica noted.

Sosi looked at Vladimir, confused.

"She is kidding," Vladimir assured him.

"Ah..." Sosi laughed. "She is to make joke with Sosi!" Sosi suddenly leered at her. "Very sexy."

"Jesus," Jessica whispered, leaning into Vladimir. "Where did you find this guy?"

"The lieutenant commander speaks for Captain Scott," Vladimir told Sosi.

"I do," Jessica confirmed.

"She is very much interested in the Sugali fighters of which you spoke," Vladimir continued. "Did you say there are one hundred of them?"

"At least," Sosi confirmed.

"These are *working* fighters," Jessica said. "Ones that can fly and fight?"

"I cannot speak on their operative state, but I see many in flight, so I think they are good, mostly."

"Mostly." Jessica did not look pleased.

"Can we see them?" Vladimir wondered.

Sosi winced. "That could to be difficult, I think."

"Why?" Jessica asked suspiciously.

"They are not here."

"No kidding."

"They are on Gatonda," Sosi explained.

"Never heard of it," Jessica muttered.

"It is not far," Sosi assured her. "Maybe two hundred light years, I think, yes."

"*Two hundred light years*?" Jessica exclaimed. "You don't call two hundred light years, far?"

"With jump drive, not far. You have jump drive, yes?"

"Yes."

"Then, no problem. We go, you see. Many Sugali fighters. Very good for you war, no?"

"There's just one *little* problem," Vladimir said. "Our ship will not be available for six hours."

"Sosi cannot wait six hours," Sosi warned. "Sosi cannot wait *four* hours. Sosi must leave very soon. Sosi very busy man."

"We need to see those fighters," Jessica insisted.

Sosi's right eye looked at Jessica, while his left remained on Vladimir. After a moment, his left eye swung over, also looking at Jessica.

"Fuck," Jessica muttered, creeped out by Sosi's independently moving eyes.

"I give you location, if you wish. But is very dangerous without Sosi to say you are good."

"Can't we just say 'Sosi sent us'?" Jessica wondered.

"You can, but they not will believe. Very dangerous for you both, *especially* for *you*," he added.

"Why me?" Jessica asked.

"Because you are female," he told her. "Not many females on Gatonda. Not many *pretty* females."

"I can handle myself," Jessica assured him.

Sosi looked at Vladimir.

"She can," Vladimir assured him.

"If you cannot, they kill you on Gatonda...or worse."

"Worse than being killed?" Vladimir wondered.

"Many things worse than death there are," Sosi insisted. "Many."

Jessica looked at Vladimir for a moment, thinking. "You have a jump ship?" she asked Sosi.

"Sosi has, yes. Very nice jump ship, Sosi has."

"Can you give us a lift?" Jessica wondered.

"Jess," Vladimir started to object, only to be shushed by a wave of her hand.

"To Gatonda?"

"Yes."

Sosi began to smile in a menacing fashion. "I take you," he replied, obviously intrigued by the idea. "But it still will to be dangerous for you."

"Even if we're with the great Sosi?" Jessica wondered.

Sosi continued smiling. "Being with Sosi only mean you make it to surface and not be shot down. You must still to prove yourself to Gatondans."

"Prove myself, how?"

"Combat," Sosi replied. "How else?"

Jessica smiled. Vladimir did not.

* * *

While the eight additional Ghatazhak and their combat gear would take considerably longer, Nathan cleared arrival inspection in a matter of minutes. Now that the Seiiki had a reserved hangar bay only minutes from Doctor Symyri's medical facility, he found himself at Miri's side fewer than ten minutes after arriving on Sanctuary.

As expected, his sister's expression was unchanged. She still looked as if she were in a deep, peaceful sleep and might wake at any moment—all of which made it harder.

"How long have you been here?" Doctor Chen asked as she entered the room.

"A few minutes," Nathan replied. "How is she?"

"Unchanged."

"Then, why am I here?"

"Doctor Symyri wants to move her to one of his medical stasis pods."

"Have you checked them out?"

"Yes, they are quite advanced."

"What's the advantage?" Nathan asked, still gazing at his sister's face through the stasis pod window.

"Our stasis pods do not provide *true* stasis, only a reduced metabolic state. Symyri's pods not only provide far better monitoring of her condition, but they can also provide *true* stasis; a complete cessation of the metabolic process. This is important, due to the corinite radiation she was exposed to in the blast. With RMS, the radiation is still degrading her tissues. With complete stasis, that degradation is halted. Even better, with Symyri's pods, her *level* of stasis can be *adjusted*."

"Adjusted?"

"Our RMS pods have two settings, on and off. Symyri's pods can change the level of metabolic reduction."

"How does that help?"

"Nanites can't just go in and repair the body, not with the level of damage Miri has suffered. They need to monitor changes and adjust their programming accordingly. This requires the patient be put into full stasis for short periods, allowing the nanites to do their work, and then brought into partial stasis to allow the patient's repaired tissues to react." Doctor Chen paused a moment. "Think of it like you're fixing leaks in a pipe, and you're turning the water on every so often to see if the repair you just made is holding, before moving on to the next repair."

"Seems simple."

"Yes, but it's not. The human body is very complex, with each component in each system relying on others to function properly. According to Doctor Symyri, if we were to simply keep her in deep stasis and let the nanites fix everything, we run the risk of incorrectly repaired tissues and systems, which could lead to even more problems."

"Then, let's move her."

"It's not that simple, Nathan," Doctor Chen insisted. "Moving her requires that we turn *off* her stasis pod and bring her *out* of stasis, before we can transfer her into one of Symyri's pods. According to the first responder's patient care reports, Miri's heart stopped *three times* before they got her into stasis."

"So, you think she might not survive the transfer process," Nathan surmised.

"It is a distinct possibility."

Nathan looked at his sister for a moment. "What if we leave her in *this* stasis pod?"

"Most likely the tissue degradation, from the corinite radiation, will progress faster than the nanites can repair the damage."

"So, she'll die."

"Most likely, yes."

"Most likely?"

Doctor Chen sighed. "If she stays in *this* stasis pod, it is not a matter of if, but when, she will die."

"Are you certain?"

"No one can be one hundred percent certain, Captain."

Nathan looked at Doctor Chen. "What would you do, Melei?"

Without hesitation, she replied, "I'd transfer her to a new pod as soon as possible."

Nathan studied his sister's face.

"If the risk must be taken, better it be taken here. Symyri appears to know more than any doctor I've ever met, and his facilities and staff are so advanced, it's hard to even compare them to ours." Melei reached out to touch Nathan's chin, turning his head toward her. "If anyone can save Miri, I believe it is Nikolori Symyri."

"Thank you, Melei," Nathan replied. He turned back to his sister again. "Miri is the strongest person I have ever known. She will survive this." Nathan walked confidently past Melei toward the exit. "Transfer her as soon as possible."

* * *

"Many worlds be willing to help Karuzari defeat Dusahn," Sosi said while he monitored his ship's flight systems. "For good price. But, is very dangerous for all. Dusahn have jump drives and long memories. Through back channels is best, maybe is only way."

"I've got no problem with back channels," Jessica replied, "as long as the price is right."

"Price is what price is. Is *not* for debate."

"The price is always negotiable," Jessica argued.

"No, no, no. This you must not do. *Especially* on Gatonda. *Especially* since you are..."

"...Female?" Jessica finished for him. "Please."

"You not understand," Sosi told her. He looked at Vladimir. "She not understand."

"Oh, she understands," Vladimir assured him. "She just refuses to accept it."

"Gatonda is part of Ilyan Gamaze. Gamaze is patriarchal, for as long as one remembers. A female not argue with male...not in public. They not allow this." Sosi looked at Vladimir with pleading eyes. "Please, Vladimir, you make her understand."

"Hey, I'm right here," Jessica objected.

"Yes, yes, yes. This I know. But you cannot. They kill you. They kill us all."

"Jess," Vladimir said, "perhaps you should just play along...just this once?"

"You're kidding, right?"

"Think of it as an undercover assignment," Vladimir suggested.

"Yes, yes, yes," Sosi agreed emphatically. "Undercover..." Sosi looked at Vladimir. "What this means? Undercover?"

"Uh, clandestine? Pretend? Incognito?"

"Ah, *Incognitaya*!" Sosi spouted. "Yes, yes, yes. This you must do. *Incognitaya*!"

"I don't believe this," Jessica scowled. "You want me to pretend to be subservient to a bunch of misogynists?"

"One hundred Sugali fighters, Jessica," Vladimir reminded her. "*One hundred.*"

"Big deal. Besides, even if we get them, who is going to fly them?"

"We have at *least* a hundred pilots among the Corinari," Vladimir told her.

"How do you know that?" Jessica challenged.

"I heard Nathan and Cameron talking about them, trying to decide how to best utilize them."

Jessica rolled her eyes. "I should have stayed on Sanctuary."

"And trust *me* to negotiate this deal?" Vladimir pointed out.

"Yeah, you're right. You'd fuck it up for sure."

"Then, you will behave?" Sosi surmised.

"Oh, wrong word," Jessica cautioned him.

"She will act appropriately," Vladimir promised.

Sosi looked at Vladimir, then back at Jessica, then back to Vladimir again. "I not sure should I believe you." Sosi sighed. "However, reward requires risk," he added, rising from the pilot's seat.

"Where are you going?" Vladimir wondered.

"It still forty minutes to we arrive," Sosi explained. "I think I would prepare for us to eat something."

"Please, allow me," Jessica insisted in a sickeningly sweet tone. "That is women's work. You must tend to your ship, Mister Orloff."

Sosi and Vladimir both watched with mouths agape as Jessica departed the cockpit.

"Very convincing," Sosi said, impressed.

"You see, there is nothing to worry about," Vladimir said. "I hope."

* * *

"Nathan," Neli greeted as she opened the door, finding Nathan standing there. "Welcome to paradise," she added, stepping aside and gesturing for him to enter.

"Holy crap," Nathan exclaimed. He looked across the main living area at the view outside. "Is that a beach?"

"A pretty convincing projection of one," Neli replied. "They've got one on every balcony. The beach is Melanie's favorite."

"Where is everyone?" Nathan wondered.

"Most of the Ghatazhak are at a briefing with Sanctuary Security. Apparently, Jessica made arrangements for them to carry weapons."

"What about Kyle and Melanie?"

"They went with Marcus to the Traibor Gardens."

"Traibor Gardens?"

"Some sort of exotic, indoor garden on deck one-forty-seven. Vasya and Brill are with them. Rezhik and Meeks are guarding Miri."

"I know; I saw them."

"How is she doing?" Neli asked.

"No real change," Nathan replied, taking a seat at

the dining table. "They want to move her into one of Symyri's medical stasis pods. They say it's the only chance she's got, but moving her might kill her."

"What did you decide?" Neli asked, sitting down next to him.

"I told them to do it," Nathan replied. He looked at Neli. "What choice did I have?"

"None, I suppose. Do you want me to call Marcus and have him bring them back, just in case..."

"No. There's no need."

"Are you sure?" Neli asked, looking somewhat perplexed.

"The weird thing is, I *am* sure."

"How is that weird?" Neli wondered.

"When have you ever known me to be *sure* of *anything*?" Nathan asked her.

"Not often, I suppose," Neli admitted. "I never really thought about it, since it never seemed to stop you from making decisions before. So, what's *different* now?"

"*Now*, I'm *certain* that Miri's going to recover."

"How can you be certain? Did Doctor Symyri say something?"

"I never even talked to Symyri, just Doctor Chen."

"Did *she* say something to make you feel this way?"

"On the contrary," Nathan replied, "she was quite clear about the risks."

"Then, how can you be so sure?" Neli wondered.

"I don't know," Nathan admitted. "That's what's weird. I have *no reason* to be certain Miri will survive, yet I can feel it in my gut that she will. It's like when you watch a vid-play that you haven't seen in a long time. You remember who lives and who dies, but you don't remember all the little details. It's like I can see the ending, and it has Miri waking up and asking what happened."

Neli thought for a moment before speaking. "You do know that it's just a feeling, right?"

"Yeah, I know," Nathan admitted, albeit reluctantly. He looked around. "Where are Vlad and Jess?"

"Uh, you're not going to like this," Neli said. "They hitched a ride with some guy named Orloff to someplace called Gatonda."

"Gatonda? That's in the Gamaze sector, another two hundred light years from here. Why the hell did they go there?"

"Apparently, this Orloff guy knows someone with over a hundred Sugali fighters for sale," Neli explained. "Marcus tried to talk them into waiting for you to arrive, but Orloff was going to leave, and they didn't want to lose the opportunity."

"And they went without any backup?"

Neli just shrugged.

"Great!" Nathan exclaimed, rising from his seat. "There's a jump comm-drone going through the inspection process right now. Once it's cleared and given a properly coded transponder, use it to update the Aurora on what's going on," he instructed as he headed toward the door.

"Where are you going?"

"To Gatonda."

"But Josh and Loki are on their way here," Neli told him, following him toward the exit.

"Then, tell them to turn around and go back to the Seiiki, and get her ready to launch. And tell Rezhik to send me a couple Ghatazhak, as well!" Nathan barked as he exited the suite.

"Jesus," Neli exclaimed, throwing her hands up.

"Josh, this is Neli," she called over her comm-set. "Nathan's headed back to the Seiiki to depart. Turn back and meet him there."

"*But we just got here!*" Josh complained.

"Just do it!"

"*Where are we going?*"

"Gatonda."

"*I don't even know where that is!*" Josh insisted.

"Nathan does, I think... I hope."

* * *

Jessica and Vladimir stood at the inner hatch of Sosi's ship, waiting for him to lead them out. After a moment, he appeared, carrying a sheer, blue wrap.

"You must wear this," Sosi said, handing Jessica the wrap.

"Why?"

"Is what women of Gatonda wear. It to hide a woman's features and sexuality from men."

"It doesn't hide much," Jessica commented. "You can practically see right through it."

"Its purpose more tradition than function," Sosi admitted. "You need this, as well," he added, reaching toward her forehead.

"What are you doing?" Jessica asked, brushing his hand away from her.

"It be easier if you bear the mark," Sosi explained, opening his hand to show her the small, flat jewel-stone in his hand.

"The mark of what?"

"Of married female."

"Married to whom?" Jessica wondered, one eyebrow raised.

"Well, to him, yes?" Sosi surmised, pointing to Vladimir.

"Do as the nice man says, honey," Vladimir told her, smiling.

"Don't make me kick your ass...*dear*," she retorted. "This is such bullshit," Jessica complained as Sosi pressed the jewel-stone onto her forehead. "How the hell do the women of this world put up with this crap?"

"Is not *crap*," Sosi argued. "Is tradition."

"The oppression of one sex by another is crap," Jessica argued as she adjusted her wrap. "Tradition or not."

"What is this *oppression*?" Sosi wondered.

"When people are treated poorly, made to serve others, like they are not of value," Vladimir explained.

"*That's* your explanation?" Jessica challenged, looking at Vladimir.

"What?"

"Why you think women of Gatonda have *oppression*?" Sosi wondered.

"Making me cover up? *Marking* me as married?"

"No one *makes* women of Gatonda do these things," Sosi insisted. "They do because it is their way. Gatondan men have great respect for their women. For their sacrifices for Gatonda. They see women as great gifts; they protect; they worship; they appreciate women for all they provide. Gatondan men *know* they nothing without Gatondan women."

"Are women allowed to do the same jobs as men?" Jessica asked.

Sosi thought for a moment. "I do not know. They do not, but by choice, I think. Women do what women do best; men do what men do best. Equal; different."

"Yeah, I've heard that before," Jessica scowled.

Sosi looked at Vladimir. "Is there problem?"

"Do not worry, Sosi," Vladimir promised. "She will be fine."

The inner door slid open, followed by the outer door, and a wave of hot air smacked them in the face. Hot, humid air that smelled of dust and rotting vegetation. The light outside was bright, with a pale yellow tint that made the expected colors seem unnatural.

"My God," Jessica exclaimed. "What the hell died here?"

"It is sulfur in atmosphere. Gatonda is mostly desert. Sand contains sulfur," Sosi explained.

"How the hell do people breathe here?"

"You get used to smell very soon."

"I have smelled worse," Vladimir insisted.

Jessica glanced at Vladimir, who shook his head, admitting he was lying.

"Please to follow me," Sosi instructed, heading down the ramp. He turned to look at them and stopped. "The female follows the male, so he may protect her from danger."

Jessica rolled her eyes, pausing for Vladimir to move in front of her. As they resumed walking, she whispered to him. "If danger comes, just step aside, and I'll deal with it."

Despite the uncertain look on his face, Sosi continued forward, leading them across the tarmac to the vehicle waiting at the perimeter. As they approached, the driver opened the back door for them. Sosi stepped to one side, then placed his hand on Vladimir's shoulder, preventing him from entering the vehicle. "Ladies, first."

Vladimir stepped aside, a confused look on his face. Jessica, on the other hand, smiled at him as she passed and stepped into the vehicle. Vladimir rolled his eyes, following her inside.

Once the three of them were safely in the vehicle, the driver secured the door, slipped into the driver's cab, and guided the vehicle toward the exit gate.

Within minutes, they found themselves cruising through the heart of the city. Although the streets and buildings were covered with a fine, pale dust, the city itself was more impressive than most that Jessica had seen as of late. The streets were logically laid out, and the buildings themselves did not have that 'slapped-together' look of most worlds. This world was more developed, more industrialized. The buildings were purposely built as complete units. In fact, many of them were rather ornate in their design, which was uncommon on all but the most heavily populated worlds.

"How many cities on Gatonda?" Jessica asked.

"I do not know," Sosi admitted. "I never to count."

"One; ten; one hundred?"

"More than ten; less than hundred," Sosi decided.

"Are they all like this?"

"Some better; some worse," Sosi replied. "Arleeto is only spaceport on Gatonda. All cities are on same part of planet."

"*All*?"

"All that matter," Sosi corrected.

"Why only the one spaceport?" Vladimir asked.

"Gatonda not have spaceships. Spaceships from other worlds visit. Bring trade, take trade. But no spaceships belong to Gatonda. They not want them."

"Why not?" Vladimir wondered.

"They not need. Plenty come from other worlds. More than they need."

"But how do they defend themselves?" Jessica asked.

"I not say Gatonda not defend Gatonda," Sosi told her. He looked out the window, then pointed. "There," he said, "very big guns. That how Gatonda defend Gatonda."

"Holy crap," Jessica exclaimed. "Are those plasma cannons?"

"They are," Vladimir confirmed, staring out the window at the massive weapons as they cruised by. "And they're even bigger than the ones on Takara." He turned to look at Sosi. "How many of them do they have?"

"I do not know," Sosi admitted. "At least one hundred, with many more in reserve."

"Do they ever use them?" Jessica wondered.

"No one attack Gatonda in Sosi's lifetime," Sosi assured her. "No one that stupid."

Jessica looked at Vladimir. "Are you thinking what I'm thinking?" she asked with a smile.

Vladimir smiled back.

* * *

Nathan bounded up the Seiiki's cargo ramp, finding Corporal Vasya and Specialist Brill waiting in the cargo bay. "Gentlemen," Nathan greeted. "I thought you were at some kind of indoor garden with Kyle and Melanie."

"We were," Corporal Vasya replied, "but the lieutenant ordered Bains and Reino to take over for us."

"So, you drew the short straws, then," Nathan joked.

"Not at all, we'd much rather go hopping across the galaxy with you. Not much chance of a good bar fight while playing bodyguards."

Nathan patted the corporal on the shoulder as he passed. "Then, button her up, boys," he instructed as he headed for the forward ladder.

"Are we it?" Specialist Brill wondered.

"Is Dalen on board?" Nathan asked as he climbed the ladder.

"Yes, sir," the specialist replied.

"Then, we're it," Nathan confirmed, pausing at the hatch and turning back toward them. "If we get into trouble en route, you two have the topside gun turrets."

"Is the starboard turret even working?" Vasya asked.

"It will be," Nathan promised.

Corporal Vasya turned and slapped the ramp control with his hand, starting the retraction cycle. "Off on another adventure," he proclaimed with a grin.

Nathan tapped his comm-set as he passed through the forward cargo bay hatch, into the central compartment. "You guys figure out where Gatonda is yet?"

"*Two sectors over,*" Loki replied. "*I got some updated star charts from a cargo ship in the next bay. They weren't cheap. Should take us about six hours.*"

"Then, let's get going," Nathan replied as he headed up the stairs to the topside gun deck. "Dalen! You up there?"

"*Yeah!*"

Nathan continued up the stairs to the gun deck, turning to starboard as he reached the top. "How's it looking?"

"The Sanctuary techs got the turret and the new gun installed, but I still have to hook everything up, including the power source. We should probably test-fire it before we use it."

"I'm hoping we won't have to use it," Nathan replied. "How long?"

"Five or six hours, I think."

"Could you use some help?"

"Sure," Dalen replied. "Just don't send Josh. He goofs around too much, and I have to double-check all of his work."

"I'll send you Vasya and Brill," Nathan replied as he turned to head back down the stairs. "And Loki, once we're away."

"Thanks, Cap'n," Dalen replied.

Nathan made his way down the stairs and across the main compartment, heading forward up the port corridor. After passing the galley, the boarding airlock, and the forward lift fan housing, he reached the cockpit ladder, quickly ascending its handful of rungs to reach the Seiiki's flight deck.

"Sanctuary Flight Control has already cleared us, Captain," Loki announced as Nathan came up behind him.

"Take us out, then, gentlemen," Nathan instructed, taking a seat at the starboard-facing engineer's station, directly behind Loki. He glanced at the displays, checking to see if his ship's systems were functioning normally, or at least as normally as could be expected. He couldn't remember the last time everything worked perfectly. Even with the help of the Aurora's engineers and technicians, her fabricators, and Vladimir's loving attention, there still was not enough time in between missions to take proper care of her. Now, without Marcus and Neli, and Vladimir being a few hundred light years away, his ship was going to receive even less maintenance.

The Seiiki rose a meter off the deck, sliding sideways as it rotated to port. Nathan turned and looked out the forward windows as the inner hangar bay doors parted, revealing the short transit tunnel leading to the surface.

"Auto-flight is taking us out," Josh stated, his usual disdain for automated flight systems obvious in his tone.

Nathan watched as his ship made its way down the tunnel, staying precisely in its center the entire way. A minute later, they approached the outer doors, which were already sliding open in anticipation of their departure. The gap between the two, massive outer doors became wide enough to allow them to pass only seconds before the Seiiki's nose crossed its threshold. Just like that, gone were the rocky, evenly lit walls of the tunnel, replaced by the myriad of buildings that littered the asteroid, threatening to hide its surface from view.

The ship cleared the doors and pitched up, its engines increasing in power to accelerate the vessel away from the station.

"Twenty seconds to release from auto-flight," Loki announced.

"So, what's the plan, Cap'n?" Josh asked as he prepared to take control of the Seiiki.

"We make best speed to Gatonda and meet up with Jess and Vlad."

"What the hell are they doing there?" Josh wondered.

"Five seconds," Loki warned.

"More importantly," Josh continued as he began flying the Seiiki, "how the hell did they get there?"

"Some guy named Orloff took them," Nathan

explained. "Says he knows a guy with a bunch of Sugali fighters for sale."

"Turn to one four seven, up fifteen relative," Loki instructed.

"One four seven, up fifteen," Josh replied. "How many is *a bunch*?"

"A hundred, or so I'm told," Nathan told him.

Josh grinned. "Man, a hundred Sugali fighters would be sweet. That thing was a blast to fly."

"Yeah, they're quick and deadly," Nathan agreed, "which makes me wonder why anyone would be looking to sell them. Especially that many of them."

"You could start your own little empire with that many fighters," Josh said, practically drooling.

Nathan looked at him. "You worry me sometimes, Josh."

"I'm just sayin'," Josh defended. "On course."

"Best speed, Captain?" Loki asked.

"Best speed," Nathan confirmed.

Josh pushed the throttles forward, bringing both engines to full power, while Loki made a few calculations.

"Bring us up to a quarter light and hold," Loki finally instructed.

"We can do at least one third light," Josh argued.

"Quarter light will be fine, Josh," Nathan agreed. "Better to save some propellant for deceleration and landing. Plus, I'd like to have enough left over to get the hell out of there in a hurry, even if we can't refuel on the surface."

"You expecting trouble, Cap'n?" Josh wondered.

"It's Jessica, remember?" Nathan replied.

"But Vlad's with her," Loki said.

"That's supposed to make me feel better?" Nathan wondered.

"Good point," Loki agreed as he made the jump calculations.

"Quarter light in two minutes," Josh reported.

"I don't suppose either of you knows anything about Gatonda?" Nathan asked.

"Never heard of it," Josh replied.

"The guys who sold us the star charts laughed when I told them where we were going," Loki told them. "They advised that we carry weapons at all times." Loki turned and looked at Nathan. "I took that as a bad sign, myself."

Nathan sighed. "As soon as you get the jump series up and running, go back and help Dalen and the others. I'd like to get that gun turret back online before we enter the Gamaze sector."

"Yes, sir," Loki replied.

"Quarter light," Josh announced, pulling the throttles back to idle.

"Starting jump series in five seconds," Loki announced.

"How much do you think a hundred Sugali fighters cost?" Josh asked.

"More than we can afford, most likely," Nathan replied as the ship made its first jump. "I just hope there really *are* a hundred of them for sale, and that it's not some kind of con that they're walking into."

* * *

At Sosi's insistence, they had stopped at a clothing store and had redressed both Jessica and Vladimir in appropriate, local attire. The result for Jessica had been a formfitting dress that stopped at mid-thigh and left very little to the imagination, even through the flowing, sheer, blue drape she wore over it. Jessica had accused Sosi of being a dirty, old man but now—following him through the crowded, upscale restaurant—she realized that hers was not the most revealing outfit in the room. The men of Gatonda took considerable pride in their appearance, but the women far outdid their male counterparts with skimpy outfits, colorful makeup, and outlandish hairstyles.

It had been some time since Jessica had worn anything other than a uniform, let alone configured her hair in anything but a ponytail. Lack of time had prevented them from visiting a salon. Had the lady at the clothiers not loaned her a brush and some clips, she'd still be wearing it that way.

At least she looked good. Vladimir, on the other hand, looked even more foolish than the rest of the men on this strange, smelly world. Long, silken, button-down robes that hung just below the knees, with high, colorful collars, and contrasting slacks seemed standard fare; the more colorful the better.

Oddly enough, Gatonda fashion stood in stark contrast to their architecture and interior decor. Their buildings were all of neutral colors, covered mostly in concrete, glass, and metals. Their interiors were just as bland, the only difference being the tapestries and long, sheer, colorful banners that draped across the ceilings and shifted lazily in the breeze of the ventilation systems. It was easy to spot service staff in the restaurant, as they were the only ones who sported no vibrant colors; only grays, whites, and blacks.

The hostess, also clad in formfitting attire, led them to the far side of the expansive dining room and up the wide staircase to the mezzanine level. Once at the top of the stairs, she steered them to the left, around the perimeter of the room, behind the private booths that lined the level.

The hostess stopped at the entrance to a booth guarded by two serious-looking men in solid blue robes and white slacks, sporting clear, one-piece glasses. By the bulges under each man's robe, Jessica knew they were armed, and likely with more than just handguns. The hostess whispered into the ear of the first man, then stepped aside. The first man reached up and touched the side of his glasses, causing the rim to glow softly. He looked Sosi up and down, then Vladimir, then Jessica, after which he smiled. The man looked to the other guard and nodded, both of them stepping aside, allowing them to enter.

Sosi was first, his arms spread wide in greeting as he uttered something in a language Jessica did not recognize. There were four people at the table when they entered, a middle-aged man, probably a bit younger than Sosi, and three considerably younger women, all of them in revealing attire, which was in line with what they had seen thus far. However, none of the young women were wearing any sheer drapes over them. At first, Jessica assumed they were the elder man's companions for the evening, but the young women's attentions seemed more focused on the diners below than on their host.

The man stood, embracing Sosi and responding in the same language. He was relatively fit, had a full head of dark, curly hair, a thick but well-groomed beard, and a medium complexion, like the majority of Gatondans. His robes were even more colorful than most and were trimmed with what appeared to be real gold that had been infused into the fabric itself. The metal caused his robes to hang cleanly, preventing the accumulation of wrinkles in the fabric and causing them to swing in a more pronounced fashion as he moved.

The table itself was set to impress, with the finest Gatondan china, crystal, and silverware. There were multiple dishes present, including fresh fruits and vegetables, many of which Jessica did not recognize. There were also several half-empty bottles of wine and partially drunk glasses, as well, making it obvious that their evening meal was well in progress.

Sosi turned toward Jessica and Vladimir, his left arm extended. "Allow I should introduce my new friends, Vladimir and his lovely wife, Jessica." Sosi turned back toward the other man. "This is Aristaeus Imburjia, most gifted trader on all Gatonda."

"You flatter me, Sosi," Aristaeus said, smiling. "I am most honored to make your acquaintance," he told Vladimir, shaking his hand as he nodded politely. "May I have the honor of paying appropriate respect to your lovely spouse?"

"A pleasure, sir, of course," Vladimir replied.

Aristaeus stepped over and took Jessica's hand, grasping it delicately, and raising it to his face, his lips barely touching the back of her fingers. "Your husband is a lucky man, my lady." He lowered her hand again, releasing it as he stepped back. "Please, you will join us?"

"We'd be delighted," Sosi exclaimed.

"These are my daughters, Yoli, Rena, and Naeni," Aristaeus introduced. After the three young women nodded respectfully, he gave them instructions, in what Jessica assumed was the Gatondan language, and the girls immediately rose from the table and departed the private dining room.

"I hope we are not intruding," Vladimir stated.

"Not at all," Aristaeus insisted. "I merely told them

what they wanted to hear, that they were free to visit the dance floor next door. Trust me, they'd rather be there than dining with their father. Besides, I prefer to keep business matters clear of family, and if you came with Sosi, then you are here on business."

"We are," Jessica confirmed. "Your wife is not dining with you?"

"My wife is long deceased, I'm afraid. Since my daughters were just children."

"My apologies," Jessica offered.

"Please, sit. Help yourself to wine and food. If there is anything you want, you need but ask, and I will provide," Aristaeus promised.

"Thank you; you are most kind," Vladimir replied as he held the chair for Jessica.

"You are not of Ilyan Gamaze, no?" Aristaeus surmised.

"You are correct," Vladimir replied, looking surprised.

"The accents, they are unfamiliar to me," Aristaeus explained. "Both of them, in fact. This does not happen often. Not on Gatonda." Aristaeus studied them both. After a moment, he turned to Vladimir. "Volon?"

Vladimir smiled, shaking his head. "I have never been there, I'm afraid."

Aristaeus looked disappointed. "I am usually spot-on." He looked at Jessica. "The name is very old, very traditional. I have not heard it used in some time." After a pause, he took a guess. "Keren Alpha?"

"Never heard of it," Jessica replied, showing no expression.

"Oh, this is most disconcerting," Aristaeus admitted. He looked at Jessica again with pleading eyes. "Please, you must share with me your place of birth."

Jessica looked at Sosi, then smiled at Aristaeus. "Florida."

"I've never heard of it," the older man admitted, surprised. "Is it in the Dori sector?"

"Sol, actually," Jessica replied.

Aristaeus looked confused, but only for a moment. His eyes widened, and his posture straightened as he looked at both of them in disbelief. "You are from *Earth*?" He looked at Vladimir. "The both of you?"

"Russia," Vladimir replied, answering his question.

"My God," he exclaimed. He looked to Sosi. "Surely, you did not travel to Earth on that tiny ship of yours."

"I met them on Sanctuary," Sosi explained.

"Incredible. I have never met anyone from Earth." Aristaeus looked concerned. "You must not divulge your true origins to anyone else on Gatonda. You will be inundated with questions, not to mention cursed with suspicions and mistrust."

"This is reason for their disguise," Sosi assured him.

"It is well that you took such precautions," Aristaeus agreed. He leaned back in his chair, taking them both in and savoring the moment. "We have heard, of course, that the people of Earth had made it as far as the Pentaurus cluster. Gatonda has only recently begun to reap the benefits of your jump drive technology. But to have the two of you here, sharing my table, is nothing short of miraculous."

"I'm happy you're so pleased," Jessica replied, having already grown tired of the older man's fascination. “But if you don’t mind, we have business to discuss.”

Sosi looked shocked and was about to object to her forwardness but was stopped by a not-so-subtle gesture from Aristaeus. “They are not of Gatonda,” he reminded Sosi. “We cannot expect them to follow our ways.” He looked at Jessica, smiling. “Then tell me, my dear, what brings you to Gatonda?”

“Sugali fighters,” Jessica replied, getting straight to the point. “We were told you might have a few to sell.”

“A few, I have,” Aristaeus confirmed. “How many were you looking to purchase?”

“All of them,” Jessica replied without hesitation.

Vladimir glanced quickly at her. “Uh, perhaps you offer a volume discount?” he asked Aristaeus.

The gentleman couldn’t help but smile at his sudden turn of fortune. He looked back at Jessica. “I have one hundred and twenty-eight Sugali fighters available for purchase. One hundred of them are fully operational. The others will require some repairs, or perhaps can be used for spare parts.”

“How much?” Jessica inquired, not wanting to waste time.

Aristaeus looked at Sosi. “She doesn’t waste much time, does she?”

“I’m right here, Mister Imburjia,” Jessica chided. “How much?”

“Two million Ilyan dracmas...” Aristaeus smiled, “...*each.*”

Jessica didn’t flinch; she simply looked at Sosi.

“Roughly half million universal credits,” Sosi told her. “Each.”

“We can cover that,” Jessica declared without pause.

"We can?" Vladimir questioned.

"I'll admit it might be stretching the budget a bit, but it sounds like a fair enough price." She turned to Aristaeus again. "Assuming you throw in the inop birds for free, of course...seeing as how we're buying the entire lot, and making you a very tidy profit, I'm sure."

"The inop birds are worth more parted out than they are as operational fighters," Aristaeus told her.

"Then part them out," Jessica dismissed. "We can always fabricate our own replacement parts after we tear one down and scan it. However, if you're not throwing in the inops, then the price is one point nine." Jessica also smiled. "*Each.*"

"I have another buyer who is willing to pay two, *and* they are willing to pay a reasonable price for the inoperative ships, as well," Aristaeus told her. "The price is two, each. However, I am willing to negotiate on the price of the inoperative ships, depending on each vessel's condition."

"Who?" Jessica asked, challenging him.

"The Ridalli system," Aristaeus replied. "They have been harassed by Ahka raiders for years."

"Ahka raiders?" Vladimir asked.

"Pirate gangs from the nearby Ahka system," Aristaeus explained. "Both worlds are just outside Ilyan Gamaze, and therefore are unprotected by the Emirates of Ilyanossa. Casbon has finally realized that they must protect themselves."

"But Casbon so small," Sosi stated, drawing an irritated look from Aristaeus.

"They are small, yes, but their world is rich in resources, particularly in rare and precious metals."

"Then, they can afford such purchase," Sosi surmised.

“Their means of payment is still in development.”

“Then, the sale is not final yet,” Jessica realized.

“Nothing is final until goods and payment are exchanged,” Aristaeus replied. “But they are quite adamant about their desire to purchase the fighters.”

Jessica thought for a moment. “Do they have pilots?”

“As part of the deal, I must provide training for their people.”

“Does Casbon even *have* any pilots?” Sosi wondered.

“They do not. They are like Gatonda and have no ships of their own,” Aristaeus admitted. “Fortunately, the Sugali fighters are quite easy to operate.”

Jessica leaned back in her chair, crossing her legs and smiling. “So, they have no combat experience, either.” She looked at Vladimir. “They’ll get slaughtered.”

“Does Casbon have any infrastructure to support these fighters?” Vladimir wondered, leaning forward, his arms on the table. “Engineers, technicians...”

“...Command and control,” Jessica added.

“Admittedly, it will take some time for them to become capable of defending their world...”

“I was right the first time,” Jessica insisted. “They’ll get slaughtered. The moment those raiders realize the Casbons are arming themselves, they’ll attack in force and obliterate every single ship.” Jessica smiled at Aristaeus. “I’d make sure you got paid in full, *up front*, before you deliver.”

Despite his best efforts to hide it, Aristaeus looked concerned. “Although peaceful, the people of Casbon are not fools. I am certain they have considered these factors in their decision to arm themselves.”

“Perhaps,” Jessica admitted. “But we *have*

considered all of these factors, and we are not only prepared *and* equipped to utilize those ships, but we have the *experience* to do so."

"Do you, now?" Aristaeus questioned, suspicious of her claims.

"We do."

Aristaeus studied Jessica for a moment. "Assume, for the time being, that you speak the truth. I do not know you, and I do not know what you will do with those fighters. The Casbons, I *do* know. Furthermore, I do business with them on a regular basis. So, you see, it is to *my* benefit that *they* receive those fighters."

"It is to *your benefit* that they *successfully* defend themselves," Jessica pointed out. She thought for a moment. "How many ships do the raiders usually attack with?"

"I am uncertain," Aristaeus admitted. "A handful at best. The Ahka have no warships, only small, short-range jump fighters. They must ferry them into strike position using small, jump cargo ships converted into carriers. However, what they lack in firepower, they make up for with ferocity."

A light went on in Jessica's head.

"What are you thinking?" Vladimir asked, noticing the glint in her eye.

"Mister Imburjia," Jessica began, "if you truly wish to continue doing business with the Casbons, you would be wise to introduce us to them *before* you sell them those fighters."

"And why would I do that?" Aristaeus countered, almost laughing. "You are their competitors."

"And we may very well be their saviors," Jessica insisted.

"Oh, really," Aristaeus chuckled.

"We can provide them with the training they need, as well as support personnel to protect them until they are able to protect themselves."

"We can?" Vladimir asked, somewhat perplexed.

"The Corinari," Jessica whispered out of the corner of her mouth.

"And why would you do that?" he wondered.

"If the Ahka are only attacking with a handful of fighters, then the Casbons don't need all one hundred Sugali fighters. Not if they're flown by properly trained pilots and supported with competent and efficient infrastructure."

"What is it you are proposing?" Aristaeus wondered, becoming curious.

"They buy the fighters from you, and we take fifty of them in exchange for providing pilots and support personnel, until their own people are properly trained and ready to take over," Jessica explained. "Everybody wins."

"Except the Ahka," Sosi pointed out.

Aristaeus examined Vladimir and Jessica for several moments before speaking. "Forgive me, but neither of you look like military experts."

"Trust me, Mister Imburjia," Jessica said, "we know what we're talking about."

Aristaeus looked at Sosi, who nodded confirmation of her claim. "Who *are* you?" he asked, looking at Jessica again.

"Take us to Casbon, and I'll tell you," she replied with a wink and a smile.

CHAPTER FOUR

"You are more introspective than usual, General," Lord Dusahn commented as he waited for the server to pour the jesauni glaze onto his dollag steak. "Something troubles you?"

General Hesson held his reply until both servers had finished glazing their entrees and left their private dining chambers. "Our lack of current intelligence on the Rogen system has me somewhat unsettled, my lord."

"The Rogen system is too far away to be an immediate threat," Lord Dusahn reminded him.

"True, but we have been unable to get a recon drone into their system for going on ten days now. They keep getting taken out by their Gunyoki fighters."

"You cannot blame them for not wanting our recon drones in their system."

"No, I cannot," General Hesson agreed. "However, if we are to destroy the Rogen system *without* suffering the loss of any of *our* ships, we need better intelligence on their defenses."

"They have a handful of jump-equipped fighters," Lord Dusahn stated as he took his first bite of the glazed dollag meat. He closed his eyes, savoring the taste and texture as he chewed. "There are many things about this world that I find distasteful," he said after he swallowed. "This creature is not one of them."

"They may have only a handful of *jump-equipped* fighters; however, they have more than five hundred Gunyoki fighters in all."

"Even their jump-equipped fighters are at a disadvantage against our Teronbah fighters."

"Our analysts estimate the Ranni plant is capable of producing five jump drives per day," the general replied. "In one hundred days, that handful of jump-equipped Gunyoki fighters will become a veritable armada. Their overwhelming numbers, alone, will render our Teronbahs ineffective."

Lord Dusahn studied the general as he enjoyed his dollag meat. "You believe the jump-equipped Gunyoki can take down one of our warships?"

"If enough of them attack in a properly coordinated fashion, yes."

Lord Dusahn picked up his glass, sipping his wine as he contemplated the general's assessment. "A frigate, perhaps," he admitted, setting his glass down, "maybe even a light cruiser, but surely not any of our heavier ships."

General Hesson cocked his head. It was obvious that he did not agree with his leader's conclusions.

"General," Lord Dusahn protested.

"Their main plasma cannons derive their energy directly from the engine aft of them," General Hesson explained. "Because of this, they have considerable firepower."

"I believe you overestimate the Gunyoki's capabilities," Lord Dusahn insisted, attacking his dollag steak again.

"After the loss of the Teyentah *and* the shipyard itself, doing so seems prudent. We cannot afford to lose any more of our warships, especially if we are to implement your plan, my lord."

Lord Dusahn sighed. "I suppose you are correct." After savoring another morsel, he looked directly at the general and spoke. "Send the Sor-Vasello. She has the best long-range sensor suite of any of our cruisers, and Captain Loray is a sneaky, little shit. Have them loiter close enough to gather signals intelligence on the Rakuen system but instruct them to avoid detection at all costs."

"Any signals they receive will be weeks old, if not months," General Hesson reminded.

Lord Dusahn held up his hand, indicating he had not finished giving instructions. "The Rakuens trade with other worlds, do they not?"

"They do."

"Then, capture a few of those ships that routinely visit their world and send them in—with their loads—and have them collect passive scans while in the Rogen system. Once they exit, they can rendezvous with Loray, who can then relay their scans to us."

"This will only work three, maybe four times at best," the general warned. "Eventually, the Rakuens will get word of the missing ships."

"Perhaps," Lord Dusahn admitted.

"We will only be able to use each captured vessel but once," General Hesson decided, "and it would be best if each captured ship was from a different world."

"That should not be a problem," Lord Dusahn said as he took another bite of his meal.

General Hesson tipped his head in agreement. "I will attempt to spread our use of captured ships over the remaining time until our ships from Orswella arrive, to ensure that our subterfuge is not discovered until it is too late."

"Good thinking, General," Lord Dusahn agreed.

* * *

Vladimir stooped over and stepped through the hatchway into the cockpit of Aristaeus's ship, moving over to sit in one of the two seats behind and to either side of the pilot's seat in the center. "It is an unusual cockpit layout," he commented as he ran his hands through his hair, trying to tame his thick mane.

"How so?" Aristaeus wondered, his eyes still on his display screens as he made adjustments to his ship's systems.

"Most ships have two seats in front, one for the pilot and one for the copilot."

"This ship's systems are mostly automated, so it only requires a single operator," Aristaeus explained.

"Was this a cargo ship at one time?" Vladimir inquired.

Aristaeus turned to face Vlad, surprised. "How did you know?"

"This cockpit and the cabin directly behind are the only parts that are double-hulled. Sleeping berths, shower, galley: all are single-hulled. Also, the storeroom between the forward cabin and the spaces that are single-hulled is actually an airlock, converted into a storeroom."

"You are very observant," Aristaeus replied.

"I'm an engineer," Vladimir boasted. "I notice such things." He glanced past his host, noticing the flight displays. "One percent light?"

"As you discovered, this ship was not originally designed as a passenger ship."

"If you are in the import/export business, you need a faster ship," Vladimir observed.

"I *had* a faster ship," Aristaeus replied. "I sold her to help close the deal on the Sugali fighters. I bought this vessel with what little was left. She was an interplanetary cargo runner, designed for week-long runs between a few of the clustered worlds on the far rim. I apologize for her lack of speed. She is not the fastest ship in the Ilyan."

"What does it mean, *Ilyan*?" Vladimir wondered.

"*Ilyan* means *realm*," Aristaeus explained.

"So, *Ilyan Gamaze* means *realm of Gamaze*?"

"Correct."

"Then, Gamaze rules this realm?"

"No, the Ilyan is ruled by all member worlds. Each is their own ruler, who have all agreed to follow a set of rules governing their interactions with other worlds of the Ilyan. Gamaze is simply the first world that was settled in the region, and therefore is the most populated and industrialized. Representatives meet regularly on Gamaze, to discuss and refine these rules, but they do not dictate to one another on how to run each individual world."

"But what if one world regularly does something that the other worlds do not like?" Vladimir wondered.

"It is of no concern to the Council of the Ilyan, unless it affects other worlds within the Ilyan."

"It seems like a recipe for conflict," Vladimir noted.

"It has its difficulties, I will admit, but it has worked for more than five hundred years. Of course, most of the worlds of the Ilyan are fairly similar in culture, ethics, and morality."

"Do all the worlds in your Ilyan have the same patriarchal structure?" Jessica asked as she stepped through the hatchway to join them.

"In the core, yes, but not all of the rim worlds share the same ways or beliefs," Aristaeus replied, doing a double-take after noticing Jessica's formfitting uniform. "Maybe it is time you told me who you *truly* are."

"Lieutenant Commander Jessica Nash," she

confessed, turning her shoulder toward Aristaeus to show him the patch. "Chief tactical and security officer for the Aurora."

One of Aristaeus's eyebrows shot up. He turned to Vladimir.

"Commander Vladimir Kamenetskiy, chief engineer."

"Where's your uniform?" Aristaeus wondered.

"I let her change first."

"But you outrank her."

"The fact that she could kick my ass with one hand tied behind her back supersedes rank."

"An odd military structure, you have."

"Yeah, it's kind of screwy, but it works for us," Jessica commented, also raising an eyebrow.

"Then, the rumors I have heard are true," Aristaeus surmised.

"Depends," Jessica replied. "What did you hear?"

"That the legendary Na-Tan somehow rose from the dead and is leading the Aurora and the Karuzari in a fight to, once again, free the Pentaurus cluster... only this time from an enemy known as the *Dusahn.*"

"Correct," Jessica replied.

"Well, the Dusahn part is true," Vladimir correct.

"Yeah, the whole 'rose from the dead' part is a little more complicated," Jessica admitted.

"But Captain Scott and the Aurora..."

"Yes, Captain Scott is back in command of the Aurora and is leading a small fleet of converted ships against the Dusahn Empire," Jessica explained.

"We also have two worlds in the Rogen system supporting us," Vladimir added.

"Just who are these *Dusahn*?" Aristaeus wondered.

"You haven't heard of them?" Jessica asked.

"I have, but only rumors. They are said to be ruthless; destroying entire worlds for no reason."

"Two, so far," Jessica explained. "Burgess and Ybara. One because it was the home of the Ghatazhak, and the other because its representatives failed to show the *proper respect* to the Dusahn leader."

Aristaeus shook his head. "It is a pity that such people still, and will most likely always, exist. We had hoped that Caius Ta'Akar would be the last to plague our quadrant of the galaxy."

"Now you know why *we* need the Sugali fighters so badly," Jessica said.

"How can one hundred light fighters help against a fleet of warships?" Aristaeus challenged.

"We lack fighters capable of atmospheric operations," Jessica explained. "We only have about twenty at the moment, and they are not as agile as the Sugali fighters, at least, not according to our captain."

"Na-Tan has *flown* one?"

"Yes," Jessica replied, "in combat, in fact. We don't have the firepower to slug it out with their entire fleet. Our only hope is to split them up by attacking surface targets, and then use the Aurora to ambush whatever warships respond. To do this, we need close air support, especially since our ground forces are limited in number."

"Fifty Sugali fighters seems an insufficient number," Aristaeus observed.

"It's a far sight better than twenty," Jessica argued.

"Perhaps, but the Casbons will argue that those fighters will guarantee their safety; whereas for you, they will be but one of many tools."

"Without proper training and experience, the only

thing those fighters will guarantee is their doom," Jessica insisted.

"I do not argue your point, even though it assumes the Ahka will also see that their only hope is to strike the Casbons in force *before* they are properly trained and capable of defending themselves. But you must see the Casbons's point of view. The raids on their world have become more frequent in recent years. Many believe the Ahka are doing more poorly than suspected and are becoming desperate. Such people can be unpredictable. Were *you* in charge of their world, would you counsel them otherwise?"

"I would," Jessica insisted.

"What would you suggest they do differently?" Aristaeus inquired.

"I would urge them to keep their newly acquired fighters a secret until their pilots can be properly trained, so as not to force their enemy's hand."

Aristaeus chuckled. "Your euphemisms are unfamiliar to me, but I think I understand your meaning. Unfortunately, it would be quite impossible to *hide* one hundred fighters on Casbon. I suspect your arguments will need to be stronger, if you hope to convince them to give up half of their fighters."

"I don't suppose they'd be willing to see the big picture here," Jessica said.

"The *big picture*?" Aristaeus wondered. "What? That if the Dusahn are not stopped, they will eventually conquer the Ilyan, as well?"

"Does the Ilyan have warships to rival the Dusahn?"

"No, the Ilyan's ships are small and meant for enforcement, not as a defense against outside invaders. However, the Pentaurus cluster is over eight hundred light years away. Even if the Dusahn are allowed to expand their empire unimpeded, they will not reach Ilyan Gamaze in my lifetime, nor that of my great-great-grandchildren."

"But they *will* reach the Ilyan, *someday*," Jessica insisted.

"It is just as likely that the Dusahn will run afoul of some other empire before they reach us. As I said, there is no shortage of power-hungry despots in the galaxy."

"Which is why we must *all* band together to stand *against* such people," Jessica replied.

"For freedom, justice, and liberty," Aristaeus surmised. He let out another laugh. "My dear, you'd be surprised how easily one gives up their liberty. *Survival* is a powerful instinct, probably the most powerful in the universe, and it exists in all living things. Promise a man his safety, and he willingly gives up his freedom."

"Not every man," Jessica argued.

"Perhaps, but most."

"So, you're saying that the people of your Ilyan would not be willing to help us?" Vladimir asked.

"It is doubtful," Aristaeus admitted. "The Ilyan has survived, *and thrived*, because it does not dictate to others, nor does it involve itself in their affairs. However, I speak of the Ilyan as a *whole*, not of each individual world. As I said, the Ilyan does not control the actions of its member worlds. It only controls their *interactions*."

"But if their actions constitute a *threat* to the Ilyan as a whole?" Vladimir wondered.

"Then yes, that could pose a problem. However, if any world within Ilyan Gamaze *wanted* to help you in your fight against the Dusahn, they would want to do so *covertly*...not only to avoid disfavor from the council, but from the Dusahn, as well."

"I thought you said they wouldn't perceive the Dusahn to be a threat, because they are too far away," Jessica said.

"Conquering and holding an entire region of space, especially a distant one, is quite different than sending a single jump ship to punish an ally of one's enemy," Aristaeus explained. "If you hope to find support within the Ilyan, that support *must* be covert."

"Jesus," Jessica scowled, turning her seat and putting her feet up against the side console. "I don't know how Nathan docs this stuff."

Aristaeus studied them both before continuing. "Might I offer you some advice?" he finally asked Jessica.

"Knock yourself out."

"I have negotiated deals on many different worlds, and one of the things I have learned is that if you want someone to compromise their position, you have to make them *want* to make that compromise."

"And how do you do that?" Jessica asked, more to be polite than because she cared.

"You must first learn what is important to them, and then craft that compromise to serve *their* needs, as well as your own."

Jessica dropped her feet back to the deck, turning to look directly at him again. "That's exactly what I'm *trying* to do."

"No, you are not. You are crafting a deal that serves *your* needs first, and not those of the Casbons, who, by the way, already have first rights to those fighters. *All* of them."

Jessica threw her hands up in frustration.

"How long until we reach Casbon?" Vladimir asked, hoping to change the subject.

"As I said, this ship is not the fastest. The journey will take approximately twelve hours," Aristaeus replied.

"Maybe we should get some rest," Vladimir suggested. "Neither of us has slept much this past week."

"As you wish."

Jessica and Vladimir both rose from their seats, but Jessica paused a moment. "Just one more question," she said. "Why are you taking us to speak to the Casbons? What's in it for you?"

"I believe you spoke the truth when you said that without proper training and preparation, those fighters present more danger to the Casbons than to the Ahka raiders."

Jessica smiled. "You see, you have a noble side. All of us do."

"Casbon is a frequent trading partner, from which I derive much profit," Aristaeus insisted. "It is merely good business."

"Uh-huh," Jessica replied, still smiling as she turned to exit.

Vladimir watched Jessica exit, then turned to Aristaeus and smiled. "Thank you for your help," he said, nodding respectfully. He glanced back at the hatchway through which Jessica had just passed. "*And* for your patience."

* * *

From the moment they entered the restaurant, they had drawn looks from every person within eyeshot. Nathan had not opted to change his Alliance uniform, and the two escorting him were still in their black, general-purpose, Ghatazhak duty uniforms.

It wasn't even the sidearms hanging from the hips of all three men that caught their attention. It was the absolute lack of vibrant color in their attire, which was in stark contrast to Gatondan fashion.

It had taken a bit of cajoling, as well as stern looks from his men, to convince the hostess to take them to the man they sought.

"How did you know where to look?" Corporal Vasya asked as he and Specialist Brill followed Nathan through the crowded restaurant.

"It's common practice to require incoming ships to register cargo, crew, and passengers with the port controller," Nathan explained. "A few units got me the hotel that this guy, Orloff, is staying in."

"But how did you know he'd be here?"

"I didn't," Nathan admitted. "But it's dinner time, so the hotel restaurant was a decent bet." He glanced back at the two men, smiling. "I got lucky."

The hostess stopped, looking back at Nathan. "In the corner, there," she told him, nodding toward the man in question.

"Thank you," Nathan replied, placing a credit chip in her hand. He made his way the last few meters unescorted and slipped into the booth next to Mister Orloff.

"What the..." Sosi exclaimed, surprised. He was even more surprised when two stern-looking, young men in black uniforms slid into the booth and sat directly across from him. "Who are you?" he asked, looking back at Nathan to his left. "What do you want?"

"In answer to your first question, I'm Nathan Scott, captain of the Aurora. This is Corporal Vasya and Specialist Brill, of the Ghatazhak."

Sosi looked at the two men, neither of whom

nodded or made any facial gestures, just sitting there like statues, staring at him.

"You're *Na-Tan*?" Sosi finally managed to mumble.

"I am."

Sosi searched for something to say, but only came up with, "I thought you be older."

"I get that a lot," Nathan replied.

"What I do for you?" Sosi wondered.

"You brought two of my crew with you, Lieutenant Commander Nash and Commander Kamenetskiy. I need to know where they are."

"Well, they not here," Sosi assured him.

"I can see that," Nathan replied, not amused.

Sosi swallowed hard. "They left with Aristaeus Imburjia."

"Where did they go?" Nathan asked.

"To Casbon."

"Why?"

"Your lieutenant commander was to speak to the Casbons, to convince them they must share fighters they are to purchase from Aristaeus with your people... I believe she is to offer help to Casbon...to the training of their pilots, but...but...of this, I not certain."

"Where is this world, Casbon?" Nathan asked.

"On the far end of the Ilyan, in Ridalli system."

"I've never heard of it," Nathan admitted. "Can you show us how to get there?"

"Yes, but, I was about to..."

All three men cast serious stares at Sosi.

"It is to be my honor," Sosi agreed. "Lead the way, Captain."

* * *

"This is BS," Jessica complained as she paced the lobby of the Leadership Council on Casbon.

"He is simply preparing them for your proposal," Vladimir insisted, trying to calm her down.

"He's finding a way to use the fact that *we* also want to buy the fighters as a way to jack up the price on whoever buys them," Jessica insisted. "*That's* what he's doing."

"He did not strike me as the type..."

"Oh, he's the type, alright," Jessica interrupted. "He's all about the deal. I know the type well."

"You may be correct, but so what? They are his ships to sell, after all. I think it is admirable that he prefers to keep his promise to the original buyer, even if someone is offering him a better deal."

"We never offered him a better deal, Vlad," Jessica pointed out. "Besides, you heard him, he just wants to keep a frequent customer alive to make more profit off them. If he *really* cares about their welfare, he'll tell them they need *our* help to keep them safe."

"And that may be exactly what he is doing, now."

"Then why are *we* out *here*?" Jessica demanded.

"Perhaps it is because he feared you would act like you are right now?"

Jessica glared at him.

"*Gospadee*," Vladimir exclaimed, noticing her scowl.

Jessica paced a bit more, and then turned back to Vladimir. "Aristaeus doesn't trust us."

"Insisting that we be allowed to carry our sidearms probably didn't help," Vladimir pointed out.

"Like you're not glad you're carrying."

"True."

The chamber doors swung open, and Aristaeus stepped through, closing them behind him. "They have agreed to hear your proposal," he told Jessica. "However, I must remind you to be careful how you phrase your points. They will not take kindly to being told they arc ignorant of the risks. Do not tell them they are doomed without your help. Tell them that their chances of success are *increased* with your help, and that their loss of life in defense of their world will likely *decrease.*"

Jessica looked at Aristaeus, one eyebrow raised in suspicion. "What did you tell them?"

"Only that your people are also interested in buying the fighters, and that you were willing to pay more."

"You see," Jessica said to Vladimir as she headed for the doors to the council chambers.

"Wait! There's more!" Aristaeus looked at Vladimir in dismay. "Is she always this headstrong?"

"This is mild," Vladimir assured him, following Jessica.

Jessica pushed the double doors open and walked into the Casbon Leadership Council's meeting chambers, looking more like a gunslinger than a salesperson.

"*Allow me to introduce Lieutenant Commander Jessica Nash,*" Aristaeus called out as he hastily followed Jessica and Vladimir into the room, "*and Commander Kamenetskiy, of the legendary Earth ship, Aurora.*"

Sitting behind podiums, arranged in a semicircle, sat fifteen men and women, each of them wearing robes bearing the emblem of the districts they represented. Gathered before them were others in attendance for various reasons, all of whom turned to watch Jessica and Vladimir as they approached the guest speaker's podium at the center of the room. Glances exchanged by various council members revealed considerable disapproval for Jessica's entrance.

"Hi, how's everyone doing?" Jessica asked as she stepped up to the podium.

"The council recognizes Lieutenant Commander Jessica Nash," the council member in the center announced.

"Thanks."

"Mister Imburjia tells us that you are concerned about our well-being?"

"He what?" Jessica replied, her eyebrows raised again.

"He also tells us that your people were interested in purchasing the Sugali fighters, as well."

"Uh…we are."

"*And* that you were *originally* willing to pay a higher price in order to secure the deal, but that you rescinded the offer when you learned of our plight."

Jessica glanced over her shoulder at Aristaeus, and then Vladimir, who had a smug look on his face. "We did," she replied, albeit unconvincingly. "What else did Mister Imburjia tell you?"

"That you were concerned that we are unprepared, and that it may take some time before our people are capable of defending our world."

"The thought had crossed my mind, yes."

"I assure you, Lieutenant Commander, we are well aware of the risks; however, we have little choice in the matter. The Ahka raids have become more frequent, and with each attack, they become bolder. In the last attack, they landed disruptor squads in the city center, to strike terror in the hearts of all Casbons. Given the escalation, we see no other alternative but to at least *attempt* to defend our world."

"Of course," Jessica said. "I completely understand, and while I am quite sure that the people of Casbon will bravely defend their world, and are willing to sacrifice themselves to do so, I believe I have a better way." She waited for a reaction.

After a moment, the lead council member said, "Continue."

"Allow us to provide you with experienced combat fighter pilots, as well as tacticians and maintenance specialists. They will use your fighters to protect Casbon while training *your* people to replace them. In this way, I believe you can not only get *immediate* protection, but you can do so with a potentially much lower loss of life... *Casbon* lives."

"And what cost would we bear for such services?" the lead council member inquired.

"In exchange for our services, you give us half of the fighters that you purchase, so we can use them in our fight to liberate the Pentaurus cluster from the clutches of the Dusahn Empire."

The lead council member did not look pleased, and by the murmurs coming from the other council members, as well as those in attendance, the others felt the same. "We need those fighters," the lead council member insisted.

"Based on what Mister Imburjia told us, you don't need all of them. Heck, you don't even need *half* of them, as long as your people know what they're doing." Jessica glanced about the room. "No offense, but I'm guessing you *don't*."

The murmurs in the room grew louder. If she had understood the local language that most in attendance were speaking, she expected she would have heard more than a few foul remarks directed at her.

"Order!" the lead council member demanded, banging his gavel on the desk. "Order!" After a few moments, the room quieted down. The council member next to him leaned in to whisper in the lead council member's ear. Once finished, the lead council member spoke once more. "The people of Casbon *might* be interested in your offer; however, with a slight adjustment in the terms."

"And they would be?"

"First, you will *purchase* the fighters from us, in *addition* to providing our people with the appropriate training. Second, you will help us *defeat* the Ahka once and for all so that we shall have no need to fear them."

Jessica looked down, shaking her head. "You don't want to do that, believe me."

"The Ahka have been killing our people and stealing our resources for years," the council member to the left spouted. "We are completely justified in our desire to put an end to it."

"I'm not saying you aren't," Jessica argued. "But you don't want to escalate things. If you do, what's to stop the Ahka from going out and buying *more* ships, or *bigger* ships? Are you prepared to then purchase additional weapons? Are you willing to potentially kill innocent civilians?"

"We would only be attacking their military assets," the council member argued.

"That's what everyone says," Jessica replied. "Yet, still, it happens. Innocents die. There's never been a war where they didn't."

"Then we are to *defend* our world against the Ahka for all eternity?" the lead council member asked. "How is that fair?"

"Whoever said the universe is *fair*?" Jessica

replied, almost laughing. "If you're going to arm up, then you have to be ready to use it. If you're going to take the fight to your enemy, you'd better be willing to *completely* annihilate them, or someday they'll come back and try to do the same to you."

"How does it serve us to let the Ahka *continue* to attack us at will?"

"If *they* attack you, you have the *right* to defend yourselves. You have the *right* to blow them out of the sky. Once they realize they are more likely to *die* than to steal your resources, they'll think twice about attacking."

"And if they do not?" the lead council member wondered.

"Trust me, they'll stop," Jessica insisted.

"How can you be certain of this?"

"Because if they have to *steal* from you in order to survive, then they can't *afford* to escalate. They don't have the *resources* to do so. If you show them that you will *no longer* allow them to attack you, and that you *will* fight back, they *will* stop."

"And why should we believe you?" one of the other council members questioned.

"Because this is what we do. This is what we are trained for."

"*You* have seen combat?" another council member wondered, looking skeptical.

"Yes, many times," Jessica confirmed.

"And you have killed?"

Jessica glared at the council member questioning her. "Many," she replied. "And unlike a fighter pilot, all my kills have been up close and personal. So, trust me when I say that I know what I'm talking about."

"Then, you are refusing our terms?" the lead council member asked directly.

"I am not. I am simply suggesting that you do not escalate matters, *unless* you are prepared for such an escalation."

The council members again began to talk among themselves. Jessica looked over at Vladimir, who shrugged.

"The council will adjourn and consider your words carefully," the lead council member announced. "Meanwhile, Mister Imburjia, the people of Casbon are prepared to make payment and complete the purchase of your Sugali fighters," he told Aristaeus. "*All* of them," he added, looking at Jessica.

Jessica stood there with her mouth open as the council members rose and filed out of the room. She turned to Vladimir. "So, now what do we do?"

Vladimir looked at Aristaeus, and then back at Jessica. "I say we get something to eat."

* * *

Nathan made his way forward through the port corridor, on his way to the Seiiki's cockpit. He had been in a foul mood since he had learned of Jessica and Vladimir's departure from Sanctuary. It was hard enough to leave his responsibilities as the leader of the Karuzari Alliance, but at least it had been for good reason. Now, he was being taken further away from both responsibilities, simply because two of his most trusted subordinates—and closest friends—had taken it upon themselves to go shopping.

It wasn't the first time Jessica had ignored the chain of command, and it certainly wouldn't be the last. This, he realized, he had no choice but to accept. It was simply her way. Luckily, she could handle herself. But it was highly unusual for Vladimir to run off with her. In fact, he was surprised that she hadn't made him stay behind. More often than not, Jessica preferred to work alone.

Nathan reached the cockpit access ladder at the bow of the ship and quickly ascended. "Relief is here," he announced as he stepped onto the cockpit deck.

Loki looked at Josh.

"I'm good," Josh insisted.

"I'll be back in an hour," Loki said as he climbed out of the copilot's seat and made his way past Nathan.

After Loki passed, Nathan stepped forward and plopped himself down in the copilot's seat, immediately looking over the various displays to orient himself with the ship's current status.

"Everything's good," Josh assured him. "Jump series sequencer is working perfectly, and the ship is humming along."

"Just getting oriented," Nathan replied. "I'm not used to sitting on this side." He looked at the sequencer display. "Looks like we'll be there in about four more hours."

"Yup."

Nathan leaned back in his chair. "Hopefully, I'll figure out what to say to them by then," he added, mostly to himself.

"What?"

"Nothing," Nathan insisted.

"Say to who?" Josh pressed. "Jess and Vlad?"

"Pretty much."

"Uh...how about 'hello'."

"Not that simple," Nathan replied, leaning forward to change displays for a moment. "They took off without properly reporting in first."

"They told Neli," Josh reminded him.

"Not good enough."

"Well, how the hell were they supposed to report in?" Josh wondered.

"They could have waited. They knew I was due back soon."

"I'm sure they had their reasons," Josh insisted. "I mean, it's Jess and Vlad, after all. I can see if me or Dalen pulled something like that. You'd have our asses."

"Still, they put me in a tight spot," Nathan explained. "I was supposed to be there for Miri; for her kids. Instead, I'm chasing Jess and Vlad across the galaxy."

"But, if they can get a bunch of Sugali fighters, it would be worth it, wouldn't it?"

"Maybe," Nathan agreed, "but it isn't their call."

"How did they know we'd come after them?" Josh asked.

Nathan looked at Josh. "Because *they* would have come after *us*. They'd have no choice, just like we had no choice. If we didn't, we'd lose their trail, and if something went wrong, they'd be screwed. Jessica *should* have known that. She probably *did* know that, but she went anyway. *That's* why I'm pissed. It's hard enough to be in charge without your subordinates going off to do their own thing."

"I guess I see your point," Josh agreed, "but isn't it *possible* that what they're chasing down is *worth* it?"

"It depends," Nathan replied.

"Depends on what?"

"On what goes wrong in the meantime. There, here, back on Sanctuary, or back in the Rogen system. That's always been Jessica's problem. She never looks at the big picture. She only sees *her* part, not everyone else's."

Josh rolled his eyes. "Kinda sounds like me, doesn't it."

"Yeah, a bit, but I *expect* that from you."

"Yeah, it's part of my charm," Josh retorted, smiling.

Nathan shot him a look, one eyebrow skeptically raised.

* * *

"Doesn't this place have any actual restaurants?" Jessica wondered as they waited in line at the mobile food vendor, outside the council building.

"Casbon does not have such extravagances," Aristaeus explained. "It is still in its early development, barely a hundred years old. The first time I came here, it was nothing more than a city of tents, and a few mining and support landers."

Jessica glanced at him as they moved forward a bit in line. "How old are you?"

"Age is nothing more than a number others attach to your name for reference. I was traveling by linear FTL using stasis pods long before your parents were born. Quite possibly before your grandparents, even. My daughters, whom you met on Gatonda, are from my third wife."

"What happened to the other two?" Vladimir wondered.

"They both led long and happy lives, most of which I was not a part of. I was present for both of their passings. I am thankful that the jump drive now allows me to be present for far more of my third family's lives."

"What about your first two families?" Vladimir asked. "Did you have children?"

"Oh, yes, many," Aristaeus replied. "Four from my first, and three from my second. I have dozens of grandchildren, great-grandchildren, and great-great-grandchildren."

"Sounds confusing," Vladimir admitted, taking a step forward again.

"Not really. It is actually quite nice. My oldest son is physically older than I. In fact, *his* oldest son is the same physical age as myself. We are quite good friends."

"Are such extended families common on Gatonda?" Vladimir asked.

"No, but they are not *uncommon.*"

The line moved again, and all three of them stepped forward.

"My oldest brother, Robert, was the captain of one of the first FTL scout ships that left Earth after the recovery," Jessica told Aristaeus. "He was twelve years older than me when he left. The next time I saw him, he was only half that."

"It almost seems a shame that such families will no longer exist," Aristaeus said. "But I suppose all things must change, for better or worse."

"You don't think the jump drive is a positive change?" Vladimir asked.

"Like all things, it is a double-edged sword. Yes, it connects us all in a way we could not imagine only a few short years ago. But it also immensely complicates things. Take the Casbons, for example. They settled this world, expecting to profit from its rich mineral resources, but also expecting a decent amount of isolation, since it was so far removed from the rest of the Ilyan. Even Ahka, their closest neighbor, was still too far away to interact with on a regular basis. Had the jump drive not been introduced to the Ilyan, Ahka would still be too far away for raids on Casbon to be logistically feasible. Their isolation all but guaranteed their safety. Now, it all but guarantees their doom. Although they are now within easy reach of Ahka, they are still too far from the core of the Ilyan to expect any protection."

"Why can't the core worlds just jump out here once in a while?" Jessica wondered, stepping forward in line again. "I'm sure if they made their presence known on a regular basis, it would be enough to make the Ahka think twice."

"The core has not yet installed jump drives on all their ships," Aristaeus explained. "And they care more about the core worlds than the ones on the rim."

"But I thought Casbon was rich in mineral resources?" Vladimir said.

"Yes, but to the Ilyan, it matters not from *whom* they buy their ores and metals. In fact, the Ahka can sell the stolen ores more cheaply than the Casbons, who must bear the cost of extraction and refinement."

"As usual, it all comes down to profit," Jessica grumbled.

"And so shall it always," Aristaeus stated. "For the strongest instinct of humanity *is* survival, and *profit* all but guarantees it."

"If these people are so poor, then why do the Ahka attack them?" Jessica wondered.

"I did not say the people of Casbon are poor," Aristaeus corrected, "I said they lacked the extravagances of more developed worlds. Casbon has huge stores of both raw and refined ores, minerals, and precious metals, but, due to their location, they are still far removed from the normal shipping routes."

"If they have so much to sell, why don't they just trade it for a few jump ships of their own?" Vladimir suggested.

"Casbon was originally started as a separatist colony, desiring limited contact with the Ilyan and its patriarchal society," Aristaeus explained as they moved up in line again.

"My kind of people," Jessica commented.

"The attacks by the Ahka have forced Casbon to rethink their separatist ideals in order to survive."

"So, the Ahka are trying to steal Casbon's resources?"

"Mostly just their precious metals," Aristaeus replied, "but they have been known to take other resources, as well, even people."

"They kidnap *people*?" Vladimir said, surprised.

"Mostly females, whom they need to grow their population. You see, about fifty years after being settled, the Ahka suffered a plague, which killed more than half their population and left the majority of their women infertile."

"They're kidnapping Casbon women to use them as *breeding stock*?" Jessica scowled as the line advanced another spot. "I'm starting to agree with the council about taking the fight to Ahka."

"The people of Casbon are quite peaceful, and most of them do not agree with the council's desire to attack Ahka."

"Not even to free their kidnapped citizens?" Jessica wondered.

"Most of these people do not see *violence* as a *solution* to violence. It is only a slim majority of the council who have voted in favor of attacking the Ahka. Most would prefer to simply defend themselves, in hopes that the Ahka will look elsewhere for an easier target."

"More likely they'll just come back in greater numbers," Jessica insisted.

"*Numbers* is something the Ahka do not have."

"How far is the next closest world to Ahka?" Jessica asked.

"At least twice as far as Casbon, if not further."

"Then bigger, more deadly ships." Jessica looked at Vladimir. "The council may be right. Attacking the Ahka, and destroying their *ability* to attack Casbon, may be the only way to stop the raids for good."

"Unfortunately, the people of Casbon lack the internal fortitude to carry out the wishes of the council," Aristaeus said. "This world does not even have organized security forces, let alone defensive ones."

"How is that even possible?" Jessica wondered.

"Such pacifism is common amongst the core worlds of the Ilyan. Everyone and everything are monitored, so crime is rare. What security forces they do have, only carry non-lethal weapons."

"Didn't you say they have patrol ships?" Jessica asked. "What about those? Do they only have non-lethal weapons, as well?"

"Of course not," Aristaeus replied. "But the Ilyan Protectorate has not fired a weapon in anger in centuries...not since long before I was born."

"If the people of the Ilyan are so non-violent, why are the Ahka raiding their neighbor and kidnapping their women?" Vladimir asked.

"Ahka was settled by those who commonly ran afoul of Ilyan law. They were of a lower class of society and chose to start their own colony, rather than conform to the expectations of Ilyan society. So, their behavior is not surprising."

"*Next!*" the man in the window yelled.

"Finally," Vladimir declared. "I'm starving."

Aristaeus stepped up to the order window. "Three wampa perinaya with white sauce."

Several distant claps of thunder sounded behind them, followed a split second later by half a dozen more. The man at the order window slammed the window shut, and the roller doors began descending over the front of the mobile food unit. People began yelling and running in all directions.

"What the hell?" Jessica wondered as she turned to look in the direction of the thunder. At least ten flashes of light appeared low on the horizon, followed seconds later by additional claps of thunder.

Alert sirens began to wail, and multiple warning cries of '*Ahka*' were heard as people ran for cover.

"What are they doing?" Jessica asked, looking around. "Why aren't they preparing to fight?"

"What are they to fight *with*?" Aristaeus asked. "Wampa rifles?"

"If that's all they've got, yes!" Jessica insisted. "Anything's better than running and hiding."

"They are hiding because they know that while those ships are raiding the storage depots, others will land here in town to take other items...and people," Aristaeus told her. "We, too, should seek..."

A brilliant, blue-white light suddenly lit up the area, and a deafening clap of thunder sounded directly over their heads. The air displaced by the arriving ship knocked the three of them to the ground and sent dust swirling in all directions.

"Jess!" Vladimir yelled over the roar of nearby thrusters.

Jessica rolled onto her back, just in time to see the underside of a small spacecraft as it descended toward her. She rolled to her left several times, moving out of the way of the landing ship, just as its gear extended and touched down beside her.

Jessica breathed a sigh of relief as more claps of thunder sounded from all around her. Her relief was short-lived when the side boarding ramp of the ship that had landed right next to her swung down toward the ground, threatening to smash her. She scrambled on her back, using her feet and elbows to quickly move out of the way, and pulled her sidearm as soon as she was clear.

The ramp hit the ground, and a bearded man carrying an assault rifle came out, followed by several more. Jessica opened fire from her supine position on the ground just aft of the boarding ramp, dropping the first three men before they realized what was happening.

The next three, now alerted to the unexpected threat, did not exit immediately, maneuvering, instead, to the side of the exit to return fire in her direction.

Jessica spotted a rifle muzzle coming around the edge of the open hatchway, angling toward her. She moved her weapon to the right to fire, just as a stream of red-orange plasma bolts came streaking from the left into the open hatchway. The rifle muzzle that had been maneuvering to bear on her suddenly fell to the deck, bouncing off the ramp, landing on the ground beside her.

"Jess! Behind you!" Vladimir shouted.

Jessica glanced in the direction of Vladimir's voice to her left, spotting him crouched low next to the mobile food vehicle, again firing into the open hatchway above her. She rolled onto her belly, grabbing the dropped assault rifle and taking aim at another ship that was landing only a few meters behind her. She peppered the front of the ship with bolts of energy, causing its pilot to abort his landing and begin climbing out again. As the climbing ship rose, it turned to starboard, away from her, showing its open port hatch. The men inside opened fire on her position, sending bolts of energy slamming into the ground around her, as well as the ship next to her, which was already firing its thrusters to lift off.

"Run!" Vladimir ordered, opening fire on the second ship to cover her escape.

Jessica jumped to her feet, rifle in one hand, sidearm in the other, firing on the second vessel as she rose. She turned, ceasing fire, and ran toward Vladimir's position as the first ship dusted off, rising quickly upward as it accelerated forward.

Vladimir continued firing on the second ship as Jessica ran to join him. His fire struck one man in the open hatch, knocking him backward into the ship. Another man stepped forward to replace him and was struck in the chest by Vladimir's continued fire. The injured man lost his balance as the ship turned further to its right, and he tumbled forward, falling to the ground fifty meters below.

After landing with a thud, the man, injured but not dead, tried to pull himself to his feet, only to be met with more weapons fire from Vladimir, ending his struggle.

"We must find shelter!" Aristaeus demanded as he crouched against the mobile food vehicle next to Vladimir and Jessica. "There are more of them landing!"

"Go ahead!" Jessica barked in reply as she handed Vladimir the energy rifle.

"What are you going to do?" Aristaeus asked.

"I'm a bit curious myself," Vladimir added.

"Whattaya think?" Jessica replied with a smile.

"Of course," Vladimir replied. He noticed she was taking off her gun belt. "What are you doing?"

"We need more firepower," she told Vladimir as she handed him her gun belt. "Don't lose this. I'm going to want it back shortly."

Vladimir looked confused. "What am I supposed to do?"

"Play along," she replied, rising to a standing position as two more landers jumped in nearby and settled in to land. "You'll know what to do."

Jessica dashed out into the open, screaming as if she were in a complete state of panic. She ran to the right, then stumbled, and changed direction to the left, when a third ship jumped in to her right. In her pretend panic, she appeared to be running directly toward a fourth ship that had just set down and was unloading a handful of armed men.

"What is she doing?" Aristaeus wondered.

"I have no idea," Vladimir admitted, raising the assault rifle she had just given him and preparing to fire.

Jessica changed direction, yet again, as if she suddenly recognized the threat of the men coming out of the fourth lander. She purposefully stumbled, falling to the ground and appearing to be confused and desperate.

Four armed men came running up to her, grabbing her from either side. Jessica fought back half-heartedly; trying to free herself, but the two men who had grabbed her knocked her down and dragged her back toward their ship.

"*This* is what you call *fighting back?*" Aristaeus wondered.

Vladimir took aim on one of the men abducting Jessica, but she shook her head not to fire.

"You must shoot!" Aristaeus insisted. "They will take her, and you will never see her again!"

"You do not know Jessica," Vladimir replied, keeping his weapon held ready.

The two men dragged her up the ramp and into the ship, while the other two men stood outside, sweeping their weapons back and forth.

"You should have fired! Now, it is too late!"

Several flashes of light came from the open hatchway of the fourth ship. The two armed men outside turned around to run back to the ship but were met with several energy bolts, killing them instantly and leaving them in smoldering heaps on the ground.

The fourth ship's engines went back to full power, and it began to rise from the ground to depart.

"Oh, no," Vladimir said, getting ready to fire on the departing ship.

More flashes of light came from inside the ship, and a body came flying out of the open hatchway. A moment later, the ship settled back down onto the surface, its engines shutting down completely.

Six armed men came running out of the shuttle that had just landed to Vladimir's right, toward the fourth shuttle that Jessica was in. Vladimir turned and opened fire, dropping three of them with the first five shots, but was forced to tuck back behind cover when the other three returned fire.

Jessica jumped out of the open hatch of the fourth

ship, an assault rifle in each hand and one slung over each shoulder. She opened fire, mowing down the other three men firing on Vladimir's position.

Vladimir smiled. "You see?"

Jessica ran over to their position, immediately handing one of the assault rifles to Vladimir.

"That was incredible," Aristaeus exclaimed.

"Thanks," Jessica replied, handing the other rifle to him.

Aristaeus took the assault rifle with a curious and fearful expression on his face. "I have never used such a thing."

"Simple," Jessica assured him. "Point it at the bad guys, press that button, and hold it until the bad guys are dead."

"What do we do now?" Vladimir asked.

"We kick some Ahka ass," Jessica replied as she turned and headed toward the sound of a woman screaming.

Jessica ran out across the square, toward several men who were dragging women toward their waiting ships. As she ran, she raised her rifle and opened fire, striking the first man in the back and the second in the side of his chest.

Vladimir was hot on her heels, firing to his right at four armed Ahka heading their way. He glanced back at Aristaeus, who was still hiding behind the edge of the mobile food vehicle. "What are you doing?" he hollered. "FIRE!"

Aristaeus closed his eyes and swung his assault rifle around the corner of the vehicle, screaming at the top of his lungs as he squeezed the trigger and held it. Vladimir hit the deck as Aristaeus's stream of energy bolts swept over his head. Aristaeus continued screaming as bolts of energy streaked from his weapon in rapid succession, slamming into the group of Ahka and cutting them to pieces. After nearly twenty seconds of firing, he took his finger off the trigger and stopped screaming. He slowly opened his eyes and saw a pile of four smoldering hulks with burning body parts strewn about. His eyes grew wide, and he looked in disbelief at the ominous weapon in his hands. “Oh, my.”

“Very good!” Vladimir yelled, climbing back to his feet. “Only, next time, keep your eyes open!”

Jessica jinked from side to side, staggering the length and direction of her strides as she ducked incoming fire. She dropped two more men with her own weapon by the time she closed on the last of the four Ahka—the one dragging a woman by her hair. Without missing a stride, she leapt up in the air, executing a backflip and coming down in a sitting position on the startled Ahka’s shoulders, his face in her crotch. Her momentum knocked him backwards, releasing his hold on the Casbon woman as he grasped at his attacker. Jessica twisted her body slightly to the right as she squeezed her thighs around the man’s head. Her momentum carried her to the man’s left, twisting his head around and snapping his neck as she tipped over upside down along his back. As her left hand touched the ground, she released her thigh-grip on the man and allowed his limp body to fall away as she cart-wheeled over and came up firing on the last two men coming out of the ship. The ship began powering up its engines, and she scrambled around to the side, sticking the muzzle of her assault rifle into one of the engine intakes and pressing the trigger. Several blasts of energy lit up the intake, causing a chain of secondary explosions deep within the ship. She stepped backwards as the ship struggled to ascend, looked up at the cockpit, and waved farewell to the pilot, just as the ship's port engine exploded, and the ship rolled to starboard, crashing into the ground.

Vladimir came running up to Jessica, stopping to help the frightened Casbon woman she had just saved. "Are you alright?" The woman nodded, albeit with some uncertainty.

"You are violent people," Aristaeus exclaimed as he came jogging up to join them, assault rifle in hand.

"Sometimes violence *is* necessary," Vladimir replied.

"Thank God, or I'd be out of a job," Jessica commented.

Six more jump flashes appeared to the east, low on the horizon, followed a few seconds later by claps of thunder.

"What's over there?" she asked, pointing toward the flashes.

"The east storage buildings," Aristaeus replied. "But I do not know what is stored in them."

"Precious metals," the Casbon woman told them. "Gold, platinum, aramenium."

"Aramenium?" Vladimir asked. "You produce aramenium here?"

"Yes," the woman replied. "My husband works in the aramenium refinery. It is one of our most valuable ores. We sell it only to the Perzans. The Ahka have yet to discover its existence on Casbon."

"If the Ahka find that aramenium, they will stop at nothing to obtain it," Aristaeus warned. "*All* of it. They will return in force, if necessary."

"What the hell is aramenium?" Jessica asked.

"It is difficult to explain," Vladimir replied. "It is

very rare and can store incredible amounts of energy. *That* is why it is so valuable."

"Then, we have to stop them," Jessica decided.

"With this?" Vladimir asked, holding up his rifle.

"How far away are the east storage buildings?" Jessica asked the woman.

"Twenty, maybe thirty, kilometers?"

"We need a vehicle," Jessica declared, looking around. "Something fast."

"Our vehicles are not fast," the Casbon woman warned. "They just go."

"By the time you get there, it will be too late," Aristaeus warned. "Even if you prevent them from making off with the aramenium, they will *know* it is there."

Jessica looked around again, spotting the first ship she had forced to land. "That's our ride!" she decided, breaking immediately into a run.

"*Gospadee*, wait!" Vladimir yelled, taking off after her.

"Who are those people?" the Casbon woman wondered as she watched Jessica and Vladimir run toward one of the Ahka ships.

"It's a long story," Aristaeus replied.

"They're crazy."

"Quite."

Vladimir ran after Jessica, calling for her to wait, but she paid no attention. She reached the ramp of the ship and ran inside, turning to her left and stepping over two dead Ahka to get to the cockpit. "Damn!" she cursed, grabbing the dead pilot and yanking him out of his seat. "I guess I shouldn't have killed you."

"What are you doing?" Vladimir yelled when he entered the ship.

"Get these bodies out of here while I figure out how to start this thing up," Jessica demanded as she plopped the dead pilot on the deck and returned to take his seat in the cockpit.

"Do you even know how to fly this thing?"

"*This* thing, not really."

"Do you know how to fly *anything*?"

"I've had a few lessons," she replied as she scanned the console, trying to figure out how to turn on the engines.

"A few?" Vladimir challenged as he dragged the pilot's body out of the hatch, dumping him alongside the other two, onto the ground next to the ship.

"Jesus, what the hell kind of writing is this?" Jessica yelled. "It looks like a bunch of worms!"

"Let me look," Vladimir insisted, climbing into the copilot's seat. "Engines are engines, and systems are systems. They all work in much the same..." He suddenly stopped, staring at the unfamiliar console.

"What?" Jessica asked.

"You are correct," Vladimir said, "their writing *does* look like worms."

* * *

"Casbon is very small colony on rim of Ilyan Gamaze," Sosi told Nathan and the others gathered in the Seiiki's galley. "It has some industry and has small city, but still needs trade with Ilyan's core worlds to survive."

"What do they trade?" Nathan asked.

"Ores; precious metals...their world is blessed with resources. Thanks to jump drive, Casbon now trade with other worlds, not just of Ilyan."

"Then, why do they need fighters?" Corporal Vasya wondered.

"Apparently, one of their neighbors isn't doing as

well," Nathan replied as he put his dirty plate into the dishwasher.

"Ahka," Sosi said. "Very bad. They kill, they steal, they kidnap women. They take what they want and not care who they hurt."

"I thought this *Ilyan* was some sort of empire, or something," the corporal said. "Why don't they do something about the Ahka?"

"Ahka outside Ilyan...barely," Sosi explained. "Casbon inside...barely. Ilyan Protectorate only have three, maybe four, jump ships, and many worlds to protect. Bigger worlds. Worlds with more money and power than Casbon. And Casbon leave Ilyan core because Casbon not like ways of Ilyan. So, Ilyan not care about Casbon...not much, anyway."

"The Casbons are buying the fighters so they can defend themselves," Nathan added.

"Do they have any pilots?" Specialist Brill asked.

"Nope," Nathan replied. "Apparently, they don't even have any ships. No transports or anything. They depend on the ships of their trading partners. Pretty common for smaller worlds that haven't reached full industrialization, yet."

"How the hell do they expect to defend themselves, then?" the corporal wondered.

"Sugali fighters are pretty easy to fly," Nathan told him. "But fly them *well* and *fight* effectively with them; that's a different matter."

"They're going to lose a lot of ships and pilots in the beginning," Vasya commented. "Maybe all of them, depending on how many ships these Ahka have."

"Not many," Sosi insisted. "They not use more than eight ships. Mostly six. But they now attack more. Maybe every six, seven days, I think."

"*Cap'n?*" Josh called over comm-sets.

"Yeah," Nathan replied.

"*We're two jumps out. Want us to hold the last jump until you're up here?*"

"Negative, I'll be there in a second," Nathan told him. "Corporal, you two man the gun turrets, just in case. Dalen, you suit up and man the bay gun."

"Yes, sir," Corporal Vasya replied as he and Specialist Brill exited the galley and headed aft.

"I'm on it, Cap'n," Dalen added, following the Ghatazhak out.

"What I to do?" Sosi wondered.

"I don't suppose Casbon has any kind of approach control," Nathan said.

"I think, no."

"Then, stay here," Nathan instructed, heading forward.

"Very well," Sosi agreed as he continued eating. "Sosi stay here."

Nathan made his way around the forward lift fan housing and was about to start up the ladder, when the ship suddenly shook violently and lurched to one side.

"*Shit!*" Josh yelled from the cockpit.

"*All hands! Man your guns!*" Loki called over comm-sets. "*We're under attack!*"

Nathan regained his balance and quickly ascended the short ladder up to the Seiiki's cockpit, hollering, "Report!" as he reached the top.

"I thought you said they didn't have any ships!" Josh yelled back at Nathan.

"We were attacked as soon as we came out of the jump, sir," Loki explained. "Small ships, about the size of a Reaper." The Seiiki rocked again as a ship coming toward them fired, striking her forward shields. "No comms, no warning, they just turned and opened fire."

"Is someone going to fire back?" Josh yelled as he jinked the ship to the left to avoid incoming fire.

"*Powering up now!*" Corporal Vasya reported over comm-sets.

Nathan quickly leaned over to the side console, patching his comm-set into the exterior comms array, and selected every known comm-channel. "This is the Seiiki. We are here on business. Break off your attack, or we will be forced to defend ourselves."

The ship rocked again as three more energy blasts slammed into their port shields.

"That answers that," Nathan decided.

"*I'm powered up!*" Vasya reported. "*Are we clear to fire?*"

"Weapons free!" Nathan ordered. "Keep those bastards off of us!"

"You got it!" Corporal Vasya replied as he swung his weapon to port and opened fire on the ship, tracking from port to starboard. He moved the gun quickly from left to right, firing constantly. The target blew apart, spreading pieces along the doomed ship's path of flight. "Hell, yeah!" the corporal cried out, looking toward the starboard gun turret. "Now, *these* are *guns*!"

"How many targets?" Nathan asked Loki.

"I'm tracking four near us and another six on the surface."

"So much for 'they never attack with more than

eight,'" Nathan mumbled as the ship rocked from another weapons impact on their shields.

"*You've got one coming under!*" Specialist Brill told Corporal Vasya. "*I couldn't get a line on him!*"

"*Josh! Roll to port!*" Vasya instructed.

"Negative!" Loki warned. "Those ships have aft-facing cannons, and our port shield is down to thirty percent."

"Sorry, Vasya," Josh replied.

"Get me a clear jump line so I can plot an escape jump," Loki suggested.

"Negative," Nathan countermanded. "Vlad and Jess are down there. Plot a jump to attack the six ships on the surface."

"Captain, we ain't a gunship," Josh reminded him.

"We are now," Nathan replied.

"For all we know, Vlad and Jess are sheltered someplace safe," Loki said, turning to look at Nathan. "If these guys are just raiders, they'll take what they came for and be on their way."

"*Jessica*...sheltered *someplace safe*?" Nathan replied.

Loki turned back around toward his console. "Plotting the attack jump now."

* * *

"Nothing is happening!" Jessica exclaimed. "It's like it's dead, or something!"

"I think it is," Vladimir agreed.

"What?" Jessica looked at him. "It was working five minutes ago!"

"Maybe the pilot locked the systems out before he died?"

"No way," Jessica insisted. "What do you think all that is!" she added, pointing at the blood and gray matter splattered all over the front window on her side.

"It could be bio-locked," Vladimir suggested, "so that only an Ahka pilot can operate it." Vladimir looked past Jessica at the blown-out section of the console to her left. "It could also be that big hole in the panel over there."

Jessica looked at the hole, then at Vladimir again.

"I thought you Ghatazhak never missed."

"Must have been a ricochet," Jessica insisted. A thunderous clap shook their ship, although there was no jump flash. Jessica looked at Vladimir again, just as a larger ship streaked over them, only thirty meters off the surface. "Fuck!" Jessica exclaimed as they both ducked instinctively.

Vladimir laughed with joy, pointing at the ship that had just buzzed over them as it sped away toward the east storage buildings. "It's the Seiiki!"

* * *

"*Seiiki! Nash! How do you copy?*"

"Jess! Is that you?" Nathan called over his comm-set.

"*Holy crap, Nathan! How the hell did you find us?*"

"Long story," Nathan replied. "What's your sit-rep?"

"*We're good. There are six Ahka raiders about to break into the east storage buildings.*"

"Yeah, we'll be on them in thirty seconds."

"*You cannot let them enter those buildings! Understood?*"

"Understood."

"*Nathan!*" Vladimir called. "*Do not shoot the buildings!*"

"Why?" Nathan wondered.

"*Trust me on this!*"

"Copy. Josh, pitch us up to get a better attack angle."

"Pitching up," Josh replied, pulling the Seiiki's nose up slightly.

"Loki, you take the forward belly turrets. I'll take the aft ones."

"Got it," Loki replied, "but three more raiders just jumped in behind us. Five clicks, slightly to port."

"I can swing it around in a hover, so our main turrets can deal with the inbounds," Josh suggested. "That should give you guys a pretty good shot at the ground targets, as well."

"Works for me," Nathan agreed as he took control of the Seiiki's aft belly turrets. "Gunners, three bandits coming in from behind. Five clicks. We'll swing around into a hover to attack ground targets and give you a good firing line. Fuck those ships up!"

"*Our pleasure,*" Corporal Vasya replied.

"Here we go," Josh announced, pushing the Seiiki's nose back down into an attack dive. His targeting system identified the six ships on the surface, just north of the storage buildings. "Boots on the ground," he reported. "They're just deboarding now." One of the targeting reticles around the ships on the screen turned green, and Josh pressed the firing button on his flight control stick, sending a stream of plasma blasts toward it. The ship exploded, sending chunks of its burning hull flying in all directions. One of the pieces struck the ship next to it, causing its starboard landing gear to snap. The ship's starboard engine immediately began smoking, and then caught fire, exploding a second later. "That's two!" Josh declared. "And with one shot!" he added as he leveled off about twenty meters above the surface, sliding into a hovering position to one side of the Ahka ships and the armed men now raising their weapons to open fire on the Seiiki. He spun the hovering ship around, bringing the nose to point toward the three raiders who were coming up from behind them. "Those ground pounders are firing," he warned.

"Oh, no, you don't," Nathan mumbled as he activated the aft turrets and opened fire on the men on the ground. "Target the ships, Loki," Nathan ordered as he continued firing, "I've got the guys on the ground with guns."

"I'm on it," Loki replied.

"One and a half clicks and closing!" Josh warned their gunners. "At our twelve and just above!"

"I've got the one on the left!" Corporal Vasya announced, lining up his turret, locking onto the approaching raider, and opening fire.

"I've got the one on the right," Specialist Brill added, also opening fire.

"And I've got the one in the middle," Josh added as the ship gently pitched up and turned slightly to port.

Corporal Vasya held his turret steady as he pounded the approaching ship. Within a few seconds, the ship's forward shields failed, and the plasma bolts tore into the target's hull, splitting it open and setting off explosions inside. The target broke apart, falling to the ground below. "ONE DOWN!" the corporal shouted triumphantly as he swung his gun toward the middle raider.

"Middle target is down!" Josh bragged, ceasing

fire as he continued to balance the Seiiki in a hover over the engagement area.

"I got another one on the ground!" Loki announced.

"The last two are trying to take off," Josh warned.

"Block them!" Nathan ordered.

"I thought you'd never ask," Josh replied, manipulating his flight controls to slide the Seiiki over and descend slightly, blocking the enemy ships' attempts to lift off.

"Keep pounding them, Loki," Nathan instructed.

"I never stopped!"

"*More ground pounders running up from behind us!*" Dalen warned over comm-sets.

"Where the hell did they come from?" Nathan wondered.

"*Beats the hell outta me!*" Dalen replied. "*Oh, shit! They're firing!*"

"Well, fire back!" Nathan ordered.

"No shit!" Dalen exclaimed as he swung the ceiling-mounted, double-barreled cannon out into the middle of the open cargo bay and took aim. Plasma bolts bounced off their aft shields, causing them to flash reddish-orange with each impact. Dalen flinched at the first few impacts, but then settled in behind his weapon and took aim, firing continuously. He swept the weapon back and forth, and up and down, spraying the area behind and below them with narrow bolts of plasma energy. "Damn!" he exclaimed as he continued firing. "Now, I know why Marcus likes this gun so much!"

"*You gonna kill that guy, or what, Brilly?*" Corporal Vasya called over comm-sets.

"The fucker's dancing around like..." His weapons fire finally overwhelmed the target's shields, and the raider came apart in three bright explosions. "Got him!"

"*It's about time,*" Vasya chided.

"Damn it!" Josh cursed. "One of them is getting up!" Josh shoved his flight control stick to one side, twisting it at the same time. The ship rose slightly and spun around. "Vasya! Tag that guy climbing out!"

"*I'm on him!*"

"Lok! Blast that other guy, will ya!"

"Hold still, and I will!"

Plasma fire streaked outside past the left side of the cockpit, slicing the fleeing raider in half, sending it crashing into the ground and exploding.

"*Got him!*" Corporal Vasya reported.

"I've got no shot!" Loki announced.

Josh swung the ship to starboard and pitched up, opening fire with the ship's forward-facing plasma cannons. He walked the fire through the air, finding the fleeing ship and tearing it open. The target tumbled over and fell toward the surface, exploding ten meters above the ground. "Scope is clear!" Josh declared triumphantly.

"Settle this ship down so I can finish off the ground pounders," Nathan instructed.

"You got it," Josh replied, doing as instructed.

Nathan adjusted the aft turrets, locking onto the last group of Ahka firing up at them from the surface. The targeting boxes around all four icons turned green. "Smile," Nathan said as he pressed the firing button. A second later, all four icons disappeared from his screen. "All targets are down," Nathan announced, leaning back in his chair with a sigh of relief. He tapped his comm-set as his ship slowly gained altitude. "Jess, you're all clear!"

"*Did they get into the storage buildings?*" she asked.

"Negative," Nathan replied. "I'm pretty sure they didn't. What's your location? We'll come to you."

"*You flew right over us when you jumped in,*" she replied. "*Meet us in the square by the council building, next to the downed raiders, and we'll buy you some wampa perinaya...with white sauce!*"

"Hell, yeah!" Josh exclaimed. "I could eat!"

CHAPTER FIVE

The Seiiki's aft cargo ramp was already partially deployed when she landed in the square a few meters away from Vladimir, Jessica, and Aristaeus. Before her engines finished spinning down, Nathan came down the ramp, an unhappy expression on his face.

"Nice job," Vladimir congratulated.

"You may have just saved this world," Jessica added as they approached. "How did you find us, anyway?"

"I had help," Nathan replied, pointing back over his shoulder.

Jessica leaned to one side to peer around Nathan, spotting Sosi Orloff coming down the ramp, along with Corporal Vasya and Specialist Brill.

"What's wrong?" Jessica asked, noticing the sour expression on Nathan's face. "I thought you'd be happy to see us."

"I *am* happy to see you," Nathan replied. "Both of you. I'm *not* happy that I had to chase you across four sectors to do so, all things considered."

"It is my fault," Vladimir admitted. "I am the one who first met Sosi. I talked Jessica into coming along."

"No one *talks* Jessica into doing *anything*," Nathan corrected.

"We couldn't wait," Jessica explained. "Sosi was going to leave before you returned, and we didn't want to lose the opportunity. I mean, we're talking about *fifty Sugali fighters*, here."

"I thought it was one hundred," Nathan commented, one eyebrow raised.

"It's complicated," Jessica admitted.

"It usually is."

"The complication is my doing, Captain," Aristaeus insisted, stepping forward to join the conversation.

"Captain, this is Aristaeus Imburjia, the seller," Jessica introduced. "Mister Imburjia, this is Captain Nathan Scott, commanding officer of the Aurora."

Aristaeus stepped forward, nodding his head in respect. "It is indeed an honor to meet you, Captain."

"A pleasure, Mister Imburjia," Nathan replied, shaking his hand. "Perhaps *you* can explain what is going on?"

"Walk and talk?" Jessica suggested.

"Where?"

"The council of leaders has requested that we return to their chambers," she replied. "I'll explain on the way."

"This should be good," Nathan said as they headed toward the council building.

* * *

Nathan, Jessica, Vladimir, and Aristaeus entered the council chambers and walked up to the center podium.

"You have brought another," the lead council member noticed.

"I have," Jessica replied. "This is my commanding officer, Captain Nathan Scott. He has only just arrived."

"Then, *you* are the pilot of the ship that defended our world and destroyed the Ahka raiders."

"I was not the *pilot*," Nathan corrected, "but I was *in command* of the Seiiki at the time. My ship's actions are my responsibility."

"Then, it seems we are in your debt, Captain Scott."

"Not at all. To be honest, my concerns were not with your world, but for my crew *on* your world."

"Nevertheless, we are grateful for your efforts, regardless of your motives," the lead council member stated. "The council is grateful for *your* efforts, as well, Lieutenant Commander."

"It was nothing," Jessica replied modestly.

"On the contrary, we may be a peaceful people, but we do appreciate the courage it takes to stand and fight. In particular, Council Member Tudo is grateful for your bravery, without which his daughter would now be in the hands of the Ahka."

Nathan looked at Jessica. "The Ahka *kidnap* people, as well?" he asked her under his breath.

"Did I leave that part out?" Jessica whispered back.

"Captain Scott," the lead council member continued, "if you were so inclined, could not the Ahka be defeated by your ship?"

"I cannot be certain," Nathan admitted. "I know very little about the Ahka's resources, fleet strength, weapons, or even tactics. If they have nothing more powerful than what we just faced, then, yes, the Seiiki could handle them. But if they have larger ships, or greater numbers than what we faced today, my answer might be different."

"We, too, have very little intelligence on the Ahka's forces," the lead council member admitted. "To the best of our knowledge, their biggest limitation is their lack of carrier ships. The Ahka raiders are numerous, perhaps as many as thirty or forty of them, but they are incapable of making the journey from Ahka to Casbon on their own and must rely on carrier ships to ferry them between our worlds. It is our understanding that the Ahka have *four* such vessels."

"And how many raiders can each carrier vessel transport?" Nathan wondered.

"That, we do not know. Until today, we have never been attacked by more than eight raiders. Our sensors only detected a single, large jump flash just prior to the attack, but our sensor technology is limited. So, we must assume they can carry at least twelve raiders, which is the number of ships that attacked us this day. So, you can see why we feel the need to purchase all one hundred working fighters from Mister Imburjia."

"I understand," Nathan assured them. "However, I must agree with the lieutenant commander's assessment of your chances. Without proper training, tactics, and support facilities, your losses will be high, if not complete, *especially* if you try to take the fight *to* the Ahka."

"Then, what would you have us do, Captain?" the lead council member asked.

"Accept our offer to provide you with experienced pilots to defend your world, and to train *your* people so they may someday defend it themselves."

"And in exchange, you get half of our fighters," the lead council member said, sounding displeased.

"Yes, but only *after* the Ahka's ability to attack your world has been eliminated."

"Then, you are willing to destroy the Ahka for us?"

"No, I am only willing to destroy their ability to attack Casbon."

"Captain," one of the other council members objected, "the Ahka have been harassing us for years. They have stolen our resources, kidnapped our citizens...surely we have the right to seek justice."

"I am not qualified to pass judgment on the Ahka," Nathan replied. "For all I know, they have a legitimate grievance with Casbon. What I *am* offering you is a *reasonable* solution to your problem, one which benefits our cause, as well. If you are interested, then I will immediately dispatch the appropriate personnel and equipment to your world. You would be protected within a few days. If not, then I wish you and your world the best of luck."

The lead council member looked over at the others on the council, then back to Nathan. "We will consider your words, Captain."

"That is certainly your right. However, I am not prepared to stand idly by while you *think* about your problem. My people have a much deadlier foe to contend with than the Ahka."

"Captain, surely you don't expect us to make such an important decision on the spur of the moment?"

"There are two kinds of people," Nathan explained, "those who act when action is necessary, and those who *think* about acting, usually until it is too late. I depart in one hour," he added. "Good day."

With that, Nathan nodded politely, then turned and headed for the exit, his astonished cohorts following him out.

* * *

"What the hell was that?" Jessica asked as she and Vladimir followed Nathan quickly down the steps leading from the council building to the square.

"It's called *negotiating*," Nathan replied with just a touch of sarcasm in his tone.

"That's not negotiating," Jessica argued. "You just gave them an ultimatum! You're supposed to have a discussion, make them realize why they need what we have to offer..."

"You *already* explained the risks to them, and I didn't feel like wasting any more time."

"So, you figured you'd insult them with all that 'those who act and those who think about acting' crap?"

"All I did was attach a time limit to your offer, which, by the way, you had no authority to make."

"I was trying to take advantage of an opportunity before it disappeared," she defended.

"That's not your job!" Nathan scolded, growing angrier by the minute.

"So, I was supposed to just sit by and watch an opportunity to acquire a much-needed resource slip through our fingers?"

"Yes! That's exactly what you were supposed to do!"

"That doesn't make any sense!" Jessica argued.

Nathan stopped as they approached the Seiiki's cargo ramp, turning to face Jessica. "It doesn't *have* to make sense to you, Jess. A command structure exists for a reason, and you're *not* in command of this alliance, *I* am."

"What?"

"You heard me!" Nathan took a deep breath, trying to calm down. "Look, the Casbons aren't stupid. They know damn well the risks you outlined are real. The question is, are they willing to pay the price to ensure success with minimal losses? Since they're primarily a non-violent people, I'm betting they'll agree to the deal. They just had to be pushed into making a decision. You? You would have negotiated back and forth with them for as long as they wanted, until they got the deal *they* wanted. Hell, both Orloff *and* Imburjia were playing you."

"They weren't *playing* us," Jessica insisted.

"Aristaeus had already promised to sell the fighters *to* the Casbons. He only agreed to bring us along to speak with them because he *wants* them to survive so he can continue trading with them."

"Don't kid yourself, Jess. Aristaeus brought you along so he could drive up the price by showing the Casbons that he had another buyer willing to pay more. Granted, you striking a deal with the Casbons that increases their chances of survival is an additional win for him, but his *primary* concern is what he gets for those fighters."

"As long as we all get what we want, who cares?" Jessica defended.

"What if the fleet had been attacked while you were running around the galaxy?"

"Was it?" Jessica asked.

"No, but what if I had already tasked the forces you'd promised to another assignment?"

"Did you?"

"No."

"Then, what's the problem?"

"The problem is, you couldn't have known that," Nathan explained. "And you know *why* you couldn't have known that? Because I don't tell you everything I'm planning, or everything Telles, Cameron, and I discuss. And you know *why* I don't tell you everything? Because I'm in command, and I don't *have* to tell you everything, nor do I have to *explain* myself *to* you. What I *expect* from you is to follow orders and do your job, which, at the time, was to protect my sister and her kids!"

"Jesus!" Jessica exclaimed. "Is that what this is about? Christ, Nathan, there are twelve Ghatazhak guarding them, *with* weapons, on a station that doesn't *allow* weapons."

"Yeah, now, but when you left there were only four."

"But I knew eight more were a day away," Jessica argued.

"That's not the point!" Nathan barked. "The point is that I *trusted* you to protect the *last* family I have left, and you broke that trust by deciding that your fighter-shopping trip was more important. *That's* your problem, Jess. You don't know how to follow orders."

"Of all people to talk about following orders..."

"The difference is that every order I've bent or broken has been within the authority of my position, and until you realize that, you're going to continue pulling stupid stunts like this one. The *only* reason I don't bust you back down to lieutenant and give you back to Telles, is because you have an amazing instinct for combat and intelligence, but that's *all* you have."

"She cleans up nice, too," Vladimir interjected, trying to lighten the mood.

Both Nathan and Jessica glared at him.

"It's true," Vladimir defended.

Nathan looked back at Jessica. "I *want* to trust you, Jess. I *need* to be able to trust you. Hell, I can't do any of this without you, without both of you, but you've *got* to know your limitations and accept them; otherwise, you're just too dangerous."

"But hot," Vladimir added, still trying to keep things friendly.

Jessica paused, swallowing hard as she got her temper under control. "Alright, what *should* I have done, Nathan?"

"You should have tried to convince Orloff to delay

his departure until I arrived or get the name and location of the seller from him."

"And if neither worked?" she asked.

"Then you shrug your shoulders, chalk it up to bad timing, and continue with your *assigned* mission. Your commanding officer, whoever they should be, needs to be absolutely certain that you will carry out their orders, and not just bail when you think there is something more important to do."

"I didn't just *bail*, Nathan..."

"Yes, you did."

"No, I didn't," Jessica insisted.

"You kind of did," Vladimir said.

"Who asked you?" Jessica snapped.

"Hey, I said you were hot, didn't I?"

Jessica took a deep breath, swallowing her pride and putting her ego in check. "I'm sorry, Nathan, I thought I was doing what *you* would've done."

"You did *exactly* what I would have done," Nathan agreed, "but you're *not* me, and I have a different set of responsibilities than you do. You *think* you understand what *my* position is about but, trust me, until you actually *have* to do it, you have no idea. So please, be that officer, *that friend*, whom I know I can trust...*completely*."

"I will," Jessica replied. "I promise."

"Me, too," Vladimir added, smiling.

Nathan looked at Vladimir, rolling his eyes. "Consider *your* ass chewed out, as well, Commander."

"Understood, sir," Vladimir replied, giving Nathan a mock salute.

"Now, everyone inside," Nathan added. "I want to be ready to depart as soon as possible."

"But what about the council?" Vladimir wondered.

"The ball is in their court," Nathan replied.

"Then, you're not bluffing?" Jessica realized. "You're really prepared to walk away?"

"I never bluff," Nathan assured her as he turned and headed up the ramp.

* * *

"I have been thinking," Vladimir said as he sat down across from Nathan in the small booth in the Seiiki's galley. "We could take a few of the mini-jump comm-drones that the Reapers use and outfit the Seiiki to use them."

"What would that entail?" Nathan wondered.

"You have two bays that were originally designed as external equipment bays. You turned them into propellant tanks. We could convert them into recovery bays and install charging systems for the jump comm-drones."

"We'd be losing propellant capacity," Nathan said, pointing out the obvious.

"Do you really need it?" Vladimir challenged. "Dalen said you added the extra tanks because you liked to carry extra, in case you weren't able to pick up another job at your destination. Something about 'always wanting to have enough gas to get away.'"

"Yeah, I guess that's not so much an issue, now," Nathan admitted. "It would be nice to have better long-range communications capabilities. Will the drones fit in those bays?"

"Actually, I believe we can fit two in each bay."

"Four comm-drones would certainly be nice," Nathan agreed. "It would give us a lot more flexibility in situations like this. I always feel guilty leaving the fleet. How long would it take?"

"A day at the most, once we get back to the Aurora."

"We would need to get clearance from Sanctuary

to use them when we're in port, or when we're trying to communicate with our people there."

"Do you think that will be a problem?" Vladimir asked.

"Let me talk to them," Jessica suggested from the doorway. "I've got experience negotiating with Sanctuary personnel."

"Yeah, I heard," Nathan retorted.

"*Captain?*" Corporal Vasya called over comm-sets.

"Yes?"

"*Council Member Garon is here and is asking to speak with you.*"

Nathan looked at Jessica. "Which one was Garon?"

Jessica shrugged. "Their nameplates were in a language I couldn't read."

"Corporal, please escort the council member to the galley."

"*Yes, sir.*"

"You're mighty pleased with yourself right about now, aren't you?" Jessica said.

"Not yet," Nathan replied. "After all, they could be coming to give a polite 'no, thank you.' I mean, we *did* take out twelve Ahka raiders for them."

"Uh-huh," Jessica said as she exited. "I'll be in *your* quarters."

Nathan watched her exit and then turned to Vladimir. "She really doesn't have any respect for chain of command, does she."

"She is who she is," Vladimir replied, patting him on the shoulder as he, too, headed for the exit. "Would you really want it any other way?"

"Maybe." Nathan rose from the booth, putting his cup into the compact dishwasher built into the galley wall, then turned to face the starboard entrance as he heard Corporal Vasya and Council Member Garon approaching.

Corporal Vasya stepped to one side of the galley's starboard entrance, gesturing to the council member. "Right in here, ma'am."

An elderly woman appeared in the doorway, still wearing her council robes. Nathan immediately recognized her from the council chambers, not thirty minutes earlier, although she had not spoken while he was present.

"Captain Scott," the council member greeted, nodding respectfully. "Thank you for seeing me."

"It is my pleasure, ma'am. Please," Nathan said, gesturing toward the dining nook. "My apologies for the cramped living spaces. We had to sacrifice quite a bit in accommodations when we armed her."

"It is quite alright," she replied. "We, on Casbon, are accustomed to spartan living. Although, I must admit, based on what your ship accomplished this day, it is not what I expected."

"The Seiiki was originally a personal yacht for a Takaran warship captain. It has been through several remodels since then and now serves as my personal ship for various missions."

"Then, you don't always travel aboard the Aurora?"

"Unfortunately, no. The Aurora's range is limited, while this ship can jump repeatedly until it reaches its destination. Plus, the Aurora has other responsibilities, at the moment."

"I see."

"How may I help you?"

"I was impressed by how you spoke your mind in our chambers."

"I apologize if I was out of line."

"Not at all," the council member replied. "Your

assessment was quite accurate, in fact. The problem with a government run by council *is* that it is often difficult to get a majority agreement. Unfortunately, the diversity of our population requires such."

"I see."

"To be honest, no one had heard of you, *or* the Aurora, until today. Mister Imburjia and Mister Orloff were kind enough to detail your accomplishments to us. Once he did so, we realized we had misjudged you and your cohorts. For that, I offer our apologies."

"No apology is necessary," Nathan assured her. "It's a very big galaxy," he added with his usual, endearing smile.

"In fact, we were even prepared to let you leave without taking you up on your offer," she continued, "had it not been for Mister Imburjia."

"Then, the council has decided to accept our offer of assistance?"

"The council is prepared to *tentatively* accept your gracious offer, on the condition that we can work out the details later."

"Our offer seemed pretty straightforward to me," Nathan told her.

"Our concern is that giving you half our fighters will leave our defenses in a weakened state, and that the Ahka will find a way to acquire other ships with which to attack us. And when they do, they will attack with intent to destroy or conquer our world, rather than simply steal from it."

"I promise you that we would never leave you unable to defend yourselves," Nathan insisted. "But the day will come when you will need to do more than just maintain an operational wing of interceptors. You will need planetary defenses and some sort of ground-based response force, if you wish to be truly safe."

Council Member Garon shook her head in dismay. "Such measures go against everything we believe in."

"I understand and admire your commitment to peace, Council Member Garon but, unfortunately, the nature of humanity is such that the only way to *ensure* peace is *with* the threat of force."

"Alas, the *threat* of force usually leads to the *use* of force."

Nathan sighed. "If good people who abhor violence do not prosper, who will change the future of humanity?"

"Very well put, Captain," the council member said.

"It is what I remind myself, every time I must fire a weapon or send my people into harm's way. It is what *you* must think as you prepare to defend yourselves."

"I suppose you're right."

"Look at it this way," Nathan said, "once you have disabled the Ahka's ability to attack others, the opportunity will exist to befriend them and show them that we can *all* survive, *and thrive*, if we work together."

"You are quite the optimist," she replied, smiling at him.

"I wouldn't be able to do my job if I wasn't."

"How soon can you provide us with assistance?"

"It will take us at least eighteen hours to reach our next destination, at which point I can send orders back to my fleet to dispatch the appropriate personnel and equipment. It would be best if Mister Imburjia held off delivery until our people arrive, as even with a full complement of pilots, it will take at least a few days for them to become familiar with the fighters and be ready to defend your world."

"Thank you, Captain Scott. I will speak to Mister Imburjia about this." The council member stood again, preparing to depart. "I trust I will see you again?"

"It is unlikely, I'm afraid," Nathan replied, also standing. "I have my own enemy to deal with."

"Of course," she replied. "The best of luck to you, Captain."

"And to you, Council Member." He turned toward the exit and called out. "Corporal."

Corporal Vasya stepped into the room. "I'll show you out, ma'am."

As soon as the council member departed the galley, Jessica entered from the opposite side.

"*Now y*ou're mighty pleased with yourself, right?"

"That's why I'm the captain," he replied, smiling as he passed her by.

* * *

Cameron stood behind the flight crew, gazing out the window at the Orochi carriers as her Reaper descended onto the landing pad of one of the decommissioned ships floating in the protected harbor off of Onaro Seykora. As soon as the Reaper's engines began to spin down, she turned to exit. "Don't go anywhere, gentlemen. I don't like being away from the ship when the captain is away."

"We'll keep her warmed up and ready for quick-launch, sir," the pilot replied.

Cameron made her way aft into the utility bay, opened the side hatch, and jumped down to the landing pad deck, not waiting for the boarding steps to deploy. She paused for a moment, looking around the topside of the ship. Even up close, the Orochi looked more like a seagoing vessel than a spaceship. In fact, it looked a lot like one of the old, deep-sea research submersibles back on Earth that had always fascinated her as a child...just considerably larger.

The Orochi carrier was about twice the length of a Cobra gunship, four times its breadth, and equally thicker from its dorsal to ventral surfaces. It had a center hull, which blended smoothly into port and starboard wing-like sections that supported seven landing pads for the original Gunyoki fighters. While the pads were too small to accommodate a modern Gunyoki, they were plenty large enough for a sizable missile launcher on each pad. The entire vessel was painted blue with yellow accents, reminding her of her high school cricket team's uniforms.

"Captain!" Deliza called as she climbed out through the open hatch on the side of the fuselage. She was followed by Abby and an older Rakuen man whom Cameron did not recognize.

"It's not as big as I thought," Cameron said as she headed toward them.

"It's a bit deceiving, as nearly a third of the fuselage is underwater," Abby told her.

"Captain Taylor, this is Danno Yasui," Deliza introduce.

"A pleasure," Cameron replied, bowing respectfully before shaking the man's hand.

"Mister Yasui is an Orochi engineer."

"Really," Cameron replied.

"Our government chose to retain a handful of us over the decades, in case the Orochi carriers ever needed to be reactivated," Mister Yasui explained.

"Good thinking," Cameron agreed. "How are things looking?"

“The decommissioning process was designed to allow rapid recommissioning,” Mister Yasui began. “All of their flight systems are still intact. It will take five to six days to make their main lift and propulsion systems operational. However, it will take a bit longer to rearm them.”

“All the guns were removed when they were decommissioned, to appease the leaders of Neramese,” Deliza added.

“Just as well, I suppose,” Cameron said. “We’ll probably want to install more current weapons.”

“That’s what I figured,” Deliza agreed.

“Abby, do you foresee any problems equipping these ships with jump drives?”

“No, but we won’t be able to install them on the surface,” Abby replied. “The only way we can fit in the jump field generators *and* energy banks is to remove four of their eight propellant tanks, and they need *all* of them to reach orbit.”

“The original engines were not as efficient as their more modern variants,” Mister Yasui explained.

“Can we replace them?” Cameron wondered.

“It would be easier to keep them and just install the jump drives in orbit,” Deliza said.

“How the hell did these things get to orbit with fourteen Gunyoki on deck?” Cameron wondered.

“They burned all their propellant to make orbit,” Mister Yasui explained. “Once in orbit, they were refueled before beginning their mission. Upon their return, they again had to be fueled, in order to return to the surface.”

“Why didn’t they just stay in orbit?”

“That would have required the construction of a massive orbital spaceport,” Mister Yasui replied. “That would have taken decades to construct, and they already had the infrastructure in place for the orbital refueling."

"The same system was used for their interplanetary transports," Deliza chimed in.

"Will they be able to lift off, loaded with jump missiles?" Cameron wondered.

"That should not be a problem," Mister Yasui assured her. "The old Gunyoki fighters were quite heavy."

"We expect to be able to put four jump missiles on each launcher," Deliza told Cameron. "Two on the top rail, two on the bottom. Including the launcher, that's still a bit less weight than a Gunyoki."

"So, fifty-six jump missiles per ship," Cameron calculated. "That's a lot of firepower for a ship this size. And there are *how many Orochis*?"

"We expect to be able to recommission at least ten of them in the next two weeks, and six more a few weeks later," Mister Yasui answered.

"I thought there were twenty of them?"

"Two were lost in the war, and two require more extensive efforts to make them operational again. Water damage, and such."

"No matter, I guess," Cameron said. "It's going to take us at least a month to manufacture enough jump missiles to outfit them all."

"The first jump missile plant on Neramese will start production the day after tomorrow," Abby stated. "They are expected to produce five jump missiles per day, after the first week of parts pre-production. And the second plant will go online a week later."

"The Rakuen plants will be online in a few days, as well," Deliza added. "If all goes well, we'll have the first ten Orochis fully loaded *and* operational within a month."

"I'll be happy if we can just get two or three of them up and running in that time," Cameron said. "Mind if I take a look inside?"

"Of course," Mister Yasui replied. "But I warn you, Captain, it is a bit cramped."

* * *

Nathan quietly entered the observation room overlooking Miri's treatment suite at Doctor Symyri's medical facility on Sanctuary. Inside, Neli was watching Kyle standing next to his mother's medical stasis pod, talking to her. "Neli," he whispered, not wanting to startle her.

Neli turned her head, smiling when she saw Nathan. "When did you get back?"

"About ten minutes ago," he replied, moving in to sit next to her. "What are you doing here?"

"Kyle insists on coming and talking to her at least twice a day," Neli explained. "I come with him for moral support. He pretends like he doesn't need it, but I can tell he does."

"He's a strong kid, just like his mother," Nathan said, gazing at his nephew in the next room.

"Did you find them?" Neli asked.

"Yeah, I found them. It wasn't easy. By the time we caught up with them, they were nearly five hundred light years away."

"Where the hell did they go?"

"Someplace called Casbon, in the Ilyan Gamaze."

"Never heard of either."

"Neither had I."

"I take it you chewed their asses?" Neli assumed.

"No more than they deserved," Nathan replied. "I felt a little guilty doing so, actually."

"Let me guess, they got the fighters."

"In a manner of speaking, yes, but they took a lot of risks doing so, and nearly got themselves killed in the process. If we hadn't arrived when we did..."

"That's what you do, Nathan," Neli said with a chuckle. "Even as Connor, you had a habit of saving people. Hell, you saved me."

"Marcus saved you, Neli. I just agreed to hire you on."

"Perhaps, but it wouldn't have worked out nearly as well, had you not."

Nathan sighed, still watching Kyle. "Where's Melanie?"

"She's back at the suite with Marcus. She's really taken a shine to him."

"To *Marcus*?"

"He's actually pretty good with little kids," Neli defended, "especially with Melanie."

"Melanie gets along with everyone."

"She is a sweetheart."

"She is so much like her mother," Nathan said, still gazing through the window. "When I look at her, I see Miri when we were kids."

"She's older than you, right?"

"By nearly two years," Nathan replied. "She was always my protector; my confidant."

Neli was silent for a moment. "She almost died yesterday, you know."

"I know. I spoke to Melei before I came in."

"They were amazing," Neli said.

"Who was amazing?"

"All three of them. Symyri, Melei, even Michi. When her heart stopped, they worked for hours to keep her alive until they could repair the damage and get it restarted." Neli looked at Nathan. "They actually had to take her heart *out* of her body for over an hour, while Symyri grafted some sort of automated patches to it before putting it back into her body. There were at least ten to fifteen people in there working away. It was like watching a perfectly choreographed dance, in the middle of a gunfight."

"God, I don't know if I could have handled that," Nathan admitted.

"Kyle did."

"What?"

"He was here the entire time, sitting right where you are."

"Why did you let him witness that?"

"I couldn't have stopped him if I'd tried," Neli insisted. "I kept asking if he was okay, and you know what he said every time?"

"What?"

"She's going to be fine."

Nathan sighed again. "I told you he was strong," he said, nearly choking up. After a moment, Nathan pulled himself together and rose from his seat.

"Where are you going?" Neli wondered, looking up at him.

"To talk to Kyle."

Nathan went over to the door and stepped into Miri's room. Just like Neli, Kyle didn't turn around... he just kept staring at his mother. Nathan walked over and put his hand on Kyle's shoulder. "How's it going, Kyle?"

Kyle looked up at his uncle, trying not to cry as he forced a smile. "She made it, Uncle Nathan. She made it."

Nathan wrapped his arms around his nephew, tears beginning to run down his cheeks. "Was there ever any doubt?"

CHAPTER SIX

The Seiiki's cargo ramp was already coming down by the time the inner doors to the Aurora's starboard hangar bay were completely open. Before it reached the deck, Nathan, Jessica, and Vladimir were already heading down.

"Welcome back," Cameron greeted as she approached the bottom of the ramp. "How's Miri?"

"It was close," Nathan replied as they reached the bottom of the ramp. "They actually lost her for more than an hour."

"What?"

"Yeah, apparently, this guy Symyri really is some kind of miracle worker, at least, according to Doc Chen."

"I figured something must have gone wrong," Cameron said. "We were expecting you back more than a day ago."

"Yeah, well, I had to go rescue *these* two from halfway across the galaxy," Nathan replied, pointing back at Jessica and Vladimir with his thumb.

"I'm sure *that's* going to be an interesting story."

"You didn't *rescue* us," Jessica insisted as she and Vladimir came to a stop alongside Nathan, "and it was only a *few hundred* light years."

"I can't wait to hear all about it," Cameron said, "*after* you've all had a chance to clean up."

"That bad, huh," Nathan said.

"Doesn't that ship of yours have showers?"

"We picked up a little damage along the way," Nathan explained. "I want to meet with you, Telles, Abby, Deliza, Prechitt, and Verbeek in the command briefing room in one hour." Nathan turned to look at Vladimir and Jessica. "You two, as well."

"I'll let everyone know," Cameron assured him.

"I'm going to want full readiness reports on all forces and all vessels, as well as what's happening on Rakuen and Neramese," Nathan added. "Also, any new intel on the Dusahn."

"Of course. What's going on?"

"We have a lot to discuss," Nathan replied, "but first, we need to wash the stink off," he added, continuing toward the exit.

* * *

"Captain on deck!" the guard at the door to the command briefing room announced as Nathan entered.

"As you were," Nathan ordered before anyone could reach a full standing position. "I've reviewed most of the readiness reports, as well as the status reports on Rakuen and Neramese," Nathan announced as he took his seat at the head of the conference table. "So, for the sake of expediency, I'll dispense with the usual formality of each of you making presentations and get straight to each topic." Nathan glanced around the room, looking for a hint of any objections from those in attendance before continuing. "Commander Kamenetskiy and Lieutenant Commander Nash made contact with a broker selling one hundred working Sugali fighters. Unfortunately, the broker had promised to sell them to a world in desperate need of the fighters to protect themselves against pirates from a neighboring system, who have been raiding their world on a regular basis. Lieutenant Commander Nash correctly recognized the increased risk the purchase of these fighters represented to the buyer, given that they have no pilots, no military, and no infrastructure in place to support them. Therefore, we offered to provide pilots, support personnel, and equipment, as well as training, in exchange for a number of fighters yet to be determined."

"You want to send one hundred pilots?" Commander Verbeek asked, surprised. "Pardon me, Captain, but do we even *have* that many pilots? I know I don't."

"Actually, there are two hundred and thirty-eight unassigned Corinari pilots at the moment," Commander Prechitt said. "More than half of them have combat fighter training." He looked at Nathan. "In fact, eleven of them are also flight instructors. I doubt it would take much time for them to become adept at piloting the Sugali fighters, and I am certain they would welcome the opportunity to serve the cause."

"Still, you'll need airframe and power plant mechanics, engineers, weapons systems technicians, avionics technicians..."

"I'm not talking about sending a combat-ready unit, capable of supporting one hundred fighters," Nathan explained. "Enough to support twenty to thirty fighters would likely be enough to get the Casbons going."

"There's also the logistics of feeding and housing that many people on a foreign world," Cameron pointed out.

"I'm not saying it's going to be easy, but I believe it is necessary."

"Just how many fighters are we talking about getting in return?" Commander Verbeek wondered.

"I'm hoping for fifty," Nathan replied, "but we need to get some intel on their enemy's forces, industrial capacity, and so on, before we can determine just how many fighters they can spare and still be able to adequately defend themselves."

"Wouldn't it be easier to simply destroy the enemy's ability to strike?" General Telles wondered.

"I am considering that option, as well," Nathan admitted. "Still, we need intel first."

"Captain, it will take at least a few days to get everything ready to move," Cameron stated. "How often do these raids occur?"

"Apparently, they have escalated to at least a weekly event," Nathan replied. "One occurred as we were arriving."

"Then, you saw this enemy in action?" Commander Verbeek asked.

"Yes, and to be honest, they weren't very impressive," Nathan replied. "Their piloting skills appeared to be rudimentary, at best, and their ships were not very maneuverable. More like armed shuttles than combat landers. Even their shields were not that powerful."

"Jump capable?" Commander Verbeek wondered.

"Short-range only. They have to be ferried over by a carrier. Initial intel indicates that each carrier can haul twelve raiders, but none of this is confirmed. It's all based on hearsay and the single attack we actually witnessed."

"That's not much upon which to base the commitment of significant resources, let alone get involved in someone else's war," General Telles warned. "Do we even know the enemy's side of the story? Perhaps there is a reason they feel justified in attacking these Casbons."

"The enemy is called the Ahka," Jessica chimed in. "They are a young colony who suffered considerable setbacks and are struggling to recover. They steal the minerals and precious metals mined and refined by the Casbons to pay for the things they need to keep their colony alive and growing. They even kidnap Casbon women to use as breeding stock."

"And where did you get this information?" General Telles wondered. "Hopefully, not from the Casbons."

"Actually, from the seller of the fighters," Jessica replied a bit defensively. "And I personally witnessed the Ahka trying to kidnap Casbon women."

"I presume you stopped them," the general remarked.

"Damn right, I did."

"I agree that we need to be certain of our intel," Nathan agreed, "which is why I'd like to send the Falcon to recon the Ahka system before we commit any resources to the Casbons."

"Then you are uncertain of the legitimacy of their claims?" General Telles asked.

"No, I believe them," Nathan replied. "I just want more intel so we're sure of what we're getting into. However, I'm not providing aid to the Casbons because I think they deserve it. I'm not even doing it for the fighters. Let's face it, fifty Sugali fighters aren't even half as deadly as fifty Gunyoki."

"Then, why?" Cameron wondered.

"Because Casbon is rich in raw ores, minerals, and precious metals, all of which we desperately need if we're going to build up the Rogen system's defenses."

"Especially the aramenium," Vladimir added.

"They have aramenium?" Abby asked, surprised.

"Apparently, a lot of it," Jessica replied. "And the Ahka don't even know about it. If they find out, they'll probably attack with a lot more firepower than before."

"I'm not familiar with aramenium," Cameron admitted.

"It is a rare element that can store tremendous amounts of energy," Abby explained. "It also stabilizes the flow of energy passing through it."

"Then, it might be something we could make use of," Nathan surmised.

"Possibly, yes," Abby confirmed. "There was also a theory about using aramenium in jump field emitters, as it helps to stabilize the distribution of energy into the jump fields, allowing for much larger instant energy dumps. This is just a theory, of course. We were never able to experiment with it because the element is so rare, especially in the Sol sector. However, I read the theorem, and if the assumptions within it are correct, it could quadruple our current single-jump range."

"By just replacing the emitters?" Cameron asked in disbelief.

"The emitters, the power distribution grid, and the energy banks," Abby replied. "The jump field generators simply modulate the energy as the fields are produced and are already designed to handle considerably more power than currently used."

"They use aramenium in the Volon system," Deliza added. "They make high-capacity batteries out of them. They recharge *very* quickly. Perhaps you could adapt their battery technology to the energy banks?"

"And reduce the recharge times," Cameron added.

"No, but they might be able to power repeated short-range jumps, just like the mini ZPEDs do for smaller ships."

"Intriguing," Abby agreed. "If we greatly reduce

the time it takes to recharge the Aurora's energy banks..."

"Then, our operational range would be improved," Nathan realized, "and without having to overhaul the emitters or the power distribution grid." He looked at Abby. "By how much?"

"That's hard to say," Abby admitted, looking to Deliza.

"We studied the idea of using aramenium in the energy banks for cargo ships. At the time, we estimated a fifty-percent reduction in the recharge time," Deliza replied.

"Why didn't you ever develop them?" Jessica wondered.

"The cost of the aramenium made the idea impractical. Cargo ships already finish recharging their energy banks faster than they can cycle cargo."

"That would reduce our transit time between Rogen and Takar to *twenty hours*," Cameron calculated.

"If that's the case, maybe we should send the Cobras along as protection, at least until the fighter wing is up and running," Jessica suggested.

"We can't spare them," Cameron argued.

"She's right," Nathan agreed. "We need the Cobras in order to continue harassing Dusahn shipping routes."

"Can't we use the Gunyoki for that?" Jessica asked.

"The Cobras are far more powerful than the octos the Dusahn usually send to guard their cargo ships," Nathan told her. "Together, they can even stand toe-to-toe with a frigate. A Gunyoki is basically an even match for an octo. Besides, it's too soon to start using the Gunyoki for anything other than protecting the Rogen system. Not until we get at least a few hundred of them fitted with jump drives."

"We need to send something," Jessica insisted. "Otherwise, our own people will be at risk, as well."

"Good point," Nathan agreed, thinking.

"Send our Eagles," Commander Verbeek suggested.

"Send *our* fighters?" Cameron asked, obviously disagreeing with the commander.

"The Aurora isn't going anywhere until the Rogen system can protect itself," the commander pointed out, "not unless you manage to increase our single-jump range. And the Dusahn octos have our Eagles outgunned anyway. *If* they should attack, the Gunyoki are better suited to take on the octos. You said so yourself, Captain."

"Sugali fighters are similar in size and capability to an Eagle," Commander Prechitt added. "The Eagle ground crews could take care of the Sugali fighters and help get the Casbon ground crews trained."

"Good thinking," Nathan agreed. "Which is why I'm sending you to command the entire operation."

"You are?"

"The Corinari are your men, Commander, and you're certainly qualified for the position."

"Of course, sir," the commander replied. "I'd be happy to."

"Very well, it's been decided," Nathan said. "Commander Prechitt, select and assemble your staff, and coordinate with Commander Verbeek."

"Yes, sir."

"Verbeek, get ready to mobilize your air wing; lock, stock, and barrel."

"Yes, sir."

"Just one question," Cameron said. "Who's

going to transport them? The Glendanon's the only ship big enough, and she's busy assembling more fabricators."

"Move the Gunyoki back to the race platform for now and move our Eagle air wing to the Inman and the Gervais. Eagles are smaller than Gunyoki, so we should be able to fit ten on each ship."

"What about the support personnel and equipment?" Commander Verbeek wondered.

"The Torrecun can haul the gear, and Hunt's ship can haul the personnel," Nathan replied.

"We should bring the Forenta, as well," Commander Verbeek added. "Unless the Casbons have a big propellant depot."

"You're talking about sending half our fleet," Cameron warned. "And with only twenty Super Eagles to protect them."

"Considering the potential rewards, I think it's worth the risk," Nathan said.

"I'm not disagreeing with you, Captain," Cameron replied. "Just pointing out the fact."

"Great. Let's make this happen, people," Nathan said, rising from his seat to exit.

* * *

"We have our first new intelligence from the Rogen system," General Hesson announced as he entered Lord Dusahn's office. "There are some disturbing developments."

"Such as?" Lord Dusahn inquired, his eyes still on the view screen on his desk.

"The entire Karuzari fleet is in stellar orbit around Rogen, near the Gunyoki base, *including* the Aurora."

"That is *good* news, is it not?" Lord Dusahn said, finally looking up. "Now that we know their location, we can destroy them."

"There is unusual activity, as well," the general continued. "There is considerable expansion of the Ranni plant," he explained, turning on the larger view screen on the wall. "They are also repairing and, apparently, *expanding* upon the Gunyoki base."

"That was to be expected," Lord Dusahn assured him while he studied the images being displayed on the large view screen.

"Also, there are indications of new factories being built on both Rakuen *and* Neramese."

"What kind of factories?"

"One would assume they are building some type of defensive weapons," General Hesson insisted.

"They could be building toilets, for all we know," Lord Dusahn commented.

"While that is certainly *possible*, my lord, it would be safer to assume they are building weapons."

"I take it you have instructed our people to leave assets on the surface before they depart."

"I have, my lord."

"Very well; then we shall soon know what they are building."

"Regardless of *what* they are building, the presence of the Karuzari fleet and the number of shuttles transiting between the fleet and the Rogen system's populated worlds, we must conclude that the Karuzari have convinced *both* worlds to join their cause."

Lord Dusahn smiled. "Then, it is time to put my plan into action."

"Of this, I am not certain," General Hesson replied. "Our reinforcements are still ten days out, and now that we know *where* the Aurora and the Karuzari fleet are located, time is on our side."

"Just because they are in the Rogen system,

now, does not mean they will *always* be there," Lord Dusahn reminded his general.

"Perhaps, but there are risks to your plan, my lord."

"Which are mitigated by our knowledge of the Aurora's location," Lord Dusahn insisted. "We set our bait, drawing her into our trap, away from her fleet and her only supporting worlds, and attack *both* at the same time. The Karuzari *and* her allies are destroyed, and we are free to expand our empire, unfettered."

"But our reinforcements are still too far away..."

"They are closer to the Rogen system than to Takara, by at least two days," Lord Dusahn pointed out. "Send word for them to reroute to within single attack-jump range of the Rogen system and await orders. We will use our own ships to destroy the Aurora, in full view of the people of Takara."

"It was my understanding that you wished our ships to be the ones to destroy the *Rogen* system," General Hesson reminded his leader.

"In war, one must be flexible," Lord Dusahn replied. "All that matters is that the Aurora and *all* her allies *are* destroyed, and that everyone *knows* it was the *Dusahn* who wiped them from existence."

* * *

"Final insertion jump in one minute," Ensign Lassen announced from the Falcon's right seat.

"Finally," Sergeant Nama exclaimed from the side-facing sensor station, directly behind the ensign. "That had to be our longest transit series yet."

"Yeah, well, it's going to be even longer on the way back," Lieutenant Teison reminded him.

"No way."

"Yup. Full evasion algos."

"Why?" the sergeant wondered. "The Ahka aren't a threat to us."

"Orders are orders," the lieutenant replied.

"Thirty seconds," Ensign Lassen reported.

"Damn, what I wouldn't give for a stasis pod," the sergeant muttered.

"Okay, boys, this one will be low and fast. We jump into atmo, buzz the colony, take a bunch of pretty pictures and scans, and jump out again."

"And if they don't like us buzzing them?" the sergeant asked.

"Then, they can file a complaint with the Ilyan," Lieutenant Teison replied.

"Ten seconds."

"Snap those shields up as soon as we hit the atmosphere, Riko."

"You got it, LT," the sergeant replied.

"Jumping in three......two......one......jump."

The Falcon shook as it jumped into the atmosphere of Ahka, suddenly slowed by the drag. All three men felt themselves thrown forward against their shoulder restraints, nearly knocking the air out of their lungs.

"Damn, the air's thick here!" the lieutenant exclaimed as he struggled to get control of the ship.

"Two thousand meters and descending!" Ensign Lassen reported. "Speed is falling rapidly!"

"Increasing power," the lieutenant replied, pushing the throttles for the Falcon's atmospheric engines forward.

"Eighteen hundred, still falling," the ensign reported. "Airspeed's coming up."

"Ahka colony dead ahead, two hundred and fifty clicks, and closing fast," Sergeant Nama reported. "They're targeting us."

"Shields up?" the lieutenant asked.

"The moment we hit atmo," the sergeant assured him.

"Fifteen hundred, rate of descent is slowing. Airspeed is holding."

"I'm picking up eight different targeting scanners," Sergeant Nama announced. "They're lighting us up!"

"Weapons type?" the lieutenant asked.

"Unknown."

"Ready all countermeasures."

"Countermeasures are armed," Ensign Lassen confirmed. "Altitude settling...one thousand meters, as planned."

"One-seventy-five to the target," the sergeant updated. "I'm picking up two missile launchers between us and the target. Suggest one one five and full power. Make them work hard to track us. Jamming their scanners now..."

"One one five," the lieutenant acknowledged, pushing his throttles wide open.

"Missile launch!" the sergeant reported. "Four... correction, *six*!"

"Track type?" Ensign Lassen inquired.

"One hundred clicks, closing *really* fast! Heat and sensor tracks! Ten seconds to impact!"

"Launching countermeasures," Ensign Lassen announced as a series of *ka-chunks* reverberated through the ship.

"Closest?"

"One two four relative!" Nama replied before the lieutenant's request had crossed his lips.

"Breaking left!" Lieutenant Teison jammed his flight control stick to the left, and pushed it down slightly, diving toward the two missiles coming at them from the left.

"Targeting inbounds with nose turret," Ensign Lassen reported. "Firing!"

Streaks of red-orange plasma leapt from their nose turret, striking the two inbound missiles and destroying them.

"Targets destroyed," the ensign reported.

"The two behind us went for the decoys!" Sergeant Nama announced. "Two more, twenty to starboard. Five seconds."

Lieutenant Lassen quickly dialed up the shortest escape jump setting and pressed the jump button on his flight control stick. The ground outside shifted as their ship jumped forward a few kilometers.

"Twenty clicks to target," Sergeant Nama reported. "The last two missiles are turning to reacquire."

"Where are those launchers?" the lieutenant asked.

"Behind us, fifty clicks now, but there could be more on the other side," the sergeant warned.

Lieutenant Teison glanced out his forward windows at the rapidly approaching colony, just as a number of plasma turrets on the edge of the city opened fire.

"Incoming plasma cannon fire," the sergeant warned as the ship rocked from the impacts against their shields.

"No kidding," the lieutenant muttered. "Recon hot?"

"Cameras and sensors are running full tilt," Ensign Lassen reported.

"Nerves of steel time, boys," the lieutenant announced as their ship continued to be bounced about, plasma blasts impacting their shields. The cockpit was bathed in irregular flashes of red-orange light as the lieutenant held his course, allowing the data collection systems to gather as much information as possible.

The ship jumped violently, and a warning buzzer sounded.

"Port forward shield is down to forty percent!" Ensign Lassen warned.

"Hang on, baby," the lieutenant said under his breath.

Another brilliant, red-orange flash lit up the cockpit as the ship jumped again, this time shifting slightly to port at the same time.

"Starboard lateral shield is offline!" Ensign Lassen reported as another alarm sounded.

"Just a few more seconds," the lieutenant muttered as his eyes darted back and forth across his flight displays.

"Missile launches!" Sergeant Nama announced. "Dead ahead! Twenty-two clicks! Fifteen seconds!"

"Targeting the inbounds!" Ensign Lassen added, firing a split second later.

"Ten seconds to jump point," the lieutenant announced.

"One inbound down!" Ensign Lassen announced.

The ship suddenly bounced and slid to the left, as if they had been hit by a large truck. Alarms sounded all over the cockpit.

"Impact! Starboard side!" Ensign Lassen reported. "Our starboard atmo-drive is overheating!"

"Shut it down!" the lieutenant ordered.

"Five seconds to missile impact!"

"I've lost the forward cannon!"

"Jumping!" Lieutenant Teison announced as he pressed the button on his control stick, jumping them to safety. A split second later, they were in space again, and everything went silent, except for the various alarms still sounding.

"Twenty hours of jumping for two minutes of terror. How are we looking?" the lieutenant asked his copilot.

"We're okay," Ensign Lassen replied as he turned off the last of the alarms. "We've lost two shields and our starboard atmo drive, but we should be able to make it back. Worst-case scenario, we set down on Casbon and make repairs."

"No, thank you," Sergeant Nama said. "I'm ready to go home."

"Agreed," Ensign Lassen concurred.

"Let's get out of here," the lieutenant said.

"Give me a cold-coast through Dusahn territory over this, any day of the week," Sergeant Nama stated from the back.

"Entering the return evasion algorithm now," the copilot replied.

* * *

"What's up, Lieutenant Commander?" Nathan questioned as he entered the Aurora's intelligence compartment.

"Something curious has turned up," Lieutenant Commander Shinoda replied. "As you know, we're constantly gathering signals intelligence from all directions. This includes comms traffic."

"Understood," Nathan replied, inviting his intelligence officer to continue.

"We picked up a message being transmitted from a jump comm-drone from the Jamayan system to the Rakuen port authority. They were asking if one of their cargo ships, the Tentibol, had made it there."

"To Rakuen?"

"Yes, sir. Apparently, it has not made it back to Jamaya and is now three days overdue."

"*Was* it here?"

"I checked with the Rakuen Port Authority, and yes, it arrived yesterday morning and departed ten hours later after off-loading her inbound cargo and loading outbound cargo."

"How long is the journey to Jamaya?" Nathan wondered.

"According to the port authority, about eighteen hours," the lieutenant commander replied. "So, she should have arrived by now."

"Was she late arriving on Rakuen?" Nathan wondered.

"Yes, sir, by twelve hours. They reported having problems with their jump drive but refused service while on Rakuen, claiming to have resolved the problem."

"Maybe they had more problems on the way to Jamaya," Nathan suggested.

"A possibility," the lieutenant commander agreed. "I would suggest sending a Reaper along her filed flight path, just in case."

"Very well, launch a Reaper and keep me informed," Nathan concurred, turning to exit.

"Aye, sir."

* * *

Sergeant Olivo stepped out onto the front porch of the run-down farmhouse. Having always been an early riser, he particularly enjoyed having his morning nutri-drink while watching the sunrise. It was about the only thing he liked about his assignment on this dusty, smelly, hellish, little world. For the life of him, he never understood why humans tended to settle on such barren rocks, especially when there were so many truly hospitable worlds out there.

Nevertheless, he had pulled the duty. It had taken him nearly a week, and several trips into town, to make the abandoned farm somewhat livable. Unfortunately, it was a constant struggle to keep the interior of his humble abode clean, due to the fierce afternoon dust storms this time of year.

Fortunately, he would soon be rotated back to the fleet, and some other poor Ghatazhak would get to spend sixty days on Haven, relaying messages from some nameless operative on whatever world he, or she, was on.

The sergeant stepped to the front edge of the porch, enjoying the soft red glow of the Haven dawn. Soon, the reds would yield to ambers, eventually blending in seamlessly with the pale amber sky. Fortunately, the day and night cycles on Haven were fast, allowing him to witness the dawn twice in a single waking period.

He watched the pale indigo illumination of Haven's parent planet begin to mix with the amber sunlight of the system's star. But, unlike most mornings, the serene transformation was interrupted by dozens of small flashes of blue-white light on the horizon, in the direction of town. Seconds later, flashes of light from surface explosions appeared, glinting in the waning light of dawn. Haven was under attack, and the sergeant was fairly certain of the aggressor's identity.

Sergeant Olivo returned to the farmhouse, quickly heading to the locked cabinet along the opposite wall. He pulled the data pad out and activated the device. A few moments later, he was hacked into Haven's security monitoring system and had confirmed his suspicions. A few more taps on the data pad, and he had sent an urgent message to the jump comm-drone lying in wait in Haven's dense ring system. In less than a minute, the comm-drone would begin a complex series of jumps and maneuvers, ensuring that it evaded pursuit before reaching its destination.

Once the sergeant received confirmation that the jump comm-drone had departed, he placed the data pad into his survival pack and headed out the door. It was only a matter of time before the Dusahn traced his signal back to the farmhouse, and he had no intention of being there when they arrived.

* * *

Lieutenant Commander Shinoda picked up the remote on the conference table in the Aurora's command briefing room, activating the view screen and lowering the lights. "The Ahka are actually better equipped than the Casbons realize. As you can see from these scans, they have missile batteries and plasma turrets, all of which can be quickly activated."

"How quickly?" Nathan asked.

"The first missiles were launched eighteen seconds after the Falcon jumped into their atmosphere."

"You did a penetration recon?" Cameron questioned.

"We needed to know how quickly they could react to an attack, as well as what they had to respond with," Commander Verbeek defended.

"Isn't that tipping the Ahka off that something is up?" Jessica wondered.

"The Super Falcon's design is quite different than anything they're used to seeing in that quadrant. Even after the Casbons take delivery of the Sugali fighters, it is unlikely that the Ahka will link a single low-level buzz by our Falcon with the Casbons.

Besides, it's better to risk a single asset than an entire squadron."

"Were we able to establish a range on those missiles?"

"Based on their acceleration rate, size, and power plants, we have to assume they can reach targets in low orbit, as well," Lieutenant Commander Shinoda replied.

"What about their ships?" General Telles asked.

"Scans and images show that they are arming more of their shuttles, turning them into raiders."

"Anything larger?" the general asked.

"Not that we could detect," the lieutenant commander replied. "However, they do *have* larger shuttles. They just weren't arming them, as of yet."

"Then, they aren't showing any signs of escalation," Nathan concluded.

"No, sir, they simply appear to be replacing the raiders that you destroyed," the lieutenant commander explained. "However, it should be noted that they have at least thirty more shuttles that they *could* arm, if necessary."

"That's good," Commander Prechitt said. "That means we have some time to prepare."

"At the very least, we have enough time to get our Eagles into position to defend the Casbons before the next attack."

Nathan looked at Commander Prechitt. "Any reservations, Commander?"

"No, sir."

"Commander Verbeek?" Nathan asked, looking at the Aurora's CAG.

"None, sir, we're ready to go."

"Very well," Nathan said. "Let's get this operation under way."

"Yes, sir," Commander Prechitt acknowledged. "We can depart within the hour."

"Lieutenant Commander Shinoda, let's return the Falcon to her Pentaurus recon duties."

"She sustained a bit of damage on her Ahka run, but she should be ready for action by tomorrow."

"Very well. Get her back up as soon as she's ready." Nathan looked around the room. "Is there anything else?"

"Yes, sir," Lieutenant Commander Shinoda replied. "There was another late arrival today. Another cargo ship, this time from the Alayan system, the Chalmer Basil. She arrived a day and a half late."

"Jump drive trouble again?" Nathan surmised.

"No, sir. Navigation error. Ended up fixing on the wrong star."

"Is that even possible?" Jessica wondered.

"Not unless they're manually calculating their jump plots," Cameron said jokingly.

"What is the significance of this?" General Telles wondered.

"Not sure there is any," Nathan admitted. "But it's the second late arrival in the last week." He turned to the lieutenant commander. "Any luck finding the Tentibol?"

"Negative," the lieutenant commander replied. "Reaper Four jumped along her filed flight path all the way back to Jamaya and turned up nothing."

"The Tentibol?" Jessica asked.

"The first ship to arrive late," the lieutenant commander explained. "The only reason we even took notice of her late arrival was because we picked up a communication from her home port asking if she arrived."

"Then, she's missing?"

"As far as we know, yes," Lieutenant Commander Shinoda replied.

"It's not enough to draw any conclusions," Nathan admitted, "but it is enough to keep an eye out for similar patterns."

"Shall we track the Chalmer Basil when she departs?" Lieutenant Commander Shinoda asked.

"Negative," Nathan replied. "If *she* turns up missing, as well, I'm sure we'll hear about it from the Alayans. Besides, with all our Eagles gone, the Reapers will be taking over their patrol duties."

"Let's hope it's nothing," Cameron commented.

* * *

Terig's wife always went to bed at twenty-two thirty. Always...except tonight, the one night he *needed* her to go to bed on time, if not early. It was well past zero two hundred by the time she was in a deep enough slumber for him to feel confident he could slip out of bed for a few minutes without being noticed.

At least he had no problem staying awake until now. Once Lord Mahtize had sent him the encrypted message about the massive number of Dusahn troops being moved from Takara to ships in orbit, all he could think about was getting home and sending word to the Karuzari. He had no idea how long it normally took for messages he hid in his fake molo twine orders to reach them, but he feared that whatever the Dusahn were preparing for would happen *before* he could warn those who were fighting them on his world's behalf.

After sliding out of bed without disturbing his sleeping wife, he had made his way to his makeshift office in the corner of their living room. It took him several minutes to recode the message, using the

Karuzari's encryption algorithms, but now he was finally ready to send it and get the proverbial latta off his back.

Terig pressed the 'submit order' button and leaned back in his chair, a welcome sigh of relief passing his lips. In his mind, he could see the message being transmitted to the sat-com ground station, then uploaded to the jump comm-drone relay satellite, and to a waiting comm-drone. It would take several minutes for that drone to series-jump to Haven, deliver its message, then jump back to Takara and download the delivery receipt that would find its way back to his terminal, seconds after it hit the sat-com ground station.

As was his normal routine, he went to the kitchen and poured himself a small glass of kava milk, the perfect complement to one of his wife's treasured senshew nut cookies. Kava milk was renowned for its sedative properties, which he would need to fall asleep after receiving confirmation. The senshew nut cookie, well, that was just because he wanted it, and his wife made such a fuss whenever he asked for one.

With the cookie devoured and the milk consumed, he rinsed the glass, placed it in the dishwasher with the rest of the evening's soiled dishes, and returned to the living room. He sat down, turned his view screen back on, and reached for his keyboard to close out the order window. That's when his mouth dropped open, and his eyes went wide.

Thank you for your order. Unfortunately, we are no longer in business. We apologize for the inconvenience.

Terig read the message at least half a dozen times before it finally sunk in. Something was wrong. Something was terribly wrong.

Terig leaned back in his chair, his heart racing. He looked around the room, wondering what he was supposed to do while a million scenarios—all of them terrible—ran though his mind. He heard the sound of a vehicle coming to a stop outside. He quickly shut off the view screen, plunging the room back into darkness, and scurried to the window. He pulled the curtain aside ever so slightly, peeking out at the street below, certain that he would see a Dusahn troop vehicle unloading an assault team. Fortunately, all he saw was an automated trash collection vehicle doing its weekly pickup.

A thought occurred to him, and he ran back to the kitchen, looking out its window, as well, which overlooked the back of the apartment building. The sound of the trash vehicle would be the perfect cover for an assault team.

Again, there was no sign of trouble. Everything appeared as one would have expected for an apartment parking lot at three in the morning.

Terig turned away from the window, his mind and pulse rate still racing. There was only one reason he had received that message. That communication method was no longer valid, which meant it had been abandoned for a reason. Unfortunately, the only reason he could think of was that it had been compromised. The question was, at which end? If it was at *his* end, he would already be facing execution.

Another thought suddenly occurred to him. *Did they have multiple orders coming in from many different worlds, to make the company seem legitimate*? It seemed such an obvious step to take, but he had never thought to ask. If they had, then he had far less to worry about...*theoretically*. If they hadn't...

One thing was certain. He wasn't going to get any sleep tonight.

* * *

Thanks to an encouraging update from Neli back on Sanctuary, Nathan had finally managed to get a decent night's sleep. For the first time in what seemed like forever, he was headed to meet Vladimir for breakfast on the Aurora's general mess deck. It had been a tradition of theirs since they first shared a stateroom as young ensigns, new to the Aurora. Somehow, that tradition had fallen by the wayside and turned into occasional meals, usually dinner, in the captain's mess. However, Nathan preferred having the same breakfast as his crew, in the same space. It made him feel more connected to those who entrusted their lives to him. He hoped his presence had a similar effect on them, as well.

Despite the fact that breakfast had been in progress for more than an hour, the mess deck was still crowded. The bustling deck was quite reassuring to him, since only a few short weeks ago his ship had been significantly undermanned. Now, they even had an extra fifty-seven techs working the day shift, who were either hot-racked or shuttled to and from Rakuen on a regular basis. The same was true of the other ships in their fledgling fleet, all of which had an abundance of crew. The result was that all of the refit projects going on throughout the fleet were ahead of schedule.

Nathan proceeded across the mess deck, nodding in response to the many greetings he received from his crew as he made his way to the table where Vladimir was already busy devouring his breakfast.

"Nathan!" Vladimir called, his mouth still half

full. "I've already got your plate for you," he told Nathan as he approached.

Nathan stepped up to the table, looking down at the plate overflowing with food. "You sure you didn't miss anything?" he asked as he sat down.

"You can go back for more, if you like," Vladimir replied. "I plan to."

"I probably should have warned the cook to prepare extra."

"I think the food has gotten better since we left Sol," Vladimir commented between bites.

"I think you just appreciate it more, after a week of meal kits on the Seiiki," Nathan replied as he started eating.

"I didn't think they were that bad."

"Why am I not surprised," Nathan said, half to himself. "Did you find space for more jump field generators?"

"I actually did one better," Vladimir bragged. "We already have two sets of jump field generators, each powering a different emitter array. Primary and backup, right?"

"Right."

"And they are cross-connected, so either set can power either array. So, I got an idea. Rather than install a *third* set of generators, why don't we just stop using them as dedicated pairs. That way, if one generator goes down, it doesn't affect the other one. We can use any *two* of *four* jump field generators to make the jump."

"Not bad," Nathan agreed. "But I'd still rather have a third set."

"And you will; they just won't be installed."

"What good will they be if they are not installed?" Nathan wondered.

"It takes more space to accommodate an *operational* jump field generator than one that is not connected. With just a little reconfiguring of the midship area between the port and starboard generator compartments—basically, widening the lateral corridor and taking out the bulkhead between compartments fifteen-twenty and fifteen-twenty-two, and installing quick-connect systems on all four field generators—we can swap out a damaged generator with a spare in *five minutes*."

"*Five minutes* is a long time in battle," Nathan reminded his friend.

"We have never lost *two* jump field generators at once," Vladimir defended, "and we are certainly not going to lose *three*."

"Still..."

"With this new cross-connecting system, we will be even *better* prepared to deal with the loss of one, or even *two*, jump field generators in battle," Vladimir insisted.

"What about when we finally get stealth-jump capabilities?" Nathan wondered.

"Abby thinks it should be installed as a separate, isolated jump system, to be used only when stealth jumping is necessary. Something about the emitters wearing out more quickly."

"Is *that* going to be a problem?" Nathan asked.

"I'm sure she will work any problems out in subsequent versions of the stealth emitters," Vladimir assured him.

"Captain," Deliza interrupted.

"Good morning," Nathan greeted.

"Sorry to bother you, sir, but do you have a minute?"

"Of course," Nathan replied. "Please, join us."

Deliza stared at Vladimir as he ate, a skeptical look on her face. “Is it safe?”

“Just keep your extremities away from his plate, and you should be fine,” Nathan joked. “What can I do for you?”

“I was thinking that we might be able to speed up development of a better energy bank system to improve the Aurora’s single-jump range, if we had a few of the Volonese, high-capacity, aramenium energy cells. It would save us a *lot* of time in research and development.”

“Do they have cells that even come *close* to our energy needs?” Vladimir wondered.

“No, but by studying the differences between their smaller, low-capacity energy cells and their industrial, high-capacity cells, we could get an idea of what aspects scale up properly and which ones have to be altered.”

“I suppose we’d have to go to Volon to get them,” Nathan surmised.

“Yes, sir,” Deliza confirmed, “but I have contacts on Volon. It shouldn’t take me more than a day to buy what we need.”

“*You* want to go?” Nathan asked, surprised.

“Considering that I’ve done business on Volon many times in the past, *and* that I know what we need, it’s logical that I be the one to go.”

“What about the plant expansion, and your R and D projects?” Nathan asked.

“My staff runs the plant, and Abby can manage R and D while I’m gone,” Deliza replied. “I just need a few hours to tie up some loose ends first.”

“It’s about seven hours to Volon,” he warned.

“I thought it was just under five,” Deliza replied.

"You'll have to skirt around Dusahn-controlled space," Nathan reminded her.

"I see."

Nathan set his spoon down, observing her. Deliza had come a long way from the teenaged farm girl he had met nearly a decade ago. "Alright, but have the Seiiki take you."

"What I need would fit on a Ranni shuttle," Deliza told him.

"Along with a couple of Ghatazhak as protection," Nathan added.

"Is that really necessary?" Deliza asked.

"Trust me; if it is, you'll be awfully glad you brought them along," Nathan insisted. "I'll make the arrangements."

* * *

"The Forenta will be ready to go in a few minutes," Commander Prechitt informed Nathan and Cameron as they walked down the ramp from the command deck to the flight operations deck.

"Did you manage to get her some defenses?" Nathan wondered.

"Thanks to Captain Taylor, yes," the commander replied.

"I gave him a few of our spare point-defense turrets," Cameron told Nathan.

"We have spares?"

"You didn't know?"

"I thought they were just parts, not entire weapons," Nathan admitted.

"All EDF ships carry spares," Cameron explained.

"How many do we have?" Nathan asked.

"None, now," Cameron replied. "But I've already ordered two of our fabricators to start producing replacements. I figured it was better to use our spares to finish arming the commander's fleet."

"Now, all five ships have point-defenses, and the Perryton has *two* plasma cannon turrets, as well," Commander Prechitt boasted.

"We even gave Hunt a pair of plasma torpedo cannons," Cameron added. "You should have seen the smile on his face when he tested them."

"I'll bet," Nathan remarked as they reached the bottom of the ramp, made an about-face, and headed aft toward the main hangar bay. "How long until you depart?"

"I got word from Commander Verbeek that all his gear is loaded aboard the Torrecun, and his crews are already on their way to the Perryton. So, we should be ready to go as soon as I depart."

"How are we on communications?" Nathan asked as they entered the main hangar bay.

"Four jump comm-drones have been tasked to maintain comms between us and Commander Prechitt's task force," Cameron told Nathan.

"Sounds like you're good to go, Commander," Nathan said as they approached his shuttle. "There's just one last thing."

"What's that, sir?" Commander Prechitt wondered.

Nathan tapped his comm-set. "Comms, Captain. Patch me through to Captain Hunt on the Perryton."

"*Aye, sir.*"

"I had intended on doing this once the Perryton was fully armed," Nathan explained, "but she's nearly there now, and if she's going to be your flagship, she needs a stronger name."

"*Captain, Comms. I have Captain Hunt on the line.*"

"Connect him," Nathan instructed.

"*Perryton, Captain Hunt.*"

"Captain Hunt, this is Captain Scott."

"*What can I do for you, sir?*" Captain Hunt asked over their comm-sets.

"Before you get under way, I'd like to change your designation."

"*Of course, sir.*"

"Congratulations, Captain," Nathan said. "You are now the commanding officer of a frigate."

"*Thank you, sir,*" Captain Hunt replied.

"And seeing that you're now a combat ship, and about to become the flagship of a task force, I think your ship needs a stronger name, something befitting her new purpose," Nathan continued. "Assuming you have no objections, your ship will henceforth be known as the KAS Sergeant Jerome Weatherly."

After a pause, Captain Hunt replied. "*A fine name, Captain. One we'll be honored to carry.*"

"Safe journey, Captain."

"*Thank you, sir. Weatherly, out.*"

Nathan glanced at his two officers, both of whom were smiling. "I take it neither of you has any objections?"

"No, sir," Commander Prechitt assured him, beaming with approval.

"Then you best get to your flagship, Commander," Nathan said, reaching to shake Commander Prechitt's hand.

"Yes, sir," the commander replied, snapping a salute to his two superiors.

Nathan and Cameron watched in silence as the commander boarded his shuttle, the hatch closing behind him.

"Nicely done," Cameron commented.

"I thought you'd approve."

"KAS?"

Nathan turned to her and smiled. "Karuzari Alliance Ship," he replied as he headed forward.

"Of course."

* * *

Deliza walked up the Seiiki's cargo ramp, her bag slung over her shoulder.

"Dressing down, Princess?" Josh joked from the top of the ramp.

"The latest in Volonese fashion, I'm told," she defended.

"By who, the guy who tricked you into buying them?"

"Volonese fashion is somewhat drab," Deliza agreed as she reached the top of the ramp. She spotted the two Ghatazhak soldiers checking their gear at the front of the cargo bay. "Are they our bodyguards?"

"Corporals Amund and Torlak," Josh replied. He turned to look at the two men. "Guys! Meet the princess!"

Deliza cast a disapproving look at Josh. "Are you ever going to stop calling me that?" she asked as she returned the polite nods from her protectors.

"Doubtful," Josh replied, grinning. "Especially since I had a date tonight." Josh looked down the ramp to see if anyone else was coming. "Where's Yanni?"

"He's managing the plant expansion for me while I'm away. Besides, the air on Volon is a little thin for him."

"Yeah, he is a bit delicate," Josh agreed as he slapped the ramp control button, activating its retraction motors. "Captain's cabin is all yours, Princess," he added as he headed forward.

"How long until we depart?"

"Wheels up in five," Josh replied as he bounded up the forward ladder. "Better strap in. I'm feeling a bit rambunctious today."

"Great," Deliza said under her breath. She followed Josh forward, passing between the two Ghatazhak soldiers. "Gentlemen."

"Ma'am."

"I trust you have something less conspicuous to wear on Volon."

Corporal Amund reached down into his bag and pulled out a Volonese jacket. "Not our first op, ma'am."

"Good to know," Deliza replied. She tossed her bag up onto the shoulder-height landing and then turned back around. "It should be an uneventful trip. I have several contacts that I trust on Volon. I expect we'll be done and on our way home within a few hours of arrival."

"Good to know, ma'am," the corporal replied.

For a moment, Deliza thought she noticed a wry smile on the corporal's face.

* * *

Three large, blue-white flashes appeared in orbit above the planet Palee, revealing two Dusahn gunships and an assault ship. Seconds later, a dozen Teronbah fighters joined them. Within half a minute of their appearance, Dusahn troop pods began dropping from the assault ship, disappearing behind tiny flashes as they jumped to the surface of Palee.

The streets were in chaos as Dusahn troop

landers jumped in, meters above the surface, slowing to a hover as four armed soldiers leapt from each pod to the ground below. Within two minutes of arrival, there were armed intruders at every tenth intersection in Palee's capital city of Dorum. Citizens ran in every direction, frantically looking for places to hide from the invaders who had, literally, fallen from the sky.

"Mister President! I have Toran on the line. They, too, have Dusahn soldiers on their streets!"

"Castell is reporting the same," another man announced, comm-unit in hand.

"It's happening everywhere," the man standing next to the President of Palee said. "What are we going to do?"

President Voros watched out the window as a Dusahn combat shuttle swooped down and landed in the square outside the capitol building. Twelve armed men jumped out and ran toward the entrance, weapons held high. "What can we do?" he sighed, turning to look at his assistant. "We have no defenses."

"We have security forces..."

"To protect us against angry citizens and political rivals," the president said, cutting his assistant off mid-sentence. "They would be killed within seconds. Order them to stand down."

"Yes, Mister President," his assistant replied, raising his comm-unit to his face.

President Voros turned to gaze out the window again as another armed shuttle appeared overhead, quickly setting down next to the first. More men came pouring out, followed by a determined-looking officer, who disembarked with alarming confidence.

The president sighed, turning to take his seat and await the man to whom he would hand over control of his world and his people.

At least no one will die, he thought as he sighed.

Captain Borra slowly paced the length of the Penta-ben's operations command center, listening to the various controllers as they communicated with Dusahn forces on the surface. His ears were tuned for any words that might indicate his troops were meeting resistance, but as of yet, he had heard none.

"Captain," a junior officer at the far end of the compartment called. "Transmission from Major Gattso."

Captain Borra turned to acknowledge his officer.

"The President of Palee has relinquished control of his world to the Dusahn."

"Casualties?" the captain asked.

"No Dusahn were lost, sir."

"What about civilian casualties?" the captain asked.

"Major Gattso reports that no shots were fired."

Captain Borra frowned. "A world that does not fight back is not worthy of the Dusahn." He turned and headed for the exit. "Dispatch the support teams and secure the planet. I want to jump to Volon by the end of the day," he ordered on his way out.

CHAPTER SEVEN

"Every time we come here, I say the same thing," Josh said, staring out the window at the planet below. "This is one weird, frickin' world."

Deliza looked at Josh as she stood between him and Loki in the Seiiki's cockpit. "Frickin?"

"He's trying not to swear as much," Loki explained.

"Really? Good for you, Josh."

"Don't congratulate him just yet," Loki insisted. "He still lets a few fly, now and then."

"Well, at least he's trying," Deliza said, gazing out the forward windows again. "I still think it's beautiful."

"Half the planet's surface is too thin to breathe," Josh argued. "Heck, it's got mountain peaks that are *in* space."

"Really?"

"How many worlds have you heard of where you could slam into the side of a mountain *while* in low orbit?" Josh asked.

"He's exaggerating," Loki told her.

"Not by much," Josh argued.

"By a *lot*," Loki insisted.

"I should have known," Deliza remarked.

"You know, I'm surprised that Yanni doesn't like the air here," Josh said, changing the subject. "Didn't he come from a mountain village, or something?"

"Where he was raised, the elevation was only about a thousand meters," Deliza explained. "So, about eight-seventy-five to nine hundred millibars. At the lowest point on the surface of Volon, the atmospheric pressure is only about six hundred millibars."

"How do you *know* this stuff?" Josh wondered.

"We were considering putting a plant here at one time," Deliza told him, "but the lower pressure would have screwed up the curing process on the hull sections. That's why the plant is on Rakuen."

"Why can't Yanni just wear a booster like everyone else?" Loki wondered.

"He doesn't like having the tubes in his nose," Deliza replied.

"Like I said, *delicate*," Josh said, laughing to himself as he guided the ship through the mountain pass.

Once they crossed between the two towering peaks, the Valley of Considor appeared before them.

"Constantatia," Josh announced, looking out at the sprawling city that covered the entire valley.

"Seven hundred and thirteen millibars," Deliza stated.

Josh glanced at her. "You're as weird as this planet."

"We're being hailed by Volonese Control," Loki interrupted. "They want to know our destination."

"Lennar Field," Deliza told him. "There are several aramenium battery manufacturers nearby. I should be able to get a transport."

"Got it," Loki replied.

"What the hell?" Josh said, noticing something on the sensor display in the center of the console. "Two fast-movers, passing to starboard, about two clicks. If I didn't know better, I'd say they're..." The tracks on the sensor screen changed course. "Shit! They're on an intercept!" he declared, reaching for the shield controls.

"Wait!" Loki insisted, reaching his hand out to

block him. He flicked a switch, putting the local communications traffic on the overhead speaker.

"Seiiki, Seiiki, this is Eti One Five Four. We have determined that you are an armed vessel. Surrender your controls to Volon Flight Control, or you will be considered a hostile vessel and dealt with appropriately. This is your only warning."

"Jesus, they're painting us," Josh realized, switching on the auto-flight system. "Nobody wants to let you hand-fly these days."

"Since when do the Volonese have interceptors?" Loki wondered.

"Eti fighters are Tonganese," Deliza said. "They must have bought some recently."

"And some pilots, too," Josh added.

"Can you blame them?" Deliza defended. "Volon's only twelve light years from Takara; well within the Dusahn's single-jump range."

"Like they could defend themselves with Eti fighters," Josh laughed.

"They probably felt like they had to do something," Loki stated. "Auto-flight link is established. They have control." He glanced at Deliza. "We'll be on the ground in five minutes."

"I'll get ready to depart," she replied, heading out.

As soon as Deliza climbed down the ladder and was out of earshot, Loki looked at Josh. "You know, if you had raised shields, they would have opened fire on us."

"And I would've jumped the fuck out of here," Josh replied.

* * *

Nathan made his way quickly to the intel shack, a few compartments aft of the Aurora's bridge. It wasn't often that his presence was required in the cramped space occupied by Lieutenant Commander Shinoda and his staff, which meant that it was either something urgent, or the lieutenant commander needed him to make a decision. When he spotted General Telles coming toward him from the opposite direction, he knew it was both. "I didn't even realize you were aboard," Nathan said.

"I only just arrived," the general replied. "I was on my way to medical when Lieutenant Commander Nash requested my presence in your intelligence shack."

"Medical? You got a cold, or something?"

"Just my monthly nanite booster."

"I had forgotten that the Ghatazhak use nanites prophylactically. How is that working out?"

"It does not make us any healthier, if that's what you're asking. It does, however, give us a better chance of survival if we get injured in combat."

"I thought they had to be programmed for specific tasks," Nathan replied as they turned the corner and headed toward the entrance to the intel shack.

"Our specialized nanites are preprogrammed to respond to any trauma that is immediately life-threatening," the general explained. "The theory is that they will stave off exsanguinations long enough to receive more precise treatments. Unfortunately, there is insufficient evidence to verify their effectiveness."

Nathan paused at the entrance, looking cockeyed at the general. "Don't you mean, *fortunately*?"

General Telles furrowed his brow. "I suppose it depends on your point of view."

"After you," Nathan said, gesturing for the general to precede him.

General Telles stepped into the compartment, followed by Nathan.

"What's up?" Nathan asked Jessica and Lieutenant Commander Shinoda.

"We received flash traffic from our comm-relay agent on Haven," the lieutenant commander explained. "They have been attacked by the Dusahn."

"When?" Nathan asked, looking concerned.

"Thirty-eight hours ago."

"Why are we just hearing about it now?" Nathan wondered.

"The message type caused the jump comm-drone to initiate a level-three evasion algorithm, which takes a bit longer," Jessica added.

"Any idea if they captured it?"

"It is highly doubtful that the Haven Syndicate's security forces would be able to repel a Dusahn invasion," General Telles opined.

"Yeah, they all but hid when the Takarans tried to take us out nine years ago," Jessica commented.

"Haven is well outside the Pentaurus cluster," Nathan said, thinking out loud. "Do you think this means they're trying to take over the entire sector?"

"Looks like it," Jessica replied.

"The most industrialized worlds, and therefore the ones of most value to the Dusahn, are *in* the Pentaurus cluster," General Telles said. "The other worlds in the sector, like Haven, Palee, and Paradar, are not of significant value, except as a buffer zone."

"A buffer zone?" Lieutenant Commander Shinoda asked.

"They know the Aurora has a limited jump range, just like their large warships do," the general explained. "By taking control of all worlds within that range, they arc preventing us from using any of them as points from which to attack."

"That means they're going to take Palee, Paradar, Ursoot, and Volon, next," Jessica surmised.

"Deliza and the Seiiki are *on* Volon by now," Nathan realized.

"We don't *know* that they're going to attack the other worlds," Jessica insisted. "Even if they do, we don't know what order they'll attack in."

"Regardless, it would be prudent to warn the Seiiki and insist that they complete their mission with due haste," General Telles insisted.

"There's another possible motive," Nathan offered. "They're trying to bait us."

"Force us to attack?" the lieutenant commander asked. "Why? Wouldn't it make more sense to just hold what they have while they build up their forces?"

"This ship is the only thing preventing them from seizing control of the entire quadrant," Nathan insisted. "They need to get rid of us, once and for all."

"Then why not just jump us while we're sitting here in the Rogen system?" Jessica wondered.

"You're assuming that they *know* we're here."

"Pretty safe bet, I'd say," Jessica replied.

"Agreed," Nathan said. "But they know our reputation for overcoming the odds, and they can't afford to keep losing ships. They've barely got enough to hold the cluster, let alone the entire sector." Nathan sighed. "No, there are only two possibilities that I can see. Either they're trying to build a buffer zone, as the general suggested, or they're trying to draw us out, so they can glass this entire system."

"Wait, I thought you said they wanted the *Aurora* gone," Jessica commented.

"What's the best way to kill off an enemy while suffering the fewest friendly casualties?" Nathan asked.

"Cut off their supply chain," Lieutenant Commander Shinoda replied.

"Attack their weaker allies," Jessica added.

"Then, you suspect the Dusahn hope to draw the Aurora away long enough to destroy Rakuen and Neramese," General Telles concluded. "A distinct possibility."

"What do we do?" Lieutenant Commander Shinoda asked.

"Nothing," Nathan replied.

"Nothing?" Jessica said, one eyebrow raised.

"For now," Nathan added. "If their objective is to draw us out so they can destroy the Rogen system, then it means they believe it's too risky to attack the system while we're here to defend it. So, as long as we're here, the Rogen system is safe."

"We can't defeat the Dusahn if we never leave the Rogen system," Jessica told him.

"I didn't say *never*," Nathan replied. "We stay put until the Rogen system can defend itself, *or* until we can increase our one-minute jump range to more than twice the distance between it and Takara."

"That could take months," Jessica pointed out.

"Yes, it could."

"And if they are simply trying to increase the buffer zone around them?" General Telles wondered.

"Like you said, none of those worlds will significantly increase the Dusahn's industrial capacity, therefore their capture does not significantly affect our chances of success," Nathan insisted.

"But what about all the people on those worlds?" Lieutenant Commander Shinoda wondered.

"If they do not resist, the Dusahn will likely not bother them," General Telles replied. "They cannot afford to keep a strong presence on worlds that do not contribute to their military buildup."

"For now," Jessica pointed out.

The general nodded his agreement.

"There could be another reason they attacked Haven," Jessica said. "They may know we have a spy on Takara, and they are trying to root him out."

"Or use him to send us false intel," Lieutenant Commander Shinoda added.

Nathan thought for a moment. "I don't believe that is the case," he finally said. "If they know our comm-relay point is Haven, then why attack the entire planet?"

"Because they know we'd hear about it right away," Jessica said.

"I suppose you could be right," Nathan admitted.

"Either way, we need to warn Terig," Jessica insisted.

"Agreed, but how?" Nathan wondered. "We can't send him a message through the Haven relay, can we?"

"Nope," Jessica replied. "Sergeant Olivo was under orders to go ghost in this situation."

"*Go ghost*?" Nathan asked.

"Stealth recon," the general clarified. "He is to spend one day monitoring developments on Haven, then report to his extraction point and await pickup."

"So, once he is picked up, we'll know more about exactly *why* the Dusahn attacked Haven."

"We will have to go to Takara ourselves to contact Mister Espan," General Telles stated.

"That's a hell of a risk," Lieutenant Commander Shinoda warned.

"No more than he took for us," Jessica insisted.

"We will be fine," General Telles promised.

Nathan looked at the general. "We?"

"Being Takaran, I am the logical choice," the general insisted.

"Who is the other logical choice?" Nathan wondered. "Or should I be afraid to ask."

"A lone man wandering the streets would be more suspect than a man and his wife," the general replied.

"I knew it," Nathan said, shaking his head.

"Besides, I wish to speak with Lord Mahtize myself," General Telles admitted.

Nathan sighed. "I don't suppose I can convince you otherwise."

"Your wisdom is what makes you such an excellent leader, Captain," the general complimented.

"Sarcasm, now?" Nathan said. "I was still getting used to Ghatazhak humor."

* * *

Jessica sat in the starboard jump seat, facing aft, staring at the nose and open canopy of the jump sub protruding into the underside of the utility cargo pod bay. As the newest addition to their little fleet, Jump Sub Four had just passed its operational-readiness tests a few days earlier. Although this was not Jessica's first time in a jump sub, it would be Jump Sub Four's first jump into enemy-controlled waters.

To her right, General Telles sat in the port jump seat, his feet resting on the nose of the jump sub, his head back against the wall, and his eyes closed. Such was his form of pre-mission meditation, or at least that was what he claimed when questioned.

Jessica just assumed he was catching a bit of rest while he could.

"*Two minutes to max jump range,*" Ensign Weston called from the cockpit.

"Time to mount up," Jessica said, rising from her seat. She grabbed the overhead railing and pulled herself up over the sub's nose and canopy, walking the few steps in a low crouch across the top to reach the boarding hatch. She placed her hands on either side of the open hatch and lowered her feet down inside, standing on the pilot's seat. After turning around to face forward, she lowered herself down into the seat and then pulled the release latch on the underside of the seat, sliding it forward into its operational position, which created the space the passengers would need to climb in behind her.

As the general lowered himself in, Jessica began powering up the tiny jump sub and checking its systems. Although this most recent iteration was perhaps the easiest to operate, it was still a complex, highly precise vessel. Jumping across light years of space was a scary enough thought to many, but jumping a few light years *directly into an ocean*? Most would consider that insane. At this particular moment, Jessica also questioned the sanity of such an act.

"It's actually roomier than I remember," the general commented as he buckled into one of the four passenger seats behind Jessica. "Weren't there supposed to be six seats back here?"

"They took the back two seats out to add more energy cells to extend its range," Jessica explained. "We're actually jumping from *outside* the cluster."

"Then we're going to set a record," the general realized, sounding pleased.

"I suppose so," she agreed as she reached up behind her head and slid the overhead hatch forward, closing and securing it. "We're buttoned up in here," she reported over comms.

"*Depressurizing the bay,*" Ensign Weston replied. "*Range in one.*"

Jessica could hear the hiss of air beyond the hull of their jump sub as the bay over them quickly lost its atmospheric pressure. Another glance at her console showed all systems were sporting green readiness lights.

"*Course and speed are good,*" Lieutenant Haddix announced over comms.

"Copy that," Jessica replied. "We're ready for release."

"*Release in three......two......one......*"

Jessica heard, and felt, a *clunk* as the clamps holding the tiny jump sub tight against its seals, on the underside of the Reaper's modified utility bay, released. There was a brief *whoosh* of air as the last of the atmosphere in the bay above them was lost to space.

Jessica looked up, watching the underside of the Reaper's utility bay move away from them. As its distance from her increased, she could easily make out the exterior details of the utility bay that had been modified to launch and retrieve jump subs.

"*Max range,*" Lieutenant Haddix reported. "*Your course and speed, or should I say lack thereof, are perfect. You're clear to jump when ready.*"

"Thanks, boys," Jessica replied. "Just make sure you come back for us in a couple days."

"*You got it,*" the lieutenant assured her. "*Pick us up a few dollag steaks while you're there.*"

"I'll see what I can do," Jessica replied. A moment later, the Reaper disappeared in a blue-white flash.

"Ready, honey?" Jessica asked.

"Honey?" the general questioned, a note of disapproval in his tone.

"Just getting into character," Jessica insisted.

"I am ready...dear," the general replied.

Jessica smiled as she reached for the jump button. "Let's do this."

* * *

"Why is it that nothing just stays working on this ship?" Loki wondered as he replaced the access cover on the Seiiki's port engine nacelle.

"This is nothing," Josh laughed. "Back in the BC, this ship was always falling apart."

Loki looked puzzled.

"That's because your pop would never let me fix anything right," Dalen defended. "Pound on this; tape up that; stick a wad of gum in here."

"That comes from too many years of trying to hold pieces of junk together on Haven," Josh chuckled. "Not a whole lot of new parts came through that place. It was pretty much where ships went to die."

"Still, it's been nice having Vlad and the Aurora's fabricators supporting us," Dalen said. "I doubt we'd still be flyin' without them."

"BC?" Loki finally asked.

"Before Conathan," Josh explained.

Loki shook his head as he continued locking down the access panel. "You really should stop calling him that."

"Lighten up, Lok. It's a joke."

A small ground transport pulled up alongside the landing pad, about ten meters from them.

"The princess has returned," Josh joked.

"You need to stop calling *her* that, as *well*," Loki told him.

"You have no sense of humor, Loki," Josh replied as he turned and headed toward Deliza. "How did it go, Your Highness?"

By now, Deliza paid little attention to Josh's inability to use her actual name. "Great."

"Sure didn't take long. Did you buy anything?"

"Four small and four industrial-sized energy cells," she replied as she closed the door behind her. "All of them made with aramenium cores."

"What, you didn't bring back lunch?" Josh asked as Deliza walked past him toward the cargo ramp.

Deliza ignored him.

Josh looked at the vehicle. "Where are they at?"

"They'll be delivered in a couple of hours," she replied as she headed up the ramp.

Josh looked at the two Ghatazhak who had escorted her into town. "How could you let her come back without food?"

The Ghatazhak just smiled as they passed, following Deliza up the ramp.

The controller attached to Josh's left forearm beeped, calling for his attention. "I'm, like, the only one who thinks about the necessities around here," he muttered as he examined the controller's display screen. "Lok!" he called out. "We've got a message from the Aurora," he added, punching in the command to pipe the message into his comm-set.

"What is it?" Deliza asked, stopping at the top of the cargo ramp.

"Uh-oh," Josh said as he listened to the message through his comm-set.

"What 'uh-oh'?" Loki questioned as he and Dalen walked around the port nacelle to join Josh.

Deliza took a few steps back down the ramp, also concerned by Josh's reaction. "What did they say?"

"The Dusahn attacked Haven," Josh told them.

"How bad?" one of the Ghatazhak asked.

"No details," Josh replied. "Just that they attacked."

"That means Ollie's gone ghost," the other Ghatazhak observed.

"They're telling us to wrap things up as quick as possible and get out of here, just in case," Josh advised.

"He thinks they're going to attack Volon, as well?"

"If the Dusahn are expanding their area of control to include the *entire* Pentaurus sector, then it is logical to assume they would start with Haven, Paradar, Palee, Ursoot, and Volon," Corporal Amund stated.

"Then, we have time," Deliza surmised, taking a few more steps down the ramp.

"That depends," the corporal replied.

"Depends on what?" Dalen wondered.

"How many strike forces they are using; the order in which they will strike. There are too many variables to calculate."

"Then, guess," Josh urged.

"Given that the Dusahn barely have enough ships to maintain control over the cluster, I suspect they will use a single task force, leaving a small contingent on each world to, at least, maintain the *appearance* of control."

"So, it all comes down to order of attack," Loki realized.

"It does not matter," Corporal Amund stated. "News of the attack is certain to be at least a day old."

"Because of the evasion algorithms," Loki surmised.

"Precisely," the corporal agreed. "If the Dusahn *are* moving to take control of the entire sector, they would not stop with Haven. Other nearby worlds have surely fallen by now. Captain Scott's instruction to depart as soon as possible is wise."

"Damn, we should have kept the transport for a while," Deliza cursed as she pulled out her comm-unit to make a call.

"I thought you said the energy cells were being delivered," Josh said.

"They are," Deliza confirmed. "Hello, this is Deliza Ta'Akar, at Lennar Field, pad one seven. We were just dropped off, but we need to make another trip into the city. Can you send our transport right back?"

"What other trip?" Josh asked.

"I'd like to know, as well," Corporal Amund added.

"Thank you." Deliza ended the call and began another. "We have to find Naralena," she explained, holding the comm-unit up to her ear again.

"I almost forgot," Loki realized, "she lives here."

"I know," Josh said to Loki. "We dropped her off *together, remember*?"

"She's not answering," Deliza said.

"She may not even live here, anymore," Josh pointed out. "Her father was on his last legs when we dropped her off."

"Josh," Deliza scolded.

"I'm just sayin'," Josh defended. "If he passed, she may have moved on."

"If she moved off-world, the call wouldn't connect," Deliza insisted. "See," she added, holding out her comm-unit. "I got her voice mail."

"You sure it's her?" Josh asked.

"I recognized her voice," Deliza insisted. "We have to go find her."

"And do what?" Josh wondered.

"Bring her with us," Deliza insisted.

"What?" Josh was shocked.

"What about her father?" Loki asked.

"Him, too."

"If he's still suckin' in air!" Josh exclaimed.

"Jesus, Josh!" Deliza scolded, coming down the ramp and walking past him toward the returning transport.

"The captain said..."

"The energy cells won't be here for at least an hour or two," Deliza yelled back at him as she continued walking toward the now-parked transport. "We'll be back by then."

"Deliza!" Josh yelled in protest.

"Don't worry, we'll keep an eye on her," Corporal Amund promised as he and Corporal Torlak followed her toward the waiting vehicle. "Just make sure you're ready to take off the minute we return."

"Yeah, no shit!" Josh exclaimed. He watched in dismay as Deliza climbed into the back of the transport, and the two Ghatazhak corporals climbed into the front. "Can you believe this?" Josh complained as they drove off.

"Could be worse," Dalen said as he returned to his work on the port engine nacelle. "You could be married to her."

Josh rolled his eyes. "Are you kidding?" he said, placing two fingers in his mouth, as if he was pointing a gun and pulling the trigger.

* * *

Commander Prechitt's shuttle jumped into the atmosphere, more than two thousand meters above the surface of Casbon. As instructed, the shuttle descended into a hover, thirty meters above the central square, waiting a moment to give those below time to vacate the area, then descending smoothly to land at the exact point the leaders of the settlement had indicated.

As the shuttle's engines powered down, the aft boarding ramp descended, and the commander and his staff disembarked. Walking out to meet him were Council Member Garon and two of her assistants.

"Welcome to Casbon," the council member greeted. "I assume you have been sent by Captain Scott?"

"Commander Prechitt, second officer of the Aurora, at your service," the commander greeted respectfully. "Allow me to introduce my second, Lieutenant Sandau, and my chief logistics officer, Ensign Kolm."

"A pleasure, gentlemen. I was under the impression that you were bringing more than just a single shuttle," the council member said. "Preferably something *armed*."

"We arrived aboard the Weatherly, an armed frigate. The remaining ships in our task force will arrive tomorrow, including twenty of the Aurora's Super Eagle jump fighters, along with flight crews, support personnel, and gear. Our goal is to secure a location on the surface of your world from which to operate. Preferably one nearby and with enough room to accommodate our forces, as well as yours, once they arrive."

"Of course," Council Member Garon replied. "There is such a place, one that we had intended for our forces. One of the first mining gorges we created. It is well concealed, with caverns that have been reinforced and plasma sealed. It should provide more than adequate space."

"Is it far from here?" the commander inquired.

"An hour by ground transport," the council member explained, gesturing toward a waiting vehicle, a few meters away.

"Perhaps it would be more expedient if we took my shuttle," the commander suggested. "Being an old fighter pilot, myself, I would like to get a look at the aerial approach, as well."

"As you wish, Commander."

"After you," the commander offered, gesturing toward his shuttle.

The council member headed toward the shuttle's aft boarding ramp, followed by her aides, Commander Prechitt, and his officers.

"Captain Scott has instructed me to ask if we might purchase a small amount of aramenium from you, for use by our research and development teams."

"I'm sure something can be arranged," she assured him as they entered the shuttle.

* * *

"This is it," Deliza told them.

"How do you know?" Corporal Torlak wondered. "There are no identifying marks on any of these homes."

"Fourth house from intersection one-forty-seven, on Dorvany Prospect."

"In which direction?"

"I've been here before," Deliza insisted.

"They all look alike to me," Corporal Amund said.

"Just stop the vehicle," Deliza insisted, opening her door.

Corporal Amund stepped on the brake, abruptly stopping the vehicle. He looked over at Corporal

Torlak, one eyebrow raised. "Fifty-fifty chance, I guess."

Deliza was already out of the vehicle and headed toward the front door of a small home. The yard was somewhat barren, with only a few scrub brushes and a lone parren tree. In sharp contrast, the house itself appeared to be well kept.

As soon as Deliza stepped onto the front porch, an overhead light came on, and she could hear a door chime playing inside the home. A moment later, a small red light, in what she thought was a peephole in the door, appeared. As the two Ghatazhak corporals stepped up onto the porch beside her, Deliza heard footsteps inside, moving quickly toward the door. Corporal Amund gently tugged at Deliza's jacket sleeve, urging her to step aside and slightly behind him, just in case. He, too, had heard the shuffle of feet from inside.

The door latch buzzed a moment, and the door cracked open, slowly at first, then swinging open wide. "Deliza?"

Deliza's eyes widened. Gone were the long dark tresses that were once Naralena's trademark. She also looked fatigued and somewhat shaken. She was not the confident woman Deliza had known so many years ago. "Naralena?"

"What are you doing here?" Naralena asked, glancing at the two Ghatazhak corporals. "And with..." Naralena covered her mouth with both hands, tears coming to her eyes. "Then...it's true? He's alive?"

"He is," Deliza replied. It hadn't occurred to her that Naralena would have heard the rumors of Nathan's resurrection and likely found them difficult to believe.

"You came all the way to Volon, just to tell *me*?"

Deliza sighed. "Now, I feel a bit guilty."

"I don't understand."

"I didn't come here to tell you Nathan is alive. I came to take you and your father away from here."

"What? Why?" Naralena wondered, wiping the tears from her eyes.

"The Dusahn are expanding their sphere of control," Deliza told her. "We just received word that they attacked Haven. Nathan believes an attack on Volon is probable."

"Then, he sent you to *rescue* me," Naralena sighed. "That is so like him."

"Actually, we were already here on business. It was my idea to find you before we left. But I'm sure Nathan would have agreed with my decision. Is your father able to travel?"

Naralena looked down for a moment. "My father passed last year," she said. "My mother, a few months later."

Deliza's voice suddenly became somber. "I am so sorry, Naralena."

"We should be going," Corporal Amund reminded Deliza.

"How quickly can you pack?" Deliza asked Naralena.

"Pack for what?"

"You're coming with us," Deliza told her. "And I'm not taking 'no' for an answer."

* * *

Lord Mahtize's day had begun as usual: breakfast, updates on markets, and a review of his daily itinerary, followed by a leisurely stroll across the gardens, sipping from a mug of kempa tea as he enjoyed the morning sun sparkling off the dewy lawns.

Despite the Dusahn occupation, and all the perils and pitfalls it created for the noble houses of Takara, his life was going quite well. Profits were up, and his position among Takaran nobility was rising faster than he had ever dreamed. It seemed that regime change was good, at least for now. It was so good, in fact, that he wondered just how long he needed to keep up the espionage game he was playing.

When he originally started his scheme, he had done so simply to give himself some protection. The right piece of intelligence, be it real or contrived, could yield significant dividends. However, those dividends had been coming without the use of his little game. Furthermore, what little information he had passed on to young Mister Espan was having no impact on his business dealings. It left him wondering if the risk was worth the reward.

Lord Mahtize passed through the gate into his private patio and then entered his business office through his private entrance. As usual, he went directly to his desk to begin his duties as the leader of House Mahtize.

"Good morning."

The voice nearly made Lord Mahtize jump. He looked toward the far side of the room, from where the voice had come, spotting a well-dressed, confident-looking man sitting next to the fireplace, and a stunning, younger woman in typical Takaran business attire standing next to him, looking equally as confident. "Who are you?" Lord Mahtize asked, his eyes narrowing as his right hand slowly slid down to the edge of his desk, "and how did you get in here?"

"It was not difficult," the steely-eyed man replied.

"Your security measures are terribly outdated, even by Takaran standards. Push the button all you want. No one will come."

Lord Mahtize glanced down at the button tucked into the scrolling, carved into the edge of his ornate balla wood desk, then back to the two intruders.

"Go ahead, we'll wait."

Lord Mahtize pressed and held the button for several seconds. After a moment, he tried it again, but still no guards came charging into his office.

"You will find that the door sensors are inoperative, as well," the man said. "However, the sound suppression fields are fully functional, in case you were thinking about yelling for help." The man rose from his chair, straightening his suit jacket as he reached a standing position. "As to your other question..."

"Which house?" Lord Mahtize interrupted.

"Pardon?"

"Which house sent you to kill me? Surely I deserve to know."

"We were not sent by a 'noble' house of Takara," the man assured him as he walked slowly toward him. "As to *killing* you, well, that need has yet to be determined."

Lord Mahtize did his best to appear composed. "So, you're not going to tell me who you are, or who sent you. Then, perhaps, you can enlighten me as to the purpose of your...overly dramatic visit."

"My name is General Lucius Telles, leader of the Ghatazhak, and second in command of the Karuzari Alliance. My cohort is Lieutenant Commander Jessica Nash, chief tactical officer and head of security for the Aurora, and the first female to be accepted into the Ghatazhak. So, do not be fooled by her lovely appearance."

"Ah," Lord Mahtize said, nodding. "So, you wish to impress me, to instill fear and respect, because of your ability to enter my offices undetected and gain an audience with me without approval."

"On the contrary," the general said, "we simply wish to avoid an official record of our meeting."

"But..."

"Your recorders have been deactivated, as well."

"I see," Lord Mahtize replied as he took his seat. "Now that we have established *who* you are, *and* who sent you, perhaps you would be kind enough to tell me *what* you want."

General Telles and Jessica moved to the chairs across from Lord Mahtize's desk. "We have reason to suspect the integrity of your arrangement with Mister Espan," the general said as he waited for Jessica to take her seat.

"The *integrity*?"

General Telles took his seat as he thought. "A nagging thought troubles me. Is he feeding us information because he *wants* to help us rid his world of the Dusahn, or does he have ulterior motives?"

"You question my honor?"

General Telles chuckled. "Please, do not insult me, Mahtize."

Lord Mahtize's expression soured, taking umbrage at the general's improper address. "The Mahtize family goes back to the first ships to settle this world. Takara is my home, just as it was once yours. The Dusahn are no more welcome on Takara than you are in my office."

General Telles smiled at Lord Mahtize's play on words. "Be that as it may, the rise in your fortunes, and in your influence in the House of Lords, has not escaped our notice."

"Is Mahtize the *only* house whose fortunes have increased under Dusahn occupation?"

"No, but it *is* doing considerably better than the others," the general replied.

"There is no crime in profit," Lord Mahtize countered.

"True, but there is cause for suspicion. One who profits so well seems an unlikely candidate to work against the very regime from which one is profiting."

"Fortune favors the bold," Lord Mahtize stated confidently.

"Indeed, it does," General Telles agreed.

Lord Mahtize studied his two guests a moment. "You still have not told me the purpose of your visit."

"Our *purpose* is to let you know that we do *not* fully trust you," General Telles explained. "More importantly, we are giving you notice that *betrayal*... would be unwise."

"Couldn't you have just sent a message through Terig?" Lord Mahtize asked.

"Yes, but we felt our presence would make you understand that your *location* does not equal *protection* from the Karuzari."

"Then you came to *threaten* me."

"Take it as you wish," General Telles stated as he rose. "Our purpose is served. I apologize for our unannounced visit, but such are the times in which we live." General Telles looked to Jessica, offering his hand. "My dear."

Lord Mahtize also stood, but out of decorum. He took a good look at Jessica. "You don't say much, do you, Lieutenant Commander."

"I'm here to do the wet work," she replied. She winked, adding, "If needed."

"I'm sure you won't mind if we use your private exit," General Telles stated.

Lord Mahtize nodded once. "As if I have a choice."

"Good day to you, my lord," General Telles said, mocking respect for the man.

Jessica smiled as she turned, blowing a kiss to Lord Mahtize on her way out.

Lord Mahtize stood there, watching, as they exited his office onto his private patio. He leaned to his left, peering through the window as they passed through the outer gate. Once out of sight, he immediately pressed the intercom button, to call his private secretary, but nothing happened. He pressed more buttons: his chief of security, his private chef, his main residence...and still nothing. He ran to the main entrance but found it locked. He ran to the private entrance, the same one the general and the lieutenant commander had just exited through, but it, too, was locked. "Damn!"

"You think it will work?" Jessica asked as she strolled across the gardens of House Mahtize, arm in arm with the general.

"We shall see," the general said. He glanced to either side, checking for onlookers. Spotting none, he slipped through the bushes, Jessica following behind him as they disappeared into the dense woods that acted as a buffer between the private gardens and the perimeter wall.

CHAPTER EIGHT

"Is that it?" Deliza asked when Naralena came out with a single bag.

"A few changes of clothes and a hygiene kit. Do I need more?"

"If the Dusahn come, I can't promise we'll be able to bring you back," Deliza told her.

"I had less than this last time; when Nathan swooped me out of my miserable life on Haven," she assured her, locking the door behind her. "Besides, everything I care about is on my comm-unit."

"About that," Deliza said as they headed for the waiting vehicle. "Why didn't you answer when I called?"

"You called? Oh, yes, you probably still have my old number."

"But it was *your* voice mail that picked up," Deliza told her as they climbed into the vehicle.

"I still have that number, but I use it as a buffer against...well, it's a long, frightening story."

"I can't wait to hear it," Deliza said as their vehicle started moving.

"I can't wait to forget about it," Naralena replied. "You know, when I heard the Aurora was fighting the Dusahn, I was certain they were just *pretending* that Nathan was still alive, in order to rally support. I mean, he *died*, didn't he?"

"That's a long, frightening story, as well," Deliza replied. "One that Nathan should tell you."

Naralena sighed as she watched the familiar buildings pass; ones that she might never see again. "You know, it devastated me when he died, but I'm sure you understand. It must have devastated you, as well."

"Not exactly," Deliza said a bit uneasily.

Naralena looked at her. "You knew he was alive?"

"Uh..."

"For how long?"

"There were good reasons to keep it a secret," Deliza defended, "from *everyone*. Even Vladimir and Cameron didn't know."

Multiple claps of thunder sounded in the distance. Corporal Torlak leaned forward, looking up at the sky as more flashes of blue-white light appeared only a few blocks ahead of them. "Uh-oh," he said as more claps sounded. "This is going to get interesting."

"Unplug the shore line!" Josh yelled at Dalen as he ran around the port engine nacelle, headed for the cargo ramp.

"Are the reactors hot?" Dalen yelled back.

"Loki!" Josh called over comm-sets as he ran up the ramp.

"*They're hot! Disconnect!*"

A thunderous clap shook the deck beneath his feet, nearly knocking him off the ramp, as blue-white light momentarily flooded the Seiiki's cargo bay. Josh spun around to see a Dusahn troop pod dropping into a hover, five meters off the surface, about fifty meters directly behind them, just on the other side of the blast wall that surrounded the landing pad. "DALEN! MOVE YOUR ASS!" Josh yelled as he reached for the boomer that Marcus kept in a small wall locker next to the cargo bay door. He raised the boomer as he pressed its power button. Just as the doors on the troop pod opened, and the soldiers inside were about to jump to the ground below, the boomer reached full power, and Josh pressed the firing button. A ball of brilliant red-orange plasma leapt from the boomer's stubby barrel, slamming into the hovering troop pod a split second later. The Dusahn soldier leaning forward to jump took the brunt of the blast, which burned through his torso in the blink of an eye, leaving only a bodiless head and a pair of legs to fall to the surface below. The pod tipped to one side, its hover-thrust destabilized, and fell to the surface, exploding as it hit the ground.

Dalen ducked instinctively at the sound of the explosion as he ran up the ramp.

"GO! GO! GO!" Josh exclaimed over his comm-set as he tossed the spent boomer aside. Two more flashes of light and claps of thunder as additional Dusahn troop pods jumped in nearby.

Josh stumbled toward the forward ladder. "Man the bay gun!" he instructed Dalen.

"Got it!" Dalen replied, scrambling across the pitching deck as Josh bounded up the short ladder and disappeared through the forward hatch.

Dalen stumbled along, grabbing the walls to steady himself as the Seiiki rose quickly into the air and began moving forward. Any minute, there would be enough power to bring the inertial dampeners online but, for now, he had to concentrate on not falling out of the gaping, open end of the cargo bay.

As soon as Dalen reached the starboard edge of the bay doors, he grabbed a safety harness and threw it around his waist. He quickly attached the tether to the overhead track and unlocked the gun arm.

Just as he pulled on the gun arm to deploy it, the ship's stern swung to the right, and Dalen found himself swinging from the gun handles, his feet straight out, horizontally. His body weight pulled the gun into place, making a loud *clunk* as the overhead support arm locked into its deployed position. The ship pitched again, going nose up, and Dalen lost his grip on the gun handles, flying out the open bay doors. The tether became taut, causing him to fall to the deck. The ship nosed down, and he tumbled forward, just as the inertial dampeners began to kick in.

Dalen struggled for a moment, still on his hands and knees, trying to get his bearings. He raised his head and glanced outside as the city below swirled about while the Seiiki maneuvered wildly. The movement outside, and the lack of inertial forces inside, were more than he could handle, and his lunch came up, spewing all over the ramp.

Corporal Amund guided their vehicle through the chaotic streets of Constantatia. People were running in all directions, in desperate attempts to find safety. Vehicles abandoned all rules, doing whatever was necessary to get to their destinations while they still could. Flashes of blue-white light appeared with frightening regularity, and the air was punctuated with constant claps of thunder. Dusahn troop pods appeared over, what seemed like, every intersection. Just as they turned onto what they thought was a clear street, another pod would appear, forcing them to make another turn.

"We need someplace large enough for the Seiiki to land!" Corporal Torlak yelled from the front passenger seat.

"You must turn to the left!" Naralcna insisted. "Toward the edge of the city!"

"Is there anything closer?" Corporal Amund asked as they approached the next intersection.

"Nothing!" she replied. "This part of the city is all buildings! No open spaces!"

"Hang on!" Corporal Amund warned, just before he yanked the wheel to the left.

The vehicle skidded, tipping to the right, the left wheels coming off the ground. Two flashes of light lit up the street, along with simultaneous claps of thunder. A Dusahn troop pod appeared over the intersection ahead of them, settling into a hover and opening its doors to drop four soldiers to the ground.

Deliza spun around, spotting another pod dropping in over the intersection behind them. "There's one behind us, too!" she warned.

"Hang on!" Amund yelled as he stepped on the throttle, accelerating toward the four soldiers jumping to the ground in front of them.

Corporal Torlak pulled his sidearm and hung it out of the window, opening fire on the soldiers as they jumped from the hovering pod. His first two shots found their targets, killing both soldiers before they hit the ground. But a bump in the road caused his third and fourth shots to miss, and both soldiers made it to the ground alive.

The two soldiers immediately turned and opened fire on the approaching vehicle, their energy bolts slamming into its front end. Corporal Amund held the wheel firm as more bolts of energy slammed into them until, finally, the entire front of their vehicle came apart, and he lost control.

The vehicle slid sideways, sparks flying off what was left of its front end. With no control left of their vehicle, Corporal Amund also pulled his sidearm, blew out the forward windshield, and joined his partner in his defensive barrage.

Ghatazhak energy bolts slammed into the two Dusahn troops, shaking their bodies with each impact. A second later, their vehicle slammed into the soldiers and came to a stop.

"Everyone out!" Corporal Amund ordered, climbing out of the vehicle.

Corporal Torlak climbed out the passenger side, pulled the back passenger door open for Naralena, and took up position between her and the Dusahn troops who had just dropped in a block behind them. "Four on our six! We gotta move!" he barked as he opened fire on the men approaching from behind.

Corporal Amund scanned the buildings around them, looking at their tops. "Rooftops!" he declared as he pulled the door open for Deliza. "That one! Go!"

Naralena ran around the front of the vehicle as Deliza climbed out her side, both of them racing for the building the corporal had pointed to while the two Ghatazhak soldiers rained fire upon the enemy to their rear. More jump flashes flooded the streets, and more sounds of thunder joined the cacophony of the firefight.

"Moving!" Corporal Torlak announced as he backpedaled around the front of the vehicle, using it for cover.

Corporal Amund tucked in between the front and rear doors of the vehicle as he continued to fire at the soldiers working their way up the street behind them. "Their armor is charged!"

"That just makes it more challenging!" Torlak replied.

Deliza and Naralena reached the front entrance

to the building, pausing to look back. "Behind you!" Deliza shouted in warning as she spotted more Dusahn soldiers dropping in at the next intersection.

Corporal Torlak turned around and opened fire on the soldiers dropping from the hovering troop pod, sending them diving for cover as soon as they hit the ground. He then targeted the pod above them, which he knew was not shielded, blasting away at it. The pod immediately broke apart, falling to the ground below and exploding.

It was the cover they needed to escape the crossfire. Corporal Torlak moved around behind Corporal Amund and opened fire toward the rear. "Go, Ams!"

"Moving!" Corporal Amund announced as he ceased fire and sprinted the few meters to join Naralena and Deliza at the doorway. "What are you doing?" he demanded.

"It's locked!" Naralena declared.

The corporal raised his weapon and blasted the door wide open. "Not anymore!" he barked. "Find the stairs and head for the roof!" he added, turning to cover his partner's retreat. "Torlak! Go!" he yelled as he started firing again.

Corporal Torlak turned and sprinted to the doorway, continuing inside the building after Naralena and Deliza. As soon as his cohort passed by, Corporal Amund ceased fire and stepped back through the doorway. He paused long enough to pull a small device out of his thigh pocket, activated it, and placed it on the floor just to the right of the doorway, where no one would notice it until it was too late.

Corporal Amund sprinted across the lobby floor, following the others to the stairwell in the back corner, knowing they had less than a minute before Dusahn troops would come charging through the door and find the surprise he had left for them. "Seiiki!" he called, tapping his comm-set. "New plan! Rooftop pickup!"

"Which rooftop?" Loki asked as he maneuvered the Seiiki to avoid slamming into a hovering troop pod.

"*You'll know!*" Corporal Amund replied. "*Just head in the direction of our comms signal!*"

"Jesus!" Josh exclaimed as he bounded up the ladder into the Seiiki's cockpit. "Can you hold it still for at least a few seconds?"

"They're dropping in all over the place!" Loki explained. "It's all I can do to keep from running into them!"

"Fuck it! Ram 'em!" Josh declared as he slid into the pilot's seat. "My controls!"

"Your controls," Loki confirmed, releasing control of the ship to Josh. "Powering up weapons and shields."

"You didn't have shields up?"

"I didn't have enough power for shields *and* inertial dampeners," Loki defended. "I figured it was better to get your ass up here. Besides, ground-pounder guns aren't powerful enough to take us out." He looked at Josh. "Right?"

Josh looked back, shrugging.

A warning beeped.

Loki glanced at the sensor screen. "Assault shuttles!"

"Where?" Josh asked as he turned toward a

Dusahn troop pod that had just jumped in to their left.

"Everywhere!"

Josh pressed the firing button, sending a pair of plasma torpedoes streaking toward the troop pod, obliterating it.

"A little overkill, don't you think?" Loki commented.

"Just get those PDs up!" Josh replied.

"Point-defenses, coming online now!"

On the underside of the Seiiki, several miniature laser turrets popped out and swung into action, the ship's automated targeting system directing the tiny weapons to target anything giving off an energy signature that looked remotely like a weapon.

Deliza's calves burned as she ran up the stairs. The building suddenly shook, causing her to stumble. "What......was......that?" she called back down the stairs.

"*A little present I left for the Dusahn!*" Corporal Amund replied from the next flight down. "*Keep going!*"

Nearly out of breath, Deliza finally reached the rooftop exit. She pushed on the crash bar, swinging the door open and tripping the alarm.

"Great," Corporal Torlak commented as he came up the stairs behind them.

Deliza stepped out onto the roof, bending over, panting as Naralena came out behind her.

"If they didn't know where we were, they know

now," Corporal Amund commented as he followed Corporal Torlak through the door, onto the roof. He tapped his comm-set as he ran out onto the middle of the roof, looking around. "Seiiki! Amund! You got me?"

"*Thirty seconds!*" Loki replied.

The corporal turned in the direction of the airfield, squinting to spot the Seiiki in the bright afternoon sun. "There!"

"Brown building, two streets over, eight down!" Loki instructed.

"*You know we have combat shuttles closing on us, right?*" Dalen called over comm-sets.

"Well, give them something to think about!" Loki replied.

Dalen flipped off the dual safety switches on the gun handle and brought the underhung weapon onto one of the three shuttles closing on them. "I'll give them something to think about." He pressed the firing button once, and three pulses of plasma energy leapt out of the weapon in earsplitting screeches. "Whoa!" he exclaimed, pressing and holding the firing button as he swept back and forth, screaming at the top of his lungs.

The shields on all three shuttles lit up as balls of plasma energy slammed into them. The shuttles jinked up and down and from side to side, trying to avoid the constant barrage of energy that Dalen was sending their way.

"This gun is great!" he exclaimed, holding his fire for a moment.

"*Yeah, but maybe you could avoid screaming through your comm-set!*" Josh replied.

The entire cargo bay flashed red in rapid succession as the shuttles pursuing them opened fire, pummeling the Seiiki's aft shields.

The Seiiki shook from the incoming fire as Josh slid the ship to the left and started a rapid descent. "I see them!" he exclaimed, looking out the forward window.

"Amund! Seiiki! We have you!" Loki called. "We'll be there in a few seconds!" Loki's eyes suddenly widened as he spotted four Dusahn soldiers coming out of a door on the far side of the rooftop. "Amund! Bandits on the opposite side! To your left!"

Corporal Amund spun around just as the four Dusahn soldiers charged toward them from an open door on the other side of the rooftop, opening fire as they approached. The corporal dropped into a crouch as he returned fire, instinctively charging toward the attackers, jinking left and right as he avoided their fire.

"Dalen! Shoot the guys on the roof!" Josh ordered as he twisted the flight control stick, causing the ship to rotate on its vertical axis.

As the view of the rooftops outside the cargo bay slid past him rapidly from left to right, Dalen felt what remained of his lunch trying to come back up. Suppressing the sensation, he concentrated on picking out his target. When the ship stopped spinning, and the charging Dusahn soldiers came into view, he shouted, "Amund! Duck!" He paused just long enough for the corporal to hit the deck, then pressed the firing button, mowing down the four charging enemy soldiers as the Seiiki began to descend to the rooftop.

"I got 'em!" Dalen shouted, ceasing fire. He pushed the gun aside and charged down the ramp, just as the Seiiki was about to touch down.

Josh's eyes darted back and forth between his flight displays and the aft camera view on the center view screen. "I can't set down!" he called over comm-sets. "There's not enough room! They've got to jump onto the ramp!"

Naralena ran toward the Seiiki's cargo ramp as it slammed against the roof, but stopped when the ramp bounced off of it. The ship wasn't landing; it was just hovering there, shaking about as energy weapons fire slammed into its forward shields. She looked at the young man balancing precariously in the middle of the moving ramp, gesturing for her to come toward him.

"You've got to jump for it!" Corporal Torlak urged. "There's not enough room for them to land!"

Naralena eyed the moving ramp, trying not to look

at the pitching ship it was connected to. She took a deep breath and charged forward, jumping to the ramp and falling onto it as it pitched upward. She reached out blindly and felt the young man's strong grasp pulling her toward him. She frantically crawled toward him, getting to her feet on the pitching ramp with his help, and finally falling into the relative safety of the Seiiki's cargo bay.

"You must be Naralena!" Dalen yelled. "I'm Dalen! Welcome aboard!"

"*Forward shields are down to forty percent!*" Loki exclaimed. "*Someone get to the gun turrets!*"

"Can you operate a plasma cannon?" Dalen asked Naralena.

"I don't know! I can try!"

"Up that ladder, through the hatch, and up the stairs! It's easy!"

"Those shuttles are closing!" Loki warned, pointing out the window as the Seiiki rotated slowly around again, her shields flashing as incoming weapons fire slammed into them. "Dalen! You see them?"

"Come on!" Dalen yelled to Deliza, standing in the middle of the pitching ramp, his hand outstretched.

Deliza watched the ship rotating around, trying to judge its rotational speed, utter fear in her eyes.

Corporal Amund fired at the troop pod hovering to his right, picking off soldiers as they tried to jump to the rooftop.

"GO!" Corporal Torlak yelled, pushing Deliza

forward, while he fired at the troop pod descending behind them.

Deliza charged forward, jumping up onto the ramp as it passed left to right. When she landed, the rotation of the ship caused her to lose her balance, and she fell to the left, tumbling off the edge of the ramp. At the last second, she grabbed hold of the port hydraulic ramp strut. As the ship swung around, she could feel the centrifugal force trying to throw her clear. She glanced toward her dangling feet, just as the ramp swung out over the edge, revealing the street more than forty meters below.

Dalen quickly disconnected his tether as he yelled, "Stop spinning! We're gonna lose her!" He slid down the ramp, face first, on his belly, stopping himself by grabbing the same strut. The ship stopped its rotation, and he grabbed the back of Deliza's jacket, pulling with all of his might.

"*Somebody, shoot those damned shuttles!*" Loki cried out over comm-sets as the ship rocked with the weapons impacts against their failing shields.

Naralena climbed up into the port gun turret, immediately reaching for the one thing that was familiar to her: a comm-set. "I'm in!"

"*Shoot!*" Josh yelled.

"How?" she asked, flinching from the flashes as incoming weapons fire impacted the shields outside her turret bubble.

"*Left handle moves the turret side to side, right handle moves the weapon up and down!*" Loki explained, trying to remain calm as their ship was pummeled.

Naralena looked at the two sticks, noticing buttons on top of each one. "Which button fires the gun?"

"*Either one!*" Loki replied urgently as the ship tracked to the right. "*Fire on the shuttles to the left!*"

Naralena reluctantly put her hands on the control sticks, pushing the left one to the side. The turret quickly rotated to port, startling her and causing her to let go of the controls. She immediately grabbed them again, tracking further left and pulling the right handle back to raise the weapon. "Is this little screen for targeting?"

"*YES! SHOOT!*" Josh begged.

The targeting reticle on the view screen turned green as she maneuvered the weapon, turning red when she went too far. She tracked back in the opposite direction, realizing the target was moving from her left to right and that she needed to lead it slightly. Again, the reticle turned green, and she pressed the firing button on the right control stick. The weapon cycled a dozen times in rapid succession, making repeated *zings,* each of which ended with a staccato *screech*, sending bolts of red-orange plasma leaping from the barrels. Left, right, left, right, the twin barrels continued to fire as she tracked the enemy shuttle, keeping the targeting reticle green. The sound of the weapon; the flashes of red-orange light; the flashes of the enemy shuttle's shields as her weapons fire struck them...it all scared her to death, but she held the button down and continued to fire until...

A brilliant explosion flashed less than a hundred meters in front of her. She screamed in fright, her weapon ceasing fire when she released the controls.

"*LOOK OUT!*" Josh warned.

Pieces of debris slammed into the Seiiki's port shields, the flashes lighting up her gun turret. Naralena instinctively held up her hands in front of her face to shield herself, never seeing the remains of the shuttle as it dove directly toward her.

Josh pulled his flight control stick back and to the right, firing the translation thrusters on the underside of the ship at the same time. The Seiiki pitched up and angled right in response, gaining just enough altitude to allow the half-destroyed shuttle to pass underneath them.

Corporal Torlak's eyes widened as he spotted the damaged Dusahn shuttle plummeting toward him. He took three running steps, then dove forward, barely escaping as the shuttle slammed into the rooftop, right where he had been standing a moment ago. The roof buckled, then gave way to the shuttle's kinetic energy.

The shuttle plowed through the roof, into the floor, and out the side wall, tumbling to the street below, and pulling half the building with it.

The Seiiki leveled off, continuing to rotate to the right, bringing its cargo ramp back around to what was left of the rooftop.

Corporal Amund watched as his fellow Ghatazhak fell with the collapsing roof. With no other option, he ran and jumped a good five meters in the air, landing perfectly on the moving ramp. Rather than run up the ramp to the safety of the cargo bay, the corporal, instead, grabbed the side hydraulic strut and turned to look for his friend amongst the rubble in the street below. "He's still alive!" he hollered over comm-sets. "He's on the street! He's in a firefight!"

"I'm in the starboard turret!" Deliza announced as she put the comm-set on her head.

"*Keep those bastards off our ass while I pick up Torlak!*" Josh ordered.

"I'm on it," Deliza replied, swinging her gun around and immediately opening fire on the other two Dusahn assault shuttles. "Come on, Naralena!" she called to her still-stunned friend. "We can do this!"

Corporal Torlak scrambled over the rubble of the collapsed building. His left leg was bleeding and searing with pain, and his back didn't feel right. Had it not been for the assistive combat bodysuit under his civvies, the fall surely would have killed him. He only hoped that his nanites were doing their job.

"*Find a clear spot!*" Loki called over the corporal's comm-set. "*We're coming for you!*"

Enemy energy weapons fire slammed into the rubble to his right, causing it to explode, sending super-heated debris flying in all directions. He returned fire as best he could, shooting over the top of the rubble, while he scrambled toward the buildings on the far side of the street. He needed to get clear, to get somewhere that the Seiiki could pick him up.

The weapons fire continued as the corporal made

it to the side of the street. Free of the rubble, he turned and ran toward the corner.

At that very moment, a Dusahn soldier came charging around the corner, nearly running into Corporal Torlak. The corporal ducked down, grabbing the charging soldier's weapon and spinning to his right, pulling hard on the enemy's weapon and the soldier holding it. A second soldier came charging around the corner, as well, unaware of the confrontation that had already begun.

As Corporal Torlak flipped the first guard over his shoulder and onto the sidewalk, he swept out his right foot, catching the second soldier just below the knees, sending him tumbling forward. Knowing the Dusahn traveled in fours, the corporal continued spinning around, tossing the captured assault rifle in the air, spinning end over end. As the weapon ascended, the corporal flat-handed the third soldier directly in the face shield with his left hand, tightening up his arm during the blow so the assistive combat bodysuit would stiffen, strengthening his blow. The soldier's helmet shifted back, the face shield striking the man's nose, bloodying it.

The weapon, still flipping end over end, came back down, and the corporal caught it with his right hand. He then slipped the shoulder strap over the third soldier's head, flipped the rifle over to twist the strap tight, and dropped to his knee, pulling downward. He could feel the man's cervical vertebrae give, shifting unevenly and severing the man's spinal cord.

With a fourth soldier due to come around the corner, the corporal took another step forward, jumped into the air, spinning around and placing his foot into the throat of the fourth soldier as he came blindly around the corner to meet his doom.

Plasma torpedo cannons sounded on the corporal's left, causing him to turn in the direction of the sound as a string of plasma torpedoes streaked past him, slamming into the building on the opposite corner, causing its massive overhang to collapse.

With barely enough room to land, the Seiiki swooped down into the rubble-strewn intersection, spinning around to point its cargo ramp at Corporal Torlak. Dalen stood inside, firing his underhung plasma cannon at the Dusahn on the other side of the rubble pile behind the corporal. Corporal Amund stood next to him, firing his own weapon with his right hand as he gestured to his friend to come aboard with his left.

Corporal Torlak broke into a run, jumping onto a large piece of the collapsed structure and launching himself toward the Seiiki's outstretched ramp. He sailed through the air, landing on the very end of the ramp, continuing up the ramp without missing a beat.

The ship rocked as its topside shields took multiple impacts.

"*We've got him!*" Corporal Amund reported over comm-sets. "*Go, go, go!*"

Josh could barely keep the ship in a hover as incoming weapons fire slammed into them, seemingly from all directions. "FUCK!" he exclaimed as he gunned the throttles and started to climb. The ship slipped to the left from the impacts and slammed into the buildings. "SHIT!"

Loki reached over, knowing that Josh's hands were full, and pushed the lift throttles to full power, as well, wanting to prevent the collapsing building from pulling them down with it.

The Seiiki screamed and moaned, feeling like she was being twisted like a pretzel, but she somehow managed to blast her way through the collapsing building and into the air again.

"YES!" Josh exclaimed. "WAY TO GO, LOK!"

"Hang on!" Loki warned over comm-sets. "We're blasting out at full power!"

Dalen braced himself, both feet planted firmly on the deck, his hands on his plasma cannon as he continued firing away at the two Dusahn assault shuttles pursuing them. The aft shields flashed red repeatedly as bolts of plasma slammed into it. Suddenly, it flashed brighter than usual, and sparks flew past the open bay doors from the sides.

Dalen's eyes widened, knowing full well what had just happened.

Two more bolts of plasma slammed into the now-unshielded stern of the Seiiki. The first impact blew the ramp into a twisted wreck, and the second passed through the open end, slamming into Dalen and his plasma cannon, sending them both flying backward toward the front end of the cargo bay.

The blast knocked both corporals to either side of the open bay, rendering them senseless for several seconds. When their senses returned, all they could hear was the rush of air, the roar of the Seiiki's engines, and the faint sound of Loki asking if they were alright.

Corporal Amund looked around. The back side of the ship was blown open. The ramp was hanging by one hinge and a strut, and was shifting back and forth. Conduit was hanging everywhere, and parts of bulkheads were warped from the intense heat. It was a miracle he had not been incinerated by the blast. He spotted Corporal Torlak, pushing a piece of the starboard bulkhead that had broken free off of him. "Torlak!" he called. "You okay?"

"Yeah!" Torlak replied. "What the fuck hit us?"

"*Cargo bay!*" Loki begged. "*Somebody! Please!*"

"Amund! I'm good!" the corporal reported over comm-sets.

"Torlak! I'm good!"

After a moment, both men looked around for Dalen. Amund was the first to spot him, his twisted body melded with the surviving portion of his plasma cannon, slammed into the lower portion of the forward bulkhead, just below the main deck landing.

Both men immediately sprang into action, rushing to Dalen. Amund was the first to reach him. "Dalen! Dalen!" he shouted, kneeling down next to him and checking for any signs of life.

"*Dalen!*" Loki called over comm-sets. "*Dalen! Check in!*"

"Dalen's dead," Corporal Amund reported.

There was no response over comm-sets.

The ship rocked again as another blast slammed into the stern, just starboard of the damaged cargo bay.

"*Clear the bay!*" Josh ordered. "*We've gotta jump to space now, or we're never gonna make it off this rock!*"

"I'm not going to be able to get his body out of here in time," Amund replied.

"*Nothing we can do about it,*" Josh insisted, his voice pained but firm. "*Leave him.*"

There was no chatter in the cockpit between Josh and Loki for some time. The ship continued to be pounded as Josh fought to keep them flying. Systems were failing right and left, and Loki was scrambling to keep everything together, but the Dusahn shuttles, still pursuing them, were doing everything within their power to prevent them from escaping.

"He'd leave you behind to save everyone else, as well," Loki said quietly.

"No, he wouldn't," Josh disagreed. "He was too stupid and too loyal."

"*Cargo bay is clear,*" Corporal Amund reported. "*Door is sealed.*"

Josh didn't say another word as he pressed the jump button on his flight control stick.

Naralena felt a tap on her foot. She glanced downward, spotting Corporal Amund standing below her.

"Ready for some relief?" he asked.

"Gladly," she replied, climbing down from her seat to the deck below.

"You did fine."

"Are you kidding?"

"You faced an attacking enemy and prevented the destruction of this ship. You could not have known the additional dangers Corporal Torlak would have to face."

"But I almost got him killed."

"Almost dying is what we do," Corporal Amund assured her. He tipped his head toward the other gun turret, which Corporal Torlak was climbing into. "He is still with us, just as all of us are."

Naralena looked down. "Not that young man... Dalen, was it?"

"Without death, war would not be something to avoid," the corporal stated, climbing up into the gun turret.

Deliza stepped over, having just vacated her turret, as well. "Come on, Naralena. We're not out of this, yet."

"Aft shields are completely gone," Loki reported. "All other shields are below fifty percent, and our port dorsal shield is fluctuating and could fail at any time."

"Any other good news?" Josh asked sarcastically as he tried to trim his controls. "Christ, this thing is flying like a brick. I've got no lateral thrusters, and my translation thrusters can't decide if they're good or bad."

"Propulsion and basic maneuvering are still working, if that helps."

"So, we can go fast and jump, but course changes are going to be slow as shit," Josh summarized. "Lovely."

"Uh, jumping might not be the greatest idea right now," Loki warned.

Josh just looked at him.

"I'm getting some odd readings from a few emitters. Three of them didn't go to full power on the last jump. I'm surprised we didn't leave anything behind."

The threat display beeped, and Josh glanced over at the view screen. "We may not have a choice."

Loki studied the screen for a moment. "Gunners, we've got four octos inbound. Directly astern, two hundred clicks, and closing fast. We've got no aft shields, and our port dorsal shields are iffy, so be ready for anything. Whatever you do, keep them off our ass *and* our port side."

"*Copy that,*" Corporal Amund replied over comm-sets.

"Great," Josh exclaimed. "I've always wanted to fly evasive...*backwards.*"

"Loki," Deliza called over comm-sets as she and Naralena made their way forward. "Can't we just jump?"

"*Uneven power on a few of the emitters,*" Loki replied. "*I'm afraid if we lose a couple of side-by-side emitters, the safeties will kick in, and we won't be able to jump at all.*"

"What about the secondary array?"

"*We lost the field generators for the secondary array when they blew our back end off,*" Loki explained.

"*They're going to split up,*" Corporal Amund warned. "*They know our aft shields are down, so they'll draw our fire and your angle with one pair, and the other pair will jump in and attack our weak side. You can't let them get a shot at it.*"

"I'll do what I can," Josh replied, "but this thing is flying like a broken-down barge."

"I can increase the power on the docking thrusters

and tie them into the maneuvering thrusters," Loki suggested. "That might help."

"I'll take anything I can get," Josh agreed.

"One hundred clicks," Loki reported, glancing at the tactical display as he worked. Two of the four icons suddenly disappeared. "Yup, two of them just jumped out. You nailed it."

"They're going to jump past us and do a one-eighty. They'll expect you to show the attackers your good side."

"Primary pair will be in attack range in thirty seconds," Loki reported. "Docking thrusters are slaved to maneuvering thrusters."

Josh killed the main engines and twisted his control stick, causing the ship to yaw round to port, into a stern-first position.

"What are you doing, Josh?" Corporal Amund wondered.

"I've got an idea."

"They're going to jump in and..."

"Both turrets, point aft and be ready to track up when I pitch down and over!" Josh ordered, cutting him off.

"I hope you know what you're doing," Corporal Amund replied.

"So do I," Josh muttered.

"Five seconds."

"Bet you weren't expecting this," Josh said as he pressed the firing button on his flight control stick. A series of red-orange plasma torpedoes leapt from their tubes on either side of the Seiiki's fuselage, lighting up the cockpit as they departed. The plasma torpedoes closed the distance to the targets in the blink of an eye, slamming into the Dusahn octo's shields and lighting them up. The octos began to maneuver wildly, not expecting such heavy firepower from what they thought was just a light cargo ship with a few guns slapped onto it. "They may be stubby, but they pack a wallop!" Josh yelled as the two attacking fighters parted ways, veering in opposite directions. Josh ceased fire and pitched down hard. "Pitch up, boys!" he yelled into his comm-set. "They're splitting left and right!" Josh held his control stick all the way forward, causing his ship to pitch down and around, back in their direction of flight. Just as his nose came up level, the other two Dusahn octos jumped in only a few kilometers away, expecting to see the defenseless aft end of their target. Instead, they were introduced to the Seiiki's twin, short-barreled, mark two plasma torpedo cannons. "EAT THIS!" he barked as he opened fire. The shields on the second pair of octos also lit up, flashing red-orange with each impact. They, too, split in opposite directions, knowing full well that their enemy could only target one of them at a time. But Josh had no interest in pressing his luck.

Corporal Amund swung his turret up and to port, locking onto one of the evading octo-fighters. The moment his targeting reticle flashed green, he opened up, adjusting his lead until he saw the target's shields flashing over and over with the impacts from his plasma cannon. "Die, you bastard!" he cursed as he continued firing. Then, without warning, the target simply vanished. "What the hell?" He looked around, noticing a planet in the distance, where there had not been one a moment ago. "Did we jump?"

"Hell, yeah, we jumped!" Josh replied.

"Shutting everything down," Loki announced.

"Just keep docking thrusters online for now," Josh reminded him. "They're cold jets, so they won't detect them."

"Uh-oh," Loki said.

"No uh-ohs," Josh insisted. "Not now."

"What uh-oh?" Deliza asked as she climbed up into the Seiiki's cockpit.

"Four emitters have been taken offline by the safeties," Loki told her. "We can't jump."

"Give me a few minutes to bypass them in the code," Deliza told him, climbing into the systems seat just behind Loki.

"They'll find us in two," Josh told her.

"Hide in the ring system," Loki suggested.

"That's the plan."

"*Guys, did you mean to power down our guns?*" Corporal Torlak asked over comm-sets.

"Everything is going down," Loki replied. "We need to be undetectable for a few minutes."

"*Are things always this crazy on this ship?*" Corporal Amund asked.

"Pretty much," Josh replied.

"That's everything," Loki announced.

Josh glanced over his shoulder at Deliza. "Princess's workstation is still up."

"She's running on battery power," Loki replied. "The chances of them detecting that tiny thing are a million to one."

"Rings coming up," Josh reported, looking out the forward windows. "More dense than I thought."

Loki also looked out the windows, his eyes widening. "Are you going to be able to maneuver through that with docking thrusters?"

"We're about to find out," Josh replied, moving his control stick slightly. "Come on, baby. Don't give out on me just yet."

The first blue-gray, icy rock, more than ten times the size of the Seiiki, closed on them rapidly. Without any instrumentation, all Josh could do was look out the window and eyeball his approach. Several times, he pushed the stick over hard, trying to get the ship to respond more quickly. Just as it looked like they were about to strike the icy rock, he rolled the ship onto its left side, and it passed over them, missing by only three meters.

"Damn, you always fly this close to things?" Corporal Torlak wondered aloud as he watched the icy rock pass overhead, barely missing his gun turret.

"*Not if I can help it,*" Josh chuckled over comm-sets.

Josh peeked back to his left, looking aft as the rock cleared the back of the ship. He spun his head back around to look forward, picking out his next imaginary line in space to fly past the next obstacle.

This time, it was two icy rocks; the first bigger than the last, and the next one half its size. Both were slowly spinning in opposite directions and had bits of debris orbiting them in odd patterns.

"Those two must have collided recently," Loki observed. He glanced at Josh, and then looked out the window again, trying to determine the flight path his friend was about to attempt. "You know, you don't *have* to go between them, Josh. You could go around the outside to the right."

"What's the fun in that?" Josh giggled, firing the docking thrusters to adjust his course.

"Not funny."

"Besides, I was planning on parking directly between them."

"The gravity of the larger one is going to pull us in," Loki warned.

"Not if I can find a stable gravity point between them."

"A gravity point." Loki shook his head. "We're being pursued by Dusahn octos, and you're looking for stable gravity points."

"If we land, we may not be able to take off again," Josh replied, "not even from these tiny rocks. If we keep flying *past* them, they'll detect us by our motion relative to the rocks."

Loki shook his head again.

"What?"

"I really hate it when you're right," Loki stated.

"Well, don't worry," Josh replied as he applied additional forward thrust to decrease their closure rate, "we both know it doesn't happen that often." Josh turned to look back over his shoulder. "How are you doing with those overrides, Princess?"

"You just worry about flying, let me worry about coding."

Josh didn't respond, just continued to guide the Seiiki in between the two icy rocks ahead, applying tiny bursts from the forward docking thrusters, slowing slightly with each burst. By the time they began to pass between the two slowly spinning rocks, they were barely moving by comparison.

Three more spurts from the forward docking

thrusters and the Seiiki came to a stop, hanging motionless between the two spinning rocks.

"The one on the right is a bit oblong," Loki pointed out.

"I know," Josh said, taking his hands off the controls. He glanced left and right at the two vastly different rocks as they spun in space. The oblong rock to the right came around, its closest end passing by them. Josh watched for a moment, and then began to smile. "I think I did it."

"Of course, you did it," Loki commented. "You're Josh Hayes."

"Damn straight."

"And I did it!" Deliza announced triumphantly. "We can jump whenever you want. Just remember, without the safeties, there's no telling what will happen, so you'd better be damn sure that all your emitters are green."

The tactical display beeped, pulling both pilots' attentions to the center display.

"Damn, that didn't take long," Loki cursed.

"What is it?" Naralena asked.

"A single contact," Loki said. "Too small to be an octo... Wait, it's gone active."

"If you can see them..." Josh said.

"I know. And now, it's gone."

"Pursuit drone," Josh surmised as he began powering up systems on his side of the cockpit.

"Time to go," Loki agreed, also powering up systems.

"And I just got us so nicely parked, too," Josh declared.

"What's going on?" Naralena wondered.

"The Dusahn have pursuit drones that are really good at following our jump trails," Deliza explained.

"They find you and then jump back to tell the others where you are," Josh added, "which means a Dusahn ship will be here any second."

Another beep sounded.

"And there it is," Loki said.

"Man, I hate being right," Josh declared as he powered up the main engines.

"Dusahn gunship, two thousand meters and closing fast," Loki reported.

"Why couldn't they send a battleship," Josh muttered as he prepared to get under way. "We could *outrun* a battleship."

"Making your guns hot again," Loki called over his comm-set. "Gunship inbound; thirty seconds."

"Here we go," Josh announced, pushing the throttles for the main engines forward. The Seiiki began to accelerate, pulling slowly out from between the two spinning rocks and then accelerating quickly as Josh continued to push the throttles to their stops.

"You may want to avoid full power, Josh," Loki warned. "I've got more than a few systems nearing max ranges."

"Gotta use 'em while we've got 'em," Josh insisted as they climbed up out of the rings.

"We're being targeted," Loki warned.

"That didn't take long."

More beeps sounded.

"Missile launch!" Loki announced with surprise.

"Missiles! Gunships aren't supposed to have missiles!"

"Shit, I lost the missiles!"

"Oh, crap," Josh declared, pushing his control stick hard to port and forcing the Seiiki into a rolling turn. Again, the ship responded sluggishly.

"I've got them!" Loki exclaimed in a near panic. "Two clicks! They're jump..."

The starboard gun opened fire, and one of the missiles exploded, rocking the entire ship.

"...missiles!"

Corporal Torlak was barely able to stay in his seat as he continued to fire, but the second missile reached the Seiiki and impacted its starboard shield, detonating and unleashing its entire fury. The turret bubble lit up with blinding, white light that seemed to last forever, before fading away. When it was safe to open his eyes again, he looked outside and saw several shield emitters on the starboard side had blown apart, overloaded by the amount of energy that had just been dumped into them. He looked to his right, his eyes widening. "The starboard engine nacelle is gone!"

"Fuck!" Josh exclaimed. "I've got no lateral control; I can't control the yaw, Lok."

"I'm cross-connecting now," Loki replied. "Try vectoring the port engine thrust as far outboard as possible, to counteract the yaw."

"You mean fly sideways," Josh realized. "I can do that."

"Jesus, the port engine is down to twenty percent thrust, and just about everything in her is redlining."

"I'm heading for the gas giant," Josh declared. "We'll slingshot around her. Try to find something along the route that we can jump to. Preferably something with a breathable atmosphere." Josh and

Loki looked at each other. "This ship isn't going to get us home."

Loki was quiet for a moment as he tried desperately to stabilize what little was still functioning. "Maybe we should launch a comm-drone and send a distress signal back to the Aurora."

"Not until we reach our final destination," Josh said. "I want to be sure they know where to find us. Besides, that damned gunship would just shoot it down."

"Got it."

"Are you sure there's not something we can do?" Naralena wondered.

Deliza shot her a look. Naralena could tell by the look on Deliza's face that Josh and Loki were doing everything they could.

"Shit!" Loki exclaimed. "Reactor is going critical. I've got to eject the core."

"Just give me twenty seconds to get on course," Josh insisted.

"I don't know if we have twenty seconds, Josh."

"That's ten right there!" Josh struggled with his flight control stick, trying to force the ship to get on a course that would take them around the gas giant, hopefully intersecting a jump line that would save their butts.

"That's it," Loki announced. "I'm ejecting the core." Two seconds later, the lights dimmed, and non-essential systems began automatically shutting down as the ship switched to emergency battery power. Loki looked at Josh. "Did you get it?"

"I hope so," Josh sighed.

Corporal Amund climbed down out of his gun turret, tapping his comm-set as he reached the deck. "Hey, why aren't they shooting at us?"

"Pity?" Corporal Torlak joked as he climbed down from his gun turret.

"*I'm picking up two new contacts,*" Loki reported over comm-sets. "*The gunship just launched two small shuttles, and they're headed our way.*"

"I was afraid of that," Corporal Amund said as he headed through the forward hatch.

"*They're going to try to board us,*" the corporal said over comm-sets.

"Why would the Dusahn want to board *this* little ship?" Naralena wondered.

"Because *this* little ship has been involved in just about every major battle against the Dusahn," Josh explained.

"Then, why not just destroy us?" Deliza wondered.

"Because they want to capture us and get us to reveal where the fleet is located," Loki said.

"Or they just want to torture us to death and send the vids to Nathan to fuck with him," Josh added.

"Really, Josh, is that helpful?" Loki complained.

"Did you find us someplace to jump to?" Josh asked.

"Maybe," Loki replied, checking the star charts again. "What about Benson One Five Nine?"

"Too far away," Josh said. "We don't know if we can make *one* jump successfully, let alone *three.*"

"The only planet along our orbital path, that's within single jump range, is an Earth-like moon called Eralit Seven Delta, but it's only eight percent oxygen and half normal pressure."

"That's..."

"Don't even tell me the millibars, Deliza," Josh interrupted.

"Hey, you didn't call me princess."

"Slip of the tongue."

"It gets colder than shit at night there," Loki added.

"It'll have to do," Josh decided. "Can you plot a jump with battery power only?"

"Yes," Loki replied. "But the real question is, do we have enough energy left in the cells to make the jump?"

"I guess we're going to find out," Josh decided.

"Please tell me the cockpit can seal up," Corporal Amund said as he pulled his combat body armor and helmet out of his kit bag.

"*Yeah, it can seal up,*" Josh replied over comm-sets. "*Why?*"

"They'll either come through the cargo bay, which is already wide open, or the port boarding hatch," the corporal said.

"I'm betting cargo bay," Corporal Torlak stated as he donned his torso piece and fastened it in place. "Path of least resistance."

"How much time until we reach the jump point?" Corporal Amund asked over comm-sets.

"*Ten minutes,*" Loki replied. "*The shuttles are three minutes out.*"

"*What are you going to do?*" Josh asked.

"We're going to give them seven minutes of

resistance," Corporal Amund replied as he donned his helmet and reached for his assault rifle.

"One minute," Loki reported.

"How big are the shuttles?" Corporal Amund asked.

"Not large. Maybe four to six men in each," Loki guessed. "Deliza, close that hatch," he instructed, looking back over his shoulder. "Should I depress your section?" Loki asked over comm-sets.

"Negative," the corporal replied. *"That'll tip them off that we're ready for them."*

"If they blast their way in, decompression may be explosive," Loki warned.

"We can handle it," the corporal assured him.

"They're maneuvering aft," Josh reported, looking out the side windows. "They're going to enter through the cargo bay."

"Copy that."

"Hatch is sealed," Deliza reported. "How long until we jump?"

"Just over seven minutes," Loki replied.

"Seven-minute firefight inside a spaceship," Josh commented. "Glad I'm not a Ghatazhak."

Loki looked at Josh.

"What?"

"I have an idea," Deliza said as she tapped her comm-set. "Hey, guys? Would it help if we turned off the gravity?"

"What are you talking about?" Josh said.

"Actually, it might," the corporal replied.

"We can't *turn off* the gravity," Loki told her. "Only the cargo bay can be turned on and off."

"The cargo bay uses active gravity plating," Deliza argued. "The rest of the ship uses passive. That's why there's still gravity, even though we're running on batteries."

"*Can we turn off the gravity, or not?*" Corporal Amund asked.

"We can't," Loki replied.

"Yes, we can," Deliza insisted. "Passive plating gets a single charge, which it holds indefinitely or until something causes it to discharge. I can *cause* it to discharge."

"*Then, you can turn off the gravity,*" the corporal tried to verify.

"Hell, I don't know," Loki replied, throwing his hands up.

"I can do it," Deliza assured them.

A metallic *clunk* reverberated throughout the ship.

"Then, you'd better get ready," Loki told her, "because the first shuttle is in position. They'll be boarding any second."

"*Wait for my signal,*" Corporal Amund ordered.

"Understood," Deliza replied as she began frantically preparing. "Just one thing, it's going to make the gravity go off everywhere, *including* the cockpit, and we won't be able to turn it back on."

"Better buckle up, ladies," Josh suggested. "It's going to be a wild ride."

"Scramble Alpha," Corporal Amund ordered as he moved into position at the hatch leading from the port-forward corner of the main cabin to the port passageway leading past the boarding airlock and galley to the cockpit.

"*Scramble Alpha,*" Corporal Torlak replied from the opposite corner. "*In position.*"

"*Cockpit is scramble Alpha,*" Loki reported.

"*Ready when you are,*" Deliza added.

Corporal Amund lowered his visor, locking it in place. A hiss of compressed air and the flash of a small, green status light in the upper right corner of his tactical visor confirmed that his combat suit was pressurized. He braced himself against the bulkhead on his left, his torso and head poking out around the edge of the hatch just enough to get a clean line of fire into the main cabin. A single thought activated the mag-locks on his boots. He moved his weapon from left to right, checking his range of motion and registering the amount of movement necessary to cover his entire range of fire. He was ready.

"*Six minutes to jump point,*" Loki reported.

As if on cue, the hatch on the aft bulkhead of the main compartment leading to the aft cargo bay blew open, and all the atmosphere in the ship was sucked out the open door, taking everything that weighed less than a few kilograms and wasn't secured with it.

The corporal held firm, his left shoulder tucked against the hatch cowling, preventing him from being sucked into the main compartment. It took only a few seconds for the compartment to become a vacuum, at which point the boarding began.

A small drone floated in through the blown-open hatch. Corporal Amund quickly ducked back out of sight, just as a laser beam came out of the drone, scanning the entire compartment. The corporal watched the icons on his visor, which indicated eight intruders still waiting inside the cargo bay.

As expected, the drone suddenly emitted a momentary stun flash, hoping to disable anyone who might be lying in wait. Either the drone had detected them, or it was just following protocol.

"Torlak," Corporal Amund called. "Take the drone; I'll lob one into the cargo bay."

"*Copy.*"

"Three......two......one......"

Both corporals swung out just enough to fire. A single bolt of energy streaked from the starboard forward corner of the main cabin, slamming into the drone, obliterating it. At the same time, a single grenade went sailing from the port forward corner, across the main cabin, and through the open hatchway leading into the cargo bay. There was a flash of light from deep within the cargo bay and an explosion, then nothing.

Five seconds later, two grenades came sailing through the hatch, bouncing off the forward bulkhead and back into the middle of the cabin before detonating. Again, the cabin was lit up by the flashes, but the Ghatazhak body armor and helmet systems protected them from its debilitating effects.

Corporal Amund remained in his firing position, despite the flashes. A split second after the flashes, two Dusahn soldiers charged through the door, weapons firing toward the two Ghatazhak who lay in wait. But their lack of familiarity caused their aim to be untrue, costing them both their lives.

As trained, Corporal Amund fired two shots into the man on the right; one in the neck, and one in the face mask. At the same moment, Corporal Torlak placed his first two shots into the same locations on the man to the left.

But the Dusahn were not afraid, and the other

six men came charging in on the heels of their fallen comrades, weapons blazing and far more accurate.

A thought crossed Corporal Amund's mind. *The first two must've been the new guys.*

After the first dozen shots, Corporal Amund changed his elevation, dropping to one knee while still staying tucked neatly in the corner to maximize his cover. Incoming fire continued to pound the hatch cowl and the corridor behind him, a meter and a half above the deck, for several seconds before tracking downward. The corporal quickly shifted his weight to the right, moving across to the other side of the hatchway as the incoming fire now focused on his previous location and elevation. As he did so, his left shoulder suddenly felt as if it had been hit by a flying rock and became incredibly hot. But it did not faze him. He continued to fire, knowing full well that his imprecise attack was not as effective as it could be, but there was little choice.

Two icons on his tactical display blinked off, indicating that another two Dusahn soldiers had fallen. There were now only four of them left.

A *clink*, then another explosion, followed by the *zinging* of a million ricochets.

Fuck, a laser ball.

Tiny laser shots bounced off the bulkheads in all directions, more than a dozen of which found soft spots in his body armor, making their way to his body underneath. Searing pain... Pain that nearly made him drop his weapon.

"Now!" he ordered over his helmet comms.

"*Gravity plating is discharging!*" Deliza replied.

"*Four minutes!*" Loki added.

The sudden cessation of gravity, while not having the planned effect, caused the laser ball's levitation fields to overcompensate for a couple seconds. It was just enough to send it crashing up into the overhead, interrupting its ability to fire its micro-lasers.

The corporal stepped out into the open, quickly firing at the device as it bounced off the ceiling. The laser ball broke apart, and the corporal continued firing, sweeping back and forth in an attempt to force the remaining four soldiers back into the cargo bay. To his surprise, his energy bolts, as well as those being fired by Corporal Torlak from the opposite corner, simply bounced off the intruders, ricocheting back toward them.

"They've got some sort of shielding!" the corporal reported.

"*Three minutes!*" Loki reported.

"*Keep firing!*" Corporal Torlak urged as he discontinued his attack momentarily.

Corporal Amund continued his barrage, causing the targets to angle their shields toward him, sending *all* ricochets back at him. Round after round of his own weapon bounced off the enemy shields, slamming into the corporal's chest, arms, legs, and even glancing off his helmet.

"*Charging!*" Corporal Torlak yelled over comms.

Corporal Amund angled his fire upward, bouncing it off the overhead and into the bulkhead behind the enemy soldiers. Two of the intruders fell as the ricochets struck the back of their calves. The corporal ceased fire, charging forward to join his comrade in the physical assault. Two clunky steps to gain momentum, and then he mentally deactivated the mag-locks on his boots and went sailing through the cabin. He slammed into one of the two Dusahn soldiers still standing, sending them both tumbling wildly into the back bulkhead.

"Shit!" Loki exclaimed. "Two more shuttles just jumped in. Bigger! They'll be on us in less than a minute!"

"How long to the jump point?" Josh asked.

"Two minutes," Loki replied.

"*Jump!*" Corporal Amund grunted in the throes of hand-to-hand, zero-gravity combat.

"I've got red lights!" Loki announced. "Starboard side, dorsal!"

"How many?" Deliza demanded.

"Two...no, three...... It keeps changing!"

"*JUMP!*" the corporal repeated, the sounds of weapons fire nearly drowning out his orders.

"It's still a minute and a half to the jump point!" Josh reminded the corporal. "Lok, lock those damned emitters down!"

"I can't!"

"*We can't hold that long!*" the corporal insisted. "*You've got to jump before those other ships reach us!*"

"If we jump with more than two emitters..."

"I know!" Loki said, interrupting Deliza.

"*DO IT NOW!*" the corporal ordered.

"SHIT!" Josh declared, pressing the jump button on his flight control stick.

"Oh, God," Loki muttered as six red lights appeared on the emitter status display.

CHAPTER NINE

Terig came out of the bathroom, a towel over his head as he vigorously dried his hair. "Is that you, hon?" he called, hearing the sound of a door close. When there was no answer, he stopped drying his hair, removing the towel to hear better. "Dori?" He listened intently for a moment, becoming concerned when he still didn't hear anything. He set the towel down on the counter and headed into the bedroom, but still saw no one. He headed for the next room, sure he would find his wife on a call with one of her friends, like usual, unable to answer him.

"Oh, my God," he exclaimed with a start when he entered the living room. Sitting there were Lieutenant Commander Jessica Nash and a steely-eyed man he did not recognize. He swallowed hard, trying to get control of his nerves, as well as his pulse-rate. "What are you doing here?" he finally managed to ask.

"You are in grave danger, Mister Espan," General Telles stated.

"What?" Terig looked confused. "Who are you?"

"This is General Lucius Telles, leader of the Ghatazhak," Jessica told him.

"Seriously?"

"Seriously," Jessica replied.

"Uh, I'm honored, sir..."

"You must prepare for immediate departure," the general said.

"Departure from where, *Takara*? How am I supposed to get off Takara? How did *you* get *on* Takara for that matter?" Terig closed his eyes for a moment, shaking his hands. "This has something to do with the relay site going down, doesn't it? Oh, my

God, I knew it!" he exclaimed, starting to pace about the room in a panic. "I haven't been able to sleep for nearly a week! I'm always looking over my shoulder! Everyone I see looks like they're a Dusahn agent! My *wife* thinks I'm *losing* it!"

Jessica looked at General Telles. "She may be right."

"What?" Terig asked, not quite sure he had heard her correctly.

"Nevertheless, we have an obligation to protect him," the general replied to Jessica.

"I can't just go," Terig argued.

"Your parents died when you were young, and your wife's parents died nine years ago, during the battle to defeat Caius Ta'Akar," General Telles explained. "Neither of you has significant ties to this world."

Terig looked to Jessica, stunned. "How does he..." He looked back at the general. "...How do you know all that?"

"I'm a general."

Jessica nodded. "He is."

General Telles reached into his coat pocket, pulling out a small device, which he activated and placed on the table.

"*It seems that Mister Espan has outlived his usefulness.*" Although somewhat distant and tinny, the voice of Lord Mahtize was unmistakable. "*It is time that we dispose of him.*"

"*I will see to it, personally,*" the other voice said.

"That's Damon Holub, the chief of House Mahtize security," Terig said, his eyes widening as he stopped pacing, concentrating on the recording.

"*It would be best if we dispose of his wife, as well,*"

Lord Mahtize added. "*She could ask uncomfortable questions.*"

"*We should thoroughly sweep his residence, as well as his accounts on the net, just to be sure he hasn't stashed any incriminating evidence to protect himself.*"

"*I doubt he is clever enough to think of such things, but I suppose it would be best.*"

Terig plopped down on the sofa, suddenly feeling drained. "He's right, I didn't."

"*When?*" Damon asked.

"*As soon as possible,*" Lord Mahtize instructed.

"*It will be completed tonight, my lord.*"

General Telles turned the device off, placing it back in his pocket.

"When did you get that?" Terig wondered.

"This morning," the general replied.

Terig sat in disbelief. His life was crashing down around him. "*How* did you get that?" Terig wondered. "His office is bug proof."

"The *method* is unimportant," the general replied. "Only the content."

Terig cast a puzzled look the general's way.

"He means it doesn't matter, Terig," Jessica explained. "It's time to go."

"What about my wife?" Terig wondered.

"She can come, as well," Jessica promised.

"How are you going to get us off Takara?" Terig asked. "Ever since the Teyentah, everyone traveling off-world is *thoroughly* checked, and I mean *thoroughly.*"

"Again, the method is unimportant," General Telles said, growing impatient.

"*Terig!*" his wife called from the back door as it opened. "*I brought benta pies from Elle's!*"

"Oh, my God, what am I going to tell her?" Terig said, jumping to his feet, back in panic mode.

"How about the truth," Jessica suggested.

"You've never been married, have you?" Terig said, lowering his voice. "She'll kill me."

"She may think you're a brave man," General Telles suggested.

"Also never been married," Terig decided, shaking his finger at the general. He spun around as his wife entered the room. "Sweetie!" he said, suddenly turning on the affection. "You're just in time."

"What's going on?" Dori asked, spotting the two new faces in her living room and wondering why her husband was acting so strange.

"These are two of my friends, Lucius Telles and Jessica Nash."

"That was a mistake," Jessica mumbled, standing along with the general.

"This is my wife, Dori."

"A pleasure to meet you both," Dori said, shaking the general's hand. She reached for Jessica's hand, a curious look on her face. "You look familiar. Are you coworkers of Terig's?"

"In a manner of speaking, yes," General Telles confirmed.

"Nash..." Dori said, still trying to remember where she had heard the name before.

Terig looked as white as a ghost.

Jessica rolled her eyes, taking control of the situation. "You probably remember me as the one who killed Caius Ta'Akar."

Now Dori's eyes widened. "Oh, my God," she exclaimed, her hands covering her mouth. She looked at her husband. "Terig, what's going on here? Why are these people in our..."

"I can explain," Terig assured her, practically pleading.

"It would probably be easier if I explained it," Jessica suggested.

Terig looked at her, his eyes wide with panic.

"Back when you two were on the Mystic Empress, your husband volunteered to use his position in House Mahtize to collect intelligence on the Dusahn and relay it to us."

"He what?" She looked at Terig. "Where was I?"

"You were unconscious, sweetie," Terig defended.

"So, instead of staying by my side, you decided to put our lives in danger—*again*—by volunteering to be a *spy*?"

"In my defense, the first danger was not of my doing," Terig insisted.

"Miss Espan," General Telles said, interrupting Terig, "your husband did an incredibly brave thing."

"You mean an incredibly *stupid* thing!" she argued, smacking Terig on the shoulder. "How could you?"

"I was only trying to do the right thing," Terig insisted.

"Oh, my God," she said, suddenly realizing something. "That's what all those molo candles were about?"

"Dori, let me explain..."

"As much as I'd love to watch you try to talk your way out of this, Terig, we don't have time. We need to go, now," Jessica insisted.

"Go?" Dori asked. "Go where?" She looked at Terig. "Where are you going, Terig?"

"Where are *we* going," Terig corrected. He looked at Jessica. "Where *are* we going?"

"I'm not going anywhere," Dori insisted. "I have to go to work in the morning!"

"We're taking you back to the Aurora and the rest of the fleet," Jessica explained.

"The hell you are!" Dori argued.

"Dori, please!" Terig pleaded, raising his voice for the first time. "Lord Mahtize is going to have us both killed."

"Why would *Mahtize* have us killed?" his wife demanded.

"Because he figured out what I was doing and began *feeding* me intel to send to them. When the relay site closed down, he somehow must have found out, and now he wants to kill *me*, so I can't tell the Dusahn that *he* was involved, as well!"

"But why would he want to kill me?"

"Because he fears that when your husband is killed, you'll ask too many questions," Jessica explained. "And he knows that neither of you have any family who will do so if *both* of you are killed. Hell, he'll probably make it look like you both died at the same time. Maybe even a murder-suicide."

"Oh, my God!" Dori exclaimed, yet again. "Terig!"

"I'm sorry!"

"Look!" Jessica interrupted, growing tired of all the drama. "We don't have time for all this. You two can hash it out later, once we're safely back on the Aurora."

"Maybe you're wrong," Dori stated.

"I heard Mahtize give the order," Terig told her. "He's sending Damon to do it."

"The guy from the party? The guy with the black, spiked hair and scary eyes?"

"Yeah."

"Oh, my God!"

"Look, are you two coming willingly or..." Jessica finally demanded.

"No, we're not!" Dori insisted.

"We're going!" Terig argued. He looked at his wife, putting both hands on her cheeks. "Look, Dori, I'm sorry I got us involved in all of this, I really am, but what's done is done. We have to go...right now."

"I can knock her out, if it'll speed things up," Jessica suggested.

Terig looked at her. "Not helping." He looked back at his wife. "I'm begging you, Dori. I can't leave without you. I'd rather stay here and die *with* you."

Dori looked into her husband's eyes. "What are we going to do?"

"We'll figure something out," Terig promised. "We always do."

"We'll set you both up nicely on another world," General Telles promised. "Good jobs, a nice place to live, everything you need."

Dori leaned forward, putting her arms around her husband, burying her face in his chest. "Okay, I'll go," she finally conceded.

"Great," Jessica said. "Grab what you need, quickly, the less the better."

"She is all I need," Terig said, kissing the top of Dori's head.

Dori pulled away from her husband, taking his hand with her right hand, and clasping at the locket hanging around her neck with her left hand. "I have all I need, as well."

"You will need coats," General Telles told them. "It is chilly where we are going."

Terig nodded and led his wife toward the bedroom to grab their coats.

"Touching, wasn't it?" General Telles commented.

Jessica just looked at him, one eyebrow raised.

* * *

Corporal Amund was thrown against the bulkhead, then to the deck, as the Seiiki violently bucked about. Air rushed through the corridor, threatening to suck him out the back of the ship. Sunlight spilled in from somewhere aft, but he didn't know where. "Torlak!" he called over his helmet comms but got no answer. "Anyone!" Again, no answer.

He glanced at his environmental readings on his tactical visor. There was oxygen around him, but it was too thin to breathe. Fortunately, his suit pressure seemed stable.

The rushing air subsided, and he managed to get to his feet, despite the violent shaking of the ship that was constantly trying to knock him over. Bracing himself against the bulkhead, he peered through the hatchway into the main cabin, not prepared for what he saw.

The starboard side of the main cabin was gone, as well as half of its aft bulkhead. From his vantage point, it appeared that the entire starboard wing and engine nacelle were also missing. There was no tearing of metal, or twisting of frames, and no dangling wires or conduit. It was as if that part of the ship had been cut cleanly away.

Shit.

The corporal struggled forward a few steps, moving into the pass-thru galley to get to the starboard side. When he reached it, he found his comrade lying on the deck, clutching the hatchway with all his might, the entire lower half of his body gone, severed cleanly at the waist.

The look on Corporal Torlak's face was one of complete anguish, one that Corporal Amund had never seen. His friend stared at him, his eyes pleading to be put out of his misery. At that moment, he knew what he had to do.

In one smooth, fluid motion, Corporal Amund pulled out his sidearm and took aim at his friend's neck, and fired. His shot found the weakest point in the Ghatazhak armor, obliterating the dying corporal's neck and ending his suffering. The doomed soldier released his grip, slid across the deck and out the gaping hole, into the atmosphere of whatever world they had jumped to.

"FUCK!" Josh cursed, struggling to gain some semblance of control as the Seiiki plummeted deeper into the atmosphere. "I've got no controls! We're falling like a fucking rock!"

"I'm trying to send power to your thrusters by cross-circuiting all batteries to them!" Deliza reported.

"I'm not getting any readings from the starboard engine nacelle!" Loki added as the ship continued to shake violently. As if someone had whispered in his ear, Loki suddenly turned to his right, looking out the window toward the starboard nacelle. His eyes widened. "The starboard nacelle is gone!"

"What?"

"It's gone! The nacelle, the wing, and part of the fuselage! All of it!"

"That explains why she doesn't want to fly straight!" Josh exclaimed.

"Mayday, Mayday, Mayday," Loki called over his comm-set. "The Seiiki is going down! Dead stick! Somewhere on Eralit Seven Delta! Six souls aboard!"

"Are you sure this is Eralit Seven Delta?" Josh wondered as he struggled to control their free fall.

"If not, the nav logs on the comm-drone will show them where we really are," Loki replied.

"I got you some power to the thrusters!" Deliza declared.

Josh tried the controls again. "It's working!" he announced. "Sort of! Can you get me more?"

"Comm-drone away!" Loki announced. "I hope."

"I'll try to tap what's left in the jump banks!"

"I'm gonna need a place to land!" Josh said.

"Don't you mean crash!" Loki replied as he frantically tried to get their terrain-following sensors to work.

"I was being optimistic!" Josh exclaimed.

"Why isn't our TFS working?" Loki wondered.

"The TFS pod was in the starboard wing!" Josh explained. "We probably lost it, as well!"

"Shit!"

"Just look out the fucking window, Lok!"

Loki strained to see outside. "We're still too high to make out any details!"

"I've tapped the jump banks!" Deliza announced.

Josh tried again to get control of the ship but found there was only marginal improvement. "Son of a bitch!" he cursed. "All I've got is a little lateral control, no pitch control whatsoever, and we're in a steep-ass dive. We'll never survive the impact. We've gotta separate and ride the chute down."

"What about the others?" Naralena asked.

"Amund! Torlak! Get your asses to the cockpit! Pronto!" Josh ordered. After a moment, he called again. "Amund! Torlak!"

"Why aren't they answering?" Naralena wondered.

"How the fuck do I know!"

"If they were in the main cabin when the jump cut it open..." Deliza began.

"They were probably sucked out into space or into the atmo after the jump!" Loki concluded.

"We don't know that!" Naralena argued. "I'll go back and look!"

"Are you nuts?" Josh exclaimed.

"You can't!" Loki told her. "We're still too high! The atmosphere is too thin! You open that door, and we'll all suffocate!"

"But we can't just leave them out there!"

"We don't even know if they're alive!" Josh argued.

"Amund! Torlak!" Loki called over his comm-set. "If you can hear me, get to the cockpit hatch and stand by! Once we get low enough, we'll pop the hatch and let you in. We're going to have to separate and ride the chute down!" He glanced out the forward windows again, trying to judge their rate of descent as best he could. "You have a minute, maybe two! We'll wait as long as we can, but if you don't get to the hatch, we'll have to eject without you!"

"Can you get me anything else?" Josh asked Deliza.

"There's nothing else to tap into," she replied.

"I see water!" Loki announced as they fell through a cloud bank. "An ocean, maybe. Can you steer us that way and follow the coast?"

"I can fucking try!" Josh replied, struggling with his flight control stick to get their wounded ship to comply. "You sure it's going to be big enough?"

"It's huge!" Loki assured him. "Keep us close to shore, and we can ride the chute down to the water and swim to shore."

Josh frowned at Loki.

"What?" Loki asked.

"I'm not much of a swimmer," he admitted.

"There's a life raft in the bulkhead compartment, right behind your seat, Josh."

"There is?"

"Jesus! How long have you been flying this thing?"

"Ditching in the water was never an issue!" Josh defended as the ship continued to fall toward the surface.

"Oh, my God!" Naralena exclaimed. "There's somebody at the hatch!" she added, moving to the hatch in the deck at the back of the cockpit.

"Who is it?" Loki asked.

"I can't tell!" Naralena replied.

"Only one?"

"Yes!"

"I think it's Corporal Amund!" Deliza exclaimed, peering through the window in the deck next to the hatch.

"Think we're low enough?" Josh wondered.

"I don't know," Loki replied, shaking his head. "I don't see that we have a choice, though." Loki turned to look at Deliza and Naralena. "Take several deep breaths, and then blow everything out of your lungs!"

Naralena and Deliza followed his instructions, as did Josh.

"Now!" Loki instructed.

Deliza blew the last of the air out of her lungs and opened the hatch. There was an immediate rush of air, indicating they were still fairly high up, as they had feared. With Naralena's help, they were able to get the hatch completely open, and Corporal Amund climbed up into the cockpit, turning around and closing it behind him.

Loki immediately reached down to the center console to flood the cabin with fresh oxygen, again.

"Where's Torlak?" Deliza asked Corporal Amund as she helped him take off his helmet.

"He didn't make it!" the corporal replied.

"Think we're slow enough for the chute?" Josh asked Loki.

Loki glanced at their dead displays, grimacing. "No idea."

"Fuck it." Josh braced himself, reaching for the ejection handle on the right side of his seat. "Everyone, hang on!" he warned. "Ejecting in three......two...... one......"

Josh twisted the handle to the left, squeezed the release lever, then yanked up on it sharply. There was a series of tiny explosions, followed by a loud *clang*, and then the firing of thrusters. At first, Josh felt himself tossed forward against his shoulder restraints, then back hard into his seat as the ejection thrusters blasted the upper portion of the Seiiki's nose, which contained the cockpit, clear of the rest of the ship. The automated system pitched the escape section upward, as if attempting to return them to space. The process slowed their rate of descent considerably, as well as their forward airspeed.

The thruster stopped, and again they found themselves free-falling. This time, however, Josh had absolutely no control over their fate. The system would either work, or not.

Suddenly, the screen directly in front of Josh lit up, but with a display he had never seen before. "YES!" he exclaimed with glee. "IT'S FUCKING WORKING!"

There was a sudden jerk, throwing him into his

shoulder restraints again. He glanced at the display screen, checking their status. "Drogue one is good!" he reported, still pushing against his restraints as the first drogue chute slowed their descent.

A few seconds later, the force against his restraints eased slightly. "Cycling!" he announced. A few more seconds, and he was again thrown forward, the restraints digging into his shoulders more forcefully than before. "Drogue two is good!"

Thirty seconds passed, and the pressure on his restraints eased again. "Cycling!" he reported as he glanced out the forward windows. The surface was getting awfully close.

Finally, after an even greater tug than before, he found himself thrown forward with so much force, he thought his shoulders would dislocate. A split second later, something gave way, and their back end seemed to fall, their nose pitching up sharply. Another snap pushed him down into his seat, and the cockpit became relatively level, with its nose a bit high, as they descended smoothly. "MAINS ARE GOOD!" he exclaimed with even more excitement than before. A message on his screen flashed, informing him that he now had steering control. Josh reached for the control stick again, twisting it left and right to test. "I've got lateral control!" he exclaimed.

"What's our rate of descent?" Loki asked.

"Eighty meters per second and falling!" Josh replied. "Three hundred KPH!"

"That's too fast," Loki warned.

"I know!" Josh replied. "I can slow us," he assured him, pulling back on his flight control stick.

Loki turned around to check on the others. "You guys alright?"

Deliza and Naralena nodded, as did Corporal Amund.

"Two-fifty," Josh reported, "sixty down."

Loki looked out the forward windows again. "I've got the coast in sight."

"I don't suppose there are any long, sandy beaches down there?" Josh asked.

"Nope."

"Two hundred, forty down." Josh looked concerned. "Winds are shifting. Crap, I've gotta turn to starboard to stay into the wind. What's the terrain like?"

"Irregular, lots of trees," Loki reported. "Can you turn around and head back? The terrain was flatter behind us."

"Not enough altitude," Josh insisted. "One-fifty forward, thirty down. It's gonna get bumpy."

Loki looked out the window one last time as they drifted over the shoreline and into the jungle. "BRACE FOR IMPACT!" he warned the others.

Several treetops brushed the underside of their escape section, before they slammed into other trees and then something far more solid.

That's when everything went black.

* * *

"*Captain, Intel,*" Lieutenant Commander Shinoda called over the intercom in the captain's ready room.

"Go ahead," Nathan replied.

"*Two of our sleeper drones have just returned. One from Palee, the other from Volon. Both have fallen to the Dusahn.*"

Nathan looked to Cameron.

"The Seiiki," Cameron said, equally concerned.

"How bad?" Nathan asked the lieutenant commander.

"Palee went down without a fight. Volon, not so much. Fighter engagements, orbit-to-surface bombardment, even firefights on the ground. What little readings we got show quite a bit of damage."

"Any sign of the Seiiki?"

"Negative, but the Volon drone arrived after the battle had already begun," the lieutenant commander replied.

"How long ago?"

"Palee looks to be several hours old. Volon only happened a few minutes ago."

"As soon as the Falcon returns, dispatch them to Volon for follow-up recon," Nathan instructed.

"Aye, sir."

"They're probably on their way back," Cameron pointed out. "Evasive returns take time."

"Let's hope," Nathan replied.

* * *

"Josh!"

There was a terrible pain in his head.

"Josh! You alive?"

He tried opening his eyes but felt something wet stinging his left eye.

"You guys alright?"

The voice sounded distant. Josh felt someone shaking his right shoulder.

"I'm okay," a female voice called from behind.

"Josh! Wake up!" Loki called, shaking him.

Josh forced his eyes open.

"Finally!" Loki exclaimed, turning to climb over Josh.

Josh's head fell to his left, the same direction that his arm was hanging. He looked around, realizing that something was askew. "What happened?"

"Naralena!" Deliza gasped, noticing that she was not responding.

"We hit something just before we landed," Loki explained.

Josh pressed the release button on his restraint harness with his right hand, and then suddenly fell to his left. "Fuck!"

"We're on our port side!" Loki told him.

"Thanks for the warning."

"Naralena's unconscious but breathing," Corporal Amund announced, checking on her.

"You're bleeding," Deliza told the corporal.

"I'm fine," he assured her as he grabbed the medical kit from the back of Josh's seat.

"Oh, my God," Deliza exclaimed. "You've got a piece of metal in your side."

"I'll be fine," Corporal Amund insisted. He glanced through the fractured forward cockpit windows, straining to make out details outside. "We need to get out of here," he added, "it may not be stable."

"Cover her up," Loki instructed, moving to the overhead emergency hatch, which was now on his left side, as he stood on the port bulkhead, facing aft.

Corporal Amund and Deliza both draped themselves over Naralena.

Loki reached over to the emergency escape hatch control panel. "It's dead," he announced. "I'm going to blow it manually." He opened the small cover and grabbed the handle, pulling it out, and twisting it. Four explosive bolts blew, and the hatch separated from the top of the cockpit, flying off to the side.

Loki pulled himself through the hatch, stepping onto the side of a fallen tree, upon which their escape section rested. "We must've hit the trees on the way down," he hollered back. He looked around a bit more, then climbed back inside. "We're stable enough for now, I think."

"Either way, we need to get moving," the corporal insisted. "The Dusahn will trace our jump, and they'll be looking for us. We need to get as far away from here as we can, before they arrive. The greater the distance we cover, the less our chances of capture."

"That's reason enough for me," Josh agreed as he struggled to get to his feet in the sideways cockpit.

"What about Naralena?" Deliza asked.

"I gave her an injection of tekemine and general trauma nanites," the corporal replied. "She should awaken shortly."

"What about you?" Josh asked, pointing to the piece of metal protruding from the corporal's right side.

Corporal Amund pulled a small spray canister out of the medical kit, then reached down and yanked the piece of metal from his side, barely grimacing in the process. "I'll be fine," he assured them, again, as he sprayed the gaping wound with the fixative.

"I didn't need to see that," Josh declared as he moved toward the escape hatch.

* * *

A blue-white flash lit up the tiny cave, and the thunderous clap that followed a split second later echoed through the narrow canyon outside. Sergeant Olivo glanced at the time on his comm-unit.

"Right on time," he said to himself as he rose from the rock serving as his seat for the last four hours. He could already hear the scream of the Reaper's thrusters while he exited his temporary refuge.

He paused momentarily at the exit, glancing left and right, scanning the distant tree line for any sign of danger as the Reaper touched down not thirty meters away.

Two Ghatazhak jumped out, taking up firing positions on either side of the Reaper, sweeping their weapons left and right as they, too, searched the area for danger.

The sergeant jogged toward the waiting Reaper, its engines spinning down to idle.

"Heard you need a ride, Sarge," the nearest Ghatazhak soldier greeted as his cohort approached.

"Just as I was getting used to the place," the sergeant commented as he climbed up into the Reaper.

Both soldiers climbed inside immediately after the sergeant, and the Reaper's engines spun back up, causing it to lift off the ground.

"At least you didn't have to do the full tour," the soldier said as he closed the hatch.

The solider on the other side closed his hatch, as well, while the Reaper continued to climb and began to move forward.

"Thank God. I don't think I could stand making any more of those damned molo twine," the sergeant said as the Reaper jumped away.

* * *

"Isn't there an easier route?" Deliza wondered as they slogged up the center of the creek. "Maybe something on dry land and, I don't know, *downhill*?"

"None of you knows how to cross terrain *without* leaving a trail for others to follow," Corporal Amund explained as he led them up the waterway, "and the Dusahn would *expect* us to go downhill."

"Who cares if we leave a trail?" Josh argued. "They'll find us with sensors, anyway."

"These mountains have something in them that

may interfere with their sensors," the corporal told him. "The range of my tactical sensors has been limited since we crashed."

"You sure they're not just broken?" Josh mused.

"I am certain."

"Of course, you are," Josh muttered, splashing through the water behind them.

Corporal Amund paused, turning around to glare at him. "Try not to splash too much."

"Why? It's just water."

"The temperature is low, and the air is humid. There is also no direct sunlight on this side of the mountain. The rocks you are wetting will not dry for hours, and with the sun about to set, they could stay wet throughout the night."

"Seriously, they're going to track us by wet rocks in a river?"

"Our job was to keep you all alive," Corporal Amund said. "Corporal Torlak died doing just that, so your cooperation would be greatly appreciated, Mister Hayes."

"Sorry," Josh apologized sheepishly. "It's been a rough day."

"It is quite alright," Corporal Amund assured him. "While you may lack the training befitting our current situation, it is unlikely that *any* of us would be alive, were it not for the skill of you and Mister Sheehan. For that, you should both be commended."

Josh stood there silently as the corporal turned around and continued up the creek. He looked at Loki. "Well, now I just feel like a dick."

"You should be used to it by now," Deliza teased as she passed by him. "Speaking of nightfall, shouldn't we be thinking about finding shelter for the night?"

"This world gets pretty cold at night," Loki added.

"We must continue," Corporal Amund insisted. "We can rest periodically, if required, but only briefly."

"We aren't Ghatazhak," Deliza reminded the corporal.

"And we don't have Ghatazhak super-suits," Josh added.

"While I agree with your strategy of using the creek to cover our departure route," Deliza continued, "by now, we should be far enough from the crash site that the benefit of making better time outweighs that of masking our trail."

Corporal Amund paused again, sighing. "An astute observation," he admitted. "Everyone, take a break. I will scout ahead a bit so that, once you are ready to continue, we will be able to make better time, as you suggested."

Without another word, the corporal exited the creek and darted off through the dense forest with surprising speed.

"We really have to get suits like that," Josh insisted as he climbed out of the creek.

"How long do you think it will take for our distress call to reach the Aurora?" Naralena asked as she sat down on the fallen log next to Josh.

"At least half a day," Loki said, helping Deliza climb out of the creek.

"Why so long?" Naralena wondered.

"The Dusahn are really good at tracking jump courses, so we use special evasive algorithms both to and from the fleet. The jump comm-drone uses the same algorithms."

"How long does it take the Dusahn to trace a jump route?" she wondered.

"I'm surprised they haven't already found us," Josh admitted.

"If they are trying to capture every inhabited world in the Pentaurus sector, they may lack the resources to track us," Loki told her.

"Perhaps they just don't care about a single little ship," Naralena suggested hopefully.

"Doubtful," Josh insisted. "I'm afraid the Seiiki has poked that dragon quite a few times."

"Knowing you, I'm not surprised," Naralena said.

"Hey, don't look at me," Josh defended. "It was Conathan's decision."

Naralena looked confused. "Conathan?"

"A long story," Deliza said.

"You really have to stop calling him that, Josh," Loki scolded.

* * *

"This is becoming a habit," Nathan stated as he entered the intel shack.

"My call," Cameron told him. "I figured you'd want to see this."

"What's up?" Nathan wondered, stepping up next to Cameron, across the plotting table from Lieutenant Commander Shinoda.

"As you know, we've got recon drones jumping in and out of every system in the Pentaurus sector," the lieutenant commander began, "and twice as frequently now that the Dusahn have begun to expand their territory. Thing is, the Dusahn pretty much know this, and there's not much they can do about it. Occasionally, they get a lucky shot, but..."

"Yeah, I understand," Nathan told him.

"Point is, they gave up trying to conceal anything from our recon drones. However, while extracting Sergeant Olivo from Haven, Reaper Six picked up something interesting, just before they jumped out of Haven's atmosphere." The lieutenant commander called up the sensor data, displaying it on the table between them.

"A cargo ship?" Nathan said, unimpressed.

"Not just *any* cargo ship," the lieutenant commander replied. "The Tentibol."

"*Really*," Nathan replied, appearing far more interested.

"And Jamaya is in the *opposite* direction."

"The Dusahn," Nathan realized.

"That's what we were thinking," Cameron agreed.

"There have been a total of three ships, not including the Tentibol, that arrived in the Rogen system more than a few hours late," the lieutenant commander reminded them. "How much you want to bet they all end up in Dusahn-held space, just like the Tentibol."

"I'll keep my credits, thanks," Nathan replied. "It appears the Dusahn have found a way to keep an eye on us."

"There's more," Cameron said. "We detected several warships about two light years outside the Takar system."

"*Dusahn* warships, I'm assuming."

"Not by the looks of them," Lieutenant Commander Shinoda said. "However, they have been running jump comm-drones between themselves and Takara so, wherever they came from, they're either *allies* of the Dusahn or ships that were *commandeered* by them."

"Why leave them parked out in the middle of nowhere?" Nathan wondered.

"So we wouldn't find them," Cameron said, as if it were obvious.

"But we did," Nathan said, sounding suspicious.

"Again, by a fluke," the lieutenant commander pointed out. "To cover the increased demand for recon jumps, we've had to come up with some creative routing, sending recon drones to several different systems before returning to the fleet. Many of those routes were considerably off the *beaten path*, if you will. *That's* why we found those ships."

"Looks like lady luck has been on our side twice, today," Cameron mused.

"*Intel, Comms,*" the voice called over the intercom speaker in the overhead.

Lieutenant Commander Shinoda reached up. "Go for Intel."

"*You asked to be notified if any ships arrived late, sir.*"

The lieutenant commander looked at the captain. "Whattaya got?"

"*A water tanker out of Treves Alpha Four, the Raffaelle.*"

"She a regular?" the lieutenant commander asked.

"*Aye, sir. According to Rakuen Port Authority, the Raffaelle was in port two weeks ago. The Rakuens sell seawater to them on a regular basis, for use in their fusion reactors.*"

"How late?" Nathan wondered.

"How late, Ensign?"

"*Six hours, sir. They claimed they were trying to conserve propellant.*"

"That's a new one," Cameron commented.

"At least the Dusahn are trying to be creative," Nathan mused.

"Thank you, Ensign," the lieutenant commander said, reaching up to turn the intercom off.

"Wait," Nathan said. "Comms, Captain. Flash

traffic for Rogen Defense Command and the fleet. Set all forces to readiness-condition two."

"*REDCON Two, aye,*" the ensign replied. "*Reason?*"

"The Aurora is leaving the system and will be gone for approximately four days. And send the message using code Two Five Echo."

"*Confirming Two Five Echo, sir.*"

"Two Five Echo, confirmed," Nathan replied.

"*Two Five Echo, aye.*"

"Captain, Two Five Echo is one of our weakest encryption algorithms," Lieutenant Commander Shinoda warned. "My kid sister could break that code."

"Let's hope," Nathan replied. He looked at Cameron, recognizing the confused look on her face. "As soon as everyone is at REDCON Two, take the Aurora to point Alpha Six Tango, but make your first jump directly toward Takara. Have all four Cobra gunships do the same."

"Are you sure about this?" Cameron asked, finally catching on to his plan.

"Sure about what?" Lieutenant Commander Shinoda wondered, confused.

"When lady luck smiles on you three times, you'd better bet big," Nathan replied, turning to exit.

Lieutenant Commander Shinoda still hadn't caught on. "Do *you* have any idea what he's up to?" he asked Cameron.

"Actually, yes," she replied. "And that's what scares me."

* * *

Three tramway connections, two cab rides, and a bit of walking had finally gotten General Telles, Jessica, and the Espans to their destination.

"A boat ride was not what I was expecting," Terig

commented as he watched the dock disappear from view behind them.

"It's a beautiful night, is it not?" General Telles said. "And a boat ride for two couples out on the town is not unusual for this time of year."

"I suppose not."

"*Five minutes*," the boat pilot called down from the steering bridge.

Jessica pulled out her comm-unit and sent a message.

Terig looked forward. No land was in sight. "Five minutes until what?"

"Until we get you both off of Takara," Jessica replied.

"On a *boat*?"

"On a submarine, actually," she answered, smiling.

"A submarine?" Terig looked at his wife in disbelief.

"I was expecting more security checkpoints," General Telles commented. "Has the Dusahn presence on Takara always been this light?"

"Actually, no," Terig replied, "only in the last week, or so. The last message I was trying to send—the one that didn't go through—was about a lot of Dusahn troops being taken off Takara."

"Any idea where they were going?" Jessica asked.

"None," Terig admitted. "Some think it is just a trick to make the population more complacent, so the Dusahn might lure those who are against the occupation out into the open."

"You *know* of such people?"

"Not personally," Terig replied. "I've heard rumors of secret meetings, mostly by anti-nobility radicals."

"There's a guy at my work who's always

complaining about the Dusahn," Dori told them. "He meets with a group of men for lunch at the café, on the street in front of the offices on Bainor, but they always get quiet when I walk by."

"No one would openly speak out against the Dusahn," Terig explained. "A few did in the beginning and were publicly executed without even a hearing. Just shot on the street."

"Most people think the nobles are cooperating with the Dusahn because they are making greater profit by doing so," Dori added.

"That's how they do it," Jessica explained. "Ensure the profits of the powerful, keeping the economy strong, and the people will put up with just about anything."

"The Dusahn offer the illusion of safety and prosperity," General Telles explained. "You'd be surprised how cheaply liberty can be purchased."

"*Port bow, about a hundred meters,*" the pilot called out.

"Wait, *he's* with you?" Terig realized, pointing at the boat pilot.

"You think you're the only operative on Takara?" Jessica said, moving to the port side to prepare.

Terig looked shocked.

"It is not only the younger, anti-nobility radicals who oppose the Dusahn," General Telles stated. "Their ranks are more diverse than you might think."

Terig moved closer to the port side as the boat idled its engines, coasting the last few meters. In the murky waters, he spotted a small, black object sticking out above the surface. As they drifted closer, he realized Jessica hadn't been joking. "That really *is* a submarine."

"Of course, it is," Jessica replied as she climbed

over the rail. The boat pulled up alongside the sleek, black submarine, and Jessica jumped over to its narrow foredeck, grabbing onto its canopy rail to keep from sliding off into the moonlit water.

"Am I missing something, here?" Terig asked General Telles.

"That ship will jump the three of you a few light years into space, where you will be picked up by one of our ships and taken back to the Aurora for debrief," General Telles explained.

"You're joking."

"I never joke," General Telles replied. "I am Ghatazhak."

Terig looked down at the sub. Jessica had already opened the hatch and lowered herself inside, her torso still above the hatch. "You've done this before, I take it."

"How do you think we *got* here?" Jessica replied. "Let's go. We've only got three minutes until the next satellite pass."

"You first," Dori insisted.

Terig climbed over the rail and stepped down onto the sub's foredeck, grabbing the handrail, and then reaching out for his wife's hand. Dori was next, stepping even more carefully over. Within seconds, the two of them had descended into the tiny jump sub's interior, disappearing from sight.

"How long?" Jessica asked the general as she stood halfway out of the jump sub's hatch.

"I cannot say," General Telles replied.

"I'll send it back to the same spot, no more than two days from now," she promised.

"That should suffice."

"Good luck, sir," she said, after which she dropped down inside the jump sub and closed the hatch.

"Take us back, Josa," the general ordered the pilot as he watched the jump sub disappear beneath the moonlit surface.

* * *

As expected, the temperature had dropped quickly after the sun had gone down, yet, despite their objections, Corporal Amund had insisted that they continue for as long as possible.

"I'm freezing," Deliza complained as they moved slowly and carefully through the dense forest, continuing up the side of the mountain.

"There is a cave not far from here," Corporal Amund promised. "A few minutes at the most."

"How do you know?" Deliza wondered.

"Yeah, I thought your tactical sensors weren't working," Josh added.

"I scouted the entire area while you were resting," the corporal replied.

"The *entire* area?" Josh asked in disbelief.

"That was two hours ago," Loki said.

"We only rested for ten minutes," Deliza insisted. "You covered everywhere between here and there in *ten minutes*?"

"It was fifteen minutes, and it was from there to ten minutes *beyond* here," the corporal corrected, "not to mention at least a click to either side."

"Unbelievable," Naralena exclaimed.

"I move quickly," the corporal said, "and in your defense, it was still light out at the time."

"Thanks," Josh replied dryly.

"There," the corporal announced, pointing ahead, "behind those trees." The corporal quickened his pace slightly.

"How can he even see that far in the darkness?" Naralena wondered.

"Super-Ghatazhak night vision, no doubt," Josh mumbled.

The corporal disappeared behind the trees, appearing again a moment later. "This is it!" he shouted, gesturing for them to come toward him.

"Thank God," Deliza exclaimed.

Loki stopped at the trees, waiting to help Naralena and Deliza down the small drop on the other side.

"The drop should prevent any sensors from seeing the cave entrance," Corporal Amund stated as they entered the cave. "Once inside, you may turn your lanterns on."

"If the rocks keep the sensors from working, then it doesn't matter," Josh pointed out, trying to be smart.

"Just because *my* sensors are affected, does not guarantee that the Dusahn's will be, as well," the corporal pointed out.

A flash of blue-white light appeared on the horizon, followed by the sound of distant thunder.

"I don't suppose that was just lightning," Josh said.

"I'm afraid not," Corporal Amund said with a sigh. "I was hoping it would take them longer."

"How long do you think we have?" Loki wondered.

"It depends on what they locate first," the corporal said, "where the ship went down or where we landed."

"As well as *if* their sensors are affected by the rocks, like yours," Josh noted.

"Use your weapons on their lowest settings to heat some rocks to warm the cave," the corporal instructed.

"If their sensors are working, they'll pick up the energy signatures," Loki warned.

"Hopefully, they will not be scanning in our

direction just yet," the corporal replied. "Besides, if we do not, we will likely freeze to death before *anyone* finds us."

"You're just a ray of sunshine, aren't you," Josh complained, following Loki toward the cave entrance. He stopped a moment, looking back at the corporal. "What about you?"

"I will stand watch."

"I can relieve you later, if you like."

"Thank you, but that will not be necessary," the corporal assured him. "Ghatazhak can go many days without sleep."

"How long can you go without pissing?" Josh wondered, a wry smile on his face.

Corporal Amund looked at Josh. "Not nearly as long," he replied, smiling.

* * *

"Production has begun at the first jump missile plant on Rakuen," Cameron stated.

Nathan looked up from his data pad. "Already?"

"The Rakuens have been working around the clock. The first missiles should start rolling off the line in about a week."

"What about Neramese?" Nathan wondered.

"Their first plant should come online in a few days," Cameron replied. "However, they already have two launchers in place, and the Rakuens don't have any yet."

"What about the Orochi?"

"Still another two weeks until the first one is ready to launch," Cameron said. "They've decided to take one of the ships—the one in the worst shape—and turn it into a training simulator. They'll start training mixed crews on her sometime next week."

"That should be interesting," Nathan commented,

setting his data pad on his desk. "Have they picked captains yet?"

"Not yet. They're still arguing about the selection criteria."

"How reassuring," Nathan said, leaning back in his chair, staring at the blank view screen on the wall.

"It's only been twelve hours, Nathan," Cameron said, noticing his distraction. "They're probably still in evasive transit."

"I know."

Jessica entered the captain's ready room, still wearing her Takaran civilian attire. "You guys having a party without me?"

"Welcome back," Cameron greeted, looking over her shoulder. "Nice outfit."

"The latest in Takaran women's wear," Jessica replied, rotating from side to side, to show off her outfit. "Perfect for an evening on the town or a jump sub ride into space. By the way, what's with the new location?"

"We discovered that the Dusahn are using captured cargo ships to spy on the Rogen system," Cameron explained.

"So, you moved the Aurora out and left the fleet behind?"

"His idea," Cameron replied, nodding toward Nathan on the other side of the desk.

"An ambush?"

"We'll see," Nathan replied. "I take it everything went well?"

"Terig Espan and his wife are in medical, getting cleared, as we speak," she replied, plopping down on the ready room couch, like usual. "Picked up a lot of useful intel, as well."

"Such as?" Nathan asked, eager for a better distraction than the daily progress reports on the state of Rogen defenses.

"We paid a visit to Terig's employer, Lord Mahtize. Downloaded his personal files. By the way, remind me to thank Deliza. The hack she gave us worked like a charm." Jessica paused, noticing the look on both their faces. "Did I miss something?"

"Volon was attacked," Cameron explained. "The Seiiki is overdue."

"How long?"

"Twelve hours," Nathan replied.

"They're probably still in evasive, then."

"That's what I keep telling him," Cameron insisted.

"Tell me more about this intel," Nathan said, wanting to change the subject.

"Well, for starters, the nobles are doing deals with the Dusahn right and left, each trying to undercut the other; absolutely no honor among thieves. I tell you, those guys make Earth politicians look like choir boys."

"Then the Dusahn are attempting to win over the Takarans with booming economies," Cameron concluded.

"And they're doing a bang-up job of it," Jessica agreed.

"Anything about these attacks?" Nathan wondered.

"Only that they are all being done by a single assault ship. The *Penta-ben.*"

"Escorts?" Cameron wondered.

"A handful of gunships and some octos. But get this: there are only *two* warships stationed in the Takar system at the moment, a cruiser and a battleship. You got any intel on the other systems in the cluster?"

"A single battleship in the Darvano system, and another cruiser in Taroa," Cameron replied.

"That leaves eight ships unaccounted for," Jessica realized.

"It gets worse," Cameron said, handing her data pad to Jessica.

"What are these?" she wondered, examining the data pad. "These aren't Dusahn ships."

"No, but they *are* parked in the middle of Dusahn territory," Cameron replied.

"*And* they are in constant contact with the Dusahn on Takara," Nathan added.

"Allies?"

"Possibly."

Jessica looked at Nathan. "You think they're trying to sucker us into attacking Takara directly. That's why they're attacking the other worlds in the Pentaurus cluster."

"We see them as spread too thin, we attack, they jump us with ships they think we don't know about and, at the same time, they attack our fleet and flatten the Rogen system," Nathan explained.

"It's quite clever, actually," Cameron admitted.

"They're basically doubling down," Nathan continued. "If we attack them and survive, they squash our support base while we're gone, so we're still out of the game. If we *don't* take the bait, they can still send the bulk of their fleet, *including* these new ships, to attack the Rogen system, in which case they will overpower us."

"Aren't you kind of *forcing* them to attack by being *away* from the Rogen system?"

"Actually, I'm using *their* trap to split their forces, thereby preventing an all..."

"*Captain, Comms. Flash traffic,*" the intercom interrupted.

Nathan pressed the intercom button. "Go ahead."

"*Distress call from the Seiiki, sir,*" Ensign deBanco reported. Without missing a beat, the ensign put the recorded call through the intercom. "*Mayday, Mayday, Mayday,*" Loki's voice called over the intercom. "*The Seiiki is going down! Dead stick! Somewhere on Eralit Seven Delta! Six souls aboard!*"

Nathan's expression suddenly soured. "Coded and time-stamped?"

"Code is verified. Message was sent eleven hours and forty-seven minutes ago. Position and flight data were included in the message. They were basically dead stick, sir. Half their starboard side was missing, including the starboard engine nacelle."

"Stand by one," Nathan ordered, pressing the mute button. "What do we have on the ready line?" he asked Cameron.

"Reaper Six is about it," she replied. "All the other Reapers are being used for stealth detection patrol."

"Want a few extra guns?" Jessica asked.

"No room," Nathan replied, rising from his seat. "Six aboard the Seiiki, and a Reaper only holds eight in the back."

"I guess it's just the two of us, then," Jessica said, also rising.

"Hold on," Cameron objected, looking at Nathan. "You're not going."

"Actually, I am," Nathan insisted, coming around his desk to head out.

"Nathan," Cameron said, standing and grabbing his arm as he passed. "We're sitting out here for a *reason*, remember? If the Dusahn attack, your place is here."

"The Dusahn are just now getting the message," Nathan insisted. "It's going to take them at least two days to get their ships into position to attack."

"Assuming they haven't already moved them," Cameron argued. "You can't go."

"That's my *ship* that went down," Nathan told her. "My *family*."

"I know, but..."

"But nothing, *I'm going*," Nathan told her.

"And if the Dusahn attack while you're gone?" she asked as he headed for the exit, with Jessica hot on his heels.

"Then you'll kick their asses," Nathan replied. He stepped through the exit, calling to the comms officer as he passed. "Notify Reaper Six to prepare for immediate takeoff," he instructed.

"Mission package?"

"Hot SAR, with two additional shooters," Cameron ordered for him.

Nathan turned to head out of the bridge, stopping to look at Cameron.

"I've got the conn, right?"

"Right."

"Then, let me handle it," she told him. "Get to the hangar bay. Everything you need will be waiting for you."

Nathan flashed a smile as he disappeared through the aft exit.

"See you soon," Jessica promised as she passed Cameron and turned to follow Nathan out the exit.

"Make sure you do," she replied. "Flight Ops, XO," she said, tapping her comm-set. "Fit Reaper Six for SAR, carrying two shooters, rescue for six. Best arms package."

"*Hot LZ?*" the dispatcher at flight ops asked.

"Unknown," she replied. "Highly probable."

"*Aye. Ready in five.*"

"Make it three," she insisted.

* * *

The young Dusahn lieutenant ran through the gardens of the Dusahn palace. Once the home of the ruling house of Takara, it now served as Lord Dusahn's personal residence and headquarters of the Dusahn Empire.

The lieutenant ran down the walkway, through the rose garden, pausing momentarily at the intersection, searching for his superiors. "My lord!" he shouted, spotting them in the distance. He continued running toward them, slowing as he grew closer. "My lord! Word has come!" he exclaimed, panting as he came to a stop.

"Lieutenant!" General Hesson scolded.

"Apologies, General. I knew you would want word. The Aurora has left the Rogen system," the lieutenant explained, handing the data pad to the general.

"Thank you, Lieutenant," the general said, taking the data pad. When the lieutenant did not immediately depart, the general added, "That will be all."

The general studied the data pad for a moment.

"Well?" Lord Dusahn asked as he enjoyed the morning sun.

"The Aurora departed the Rogen system twenty hours ago," the general reported. "Their departure heading was in the direction of the Pentaurus cluster."

"Then, our plan is working," Lord Dusahn commented without show of emotion.

"Possibly," the general said. "Prior to her departure, the Rogen system's readiness state was increased. She is expected to be gone for as long as four days."

"Precisely the amount of time required for a round trip to Takara." Lord Dusahn smiled. "Captain Scott is a confident young man, I'll give him that."

"It appears his gunships have departed, as well," General Hesson added.

"His gunships are of little concern. How long until our ships are in position to attack?"

"If the Aurora is *indeed* on her way here, then we already have enough ships within striking distance to destroy the Rogen system, twice over."

"Then give the order to attack, my dear general," Lord Dusahn ordered, the slightest of smiles on his lips. "It's time the entire quadrant learns the fate of those who oppose the Dusahn."

"My lord, if I may, would it not be prudent to *confirm* the Aurora's position, *prior* to launching the attack?"

"Nonsense."

"Respectfully, my lord," General Hesson pressed, "with the reinforcement fleet so close to the Rogen system, delaying the attack a mere day would not only guarantee our success, but would provide a victory so overwhelming, the Dusahn would never again be challenged."

Lord Dusahn cast a menacing gaze the general's way.

"That *is* the effect you seek, is it not?"

"Keep in mind, General, that I occasionally do not

share *all* of my plans with you," Lord Dusahn stated. "However, I shall consider your words."

"Your consideration honors me, my lord," the general said, bowing respectfully.

"I shall give you my answer within the hour," Lord Dusahn promised.

"I shall alert our forces to be ready, once word is given," the general added, withdrawing carefully. It was a delicate game that he played with the leader of his caste. One that was both necessary *and* dangerous.

CHAPTER TEN

Nathan and Jessica passed through the forward hatch to the Aurora's main hangar bay and moved briskly out across the deck, turning left toward the waiting Reaper.

"*Nash!*" a voice called from their right.

Jessica turned her head to see Lieutenant Commander Hechler and Master Sergeant Willem coming toward them, carrying gear bags. The two men doubled their pace to catch up, intercepting Nathan and Jessica halfway to Reaper Six.

"I brought your combat gear," the lieutenant commander told her. "We brought gear for you, as well," he informed Nathan. "You're about the same size as us. Might be a little snug around the middle," the lieutenant commander added in jest.

Nathan took the bag from Master Sergeant Willem. "This is the general's gear?" he asked, noticing the label on the bag.

"None of the backup gear has been equipped with personal shields yet," the master sergeant explained. "I figured the general wouldn't mind...much."

"Just be sure to clean it when you get back," the lieutenant commander joked.

"Thanks," Nathan replied. "How are we looking?" he asked the chief in charge of the Reaper's deck crew as they approached the ship.

"Double-teamed her to change her load," the chief replied. "Pretty sure we set a record."

"Good job," Nathan replied, patting the chief on the shoulder as he passed. Nathan quickly tossed his gear bag into the Reaper's open side door and jumped up inside, with Jessica doing the same immediately after.

"Bring 'em all back, Jess!" the lieutenant commander barked from outside the Reaper.

"Damn straight!" Jessica replied as she slid the door closed.

"Let's get going!" Nathan ordered to the Reaper's flight crew as he opened the general's gear bag and pulled out his combat helmet. "I hope you're going to show me how to use this stuff."

"I'll have you chewing glass and spitting shards before we get there," Jessica promised.

Nathan scowled at the expression.

"A Ghatazhak expression," she explained as she opened her own gear bag. "Doesn't translate well from Takaran; do as I do."

"*Captain, XO,*" Cameron called over comms.

"Go ahead," Nathan replied, watching Jessica and pulling out the bodysuit as she had.

"*I managed to get you four Gunyoki, and I sent a comm-drone to contact the Falcon and redirect her to Eralit Seven Delta.*"

"Good thinking," Nathan replied. "Where are we going to rendezvous?"

"*I took the liberty of making a quick mission plan and sending it to all the elements involved. Everyone should know what to do.*"

"Thanks, Cam."

"*Good luck.*"

"*We're cleared for emergency departure,*" Ensign Weston reported over Nathan's comm-set. "*Hang on.*"

Nathan and Jessica both braced themselves, knowing the Reaper's inertial dampening systems would not be active while she was still within the influence of the Aurora's artificial gravity. They both swayed to their right as the ship turned sharply from the airlock into the unpressurized starboard departure deck. Nathan turned to look between the bulkheads and out the forward windows, just as the ship began to float up off the deck. Lieutenant Haddix pushed the Reaper's throttles forward just a bit, and the ship quickly accelerated through the remainder of the open-ended compartment, shooting out into space as the bow of the Aurora quickly slid past on their port side. A split second later, the ship turned sharply and jumped.

Nathan turned back around, surprised to see Jessica already stripped down to her bra and panties.

"What are you waiting for?" she asked. "Strip."

Nathan smiled. "Yes, ma'am."

"Shouldn't you send another crew?" Tariq suggested as the eight of them moved quickly toward their waiting Gunyoki fighters.

"She said to send her four best crews," Vol replied.

"Then why are you here?" Alayna joked.

"Any idea of our mission profile?" Tham wondered.

"Not a clue," Vol replied.

"Captain Taylor sent over a loose plan," Isa said, holding up his data pad. "Nothing more than a few waypoints and alternates."

"What's the mission objective?" Gento asked.

"Fly cover for a SAR mission, rescuing the crew of the Seiiki from some moon called Eralit Seven Delta," Isa explained.

"They went down?" Alayna asked.

"Hard. Had to eject."

"Rules of engagement?" Isanu inquired.

"If they aren't ours, kill them," Vol instructed.

"Understood," Tariq replied as he and his weapons officer peeled off from the group to board their fighter.

"See you at the departure rally point," Alayna called out as she and Isanu headed for their fighter.

"Hot LZ?" Tham asked Vol as they approached their fighters.

"Unknown," Vol replied. "But if the captain is asking for cover, I'd assume so."

"Let's do it," Tham stated confidently, turning to climb aboard his fighter.

Vol looked back at the other two Gunyoki fighters. The newly remodeled ready deck was being tested for the first time, and the design seemed good. He turned and continued the last few steps to his cockpit, which was sticking up through the ready deck like all the others. He stepped over the edge and dropped into his seat, the deck chief handing him his helmet from the opposite side.

"She's good to go, sir," the chief assured him as he waited for Vol to put on his helmet, and then connected it to the Gunyoki fighter's systems. "*Good luck,*" he added over the helmet comms. The chief stepped back, and the canopy quickly closed. Two seconds later, the deck shells slid forward and covered the canopy from the outside.

"All systems show ready. All elements show ready. Cleared for combat launch," Isa reported from the back seat.

"Shenza Leader; launching," Vol announced. He pressed a button, and his ship dropped away from the underside of the ready deck. The well-lit departure corridor appeared before him, and Vol pressed the combat departure button, sending his ship barreling down the long corridor toward the opening at the far end. Five seconds later, his ship shot out the end of the departure corridor and turned toward the departure rally point.

"Shenza One, away."

Corporal Amund scanned the area from his perch atop an outcropping of rock, fifteen meters from the cave entrance. From his position, he could see all three routes up the side of the mountain. Unless the Dusahn decided to blaze their own path through the dense forest, there was no way they could approach without him knowing.

Planet rise had come sooner than he had expected. Eralit Seven's angry, amber light had come on quickly, already washing away the pale shadows from her third moon that had provided their nighttime illumination. By the time Eralit Seven's horizon spanned the entire length of the valley below, the nearest group of Dusahn soldiers had closed to within a few kilometers. They could no longer afford to wait. He only hoped that the minerals obscuring his sensors equally interfered with those of their enemy. If not, their demise would come sooner than expected.

The corporal slid down from his perch, sliding backwards on his belly, being careful not to stir up any dust that might be detected by his approaching enemy. Once down from his perch, he turned and moved quickly back into the cave.

"Time to go," he ordered, waking the others.

"What's wrong?" Loki asked, snapping awake.

"The Dusahn are approaching. The nearest party is about three to four kilometers away."

"The nearest?" Josh said, realizing the implication as he rubbed the sleep from his eyes. "There are more?"

"Two others, but they are further away and headed to either side of our position."

"Wait, you can see three or four clicks?" Josh asked in disbelief.

"The Ghatazhak have very good eyesight," the corporal replied. "I will act as a decoy and lead them away, while the rest of you continue up the mountain. Try to remain under the trees at all times and mask your trail."

"Wait, what about you?" Loki asked.

"I will be fine," the corporal assured him. "If you see a friendly ship, find a clearing big enough for them to land, and fire in the air at opposing angles so they can locate you." Without another word, the corporal disappeared out the cave's entrance.

"I think that guy is a robot, or something," Josh stated as he rose to his feet.

"Let's get going," Deliza insisted.

"After you, Princess," Josh said, gesturing for her to go ahead of him.

"How does it fit?" Jessica asked.

"A little snug in the crotch, actually," Nathan replied.

"Yeah, right."

"How do these pajamas work?" he wondered as he snapped the last of his leg armor onto the assistive undergarment.

"They sense what you're doing with your body and adjust the tension, and the direction of that tension, to help you out."

"This thin, little fabric?"

"You played hockey, right?"

"Yeah."

"Don't all hockey players wear that second-skin stuff?"

"Knees, ankles, and elbows," Nathan replied as he donned his pelvic armor. "Never hit the ice without them."

"Think of it as a high-tech version of that, then."

"So, it protects me from getting hurt?"

"Oh, it does a lot more than that," she assured him as she donned her chest and shoulder armor. "Everything you can do: run, jump, punch, kick... with that, you can do it all better. Just take it easy at first," she warned. "It takes a bit of getting used to."

"I'll try to remember that," Nathan promised as he wrapped the abdominal section around himself. "Tell me about the personal shield."

"You activate it with this button," she showed him, pointing to the button at the center of her chest. "Just remember, it's a single, flat shield that always runs parallel to your chest."

"How wide is it?" Nathan wondered.

"About a meter, so don't go flailing your arms about, or you just might end up without one of them."

"And I can shoot through it?" Nathan asked.

"Yup, but always try to poke your barrel through the shield first. Shooting from behind it tends to drain it faster."

"It drains?"

Jessica sighed. "This is going to take longer than I thought."

Josh moved quickly through the forest as he led the others up the side of the mountain. Behind him, Deliza, Naralena, and Loki were keeping up, but the pace was taking its toll on them all, including Josh.

"Didn't Amund......say to......mask our......trail?" Deliza reminded Josh, noticing that he was sticking to animal trails as much as possible.

"Our distress beacon......should have reached the Aurora......by now," Josh replied between breaths. "We need to find......a safe LZ for extract."

Two distant booms interrupted Josh, stopping him dead in his tracks, spinning around to look at the sky behind them. Seconds later, two flashes of blue-white light, just above the treetops behind them, followed a split second later by two more thunderous booms.

"That's eight in the......last five minutes," Loki said.

"Those last two......were right over......Amund," Josh noted, a concerned look on his face.

"No, Josh......just no," Loki warned.

"What?"

"I know......that look. Amund told us......to head up the mountain......for a reason. If the Dusahn's sensors aren't working......they'll start at the crash site......and work their way out......based on how fast they think......we can travel over this terrain. They won't be looking......on the other side of that ridge," Loki explained, pointing up the mountain toward the summit less than a kilometer away.

Distant energy weapons fire sounded down the mountain, in the direction from which they had come, grabbing Josh's attention.

"No," Loki reiterated, this time more sternly. "Amund knows what he is doing."

"He's sacrificing himself for us, Lok!" Josh argued.

"Maybe......maybe not. Either way......he's counting on us to get our asses......up this mountain and over to the other side."

Two more flashes of light, followed by claps of thunder.

"Those are troop pods, Loki!" Josh exclaimed. "That means there are at least twenty men on the ground......all of them hunting Amund!"

"Which he can probably handle!" Loki argued. "He's Ghatazhak, remember? Besides......if you go back to help him......all you're going to do is get him, *and* yourself, *killed*!" Loki scolded.

"Lok!"

"He's right, Josh," Deliza stated.

"Get your ass up that mountain!" Loki ordered.

Deliza stepped up and put her hand on Josh's shoulder, looking at him with pleading eyes. "You're very brave......to want to go back and help Corporal Amund," she told him softly, "but now you must be even braver......and follow his instructions."

Josh looked into Deliza's eyes for a moment, saying nothing. Finally, he turned back around and continued up the mountainside.

The amber hues cast by Eralit Seven yielded momentarily to a ghostly, blue-white flash. The corporal glanced skyward, not missing a step as he zigzagged through the dense forest, spotting yet another Dusahn troop pod descending into a hovering position in a small clearing not twenty meters ahead.

The corporal raised his assault rifle with one hand as he dodged between trees, firing three shots at the hovering pod as all four sides opened up to reveal its passengers. The first shot slammed into one of the pod's lift thrusters, causing it to fail, but the other thrusters compensated, and the pod remained level. His second shot struck one of the jump field emitters on the near side, rendering the pod unable to jump back to its mother ship and deliver another load of soldiers. His third shot struck an occupant in the neck, just as the door that protected the soldier had opened enough to reveal his upper half.

The corporal broke out into the clearing, stepping up onto a pile of rocks and firing two more times, the shots finding two of the three remaining soldiers as they jumped from the hovering pod toward the surface below. Without missing a step, the corporal bounded up the last rock and leapt into the air, slamming into the fourth soldier as he dropped to the surface. The two men tumbled through the air, intertwined, landing in the underbrush on the far side of the tiny clearing. As they landed, the corporal twisted the enemy soldier's neck in a smooth motion, using the kinetic energy of his landing, as well as the added force of his suit, to snap the man's neck.

The corporal held the man tightly, rolling over and placing the dead man's body between him and the other two soldiers who, although they had both been hit by his weapons fire, were still in the fight. Two bolts of energy slammed into the dead man's back armor, ricocheting off into the trees, setting one of them ablaze. The corporal brought his weapon over, laying it across the dead man's side, and fired two shots of his own, killing one of the two remaining soldiers.

Two more energy blasts came at him, one glancing off the corporal's right shoulder armor, the other missing him completely and slamming into the dirt well past him. The remaining soldier came charging toward him, sounding a ferocious battle cry.

Corporal Amund released the dead man and scrambled to his knees, just in time to drop his assault rifle and accept the lunging attacker with both hands. They rolled over, the corporal pulling his combat blade from its sheath on his right thigh, coming over atop the soldier and dispatching him with a blade placed neatly between the protective bands around the enemy soldier's neck.

The corporal immediately leapt from the convulsing body, withdrawing his bloody knife and replacing it in its sheath while he ran. Two steps later, he scooped his assault rifle up and disappeared into the forest once again, seeking yet another target of opportunity.

"Jump series complete," Isa announced from Shenza One's back seat. "We're at the insertion rally point on the outer edge of the Eralit system."

"Any contacts?" Vol inquired as the other three ships in his formation appeared on either side of him.

"Just Shenzas."

"Dispatch a recon drone to do a quick sweep of Eralit Seven and return," he ordered.

"Right away," Isa replied.

"*Where is everyone?*" Tariq asked over comms.

"Recon drone away," Isa reported.

"I am certain they will be here shortly," Vol assured his pilots.

"*I hate being the first one to arrive at a party,*" Alayna added.

Josh ducked instinctively as a blue-white flash appeared just above the treetops, one hundred meters ahead of them. Deafening thunder shook the mountain, and a Dusahn troop shuttle appeared, streaking directly overhead toward the valley behind them. "Damn!" he cursed. "Either they're really lucky......or their sensors are better than ours!"

Two more flashes of light appeared ahead of them and slightly to their left, revealing Dusahn troop pods just above the ridgeline. Josh paused, watching in horror as eight soldiers leapt from the hovering pods to the surface below. "This way!" he ordered, veering to the right as he continued up the mountain. "We're almost to the top!"

"Recon drone has returned," Isa announced. "Damn."

"What is it?" Vol asked, noticing the concern in his weapons officer's voice.

"Dusahn assault ship in low orbit over the estimated crash site. They're dropping troop pods and shuttles."

A jump flash appeared a few kilometers to their port side.

"Reaper," Isa reported.

"*Shenza Leader, Reaper Six,*" Lieutenant Haddix called over comms.

"Reaper Six, Shenza Leader. There is a Dusahn assault ship over the crash site. They have launched several shuttles and are dropping troop pods."

"*Shenza Leader, Scott,*" Nathan called. "*Engage the assault ship. Try to prevent them from sending any more forces to the surface. We're going in.*"

"Understood, Captain." Vol checked his displays. "Shenza Flight, Leader; sending you target data now. Split attack, left high, right low, double reverse, in ten."

Corporal Amund dove over a fallen tree as energy bolts streaked through the air all around him, their sizzling sound filling his ears. Several bolts slammed into the log as he landed on the far side, sending splintered wood flying in all directions, and lighting the massive log on fire.

The corporal came up a split second later, his helmet barely protruding above the top of the log. He brought his weapon over the burning log, laying it on its side in the flames. He opened up, firing in a non-precise sweeping motion, hoping to slow the advance of the eight men who were fewer than twenty meters behind him.

The corporal continued to fire, knowing the Dusahn would send men to either side, to encircle and trap him. After nearly a full minute of firing wildly, he stopped, poked his head up a bit more, and scanned the dense forest for signs of movement. As suspected, two men had headed to his left.

The corporal fired for another thirty seconds, then took off to his left, remaining in a crouch as he ran. He immediately drew fire from the main group, taking several shots to his thigh and pelvic armor, causing him to stumble slightly. He jumped down into a ravine and continued running, coming back up the side, ten meters further down. As he ascended into the open, he slapped the shield button on his chest, just as a barrage of weapons fire from the two men attempting to flank him came his way. His personal shield flashed red-orange with each impact. The corporal raised his weapon and opened fire, riddling the surprised soldiers with his own energy weapon, dropping them both to the ground in smoldering heaps, before disappearing off into the forest, yet again.

"Jesus! They've gotta be tracking us!" Josh exclaimed as two more troop pods appeared directly ahead of them. "Cut back!" he barked.

Another troop pod appeared in the sky just above the tree line directly behind them, cutting off their only escape route.

"Son of a bitch!" he barked, pulling his sidearm. "Take cover!" he added, opening fire on the newly arrived pod hovering behind them.

Two Gunyoki fighters suddenly appeared less than a kilometer away and slightly above the Dusahn assault ship in low orbit over Eralit Seven Delta. Both ships immediately opened fire on the unsuspecting vessel, sending a constant barrage of plasma bolts into the shields of the massive ship.

A split second later, two more Gunyoki fighters appeared on the opposite side, opening fire, as well.

The assault ship responded with point-defense cannons located all around its hull, sending angry streaks of red-orange back at the attacking fighters, causing their shields to flash, as well. Yet, the ship repeatedly launched troop pods as it continued to swat at the pests swarming about it.

Reaper Six shook violently as it jumped into Eralit Seven Delta's atmosphere.

"Oh, shit!" Lieutenant Haddix exclaimed.

Nathan immediately turned his head to look forward through the short, narrow passageway leading from the Reaper's aft utility bay to its cockpit. As he did so, their forward shields flashed red-orange, and the ship lurched to the right from weapons fire impact.

"Crash site directly under us!" Ensign Weston reported. "Combat shuttle moving into our six!"

"Any sign of our people?" Nathan asked as the ship took another hit.

"Not at the crash site!" the ensign replied. "But I'm picking up signs of firefights on the surface, just below the south ridge!"

"That's them!" Nathan replied. "Get us to them!"

"Hold on, sir!" Lieutenant Haddix replied as he yanked his flight control stick over to the right.

Jessica was already up and opening the door on her side. A rush of air filled the compartment as

Nathan dropped his helmet visor, sealing it up, and moved to the other side, opening his door, as well.

"*Your boots and gloves have mag-locks!*" Jessica told him over their helmet comms. "*The ones in your hands work automatically. To activate the ones in your boots, just think 'boots-lock'.*"

Sounds easy enough, Nathan thought as he prepared to lean out the door just as she was.

The Reaper's utility bay filled with blue-white light as they jumped from the main crash site to the south side of the valley. The side of the mountain suddenly seemed dangerously close, and Nathan's eyes widened. He grabbed the overhead rail and leaned out, his assault rifle in hand and ready to fire, as their Reaper skimmed the treetops and decelerated.

As his ship came out of its escape jump, Vol pulled it into a hard, right turn to come about. "Target those drop pods on the next pass," he instructed his weapons officer. "I'll come in from underneath and loiter as long as possible. Their point-defenses may not fire as freely in the area where they are dropping troop pods."

"Understood," Isa replied as the ship completed its turn.

Vol spun up his jump distance and pressed the jump button on his flight control stick. Eralit Seven Delta appeared in front of him, filling the entire canopy. He killed his throttle and pulled back on his flight control stick, pitching their nose upward. The Dusahn assault ship above them swung into view, as well as more than a dozen drop pods falling from her underside.

Isa used his finger to draw a circle around the group of icons on his targeting screen, and then assigned them as missile targets. "Missiles away!" he announced as he pressed the launch button.

More than a dozen tiny missiles leapt from the rectangular missile pods, slung under either side of the Gunyoki fighter, slamming into their targets a few seconds later. What were, at least, fifteen troop pods about to jump to the surface, suddenly became three.

Their fighter shook violently, their shields lighting up, as they absorbed an incoming barrage of point-defense fire from the enemy ship.

"What were you saying about them not firing as much in this area?" Isa wondered.

"Funny," Vol replied as he pressed the jump button on his flight control stick.

Josh ran across the tiny clearing and dove toward Deliza, knocking her to the ground as a red-orange energy bolt streaked over her, narrowly missing her head, and slamming into the mountainside a few meters away. "I said get to cover!" he barked as he rolled over onto his back and returned fire.

"I was trying!" Deliza insisted, scrambling on her hands and knees to get to the rocks a few meters away.

"COVER FIRE!" Josh begged.

Loki swung out from behind the thick tree trunk to the right of the boulders and opened fire. "*GO!*"

Josh rolled back over, scrambling into a low run

behind Deliza, both of them arriving at the group of rocks simultaneously.

"*JOSH!*" Loki called out as he continued firing. "*YOU GOOD?*"

"YEAH!"

"*MOVING RIGHT!*" Loki announced. "*COVER ME!*"

"GO!" Josh replied, bringing his weapon up over the rocks and firing in the direction of the incoming fire as bolts of enemy fire ricocheted off the rocks to his right.

Loki ran to his right, jumping over obstacles as he made his way to a fallen tree trunk to join Naralena, who was also firing. He fell to the ground next to her and then fired blindly several times back over the fallen log. "*THEY ARE GOING TO COME DOWN FROM THE RIDGELINE AND FLANK US!*" he yelled back to Josh.

"I FUCKING KNOW!" Josh replied. He glanced at Deliza. "Are you going to use that thing, or what, Princess?"

Deliza looked down at her sidearm, embarrassed that she hadn't thought to at least pull it from its holster. She pulled it out and swallowed hard.

"You do know how to use it, right?" Josh asked as he continued firing.

"Of course, I know how to use it!" she retorted.

"Good! Shoot that way! I'll cover our flank!"

Vol rolled out of his turn and pressed the jump button again, this time arriving behind and above the Dusahn assault ship. Before he could get his first shot off, his starboard shields lit up, and his ship slid sideways.

"Octos!" Isa warned. "Six of them to starboard!"

"*Bandits in sight!*" Tham reported. "*To your starboard, Vol! I'm on them! Break down and left!*"

Vol did as instructed, pushing his control stick forward and to the left, twisting it at the same time. The computers in his Gunyoki fighter fired the appropriate thrusters to complete the maneuver, while yawing his ship around to bring his main guns onto the flight of octo-fighters attacking him. As the enemy fighters came into sight, one of them exploded.

"*That's one!*" Tham exclaimed.

Vol pressed his firing button, sending a stream of plasma bolts from the main cannons on the front of his engine nacelles toward the attackers. Another octo fell to his fire, exploding with equal brilliance. "That's two," he proclaimed, pressing his jump button.

Energy weapons fire streaked over their heads from all directions, slamming into the trees around them and the rocks that protected Josh and Deliza, sending shards of the gray-blue rocks flying.

"They've got us surrounded!" Deliza exclaimed.

"Just keep firing!" Josh insisted as he continued firing at the Dusahn soldiers making their way down the mountainside toward them. "LOK!" he called out.

"*STILL HERE!*"

"IT DOESN'T LOOK GOOD!" Josh exclaimed.

"*IT NEVER DOES!*" Loki replied.

Reaper Six bounced violently, nearly knocking

Nathan out of the open doorway on its starboard side.

"*I can't get in there!*" Lieutenant Haddix exclaimed. "*There's too much fire coming from the ground, and we're down to forty percent on our shields!*"

Jessica opened fire from her side of the Reaper, spraying the area from where she spotted weapons fire.

"Can you take them out?" Nathan asked as he, too, fired at the surface from the starboard side.

"*All I have are forward guns,*" Ensign Weston replied. "*We're fitted for SAR, not close air support.*"

"I see them!" Jessica announced. "They're surrounded!"

The Reaper's port shields flashed, then fizzled out.

"*Port shields are down!*" Ensign Weston warned. "*Watch out, Nash!*"

Incoming fire continued to come up from the ground on their port side, barely missing Jessica as it entered the Reaper's utility bay and slammed into the overhead, sending sparks flying in all directions.

"FUCK!" Jessica exclaimed in frustration. "THEY'RE RIGHT THERE!"

Energy weapons fire continued to pound their position with increasing intensity. A bolt struck the rock directly in front of Deliza, knocking her weapon from her hand and spraying her face with tiny shards of rock and dust. She screamed in pain, falling back to the ground next to Josh.

More fire came from their rear, forcing Josh to duck down behind the rock, facing the uphill slope behind them to avoid taking hits. Explosions of rock showered them, and he instinctively found himself covering Deliza to shield her from the red-hot shards.

In all his years, Josh had never felt that he was about to die...until today. Burning bits of rock and debris singed his back. His body dripped with the kind of sweat that only fear can bring. His eyes cringed tightly as he tried to ignore the stinging pain. The time between the sound of energy weapons fire and the impact of plasma bolts against the rocks around them grew shorter. At any moment, the rocks that were protecting them would be overheated and would explode. If that didn't kill them, the following blasts certainly would.

Josh opened his eyes and found himself looking into Deliza's. *What the hell*, he decided and began kissing her passionately. To his surprise, she did not resist.

The ground shook as pale, blue-white light momentarily washed away the ambers of Eralit Seven. A split second later, there was the sound of distant weapons fire. Explosions all around them shook them both to their very souls, after which something swooped over their heads, sending dust swirling in all directions. As they were showered with hot thruster exhaust, a pair of familiar-sounding engines filled Josh's ears.

"*Seiiki! Falcon! Do you copy?*"

Josh raised himself from their embrace, looking to the sky, and spotted the Falcon's distinct, stern silhouette as it climbed toward the sky. "YES!"

"Falcon, Scott," the captain called over comms. *"How does it look?"*

Ensign Lassen looked at the sensor display. Four green triangles surrounded by at least twenty red ones, all of them close by. "Not good, sir. The Dusahn have them surrounded and outnumbered."

"Can you do anything to help them?"

"We can drop in a line buster, but it's going to be danger-close, and it's only going to help them with the bandits downhill of their position. If we try to drop on the uphill ones, it'll kill our people, as well."

"Understood," Nathan replied. *"Set up for your attack run, and I'll get back to you."*

"Copy that." Ensign Lassen and Lieutenant Teison exchanged worried glances.

"Seiiki, Seiiki. This is Scott!" Josh's comm-set squawked. The amount of energy weapons fire coming directly at their position had decreased noticeably, now that the Dusahn soldiers had something else to worry about. Unfortunately, it hadn't stopped completely, and the four of them were still pinned down and taking fire from all sides. "Is that you, Cap'n?"

"Josh, the Falcon is going to drop a line buster between you and the guys downhill of your position."

"Uh, don't you think that's cutting it a little close?" Josh replied as he fired at one of the Dusahn soldiers moving laterally, uphill of their position. Two shots streaked past him to his right, slamming into the tree next to him, cutting it in half and sending the tree falling. Josh's eyes widened. "LOOK OUT!" he yelled, diving at Deliza and knocking her out of the way. The tree landed on top of him, slamming into the rocks on either side.

"Josh!" Deliza cried, scrambling over to him, frantically digging through the broken branches until she reached him. "Are you alright?"

"Yeah, I think so," Josh replied as weapons fire continued to slam into the rocks around them.

"*Josh, it's your call,*" Nathan said over his comm-set.

"Copy, my call!" Josh replied. "LOKI! LIVE ORDNANCE COMING IN! KEEP YOUR HEAD DOWN!" Josh grabbed Deliza's hand and pulled. "Get in here," he ordered as he tapped his comm-set again. "Falcon! Seiiki! Danger-close! Drop on me!"

"*Seiiki, Falcon. Copy danger-close, drop on your position. Heads down. Drop in ten.*"

"TEN SECONDS, LOKI!" Josh yelled. He pulled Deliza in under the branches, holding her close. "I've got you, Princess," he whispered, closing his eyes tightly as he pulled her against him, and rolled slightly to put his body over hers.

"Go in from the opposite direction, just east of the Falcon's flight path," Nathan instructed Lieutenant Haddix. "They'll drop and jump, big boom, we fly through the shit cloud, and then blast the guys uphill of them. Then hover, and drop us in, so we can clean up the others." He looked at Jessica. "Sound good?"

"Sounds great." She replied. "Just remember to bend your knees when you land."

"Are you sure this suit will work?"

"I've jumped from twice the height of those trees down there," Jessica assured him.

"Five seconds!" Lieutenant Haddix warned.

The Falcon completed its one-hundred-and-eighty-degree turn and then jumped the two kilometers to the engagement area. It came out of its jump only a few meters above the ridgeline and released its ordnance a split second after jumping in. The weapon fell away, and the Falcon pitched up and jumped away in a blue-white flash.

The weapon struck the mountainside fewer than ten meters away from Josh and the others, exploding on impact, erupting into a massive fireball that swept down the mountainside, consuming everything in its path, including the Dusahn soldiers.

Lieutenant Haddix pressed his jump button and suddenly found their ship a few meters away from a fiery cloud, flying straight for it. "Hang on!" he warned, holding firm on his flight control stick.

Nathan and Jessica both swung back inside the Reaper's utility bay, putting their backs against the forward bulkhead. Fire and smoke suddenly poured into the open sides of the bay, swirling about them. Nathan could feel the intense heat, despite the fact that his Ghatazhak combat suit was doing everything it could to cool him.

The heat only lasted seconds, and then the fire departed the bay as quickly as it had come. He heard the sound of the Reaper's forward plasma cannons as they fired. He swung back out, hanging out of the side of the Reaper, looking forward as the lieutenant's plasma cannons pounded the Dusahn forces uphill of his friends.

The firing stopped, and the Reaper pitched upward sharply, its thrusters screaming as it came to a hover just above the trees.

"*Go!*" the lieutenant ordered.

Nathan glanced to his left, catching a glimpse of Jessica as she let go of the Reaper and fell. He, too, released his grip, falling toward the surface. He tucked his arms in close and kept his feet together to pass through the trees. Branches and leaves brushed at his armor, some of them slapping him hard as he fell. A split second later, he was through the dense canopy of leaves and could see the rocky ground rushing up at him. He spread his feet to shoulder-width and bent his legs, tensing up to prepare for touchdown. When he did, he could feel the assistive undergarment squeeze him, applying pressure in all the right places.

Nathan landed, tucked, and rolled to his left, and came up with his weapon ready to fire. The screech of gunfire sounded to his left.

"*Contact left,*" Jessica announced calmly over his helmet comms, reporting that she had engaged the Dusahn soldiers to the left of the Seiiki crew's position.

Nathan glanced to his right but saw nothing but smoke. Red icons suddenly appeared on his tactical visor, and Nathan took aim in their general direction. Squaring up his body to the enemy's position, he slapped the button on his chest to activate his personal shield and charged forward. Within seconds, he was taking fire, his personal shield flashing red-orange with each weapons impact. "Contact right," he reported, trying to sound just as calm.

The swirling smoke cleared, and Nathan found himself face-to-face with three Dusahn soldiers, all of them equally stunned. He barreled into the middle soldier, knocking him to the left, shooting the one to the right. He dove forward and rolled, coming up and spinning around just in time for his shield to take three more energy blasts. He dropped to one knee, fired three shots into the chest, neck, and head of the soldier to the right, then two more shots to the abdomen and chest of the guy to the left. The first one dropped immediately, but the second one managed to remain standing and brought his weapon to bear on Nathan. The soldier fired a single shot, causing Nathan's shield to flash again. Nathan also fired, this time sending half a dozen shots into his enemy. The Dusahn soldier shook violently as the impacts overloaded his combat armor and found their way into his body. The soldier fell to the right in a smoldering pile atop his dead comrade.

"*Clear left,*" Jessica reported, again calm.

Nathan looked at the three dead soldiers, then up through the swirling smoke at the treetops, some fifteen meters above him. "Shit."

"*You okay?*" Jessica asked over his helmet comms.

"Yeah, I mean, clear right," Nathan replied. "Josh! Loki!" he called, raising his assault rifle back to ready position and charging back through the smoke toward the green blips on his tactical visor. "You guys still alive?"

"*I've got Josh and Deliza,*" Jessica reported. "*They're a little crispy, but they're alive.*"

Nathan recognized the three-green blips as Jessica, Josh, and Deliza, and headed toward the remaining two blips, expecting to find Loki and Dalen. Instead, when the smoke cleared, he found Loki and Naralena.

Nathan reached out to take Naralena's hand, helping her to her feet.

Naralena glanced at him, not recognizing him at first. Then she saw Nathan's face through the combat visor. "Nathan?" She couldn't believe her eyes. "Oh, my God!" she exclaimed, throwing her arms around him.

"It's good to see you, Naralena," Nathan said. He pulled away and turned to Loki. "Are you alright?"

"I've had better days," Loki replied.

Nathan looked around, also checking his visor display. "Where's Dalen?"

"He didn't make it, Captain," Loki replied soberly. "We lost Torlak as well." He looked at Nathan. "I'm sorry."

A million images flashed through Nathan's mind. A young man looking for his first, real job as a ship's mechanic. A million jokes, the hearty laughter. The constant arguing between Dalen and Marcus about how to fix the Seiiki. The times when Dalen, Josh, and Connor had gone to bars, hitting on countless women on dozens of worlds. Meeting Dalen's aunt on Cheraming Four.

"*Four Dusahn troop pods just dropped in on the ridgeline,*" Ensign Weston called from Reaper Six, interrupting the flood of memories. "*They'll have uphill position on you in two minutes, sir.*"

"Time to go," Nathan told Loki and Naralena. "Reaper Six, can you land?"

"*Negative, sir. Not enough room,*" the ensign replied.

Nathan lifted his assault rifle. "Everyone, get

down!" he barked, then opened fire on the nearby trees, cleanly cutting through a half dozen of them, half a meter above the surface. The trees fell, slowly at first, and then accelerated toward the surface. They crashed down in near unison, swirling the smoke about on their way down. Nathan looked around. "How about now?"

"*That'll work,*" Lieutenant Haddix replied over comms, almost laughing.

"Jess! Time to go!"

"*On our way,*" she replied over comms.

"Huddle down," Nathan instructed as Reaper Six descended into a hover, half a meter above the fallen trees, their thruster wash blasting the surface and spreading out in all directions.

"*That's as close as we can get,*" Lieutenant Haddix reported over comms.

"That'll work," Nathan replied. "Just hold it steady."

"*Make it quick,*" Ensign Weston urged. "*Eight bandits are moving down the mountainside toward you. Less than a click away and moving fast.*"

"Go!" Nathan instructed Loki and Naralena. "Jess!"

"*I heard!*" she replied over comms.

Nathan looked to his left, spotting Jessica, Josh, and Deliza running through the smoke toward them.

"Nice outfit!" Josh yelled at Nathan as they approached.

"You broke my ship, Josh!" Nathan replied, smiling.

"Send the bill to Lord Dusahn!" Josh laughed.

Weapons fire came from higher up the mountainside, slamming into the fallen trees around them.

"Get them aboard!" Nathan instructed Josh as he and Jessica both turned to face the incoming fire, reactivating their personal shields as they turned. Weapons fire slammed into their shields, causing them to flash red-orange repeatedly as they both returned fire. The targets were too far away to see through the swirling smoke, but as he moved his weapon around, little red circles would appear momentarily around the red blips that indicated enemy troops. *Nice,* Nathan thought, lining up his weapon until he got one of the circles to stay on. He pressed and held his trigger, sending a stream of plasma fire at the distant target. A few seconds later, the target disappeared.

"*Scott, Falcon,*" Lieutenant Teison called over comms. "*Shenza Leader reports they have engaged Dusahn octos.*"

"Falcon, Scott. Order Shenza Flight to retreat using the evasion algorithm and get back to base."

"*Understood.*"

"*Go!*" Jessica told Nathan. "*I'll cover you!*"

"You first," Nathan insisted as he continued firing.

"*I'm going after Amund!*"

"Not without me, you're not!" Nathan replied. "Reaper Six, you've got four aboard! Rotate and pound those troops coming down the mountainside. Nash and I are going after Corporal Amund. Once you kill those bastards, circle the area and be ready to pick us up!"

"*Understood,*" Lieutenant Haddix replied.

Nathan looked up as he continued firing at the distant targets. Reaper Six yawed quickly around and opened fire, peppering the mountainside uphill from them with plasma fire.

"*Let's move!*" Jessica barked, turning to run down the mountainside in the direction of Corporal Amund.

Lieutenant Haddix ceased fire once all the red triangles, representing Dusahn soldiers, disappeared from their tactical display.

"How are you guys doing back there?" Ensign Weston yelled toward the back of the Reaper.

"*Where are Jessica and Nathan?*" Deliza yelled back.

"They went after Corporal Amund!"

"Uh-oh," the lieutenant said as he looked down out the window. A dozen flashes of blue-white light appeared above the trees, one kilometer downhill from them, in the direction of Corporal Amund.

"*What's wrong?*" Josh asked over comm-sets.

"Forty-plus men just dropped in on Amund's position."

"Captain! You've got a butt-load of troops dropping in on you!" Ensign Weston warned over comms.

"*Reaper Six! Scott!*" Nathan called over comms, energy weapons fire in the background. His voice sounded tense, his breathing heavy and labored. "*Get them back to the Aurora!*"

"We're not leaving you behind, sir!" Lieutenant Haddix argued.

"*I just gave you an order, Lieutenant!*"

"I'll be happy to face a court-martial later, Captain," the lieutenant replied. "Falcon! Reaper Six! Attack new ground targets from the north! We'll attack from the south!"

"Copy that," Ensign Lassen replied. *"Falcon is coming in from the north."*

"Heads up, Captain!" the lieutenant warned. "It's going to get interesting down there!"

Nathan and Jessica charged forward through the burning forest and the swirling smoke, incoming energy weapons fire lighting up their personal shields as they fired.

"Our shields can't take more than a few more minutes of this!" Jessica warned.

Nathan said nothing, only continued charging forward and firing at any Dusahn soldier he spotted. A green blip suddenly appeared on his tactical display. "I've got him!" Nathan announced.

"Where?" Jessica asked. *"I've got nothing!"*

"Three o'clock; twenty meters!" Nathan replied, veering right as he ran and fired. "He's surrounded."

"Combat shuttles inbound!" Ensign Weston announced from Reaper Six.

Lieutenant Teison pressed the jump button on his control stick, jumping the Falcon into position to start their attack run. His targeting screen immediately lit up with multiple targets, all of them surrounding the three green icons. "Holy shit! Riko! Can you kill those bastards without killing our people?"

"No way, Jas."

Lieutenant Haddix opened fire, sending a steady stream of plasma cannon fire into eight Dusahn troops charging toward Nathan and Jessica from the east.

"Jesus, there are too many of them!" Ensign Weston exclaimed. "They're surrounded!"

"Damn it!" the lieutenant cursed, ceasing fire for fear of shooting his own people. "Where are those fucking combat shuttles?"

"They'll be on us in thirty seconds."

Nathan and Jessica had slowed their pace, taking the time to fire more accurately as they blasted through the Dusahn line surrounding Corporal Amund.

"AMUND! NASH!" Jessica called over comms. "TWO FRIENDLIES TO THE SOUTH, COMING TO YOU!"

"*Challenge!*" the corporal barked over comms.

"Whiskey seven, echo tango one seven two five," Jessica replied.

"*Finally!*"

Jessica charged forward, Nathan following close behind. They broke through the Dusahn line and, after a few more meters, found themselves kneeling beside the corporal, firing at the thirty-some-odd enemy combatants still out there in the forest.

"*Scott! Falcon! The enemy is too close!*"

"Drop on us!" Nathan ordered as all three of them fired away relentlessly. "Drop on us, NOW!"

"*Nathan!*" Josh called over comms.

"Get them the fuck out of here, Haddix!" Nathan barked as he continued sending an endless stream of plasma bolts toward the advancing enemy.

"Ten seconds!" Ensign Weston warned.

Lieutenant Haddix stared out the window as the Falcon swooped in, fired its weapons, and then disappeared into the explosion.

"They're firing!" the ensign announced.

The Reaper's starboard shields flashed with the incoming fire, and the ship shook violently. The lieutenant glanced down at the tactical display, seeing no icons of any kind. No red triangles, no green ones. Not even one for the Falcon.

"We gotta go, Lieutenant!"

Lieutenant Haddix said nothing as he gunned his engines, pitched up, and pressed the jump button.

* * *

Cameron stood patiently as Reaper Six rolled out of the transfer airlock and into the Aurora's main hangar bay. No communications had been received from the Reaper on her approach, but they had detected significant battle damage to the ship.

The Reaper's port hatch slid open, and Josh stepped out. He turned around to help Deliza and Naralena down, then Loki hopped out to join them. The four of them walked over to Cameron, all looking considerably worse for the wear.

"Naralena," Cameron said, surprised to see her. "I wasn't expecting you. I am happy to see you, though."

"Me, too," Naralena replied somberly. "I only wish it were under better circumstances."

Cameron looked past them, noticing that Lieutenant Haddix and Ensign Weston were also climbing down out of the Reaper. She looked at Josh.

"I'm sorry, Cam," Josh replied. "We lost all three of them...even the Falcon."

"What?"

"The captain and Jess went back to try to save Corporal Amund," Loki explained. "The Falcon tried to help them, but..." Loki paused a moment. "They flew into their own ordnance detonation and didn't come back out."

"But the Falcon is here," Cameron said.

"What?" Josh said, shocked.

"She's rolling out of airlock four behind you."

Josh and the others turned around as the Falcon pulled out of airlock four and rolled into the main hangar bay. The ship was scorched, with black scarring all across her underside and extensive plasma damage to her hull from nose to tail. There were even pieces of her port wing missing.

The ship pulled to a stop, not three meters away from them, and the main weapons bay door in its belly slowly opened, allowing three Ghatazhak soldiers to fall out onto the deck below.

Cameron and the others watched as the three soldiers, all of whom had similar signs of battle damage, crawled out from under the Falcon and rose to their feet, removing their helmets.

The first helmet to come off was no surprise, as it was the smaller of the three soldiers. Jessica's long, brown hair, wet and matted as it was, fell about her scuffed body armor.

Corporal Amund's helmet was next, and he, too, looked similarly spent.

Finally, Nathan's helmet came off, and he was all smiles.

CHAPTER ELEVEN

"Jump complete," Isa announced from Shenza One's back seat. "We are in the Shinxo arrival corridor, five light hours from base."

"*It's good to be home,*" Tariq remarked over comms from Shenza Two.

"We're not home, yet," Vol reminded him.

"*Anybody know if they rescued everyone?*" Tham asked from Shenza Three.

"*I was monitoring their comms,*" Jova said from Shenza Two. "*They were boarding the Reaper when we received the order to withdraw and return, but they did not say how many survivors there were.*"

"*Well, we all made it back,*" Alayna pointed out from Shenza Four.

"Alayna," Vol scolded.

"*You know what I mean.*"

"*Eight hours of jumping, followed by eight minutes of combat, and then another eight hours to get back,*" Tariq complained. "*My ass is killing me.*"

"*Mine, too,*" Alayna agreed.

"*Seriously, Vol,*" Tham added, "*if we're going to fly such long missions, we need to get more comfortable seats.*"

"I'll see what I can do," Vol promised. "To be honest, my backside has seen better days."

"*What we need is a squadron massage therapist,*" Tariq said, half-joking.

"*Oh, I know just who we should get!*" Tham said. "*There's a place on Hino and Paramin...*"

"*KUMI!*" Gento barked.

"*That's her!*" Tham agreed.

"Gentlemen, need I remind you that there is a lady among us?" Vol scolded.

"*There is? Where?*" Tariq joked.

"*I heard that,*" Alayna warned.

"Uh, Vol?" Isa called from behind.

Vol immediately noticed the change in his weapons officer's tone of voice. "What is it?"

"I'm picking up jump flashes. One four seven by one five. Three, four, six... Six contacts, big ones......" Isa's voice suddenly became deadly serious. "Dusahn warships... Two heavy cruisers, four frigates... Shit... Eight more! All gunships! That's fourteen contacts, and they're heading straight for the core!"

"Tariq, Alayna, stealth jump ahead and alert command," Vol ordered. "Then, stealth jump back and meet us at..." Vol quickly scanned his tactical display, "tac-point Dokati Seven Five for stealth intercept."

"*Shenza Two copies,*" Tariq replied.

"*Don't start the party without us,*" Alayna added, just before both ships disappeared.

"Tham, on me," Vol instructed, turning to the tac-point.

"*No massage today, I guess,*" Tham replied, turning with him.

* * *

"This stuff is amazing," Abby said as she studied the readings on the view screen.

"How so?" her assistant, Deka, asked.

"Initial testing shows less than three percent transmission loss, and oscillations are almost undetectable, even at maximum line distances."

"So, that means?"

"I'm sorry," Abby said, feeling somewhat

embarrassed. "I keep forgetting that many of our terminologies are unfamiliar to you."

"That's alright," Deka assured her. "I'm honored to be working with the inventor of the jump drive."

"*I* didn't invent the jump drive," Abby corrected.

"You are too modest, Doctor Sorenson. You worked side by side with your father, for more than a decade, to make the jump drive a reality, did you not?"

"Yes..."

"Then, you deserve as much credit as your father does."

"*He* didn't invent it either," Abby insisted.

"All science and technology is built upon the work of those who came before us," Deka told her. "It still takes hard work to make it happen."

"I suppose you're right," Abby admitted. "I've just never been comfortable with all the notoriety. My father was the same way."

"Most true scientists are," Deka said. "They live for the discovery, not for the fame that it brings." Deka stared at the view screen. "So, what do these results mean?"

Abby smiled. "They mean we will be able to greatly increase the range *and* accuracy of the jump drive."

"That's wonderful!" Deka congratulated. "By how much?"

"Based on these initial tests, at least ten, maybe twenty times the current range. Perhaps even further, once we are able to solve the gravitational warping effects of large-scale ZPEDs."

"Didn't the Avendahl use such devices?" Deka wondered.

"Yes, but not to power their jump drives directly," Abby explained. "They used them to quickly recharge the energy banks for their jump drive, but had to take them down to almost zero output, barely enough to keep them from shutting down completely, before they could jump."

"But, there *are* ships using ZPEDs that directly feed their jump drives."

"Yes, but their output, while enough to power repeated short-range jumps, is not enough to create gravitational warping."

"Interesting..." Deka observed.

Suddenly the doors to the lab burst open, and Abby's security team charged in.

"We must go," one of the men told her.

"What is it?" Abby asked, her eyes wide.

"The Rogen system is about to be attacked, Doctor," the man explained. "We have to get you to safety."

"What about my family?" she asked as she rose to follow them out.

"They are being evacuated as we speak," the man assured her.

"Wait!" Abby objected. "My research!"

"There is no time, Doctor!" the man objected. "We must go, now!"

"NO!" Abby insisted, turning back to her terminal. "It will just take a second." She tapped several keys and watched the screen for a moment. "There; everything has been backed up to the data vault," she said, again turning to follow them out. "Let's go, Deka."

"We cannot bring her along," the man warned.

"The hell we can't," Abby argued.

"I will be fine, Doctor. I will go to the shelter with everyone else."

Abby followed the men out, looking back over her

shoulder at Deka, hoping it wouldn't be the last time she saw her.

* * *

"Two and Four are back," Isa reported from the back seat of Shenza One.

"*Miss us?*" Tariq asked.

"Terribly," Vol replied sarcastically.

"*We brought friends,*" Alayna reported.

Vol looked around as Gunyoki fighters began jumping in all around them. "How many?"

"Looks like the ready flight," Isa replied. "Eight added, twelve total."

"Welcome Gunyoki," Vol called over comms. "This is Leader. Time to defend our home."

"Transmitting intercept coordinates to all elements," Isa announced.

Vol glanced at his tactical display one last time. The data on the Dusahn ships was at least three minutes old. If they were still there, he and his fellow Gunyoki were about to challenge a vastly superior force. If they were not there, his world was already under attack.

Vol took a deep breath. "Time to go to work, people."

* * *

"How did he die?" Nathan asked Josh.

"Amund didn't tell you?"

"He lost comms just before we were picked up," Nathan explained. "Did...did he suffer?"

Josh started to tear up. "He was on the cargo deck gun, Cap'n," Josh began somberly. "We had just taken off, we didn't have enough power to jump yet...we were being chased..."

Loki noticed his friend struggling and took over for him. "We lost our aft shields."

"He died bravely and with honor," Corporal Amund assured Nathan. "I am proud to have fought by his side, just as I am proud to have fought alongside all of you," the corporal added, looking at the others.

"I'm sorry, Cap'n," Josh said, his voice wavering. "It's my fault. He was my responsibility."

Nathan stepped forward, still wearing General Telles's combat armor, and put his hands on either side of Josh's head. "You did nothing wrong, Josh," he told him, looking straight into his eyes. "You were in command. You made the decisions necessary to save as many as possible. That's all anyone can ask of you. If *anyone* is to blame, it's me. *I* should have sent him home from the start." Nathan ducked down slightly, trying to get Josh to look him in the eyes. "Let me carry this guilt, Josh."

Josh nodded, and Nathan pulled him in tight, putting his arms around him.

"He was my friend," Josh cried as he hugged his captain.

"Mine, too," Nathan whispered. "And I'll miss him greatly."

An alarm klaxon sounded, echoing through the Aurora's main hangar bay. "*General quarters, general quarters,*" Ensign deBanco called over the loudspeakers. "*All hands, man your battle stations. This is not a drill.*"

"*XO, Tactical,*" Lieutenant Commander Vidmar called over Cameron's comm-set.

"Go for XO," Cameron replied.

"*Flash traffic from Rogen Defense Command. Dusahn warships have been detected on the outer edge of the system. Gunyoki are moving to intercept.*"

"Understood," Cameron replied. "Prepare to jump back to the Rogen system. We're on our way."

"Comms, Captain," Nathan called over his comm-set. "Patch me through to Striker One."

"*Aye, sir,*" the ensign replied, "*one moment.*"

Nathan immediately began moving toward the forward exit, with Cameron and Jessica following.

"What do we do?" Josh asked, wiping his tears.

Nathan turned around and walked backwards. "Look behind you."

Josh and Loki both turned around, spotting the Sugali fighter at the back of the bay.

"That's yours now," Nathan added.

Josh wanted to smile, but he was still upset about the loss of his friend. He looked at Loki. "You game?"

Loki looked back at Josh. "Always."

"The Aurora just went to general quarters," Lieutenant Kraska reported from Striker One's right seat.

"*Striker One, Aurora,*" Ensign deBanco called over comms.

"Aurora, Striker One, Nash," Robert replied.

"*Standby for Aurora Actual, sir.*"

"Set general quarters, Sasha," Robert told his copilot.

"*Nash, Scott,*" Nathan called.

"Go ahead."

"*Dusahn warships have been spotted inside the Rogen system, and I'm pretty sure they're not looking for a liberty port.*"

"What's the plan?" Robert asked.

"*I'm sending the Strikers in first to engage them; feel them out.*"

"You think they're holding some ships back in reserve?"

"*Wouldn't you?*" Nathan replied. "*No heroics, Robert, just harass the hell out of them.*"

"We can do that," Robert replied. "Just don't wait too long."

* * *

"Jump complete," Isa reported from Shenza One's back seat. "Their shields are up, and we're being targeted."

"All known comms channels and frequencies," Vol instructed.

"You're live across the spectrum."

"Attention Dusahn vessels, this is Commander Kaguchi of the Rogen Defense Force. You are ordered to lower your shields and power down your weapons systems, and to immediately exit the Rogen system, or you will be fired upon."

"*Yeah, I'll bet they're shaking in their boots,*" Tham joked.

"They're firing," Isa warned just as the first of a series of plasma bolts lit up their forward shields.

"Leader to all Shenzas, weapons hot, maximum force, intercept pattern Shiza Two...break, break, break." On the last *break*, Vol pressed the jump button on his flight control stick, jumping ahead to less than a kilometer outside the lead cruiser's forward shields. The other three ships in his group jumped, as well, and all of them opened fire with their main plasma torpedo cannons on the front of their engine nacelles.

"Three small contacts from the lead ship," Isa reported. "All three just jumped. Same course."

"Missiles, please," Vol instructed.

"Buster pattern, launching," Isa replied.

The remainder of the missiles in both pods streaked away, their guidance systems lining them up to hit the same point on the enemy target's shields.

Vol didn't wait to see the results, immediately turning to his escape heading and executing his next jump. In the few seconds since the first shot had been fired by the lead Dusahn warship, his forward shields had already taken a dozen direct hits and had been drained by more than fifty percent. The Dusahn had no intention of playing games with them. They were here for one reason: to destroy Rakuen and Neramese.

* * *

"Shouldn't we be wearing flight suits?" Loki suggested as they climbed up into the Sugali fighter's cockpit.

"We didn't have any last time we flew this thing," Josh pointed out as he dropped down into the front seat. He looked around, refreshing his memory from his prior flight experience. "This thing is so damned cool, it hurts," he exclaimed as he fired up the ship's main reactor.

"I still think we need flight suits."

"Next flight, I promise," Josh told him. "You good?" he asked as he fired up the fighter's main propulsion.

"If you mean, am I *inside*, then yes."

"Aurora Flight..." Josh suddenly stopped. "What do we call ourselves?" he asked Loki.

"Sugali One?"

"Naw, that sucks."

"*Unit calling Aurora flight ops, repeat.*"

"Uh, this is Josh Hayes in the Sugali fighter," Josh replied. "I'm not sure what to call ourselves."

"Okay, I'm loving this," Loki remarked as he powered up his console, "Josh Hayes at a loss for words."

"No designator has been given," the flight controller stated. "Your choice."

"Hmm." Josh thought for a moment. "What do you think of Talon, Loki?"

"That was the designator used by the Corinari fighters."

"Okay, what other birds of prey can you think of?"

"Jenno bats?" Loki suggested.

"That's dumb."

"Klytes?"

"Never heard of it."

"A big ugly bird that swoops down and kills house pets on Dennimen Five."

"That's even dumber," Josh replied. "Come on, Lok, think of something flashy, something sharp."

"Sharp? Like a razor?" Loki asked.

"That's it!" Josh exclaimed. "Razor One!"

"Why One? There's only *one* of us."

"Fine, just Razor then," Josh agreed. "Flight Ops, *Razor* is ready for departure."

"*Just Razor?*" The flight controller asked.

"You see!" Josh complained. "Yes, just Razor," he told the controller.

"*Copy that.*"

"Any idea what our mission is?" Loki asked.

"I'm guessing we're going to shoot at the bad guys," Josh replied.

"Maybe we should ask?"

Josh rolled his eyes as he activated the canopy motor. "Flight, Razor. Any idea what our mission is?"

"Razor, Flight. Combat recon; you are to be the captain's eyes and ears."

"Lovely," Josh complained.

"Razor, you are cleared for transfer airlock three, with immediate launch aft," the controller instructed.

"I should have asked about our mission *before* I accepted it," Josh cursed. "Airlock three, aft departure."

"What are you complaining about?" Loki wondered. "We've got another ship, and it's a beauty."

"Yeah," Josh agreed as he watched the deck slide by through the floor view port, beneath his feet. "This thing is pretty cool. Not as cool as the Falcon, of course."

"Of course." Loki giggled to himself.

"What?" Josh asked.

"Maybe we should have called ourselves *Peeper.*"

* * *

"Jump complete," Sasha reported. "All Strikers are with us."

Robert glanced at the tactical display in the center of their console. "Fourteen enemy ships, thirty light seconds out. Leader to all Strikers, we'll jump in two clicks out and assess. The Gunyoki are probably engaged. Weapons hot, range will be fifteen hundred meters. Check your field of fire. We'll go after cruisers and leave the rest to the Gunyoki. Target the lead ship, near side, attack in order, ten-second intervals, alternating direction breaks. We'll keep pounding the same shield section until it gives. Jump in ten seconds."

Robert waited for all three confirmation indicators from the other ships, then checked the tactical screen one last time. "Here we go," he announced as he pressed the jump button.

The stars in the forward windows shifted almost imperceptibly; the main difference being that now there were continuous flashes of red-orange in the distance as the Gunyoki engaged the lead ship of the Dusahn's fleet.

"Shenzas, Striker Leader. Target the frigates. We'll handle the cruisers," Robert instructed over comms.

"We're being targeted," Sasha warned.

"By which ship?"

"Take your pick."

Robert adjusted their course slightly, turning toward the lead cruiser.

"They're firing," Sasha announced.

Robert quickly fired his topside translation thrusters, pushing his Cobra gunship downward, while adjusting his pitch to bring their nose back onto the target. Their forward shields immediately lit up, flashing red-orange as the first rounds of enemy fire slammed into them.

"Range in five," Sasha reported.

Robert waited five seconds, then pressed and held his firing button for several seconds. A series of red-orange balls of plasma leapt from under their nose, in rows of four across, firing in groups of three. By the fourth set of triplets, the temperature on his plasma torpedo cannons was approaching critical, and he ceased fire and pitched down and to port, hard, before pressing his jump button again.

Gil Roselle watched his tactical screen, holding his course directly behind Robert's gunship, waiting until it broke off and jumped away, clearing his line of fire. He pressed and held the firing button on his flight control stick, sending waves of triplets of plasma torpedoes toward the exact spot on the lead cruiser's shields that Robert had been firing at. The problem was that with all four ships coming in on the same attack path, the target did not have to adjust their defensive fire very much to acquire the next attacker. They, too, took direct hits on their forward shields, enduring more than a dozen impacts before they dove to starboard and jumped away.

"Sixteen hundred meters," Kenji reported. "Two has jumped."

"Firing," Aiden announced, holding his firing button. He brought his ventral thrusters to full power, translating the ship rapidly upward as he pitched his nose down to keep his stream of plasma torpedoes on the target point. "Damn!" he exclaimed as he pitched up and to starboard. "That's seventy-two hits!" he added as he pressed his jump button. "What kind of shields does that ship have?"

"Target's shields are at twenty percent," Sari reported. "Three has jumped."

Charnelle fired her translation thrusters, sliding upward as she slid the ship to port, trying to take a slightly different firing line, to avoid some of the incoming fire originally intended for Striker Three just before they jumped away. At best, it bought her a few seconds. By the time she adjusted pitch to bring her barrels on the target point, her shields were already being lit up. "Firing," she announced, pressing the firing button on her flight control stick.

The cockpit of the Cobra gunship was bathed in red-orange light from both their outgoing plasma torpedoes, as well as the flashing of their own shields as incoming weapons fire pounded them relentlessly. Ten seconds of exchanging weapons fire felt like a lifetime and, finally, she peeled off high left and jumped away, breathing a sigh of relief. She looked at her copilot. "Man, I really thought we were going to get the money shot," she said in frustration.

"At least Aiden didn't get it," Sari pointed out.

* * *

"Man, I love the way this ship handles," Josh exclaimed as he executed a snap roll, immediately after clearing the Aurora's aft, starboard flight deck threshold. He pulled out of the roll at a forty-five-degree angle to port, pulled up slightly on his stick to turn away from the Aurora, and pressed his jump button, instantly advancing the tiny fighter five light seconds. "You got a heading for me?"

"One moment," Loki replied. "We need to come in from a different location than the Aurora's current position." Loki studied his display, making some quick calculations. "Turn to one five seven, twenty down relative, then jump straight ahead five light years."

"One five seven," Josh replied, pulling into another left turn and pitching down. "Twenty down." He dialed up five light years, waited to come to the new course, and then pressed the jump button. The Sugali had a different take on jump drives, similar to the ones on the Contra ships they used to kidnap Maximilian Senah. All jumps over a tenth of a light year were accomplished using a series of jumps executed automatically by the jump control computers.

The Sugali fighter also didn't have actual windows. Instead, a wraparound view screen provided the same view but afforded them the protection of an actual hull, as well as the added advantage of touch-screen targeting and zoom. Even the window wrapping around the front center of the fuselage, between the twin noses of the fighter and around under the pilot's feet, was a sophisticated view screen.

A rapid series of subdued flashes of light announced the sequence of jumps, and ten seconds later, they found themselves at their next turn.

"Come about to two one five, thirty degrees up relative," Loki instructed.

"Two one five, thirty up," Josh replied, bringing the ship around and pitching up. "Jump range?"

"Two point four one five," Loki replied.

Josh adjusted his jump range as the fighter came about. "You ready?"

"No, but don't let that stop you," Loki replied.

Josh pressed the jump button on his flight control stick again. Three flashes of light, and they found themselves in the middle of the Rogen system, halfway between Neramese and Rakuen. "Whattaya see?"

"A butt-load of Gunyoki, launching from the race platform," Loki replied.

"How many of them are jump-equipped?"

"Forty, I think."

"What the hell are they thinking?" Josh wondered. "If they try to attack without jump drives, the Dusahn guns will annihilate them."

"They're defending their world with whatever

they have, Josh. Don't forget, there is strength in numbers."

"Might as well be using bows and arrows," Josh decided.

"What?"

"An old, Earth weapon, back before *anything* was invented."

"Jump flashes," Loki announced, "over Rakuen. Three contacts, a heavy cruiser and two frigates. Three more over Neramese. Same configuration. Heavy cruiser and two frigates."

"Which means they jumped in, what, two minutes ago?"

"More like two and a half," Loki corrected.

"I'm turning toward Rakuen to take a closer look," Josh decided.

"Are you sure that's a good idea, Josh?"

"Hey, the captain wants us to be his eyes and ears, right?" Josh defended as he finished his turn and pressed the jump button. Suddenly, directly ahead of him was the planet Rakuen. "I thought you said there were three ships!" Josh exclaimed as multiple threat alerts sounded.

"Four gunships and eight octos!" Loki warned. "We're being painted!"

Josh snap-rolled the Sugali fighter to the left as bolts of plasma streaked past their right side. Icons began appearing all over their window-like, wraparound view screen, marking the location of the other ships around them. The icons moved across the screens, some of them disappearing as they slid up and off the screen as they rolled. Josh pushed their nose down and fired his dorsal translation thrusters at the same time, diving toward the planet and sliding quickly below their original flight path, trying to avoid incoming fire. Their shields flashed repeatedly from incoming weapons impacts, shaking them violently. “Man, this ship may look cool, but its dampeners suck!”

Loki glanced at the big, blue planet below as explosions began dotting the surface. “They’re bombarding the surface, Josh. Head for Neramese and jump.”

“Why the hell would I do that?” Josh wondered as he turned in the direction Loki had suggested.

“Eyes and ears, remember? We need to see if Neramese is being pounded, as well.”

“I’ll give you three guesses,” Josh mumbled as he pressed the jump button.

* * *

“Captain on the bridge,” the Ghatazhak guard at the port entrance announced as Nathan and Jessica entered, still in their black combat armor. More than a few double-takes occurred. Most were accustomed to the menacing look of Ghatazhak body armor; they just weren’t expecting it on their captain.

“All stations report general quarters,” Lieutenant Commander Vidmar reported, stepping aside to make room for Jessica to take over the tactical console. “XO is in combat, chief of the boat is in damage control.”

“Don’t go anywhere,” Jessica told the lieutenant commander. “I have a feeling I’m going to need an extra set of hands for this one.”

The lieutenant commander nodded his understanding and stood to the right, making room for Jessica on the left side of the wide, standing-height tactical console.

“Jump to Rogen, plotted and locked,” Ensign Bickle reported from the navigator’s station.

"On course and speed for jump," Lieutenant Dinev reported from the helm.

"All weapons are charged and ready," Jessica announced. "Shields are up and at full power."

"Flight reports seven Reapers on the apron and ready for launch. Reaper Six will be ready in five."

"Any updates from Rogen Defense Command?" Nathan asked his communications officer.

"Nothing since the original message," the ensign replied.

Nathan turned to face forward, standing to the left of the tactical station. "Show me the Rogen system and the reported position of the Dusahn attack force."

A moment later, a map of the Rogen system appeared in the middle of the main view screen that wrapped around and over the front half of the Aurora's bridge. A cluster of red dots appeared on the outer edge of the system, and a line indicating the course of the group of ships extended across the screen to the icon representing the former Gunyoki race platform, now turned base of operations, which sat halfway between Rakuen and Neramese.

"They'll launch recon drones first," Nathan said, thinking out loud. "Probably three of them; one to each planet, and one to the Gunyoki base. From that distance, their sensor readings will be too outdated for tactical use. Once they get the updated scans, they'll jump in and start the attack."

"They'll probably attack the Gunyoki base first," Jessica opined.

"I don't think so," Nathan disagreed.

"It's the system's only defense," Jessica reminded him.

"I doubt the Dusahn see the Gunyoki as much

of a threat," Nathan explained. "If they did, they would have attacked them directly, without warning. Jumping to the outskirts and doing recon first tells me one thing. They expect to walk all over them."

"What about our fleet?" Jessica wondered.

"We moved them out of the system as soon as the Raffaelle departed," Nathan told her. "The only ships we have left in the area are the four flatbed cargo ships we equipped with plasma cannon turrets. They're on the other side of the system, directly opposite us." He turned back to the comms officer. "I assume you've alerted them?"

"Aye, sir," Ensign deBanco replied. "Per protocol."

"Sensor contact," Lieutenant Commander Kono reported from the sensor station. "Jump flash. It's Razor."

"Incoming hail from Razor," Ensign deBanco announced.

Nathan tapped his comm-set, tying it to the comms channel. "Razor, Aurora Actual, sit rep."

"*One heavy cruiser and two frigates over Rakuen,*" Loki reported. "*The same over Neramese. They've started orbital bombardment of both worlds, sir.*"

"Nothing at the Gunyoki base?" Nathan asked.

"*Negative, sir, but there were fourteen ships total at the original arrival point so, as of our departure from the system, there were still eight gunships that hadn't jumped deeper into the system, yet.*"

"What about our gunships?"

"*Strikers were attacking the lead heavy cruiser when we first jumped in. The Dusahn ships jumped in to attack Rakuen and Neramese just after we jumped into the heart of the system. I expect the Cobras followed.*"

"Jump back to the Gunyoki base and report back in two minutes," Nathan ordered.

"*Aye, sir,*" Loki acknowledged. "*Razor, out.*"

"Comms, launch a comm-drone and order our flatbed gunships to jump in to protect the Gunyoki platform. Also, send a comm-drone to Rogen Defense Command, but from the Octonai approach corridor. Tell them to order the jump-equipped Gunyoki to attack the frigates over Rakuen and Neramese, and the rest of the Gunyoki stay near their base. The Dusahn will probably attack the Gunyoki base with their gunships. If our flatbed gunships help, a few hundred Gunyoki fighters, even *without* jump drives, *should* be able to take on eight gunships."

"What about those heavy cruisers?" Jessica wondered.

"With the jump-equipped Gunyoki, the Strikers *should* be able to handle them without us," Nathan said, appearing somewhat optimistic.

Jessica didn't look as convinced.

* * *

"I can't believe we're doing this," Quarren said under his breath as the Morsiko-Tavi jumped from its position outside the Rogen system, into the distal end of the Dikona approach corridor to the Gunyoki base.

"They put guns on our deck for a reason," Captain Tobas commented.

"Easy for you to say," the XO replied. "You've seen combat."

"Jump complete," the helmsman reported.

"Oh, my God," Baen said as he gazed at the sensor display.

"Mister Kellog?" the captain called, prodding his sensor officer to report.

"Sorry, sir," Baen said. "Multiple contacts, eight Dusahn gunships are attacking the Gunyoki base. Dozens of Gunyoki are defending, and more are launching every second. Eight...make that twelve octo-fighters are attacking the Gunyoki defenders." He looked at his captain with concern. "It is too congested to jump to the transition point."

"We will approach at normal speed," the captain replied. "Mister Das, put us on station at the Dikona transition point, then spin us around to face away from the Gunyoki base. Choose a relative altitude below that of the main battle, to give our deck guns the best angle. We'll target those gunships as best we can."

"That's *inside* the battle, Captain," the helmsman warned. "And we'll have to fly straight through it to get there."

"I know, Geo," the captain replied as he punched in a comms channel. "Baltus, Tavi, take position at the Mikona transition point, and defend the Gunyoki platform."

"*Tavi, Baltus, we copy. Moving to Mikona transition,*" the captain of the Baltus replied.

"Lorino, Tavi," Captain Tobas continued. "Take position at the Okano transition point and defend the Gunyoki platform."

"*Tavi, Lorino. We will stand at Okano transition,*" the captain of the Lorino replied, sounding nervous.

"You've got this, Deta," Captain Tobas added, trying to calm the young captain's nerves. "Just keep your shields toward any attackers, and keep your guns firing. If you lose your shields, jump to safety and return once your shields are back up."

"*Yes, yes, I understand. Thank you.*"

"Gannimay, Tavi," Captain Tobas called over

comms, "take position at the Sakuma transition point and defend the Gunyoki platform."

"*Tavi, Gannimay, defend Gunyoki base from the Sakuma transition point. Good luck, Effry,*" the captain of the Gannimay replied.

"To you, as well, my friend," Captain Tobas replied. Effry glanced at his helmsman's console to his right, noticing their flight path was askew. "What are you doing, Geo?" he asked. "You are leaving the approach corridor."

"I thought we could avoid taking additional fire on the way in if we dove below the approach path, jumped forward, then translated upward toward the transition point, guns firing."

"Good thinking," the captain agreed.

* * *

"Whoa!" Josh exclaimed as they came out of the jump, only a few hundred meters from a battle between a Dusahn gunship and half a dozen Gunyoki fighters. "A little close, Lok!"

"Sorry," Loki replied. "I'm still getting used to the Sugali jump control interface. "Shit!" he suddenly exclaimed. "Break left and dive!"

Josh immediately complied, pushing his flight control stick forward and to the left as he went to full thrust.

"Gunyoki! Gunyoki! This is Razor! Do not target us! We are friendly! Check our squawk! Check our squawk!"

Josh pulled out of his dive, then turned toward another Dusahn gunship not far from them. "Guess we have to prove ourselves," he declared as he jumped forward just enough to get into weapons range. The icon on the forward window screen, around the visible enemy gunship, flashed green, and Josh opened fire with his main cannons, sending streams of bright red plasma into the shields of the target, causing them to flash repeatedly. Their own shields flashed, as well, as the Dusahn gunship returned fire, and Josh pushed the Sugali fighter into a continually-widening-corkscrew roll as he continued to pound the enemy. After several revolutions, he broke off his attack, pitching away from the target, again pushing his throttles all the way forward, glancing at his tactical display to check his jump line, and then jumped a light minute ahead to the opposite side of the target.

"That was a sweet move," Loki complimented.

"Thanks, I just thought of it. Gets a little hard to keep your guns on target after a few revolutions though."

"I can program that maneuver into the auto-flight if you want," Loki suggested.

"And take all the fun out of it?" Josh exclaimed as he brought the ship around to jump back into the fray.

"What are you doing?" Loki wondered. "We're supposed to be doing recon, remember?"

"Party pooper."

"Uh-oh," Loki said as he studied his sensor display.

"I really don't like that phrase."

"A Dusahn battleship just jumped in over Rakuen."

"And that's why I don't like *uh-oh*," Josh declared. "It never precedes *good* news, only bad."

"We'd better jump back and report this," Loki decided.

"But it hasn't been two minutes yet," Josh argued.

"I'm pretty sure the captain would want to know about this sooner, rather than later."

Josh sighed. "I hate recon."

* * *

"*I've got three octos at nine high!*" Ledge reported over comm-sets. "*They're coming across to you, Ali!*"

"*Striker Two! Break right! Break right!*" one of the Gunyoki pilots barked over comms.

"*I'm ready for them!*" Ali announced.

Striker Three's shields flashed repeatedly as energy weapons fire, from at least six different enemy targets, pounded the gunship from every angle.

"Jesus!" Aiden exclaimed as his gunship shook violently from the impacts.

"*Starboard jump field generators are showing intermittent power fluctuations,*" Chief Benetti warned.

"Shields are down to fifty percent across the board!" Kenji reported. "Get your shots off, and let's jump the fuck out of here while we still can!"

"I'm trying!" Aiden replied as he struggled to get his nose onto the Dusahn gunship, directly ahead of him. "Ash, lock that shit down, or we're done for!"

"*Three octos just jumped in directly astern!*" Sergeant Dagata reported. "*They're firing!*"

"*What the hell do you think I'm doing, Aiden!*" the engineer replied.

A Dusahn octo-fighter suddenly jumped in directly in front of him, blasting away and lighting up their forward shields. "FUCK!" Aiden exclaimed, instinctively ducking.

"Hold your course, Aiden!" Kenji urged.

"I AM!" A split second later, his targeting reticle flashed green, and Aiden pressed and held the firing button on his flight control stick. Waves of red-orange plasma torpedoes leapt out from under their bow in columns of four, streaking toward the enemy cruiser and slamming into the shields, causing them to glow brilliantly with each group of impacts. Yet, still, the cruiser's shields held. "DAMN IT!" Aiden cursed, pitching down and left to get a clear jump line.

"*They're coming over now, Ali!*" Ledge warned, the sound of his own plasma cannon nearly drowning him out.

"Wait!" Kenji warned. "You're not clear!"

"I know! I know!" Aiden replied, maneuvering back and forth until he found a clear path along which to jump. He pressed the jump button, and his threat board immediately cleared once they jumped out of the engagement area.

"*Strikers Three and Four, Striker Leader,*" Robert called over comms. "*Attack target foxtrot four. High low, opposing odd and even. Two-ship attack. One and Two will take foxtrot three. Once your target is destroyed, engage the next odd foxtrot.*"

"We're giving up on the cruisers?" Sergeant Dagata asked in disbelief.

"It's about time," Aiden stated, adjusting his course to attack the new target. "Somebody bigger than us is going to have deal with those cruisers."

* * *

"*Rakuen and Neramese are both getting pounded!*" Loki reported over the loudspeakers on the Aurora's bridge. "*Strikers are keeping up the attack, but the heavy cruisers' shield-recharge rate is keeping pace, and the frigates guarding them are making it impossible for them to stay on target for more than five seconds! Striker One ordered all Strikers to switch their attack to the frigates escorting the heavies!*"

"Understood," Nathan replied. "Razor, return to the engagement area. Continue to jump between Rakuen, Neramese, and the Gunyoki platform. Update Cam every minute, starting at Whiskey Four in three minutes, point rotation Alpha Two."

"*Three-point, quick recon, update every minute, starting with Whiskey Four in three, rotation Alpha Two,*" Loki confirmed. "*Razor, out.*"

"XO, Captain."

"*Go for XO,*" Cameron replied over comm-sets.

"Cam, we're about to jump in. Get to Reaper Six and jump to Whiskey Four. Razor will update recon data every minute, starting in three. Point rotation Alpha Two."

"*Already on my way,*" Cameron replied.

"Lieutenant Commander Vidmar," Nathan said, "take the XO's place in combat command."

"Aye, sir," the lieutenant commander replied, heading for the exit.

"As soon as Reaper Six launches, we jump," Nathan instructed his flight team.

Cameron ran toward the stair ladder at the end of the corridor. "Down ladder! Make a hole!" she barked, warning anyone on the ladder to move to the outside edge to give her room. Since most of the crew were already at their combat stations, there were only two crewmen on that particular ladder. Cameron whizzed past them both without saying a word, taking the steps in rapid-fire fashion. She reached the bottom, ran across the corridor, and darted through the starboard personnel airlock leading to the main hangar bay. After passing through it, she entered the bay only a few meters from Reaper Six, standing just inside the starboard aft transfer airlock's inner door. Its engines were already spooled up, its top and bottom beacons flashing red every second.

Without missing a step, Cameron jumped through the hatch into the main hangar bay and then sprinted across the open deck, ducking between the starboard transfer airlock's inner doors just before they closed. She could already hear the air being sucked out of the airlock as she jumped up into the Reaper's open port hatch. "Let's go!" she barked as she moved inside, and the crew chief closed the door behind her.

Cameron took her seat in the middle of the tactical bay, facing the plotting table in front of her. Two other officers were already at their workstations at the aft end of the bay, and the crew chief was moving to his seat at the front of the bay, after closing and securing the port hatch.

"*We're rolling,*" Lieutenant Haddix announced over comm-sets.

Cameron secured her restraints and spun her seat around to face forward, sliding herself up to the plotting table. She peered past the crew chief, through the narrow passageway that led to the Reaper's cockpit, looking through the front windows as the outer doors opened to reveal the aft starboard flight deck. She glanced at her watch as the Reaper pulled out of the transfer airlock and turned aft toward the open end of the flight deck. Exactly two minutes and fifteen seconds had passed since Nathan had ordered her to the Reaper. They would barely get to the first intel relay point in time.

"Reaper Six is away," Ensign deBanco announced from the Aurora's comm-station.

"Tactical, weapons free, engage targets at will. I'll call our torpedo shots," Nathan instructed.

"Aye, sir. All weapons ready," Jessica replied.

"Take us in, Lieutenant."

"Jumping to the approach-end of the Nonaka corridor," Lieutenant Dinev replied from the helm.

The subdued, blue-white jump flash washed over the Aurora's bridge. A second later, new tactical data began popping up on various display windows that floated on the main spherical view screen to the right and left of center.

"Jump complete," Ensign Bickle reported.

"Gunyoki platform directly ahead," Lieutenant Commander Kono reported from the sensor station.

"Several dozen targets to choose from," Jessica reported from the tactical station behind Nathan.

"Let's clear a path as we pass," Nathan instructed.

"Targeting gunships with plasma cannons and octos with point-defenses," Jessica reported. "Nothing larger in the immediate area."

"I'm still showing a heavy cruiser and two frigates at both Rakuen and Neramese," Lieutenant Commander Kono reported. "Multiple surface detonations on both worlds."

"Is either one getting the worst of it?" Nathan asked.

"I'd say Rakuen is getting the worst," the lieutenant commander replied. "Neramese has far more land and is more spread out, making them more difficult to target. Rakuen's floating cities are much easier to take out."

"As soon as we pass the Gunyoki platform, turn toward Rakuen and prepare to jump in just ahead of the heavy cruiser, five kilometers from the intercept point."

"Aye, sir," the helmsman acknowledged.

"Weapons range," Jessica announced. "Engaging all targets."

"Comms, warn the Gunyoki, the Aurora is plowing through."

The Aurora continued straight up, toward the underside of the Gunyoki race platform, her forward plasma cannons and point-defense turrets firing away at the enemy targets buzzing about the fighter base. One by one, Dusahn octos took multiple point-defense strikes. Those that jumped away likely survived and would return to the battle in seconds. Those that did not were quickly overcome by the incoming fire, lost their shields, and exploded.

The Aurora veered slightly to port and rolled to the left, putting her belly toward the Gunyoki base and her topside guns toward its swarm of attackers. She plowed through the ships, her shields slamming into several octo-fighters that failed to notice her approach in time, breaking them apart.

As they passed through the swarm, the Aurora's massive, topside rail guns joined in, plowing through the Dusahn gunships' inadequate shielding, which had been designed to withstand plasma and laser energy, not kinetic. Three gunships were destroyed within seconds, two more jumping away as the Aurora cleared the top of the Gunyoki base and pitched over toward Rakuen, still firing with all available weapons.

"That was for Torlak!" Jessica exclaimed with satisfaction.

"On course for intercept over Rakuen," Lieutenant Dinev reported from the helm.

"And this is for Dalen," Nathan added. "Jump."

Again, the blue-white flash washed over the bridge, and Rakuen appeared before them, filling the bottom-third of the view screen. Three tiny, black dots appeared in orbit against the white clouds and brilliant topaz oceans below.

"Lock onto the heavy and prepare to fire," Nathan ordered. "Layla?" he said, summoning the opinion of his sensor officer to his left.

"The heavy's starboard, midship shields are the lowest, at fifty percent and climbing."

"That's your target, Jess," Nathan instructed.

"Got it."

"Prepare to jump forward, one kilometer at a time," Nathan added.

"Aye, sir," Ensign Bickle acknowledged.

"Good lock!" Jessica announced.

"Full power, single round, on my command only......FIRE!"

"Firing four!" Jessica replied as four red-orange balls of highly charged plasma streaked out from under their bow.

Nathan waited two seconds, then spoke again, "Jump." The bridge flashed blue-white. "Another round......Fire!"

"Firing!"

More red-orange torpedoes streaked away.

Nathan waited again. "Jump......FIRE!"

"Firing."

"Be ready to pull up to a clear jump line after the

next round," Nathan ordered. "Jump...and...FIRE!" he barked as their next jump flash cleared.

"Firing!" Jessica replied.

"Incoming missiles!" Lieutenant Commander Kono warned.

"Turn to a clear jump line and ahead two clicks!" Nathan ordered. "Stand by, all aft tubes, full power triplets!"

"Aft tubes, aye!" Jessica replied.

Lieutenant Dinev was already pulling her flight control stick backward and to the right, flying manually just as Nathan would have.

"Clear jump line!" Lieutenant Commander Kono reported.

"Jumping," Ensign Bickle announced.

"Ready on aft tubes," Jessica reported as the jump flash washed over the bridge.

"FIRE!" Nathan ordered.

"Torpedoes away!"

"One of the frigates just exploded!" Lieutenant Commander Kono announced. "It must have been one of the Strikers!"

"What about the heavy?" Nathan asked.

"Multiple shield failures!" the lieutenant commander replied. "She's hurt, but she's still in the fight!"

"Helm, ninety to port, roll onto our port side," Nathan ordered. "Jess, rail guns on the heavy's unprotected areas."

"Ninety to port..." the lieutenant stated.

"Rail guns, aye," Jessica acknowledged.

"Rolling to port," the helmsman added.

"Flash traffic from tactical command," Ensign deBanco reported. "They're sending us targeting coordinates for jump missiles......over Neramese."

"Jess?" Nathan called.

"I'm on it," she replied. "How many are they asking for?"

"Four," the ensign replied. "All on the heavy."

"The target's shields must already be weakened," Nathan realized. "What about the frigate escorts?"

"TAC-COM reports the frigates over Neramese have already been destroyed," the ensign reported.

"What about our gunships?"

"No Strikers have been lost as of yet," Ensign deBanco assured his captain.

"Firing rail guns," Jessica reported. "Jump missiles are loaded with the targeting coordinates."

"Launch the missiles," Nathan instructed.

"Launching missiles."

"Four octos just jumped in at our three high," Lieutenant Commander Kono reported.

"Point-defenses already have them acquired," Jessica reported. "Missiles are away."

"Multiple secondaries on the heavy cruiser," Lieutenant Commander Kono reported. "She's losing main power."

"Keep pounding her," Nathan ordered sternly, the face of Dalen Voss in his mind. "Add plasma cannons."

"Adding plasma cannons," Jessica acknowledged.

The Aurora flew past the wounded Dusahn heavy cruiser, passing in the opposite direction over Rakuen. Plasma fire streaked from the Aurora's forward guns as her massive midship rail guns sent a constant barrage of exploding slugs the size of a man's torso into the target.

More secondary explosions came from all over the doomed cruiser, and within seconds, it began to break apart. First in two sections, then three, then five, and then several of the sections exploded, starting a chain reaction that quickly consumed the entire ship.

"Cruiser is destroyed!" Lieutenant Commander Kono announced.

"Switching to the other escort frigate," Jessica reported.

"Frigate is jumping!" the lieutenant commander warned.

"Not so fast, you little bastard," Jessica cursed.

"Frigate has jumped," the lieutenant commander reported.

"Damn it!" Jessica yelled, pounding her fist on her tactical console.

"Comms, any word on our missiles?"

"Negative, sir," the ensign replied.

* * *

"Heavy cruiser over Neramese has been destroyed," one of the officers in the Reaper's tactical utility bay reported. "Strikers are dealing with the frigates."

"Any word on the targets over Rakuen?" Cameron wondered.

"Not yet, sir."

"All gunships attacking the Gunyoki platform have been destroyed," the other officer announced. "Gunyoki are still dealing with the octos."

"How many Gunyoki have we lost?" Cameron wondered.

"Fifty-eight," the officer reported. "All of them without jump drives."

"Survivors?"

"Unknown."

"Dispatch a jump comm-drone to update the Aurora," Cameron ordered. "Tell them they can stay over Rakuen for the time being."

"Aye, sir."

* * *

"New message from TAC-COM," Ensign deBanco reported from the Aurora's communications station. "Heavy cruiser over Neramese has been destroyed. Strikers are dealing with the escort frigates. Gunyoki have suffered heavy losses but have destroyed all enemy gunships. They are cleaning up the last of the octo-fighters now."

"Looks like we've got the upper hand, already," Jessica surmised.

"TAC-COM is suggesting we remain over Rakuen for now."

"Send a comm-drone to TAC-COM to acknowledge, and let them know one of the frigates escaped, and its whereabouts are unknown," Nathan ordered.

"Aye, sir."

"We'll stay at general quarters until both Neramese and the Gunyoki platform are completely cleared of enemy targets," he added.

"You got it," Jessica replied.

"Did TAC-COM report losses?" Nathan asked his comms officer.

"Only that fifty-eight Gunyoki were lost," the ensign replied. "Unknown if any of their flight crews survived."

"What about our flatbed gunships?" Jessica wondered.

"Still on station around the Gunyoki base," Ensign deBanco reported.

"Those ships deserve praise," Jessica decided. "It took guts to stand their ground in converted cargo ships, and only Tobas has combat experience."

"I'll be sure to give them each a pat on the back after this is all over," Nathan agreed.

"CONTACT!" Lieutenant Commander Kono reported urgently. "Twenty jump missiles! Three seconds!"

Nathan's eyes widened. "All hands! Brace for impact!"

* * *

"Gunyoki report the base is secure," one of Cameron's officers reported.

"The second frigate over Neramese has jumped away," the other officer updated.

"That makes two frigates unaccounted for," Cameron stated.

"Strikers are asking for tasking orders," the officer added.

"Tell them to remain over Neramese for now," Cameron instructed. "Send word to Rogen Defense Command to have the jump-equipped Gunyoki start searching the system for those frigates, just in case."

* * *

"This dance is almost over," Josh declared as he turned away from Reaper Six's position, toward Rakuen, for their next recon jump.

"Thank God," Loki commented.

"To be honest, I didn't expect it to go as well as it did."

"We lost fifty-eight Gunyoki," Loki reminded him. "That's one hundred and sixteen people. I wouldn't call that 'going well'."

"You know what I mean, Loki."

"Yes, *I* know," Loki replied. "But don't expect the Gunyoki to feel the same way."

"Noted," Josh agreed. "Jumping."

The wraparound window screens blinked momentarily, and the planet appeared before them. They could barely make out the Aurora in the distance, against the brilliant topaz waters of Rakuen.

"Aurora, Razor," Loki called over comms, "anything new to report?"

Josh visually scanned the surface of Rakuen, touching the view screen in front of him with two fingers and spreading them to zoom in. "Man, some of their floating cities really got pounded," he commented, noting the fires and heavy smoke.

"Aurora, Razor," Loki repeated. "How do you copy?"

"Maybe they don't want to talk to you," Josh teased.

"I'm going to try a different channel," Loki decided. "They might have lost a comm-dish, or something."

Josh adjusted his course slightly, turning to intercept the Aurora as it grew larger in his forward window screen.

"Aurora, Razor, on one one seven. Do you read?"

Josh squinted, noticing something askew. He reached forward and touched his forward window screen, zooming in on the Aurora. "Uh-oh."

"I'm sure it's nothing," Loki said, changing frequencies again.

"Loki, look."

Loki looked up, peering over his console and Josh's left shoulder to see the forward window screen. "Oh, shit," he exclaimed, quickly looking back down at his sensor display and making some quick adjustments. "She's hurt, Josh."

"How bad?" Josh asked, his tone uncharacteristically somber.

"All her reactors are offline. Multiple hull breaches. Secondary explosions in several areas. No shields and no weapons. Shit, Josh, she's dead stick and losing altitude."

Josh immediately pulled their ship into a tight one-hundred-and-eighty-degree turn, gunning his main propulsion in the process.

"What are you doing?" Loki asked.

"Getting help," Josh replied.

"Aurora, Aurora. This is Razor. We're getting help."

A brilliant, blue-white flash suddenly whited out their window screens, lighting up the interior of their cockpit for a split second. Josh instinctively covered his eyes with both hands, lowering them again once the flash had subsided. "What the fuck..." He struggled for a moment, trying to see clearly.

"JOSH! HARD ABOUT!" Loki yelled.

Without thinking, Josh grabbed his flight control stick and throttles. He yanked the throttles to zero and spun the ship around, pushing the throttles to full power again. "What the fuck!" he barked.

"A Dusahn battleship jumped in right in front of us! We're about to collide! You've got to jump!"

"I can't!" Josh replied frantically, "Not until we change direction! We'll jump right into them!"

"Fifty meters to their shield thresholds!" Loki warned.

"Why aren't they firing at us?" Josh wondered.

"Thirty meters!"

"We're not going to make it, Lok!" Josh realized.

"TWENTY METERS!"

"SHIT!"

"TEN!"

"Sorry, buddy," Josh said as they were about to collide.

Their ship shook violently, and Josh felt himself being pushed into his seat with so much force, he thought his back would break. The wraparound window screens blinked repeatedly, then went dark. A moment later, so did everything else. Then, the shaking stopped, and everything was quiet.

Josh looked around, the only illumination coming from small, battery-powered lights in the top of the cockpit canopy, on either side of his head. "What the hell just happened?"

"I think we passed right through their shields," Loki surmised.

"Is that even possible?"

"Apparently," Loki replied as he attempted to restart their systems. "If we did, we need to get maneuvering back, quickly, or we're going to slam into their hull in less than a minute."

"Reactor is restarting," Josh commented as his reactor status screen came back to life.

"Ten seconds to engine restart," Loki added.

"Power levels are rising," Josh announced as his console flickered, coming back to life. The forward section of his window screens also snapped on. "Whoa!" Josh grabbed his flight control stick, immediately sliding it to the left, but nothing happened. The forward screen was filled with the side of a Dusahn battleship, closer than he ever wanted to see one. He tried his control stick again, but still nothing. "Come on!"

"Diverting what little power we have to maneuvering," Loki announced.

Josh pushed the stick again and got the smallest of response from his starboard translation thrusters. The view before him began to move slowly to the right, but it was still coming at him at a frightening speed. "I need more power, Loki!"

"I'm trying!"

Josh held the stick to the left and, finally, the translation thrusters began having a more noticeable effect.

"Reactor is back online," Loki announced with relief. "All systems are coming back up."

"What about weapons!" Josh barked.

"They're up! Why?"

"We're *inside* their shields, Loki. This may be our only chance to do some real damage."

"Are you nuts?"

Josh paid no attention, instead yawing his ship to the right to face the massive passing vessel. "Find me some shield emitters, Loki!"

"Hold on!" Loki replied, frantically working at his sensors.

On his forward window screen, small, red targeting brackets began appearing in regular patterns, marking the location of the battleship's shield emitters. Josh immediately opened fire, sending bolts of plasma energy into the targets, one by one. Unprotected by the very shield energy they were emitting, the result was instantaneous, and the emitters began exploding with each weapons impact.

"How do you like that!" Josh exclaimed.

"Oh, they've noticed us now," Loki warned. "They're targeting us."

"Will our jump drive work through shields?" Josh wondered.

"Let's find out, quickly!" Loki yelled.

Josh pressed his jump button, mentally cursing himself that he hadn't checked their jump line to make sure some protrusion from the massive battleship wasn't going to end their escape jump prematurely, and with tragic results. A split second later, he had his answer.

"WOO-HOO!" Josh exclaimed at the top of his lungs.

"Get us to TAC-COM!" Loki barked.

* * *

Nathan opened his eyes slowly. The first thing he noticed was the smell. Burning, acrid, metallic. It burned his nose and throat with each breath.

It was dark. He could barely see. Flashes of light, provided by shorted circuits spewing sparks, seemed to be the only source of illumination.

He quickly took a mental inventory. Head, arms, legs. Everything seemed to work. Some soreness, but nothing more. "Report!" he barked. Oddly enough, he didn't remember thinking before he spoke.

There was no response. Nathan realized he was on the floor and raised himself to his hands and knees. To his right was Lieutenant Dinev, with open, lifeless eyes, her pupils dilated and unresponsive to the intermittent flashes of light. He reached out to touch her head, but it fell to the side, limply, her neck most likely shattered.

"*Captain!*" a female voice called from behind while fizzles and pops threatened to obscure her cries.

"I'm okay!" Nathan replied.

"*Weapons and shields are down!*" the voice reported.

It was Jessica. “Are you alright?”

“I’m fine!” she replied. “My combat suit protected me.”

Nathan had forgotten he was still wearing the general’s combat gear. He struggled to his feet, using the Ghatazhak assistive undergarment to his advantage. He looked to his left, spotting Ensign Bickle’s legs, his torso smashed by a section of the overhead that had fallen. Judging by the amount of blood pooled under him, he was certain the ensign was also dead. “Kono!” he called.

“I’m here!” the lieutenant commander replied.

Nathan moved to his left, stepping over the ensign’s body and the debris that had killed him. On the other side was his sensor officer, bent over Pol Bickle’s head.

“He’s dead, sir,” she told him.

“So is Marsi,” Nathan replied. “I need you to see if you can get your sensors working, Layla. I need to know who fired those missiles,” he instructed, reaching out to help her up.

“Yes, sir,” she replied, taking his hand.

Nathan helped her up and then turned toward the back of the bridge. “Sergeant!” he barked. When there was no response, he looked to the starboard side and called out again. “Corporal!”

“Both hatches auto-sealed,” Jessica told him. “If they’re alive, they’re on the other side.”

“deBanco!”

Jessica moved to the comm-station, stepping over a fallen structural beam to make her way behind the console. She knelt down next to the ensign. “He’s alive but unconscious. He’s bleeding from the head and torso.”

“Is anyone else alive?” Nathan wondered.

"I think we're it, Nathan," Jessica replied. "At least on the bridge."

Emergency lighting suddenly snapped on, offering steady, albeit barely adequate, lighting.

Nathan tapped his comm-set. "Vlad! You still with us?"

"*Yes, Nathan!*" Vladimir replied. "*I am here!*"

"How bad?" Nathan asked.

"*Two reactors are damaged. Not badly, but more than I can fix now. I'm trying to restart reactor three now.*"

"What about propulsion and maneuvering?" Nathan asked.

"*I do not know,*" Vladimir replied. "*Once I get number three working, I will know more. Give me a few minutes.*"

"We may not have a few minutes, my friend," Nathan replied. "Whoever fired those missiles will be on us any second. Can you at least get me shields?"

"*Without any power, I can do nothing,*" Vladimir replied. "*Now please, let me work. I will give you shields as soon as I can.*"

The bridge shook.

"What was that?" Lieutenant Commander Kono wondered.

"It sounded like something struck the hull," Nathan said, "hard."

The bridge shook again, and again.

"*Bridge! Medical!*"

"Go ahead!" Nathan replied after tapping his comm-set again.

"*Med-tech Bates here, sir. There are Dusahn troops in the corridor outside of the surgical ward! They are moving forward!*"

"Lockdown procedures," Nathan ordered.

"Aye, sir!"

"Eagle Squad, Nash," Jessica called over her comm-set. "We've been boarded. Prepare to defend the bridge."

"Nash, Penwell. Hinistrosa and Hoca are trapped in the port airlock, and the doors are jammed. It's just me and Penton, and I can't raise First Platoon on comms."

"I'll try to reach them and get you some backup," Jessica promised. "Meanwhile, be ready. We have no idea how many intruders we have on board or from how many points they have entered."

"They won't get past us without a hell of a fight, sir," the corporal promised.

"I managed to get one of the forward cameras working, sir," Lieutenant Commander Kono announced.

One small section in the center of the Aurora's spherical view screen came to life, and an image appeared. Despite the distortion, Nathan had his answer. "I should have waited," he said, cursing himself.

"Is that a..."

"A fucking, Dusahn battleship," Jessica swore.

"They must've jumped in only a few light minutes out, at the most," Nathan said. "Just close enough to plot our course and launch, but far enough out to do so before being detected." Nathan shook his head. "That's exactly what I would have done."

"Why haven't they finished us off?" the lieutenant commander wondered.

"Because they want this ship," Nathan replied. "More importantly, they want me so they can publicly execute me in front of the *entire* Pentaurus sector, *after* destroying this entire system." Nathan turned around to look at Jessica. "That's the *only* thing in our favor right now."

"That's not much," Jessica remarked.

"No, but it's better than nothing," Nathan said, tapping his comm-set again. "Vlad, as soon as you get reactor three working, I need you to figure out how to force the containment fields on one and two to fail on command."

"*Are you joking?*" Vladimir replied. "*I'm surprised they haven't already failed.*"

"Good, then it should be easy."

"*TAC-COM, Razor!*" Loki called urgently over comms. "*The Aurora is dead stick! No power! No weapons! No shields! She's losing altitude, and a Dusahn battleship just jumped in only a click away from her!*"

Cameron sprang into action. "Flash traffic to all forces," she ordered. "Converge on Rakuen and defend the Aurora! Razor, Taylor! Were you able to raise anyone on board?"

"*Negative!*" Loki replied. "*But we may have found a way to get inside the battleship's shields!*"

"What?"

"*They jumped in no more than fifty meters from us,*" Loki explained. "*We tried to come about and make a run for it, but we collided with their shields, tail first! I think it had something to do with this ship's gravitational drive. When we passed through, everything shut down. We managed to get everything restarted and jump away, but Josh managed to take out quite a few emitters on the battleship's starboard side, first! If we could get back in there and do some more damage...*"

"Lieutenant Haddix," Cameron called to her pilot. "Jump us to Rakuen but stay out of range of that battleship."

"*What battleship?*" the lieutenant replied.

"Get us there now!" she ordered.

"*Razor, TAC-COM,*" Cameron replied over comms. "*We're jumping to Rakuen. Stay with us but stay out of range of their guns. You may be the Aurora's only hope.*"

"TAC-COM, Razor, understood," Loki acknowledged.

"*Now* we're having *fun*!" Josh exclaimed.

"Protect engineering, power generation, life support, and the bridge," Jessica instructed over comm-sets.

"What about Eagle Squad?" Lieutenant Brons asked as he and Master Sergeant Willem marched between the two rows of combat-ready Ghatazhak soldiers.

"Two trapped, two active," Jessica replied. "Not enough if they come in force."

"How many alive in the bridge?"

"Three active, including myself. One alive, but down."

"And the captain?"

"He's fine, thanks to the general's armor."

"Good to hear," the lieutenant replied. "Don't

worry, Lieutenant Commander. Those bastards won't take this ship while I still draw breath."

"Damn straight, Lieutenant."

"LISTEN UP!" the lieutenant barked as he reached the front of the line. "Multiple Dusahn boarding pods have pierced the hull. Unknown number of intruders, unknown number of entry points. The only confirmed sightings were in the medical section, but you can bet your ass they're busting in all over the place. They'll go for the bridge and engineering first; power gen and life support, second. Blue Squad protects the command deck. Red Squad protects engineering and power gen. Gold will be hunter-killers."

"What if they go after life support?" Sergeant Rossi asked.

"This ship has separate life support for every major compartment; the bridge included. If they *do* go after main life support, they'll be doing us a favor by making themselves easier to find and kill," the lieutenant insisted. "Rules of engagement are simple. If it carries a gun, kill it. If it looks like a threat, kill it. If you don't like the way it looks at you, fucking kill it."

"We've got a lot of non-combatants on board, Lieutenant," Sergeant Estabol warned.

"And if they've got half a brain, they'll find a place to hide and stay the fuck out of the way!" the lieutenant barked. "This is the shit, gentlemen! We are fighting for survival! OUR survival! If a few friendlies have to die to ensure our success, so fucking be it! Now MOVE!"

Without another word, thirty-nine highly trained, well-equipped, and well-armed warriors double-timed it out of their ready bay and toward the enemy, wherever they might be.

The Aurora shook repeatedly...three, four, five times, at least.

"Please tell me those aren't more boarding pods," Nathan said, pacing back and forth nervously.

"We don't even know how many one of them holds," Jessica reminded him. "What if they're like their drop pods and only carry four each. We've got more than forty fully armed Ghatazhak on board."

"I need power," Nathan complained. "I feel helpless in here, with no control over my own ship."

Several overhead lights flickered to life.

"Finally," Nathan exclaimed, moving to the helm station and pushing fallen debris out of the way. "Reactor three is up at one percent and climbing slowly. Jesus, half this panel is busted." He got up and shoved the rest of the debris forward, using the extra strength provided by the Ghatazhak suit to push it off the navigation-side of the console. "Jump drive is offline, plotting, position calc...this whole side is useless." Nathan sat back down at the helm station, checking what still worked. "I've got no flight dynamics data, no thruster status, no main propulsion control. About the only thing I *do* have is a control stick and docking thrusters, and I don't even know if the control stick works without the flight dynamics display."

"Maybe I can help," Lieutenant Commander Kono suggested. "I've got some short-range sensors. I can determine position somewhat accurately, using our accelerometers to calculate rate of motion on all axes, and extrapolate all that into course and speed data."

"Can't you just look out the window and fly it?" Jessica wondered.

"Look out the window?" Nathan asked.

"I can probably get you a few forward cameras and channel them into your heads-up screen," the lieutenant commander suggested.

"Why not the main view screen?" Nathan asked.

"It uses a lot of power, and it requires special computers to stitch the views together into a seamless, three-dimensional image," Lieutenant Commander Kono explained. "If it fluctuates or distorts, it could be misleading."

"Okay, the heads-up screen it is," Nathan agreed.

"Give me a minute," the lieutenant commander replied.

Vol's forward window was suddenly filled with a Dusahn battleship, nose-to-nose, only a few hundred meters away from the Aurora. Small, pointed, cylindrical pods were being dispatched, immediately turning toward the Aurora upon departure, from the underside of the massive black and crimson warship. "What are those?"

"Some sort of breach pods," Isa said. "I'm picking up six life signs in each of them."

Vol stared at the battle as several of the pods slammed into the hull of the Aurora, driving down so deep that barely a meter of them remained visible above her outer hull line.

"The battleship is targeting us," Isa warned. "And they're launching octos."

"Shenzas Two through Twelve, attack the breach pods," Vol ordered over comms. "Everyone else, attack either the octos or the battleship itself. Jump around like a kala bug on a hot deck, and don't let them target you for more than a few seconds!"

"*Let's do this!*" Tariq shouted.

Vol twisted his ship into a spiraling turn to port, diving toward the Aurora as point-defense fire from the enemy battleship lit up their starboard shields. Within seconds, the commander had acquired his first breach pod and blasted it out of existence with a single burst of cannon fire. "They're not shielded!" he announced with glee. "How many of them have already made it in?" he asked his weapons officer.

"I count thirteen," Isa replied. "Make that fourteen."

"That's eighty-four men. They can handle that, right?"

"They say a single Ghatazhak is equal to ten regular men in combat," Isa replied.

"Well, no more of them get aboard," Vol insisted. "Not while the Gunyoki are here!"

"Jump complete," Sasha reported.

Robert looked out the forward window of his Cobra gunship as the Gunyoki pressed their attack on the Dusahn warship and her auxiliary ships. "What the hell? Kas, what are those pointy things?"

"*Some sort of breach pods, sir,*" the sensor officer replied over comm-sets. "*Six bodies on each. The battleship is launching dozens of them, but the Gunyoki are shooting them down as fast as the Dusahn can spit 'em out.*"

"Striker Leader to all Strikers. Pound that battleship! We need to drive her away from the

Aurora! Cycle your angles, odds by evens, high to low, port to starboard! Follow me in!"

"Looks like the cavalry has arrived!" Nathan exclaimed as his heads-up tactical screen lit up, displaying a limited view forward.

"I'm picking up a lot of weapons fire!" Lieutenant Commander Kono reported. "None of it directed at us!"

"Nathan, we've still got a full charge on all four forward tubes!" Jessica reported urgently. "We can fire one round from each tube whenever we want."

"I'm afraid it won't be enough to get through their shields," Nathan said, "let alone, do any damage. Not by a long shot."

"At least we'll bloody that fucker's nose before we go down," Jessica insisted.

"Oh, I'm planning on doing a lot more than bloodying their nose," Nathan assured her.

Jessica and Lieutenant Commander Kono exchanged concerned glances, both well aware of what that meant.

Sergeant Rossi led his squad charging up the zigzagging central ramp structure that connected every deck on the Aurora. The longest run was the section that tied the lower hangar deck with the main flight operations deck. While most decks only had two switchbacks, this one had six, as it had to pass through the main fore-aft truss structure and machinery corridor running the length and width of the ship.

At each reverse of direction, the sergeant and his fire team had to stop, take up firing positions facing up the next run, and wait for the next two fire teams to pass them. The process repeated as they ascended, and with each ramp, they grew closer to the upper decks; the ones on which intruders had already been spotted.

With only one ramp left before they reached the flight operations deck, otherwise known as the main deck, they encountered their first obstacle. Energy weapons fire rained down from above, ricocheting all over the place, cutting down two of his men in the first few seconds of the engagement.

"Siewert! Haycook!" the sergeant barked, calling on two of his men carrying the most firepower.

The two men quickly joined their sergeant at the front line, tucked around the corner from the enemy firing down toward them. They raised their weapons, adjusting them slightly, and then nodded their readiness to the sergeant. The sergeant looked at the corporal next to him, and each man pulled out a small, flat, metallic disk. They activated the disks, and the sergeant nodded at the two shooters.

As the energy weapons fire continued to rain down around them, the two specialists leaned out slightly, firing four times each. Their bolts of energy ricocheted off the wall, then off the overhead, above the enemy's position, raining down and striking several of the shooters, dropping them.

The pause in the rain of enemy fire was all the sergeant and corporal needed. Both men stepped out and tossed the small, metallic disks upward. The disks stuck to the wall in line with the deck the enemy was on. The sergeant and corporal ducked back around the corner as both disks exploded, sending a wave of red-hot shrapnel spraying into the group of unwelcome visitors, cutting through their armor and their tissues underneath. The men fell, screaming in pain as their bodies burned inside their combat armor.

"Go!" Sergeant Rossi ordered, charging up the ramp. In four bounding steps, he reached the next corner and opened fire as he and his fire team charged up the last section of ramp, mowing through the remaining Dusahn soldiers on the next level.

The sergeant leapt over the fallen bodies of the enemy, immediately diving into the main corridor of the flight ops deck, tucking and rolling, coming up shooting forward down the corridor, until he reached the other side of the corridor unharmed. He held up two fingers, and the corporal, still on the previous side, tossed him two grenades, activating each as he passed them to his sergeant. The sergeant caught each grenade, immediately throwing them down the corridor, bouncing them off the opposite wall. The first one entered the corridor bouncing to starboard, while the second one was angled just enough to cause it to bounce down the corridor going to port. The grenades exploded a mere second apart, and the rest of his men charged into the corridor, the first four laying down suppression fire, while the rest of them crossed the main corridor to join the sergeant on the opposite side and head up the ramp to the command deck.

"Blue Charlie, hold this position," the sergeant ordered as he followed his men up the ramp.

"Blue Charlie One, we've got you covered, Sarge."

"Jump complete," Ensign Weston reported from the cockpit of Reaper Six.

"That does not look good," Lieutenant Haddix said, half under his breath.

"Multiple contacts," the ensign reported. "Octos, Gunyoki, Strikers, flatbed gunships, and some long, cylindrical things that I'm guessing are some sort of breach pods, since they're showing six life signs in each, and they're all diving toward the Aurora."

"How bad does she look?" Cameron asked, standing behind the ensign, peering over his shoulder at the distant battle.

"She's got power again, but not much. I'm showing one reactor is back up, but only at two percent."

"That's barely enough to run life support, let alone maneuver or raise shields," Cameron realized. "How many of those breach pods made it to the Aurora?"

"It looks like six or seven," the ensign replied. "Hard to tell without getting a look at all sides of her."

"They're trying to capture her," Cameron said as she tapped her data pad, tying her comm-set into the local combat communications channel. As soon as she did, her comm-set became alive with chatter from the Alliance forces battling to defend the Aurora. "TAC-COM to all Alliance forces," she called over her comm-set. "Do not allow anymore breach pods to reach the Aurora. Strikers and flatbed gunships, try to force that battleship away from her. Gunyoki are to engage the octos that are trying to provide cover for the breach pods."

"How many Ghatazhak are aboard?" Lieutenant Haddix asked.

"Forty," Cameron replied. "If there are six pods

on each side, that's one hundred and forty-four men they'll have to fight off."

"Can they do that?"

"I don't know," Cameron admitted. "One thing's for sure, the captain won't let them take the ship. He'll try to get close, and then blow the ship."

"He can do that?" the lieutenant said, surprised.

"*He* can't, but the cheng can. All he has to do is force one of the reactor cores to breach and let physics do the rest."

"Uh, won't that affect the planet, as well?"

"Probably," Cameron replied, unsure of her answer. "But if that battleship survives, the entire system is doomed."

"If the Aurora is lost, it's the same result," the lieutenant pointed out.

"I'm pretty sure he knows that, Lieutenant," Cameron said. After a sigh, she added, "Limited options, and none of them good."

Ghatazhak forces pressed their attack down the Aurora's main engineering corridor, exchanging heavy energy weapons fire with Dusahn boarding parties. In practiced fashion, Ghatazhak troops in full, flat-black combat armor, rotated between laying down cover fire and advancing toward the enemy position.

Unlike other parts of the ship, the corridor leading from the main junction, just aft of the flight deck to the engineering section in the back half of the ship, was considerably larger. Its vertical structural members stuck out half a meter from the corridor walls, providing excellent protection against enemy fire. Unfortunately, it provided excellent cover for the enemy, as well, and the Dusahn had the advantage. All they needed to do was slow the Ghatazhak's advance long enough for the rest of their forces to capture the Aurora's engineering and power generation sections. Once they were firmly entrenched in those sections, they would have control of all the Aurora's resources. Then, it would only be a matter of time until they had control of the entire ship.

"*They're not going to give up their ground easily,*" Corporal DaPra commented as he fired around the vertical beam at the Dusahn position, ten meters down the corridor.

"Just keep them focused on us," Sergeant Estabol told him. "Red Bravo, report!"

"*Red Bravo is engaged!*" Corporal Prater replied over the sergeant's helmet comms. "*Deck E, corridor one one eight, section fourteen! Just forward of power gen! Estimate six! Heavy guns and well shielded.*"

"Keep them busy," the sergeant ordered.

"*We'll make them hurt!*"

"Red Charlie, report!"

"*Red Charlie, in pursuit of four! Deck D! Corridor forty-two! Approaching junction seventy-five!*"

Sergeant Estabol touched the control pad on the side of his helmet, calling up the Aurora's deck plan. "Red Charlie! Right turn at junction seventy-five, then left at sixty-seven. Double-time it, and you should be able to cut them off!"

"*Right at seventy-five and left at sixty-seven!*" Corporal Robson replied.

"*Moving!*" Corporal DaPra barked.

"Go!" the sergeant replied, bringing his weapon around the vertical beam and firing over the head of the advancing corporal.

"Aurora, TAC-COM, do you copy?" Cameron repeated, her frustration growing. "Are you having any luck?" she asked the flight crew.

"*Negative,*" Ensign Weston replied. "*I've tried every channel and nothing, but we've been jumping about to stay out of weapons range, so we could have missed their reply.*"

"If their comms were working, they'd be broadcasting something. A repeated hail, a Mayday... *something,*" Cameron insisted.

"*Razor just jumped in off our starboard quarter,*" Lieutenant Haddix reported.

"*TAC-COM, Striker One!*" Robert called over comms. "*The battleship's shields are holding fast, and we're throwing everything we have at them!*"

"*TAC-COM, Razor,*" Josh called over comms. "*We can do this, Cam!*"

"Razor, TAC-COM, are you certain?"

"*Of course not!*" Josh replied. "*You got a better idea?*"

Cameron was growing more frustrated by the moment. "No," she replied, "I don't." She shook her head. "I can't believe I'm agreeing to this," she said to herself, just before keying her comm-set. "Razor, TAC-COM. You're cleared to penetrate their shields. Take out as many emitters as possible."

"*Any preference on shields?*" Loki wondered.

"Your choice," she replied. "Maybe whichever one is weakest?"

"*How about everyone else attacks whichever one is weakest, as a diversion, and we'll attack the opposite side,*" Josh suggested.

"Good idea," Cameron agreed. "I'll pass the word. Attack in two minutes."

"*Copy that.*"

"TAC-COM to all Alliance forces..." she called over comms.

"I can't believe those idiots didn't know about these tunnels," Corporal Chodan commented as all three fire teams of Gold Squad moved swiftly, but carefully, down the Aurora's machinery corridors, between decks D and E.

"With all the shit running through here, they probably didn't even detect it," Sergeant Doray surmised. "Those big yellow pipes up there are main power conduits. The EM field from those alone scrambles the hell out of sensors. That's why we can't see the enemy positions on the deck above us on our tac-visors."

"Guns, brawn, and brains," the corporal replied. "That's what wins battles."

"That's it!" the sergeant barked. "Ladder two four seven!" The sergeant ran up to the ladder and looked up, pointing his assault rifle up the tube. "This will put us aft of the Dusahn element attacking engineering." He looked at the corporal. "You first, Chodie. You've got the big gun."

Corporal Chodan smiled as he stepped up to the ladder. He pointed his large-bore assault rifle up the ladder with his right hand, and started up, using his left hand to make a one-handed climb up the ladder.

"Gold Alpha, you're the brawn," the sergeant announced, pointing up the ladder.

The three specialists slung their weapons over

their shoulders and headed up the ladder after their team leader.

The next fire team stepped up, ready to head up the ladder, as well.

Sergeant Doray held up his hand, stopping them. "Now, for the brains," he said, smiling as he headed up the ladder himself.

"We've done pulled some crazy stunts in the past, but this one has got to be the craziest," Loki commented as he calculated their intercept jump.

"Crazier than flying through a waterfall?" Josh asked.

"Yup."

"Crazier than a series jump without a canopy?"

"Yup."

"Crazier than..."

"Crazier than all of them," Loki interrupted. "Turn to two five seven, eleven down relative, and slow to seven five eight. That should give us a closure rate that is so slow, they may think we're dead."

"I can't believe we're about to jump in a meter away from a Dusahn battleship's shields...*backwards* no less, in the middle of a battle."

"I told you," Loki said. "Craziest stunt yet."

"You could be right, Lok," Josh agreed. "On two five seven by eleven down, at seven five eight." Josh twisted his flight control stick to the right, causing the Sugali fighter to yaw around one hundred and eighty degrees, so they were flying backwards.

"Ten seconds," Loki announced.

Sergeant Rossi slowed as he neared the top of the ramp, pausing to peek over the edge of the deck and down the command deck's central corridor. He could see several Dusahn soldiers running toward the Aurora's bridge and hear the sound of energy weapons fire from around the starboard corner. "Eagle Squad, Blue Leader," the sergeant called at a low volume. "Sit rep."

"*Eagle is down to two!*" Corporal Penwell reported over comms, the sound of his own weapon screeching in the background as he defended his position. "*Port airlock is jammed! Hini and Hoca are unknown status! We're engaged with eight! Maybe more! What's your position?*"

"Command deck, main ramp, full squad," Sergeant Rossi replied. "Keep them busy for a minute while we get into position to mow them down."

"*Make it quick, Sarge!*"

Sergeant Rossi looked back at his squad. "Bravo circles to port, Charlie to starboard, Alpha up the middle with me. We attack in one." He looked down the corridor again, checking to make sure it was clear, then added, "Go, go, go!"

Corporal Penwell and Specialist Penton continued firing from their position in the starboard airlock leading to the Aurora's bridge. They moved their weapons left and right with precision, trying to hold the Dusahn back while Blue Squad got into position.

A Dusahn soldier leaned out and tossed something in their direction, and Corporal Penwell cut him down with two shots to the neck and face. The object the soldier tossed bounced off the deck and over the airlock hatch threshold, into the airlock itself.

"GRENADE!" Specialist Penton yelled, scrambling to grab it as it bounced off the back wall and back toward him. He grabbed it and spun around, throwing it back toward the open hatch toward the Dusahn, but the grenade detonated before it exited the airlock.

The blast knocked both men off their feet, slamming them into the walls of the airlock, knocking them unconscious. Seconds later, the Dusahn charged forward, cutting both men down as they entered the airlock.

"What was that?" Nathan wondered, hearing the muffled explosion.

Jessica didn't respond but grabbed one of the weapons Nathan had pulled from the weapons locker in his ready room and moved around to the left side of the tactical console, opposite from the starboard entrance.

Nathan grabbed his weapon, as well, moving around to take cover on the forward side of the helm console. "Get down!" he ordered Lieutenant Commander Kono.

His warning came too late. Several Dusahn soldiers charged through the door, their guns blazing. Energy bolts ricocheted off the walls, breaking displays and damaging the main spherical view screen. One of the ricochets slammed into the lieutenant commander's chest as she scrambled for cover, twisting her around as she fell to the floor next to Ensign Bickle's body.

Nathan and Jessica both returned fire, dropping

the first three soldiers who entered. Nathan glanced at the lieutenant commander as he fired but saw by the blank stare in her eyes that she, too, was dead.

Four more men charged in, their shields flashing as they absorbed the incoming weapons fire.

Jessica charged out from around the tactical console, plowing into the first soldier, knocking him into the starboard auxiliary console. The next soldier turned his weapon toward Jessica, but Nathan's next shot slipped past the man's shield and caught the enemy soldier in the gut, doubling him over.

Jessica raised her weapon and drove its butt into the first soldier's face, breaking his nose and tearing his cheek open, sending blood squirting into the air and across the nearby console. In a smooth motion, she rolled over on the deck, drew her combat knife as she rolled, and drove it into the face of the second soldier, who was writhing in pain from his gut wound.

Nathan fired again, his blast slamming into the third soldier's shield. Jessica swept her foot, catching the third soldier's foot and sending him toppling. Nathan's next shot caught the tumbling soldier in the left shoulder after he inadvertently lowered his shield. The impact caused him to release his shield completely, and Nathan put two more shots into the man, killing him.

A series of energy weapons fire sounded from outside the bridge, and the next three soldiers attempting to enter fell forward with massive, sizzling wounds in their backs.

The weapons fire continued as Jessica scrambled to her feet and tucked in behind the edge of the starboard hatch cowling, preparing to attack the next Dusahn soldier who tried to enter.

"NASH!" Sergeant Rossi yelled from the corridor

on the far side of the starboard airlock. "ROSSI! HOLD YOUR FIRE!"

"CHALLENGE!" Jessica barked.

"WHISKEY SEVEN!" the sergeant barked, "ECHO TANGO, ONE SEVEN TWO FIVE!"

Jessica breathed a sigh of relief, her body relaxing. "GET YOUR ASS IN HERE, SERGEANT!" she ordered, moving back toward her tactical console.

Nathan moved over to check on Lieutenant Commander Kono, putting his fingers on the carotid artery on her neck.

Jessica looked in Nathan's direction as he shook his head. "Damn it!"

"Holy shit!" Sergeant Rossi exclaimed from the starboard entrance. He looked around at the damage to the bridge. "How the fuck did you two survive?"

Jessica thumped the chest of her body armor twice to answer his rhetorical question.

"Secure this deck, Sergeant," Nathan ordered as he rose and stepped over the lieutenant commander's body, moving back toward the helm.

"Aye, sir," the sergeant acknowledged. "Blue Squad! Secure the command deck! Seal all entrance points. Emergency ladder one alpha will be the only access point to this deck until further notice."

"Check flight ops for survivors," Nathan added.

"As soon as I secure this deck, sir," the sergeant replied as he headed back into the starboard airlock tunnel to direct his men.

"Now what?" Jessica wondered.

"As soon as that battleship realizes their boarding attempt failed, they're going to blast the hell out of us," Nathan replied as he sat back down at the helm. "Jesus, the helm took a direct hit. Everything is fried!" Nathan tapped his comm-set. "Vlad! You still with us?" he called. "I need some kind of forward propulsion!"

"If you can't steer, what good is propulsion?" Jessica wondered.

"They're right in front of us," Nathan replied. "All we need to do is get close, maybe even ram them."

"What the hell is it with you and ramming things?" Jessica demanded. "What, is it a man thing?"

"We'll attack their port midship shields," Robert instructed over comms. "Razor, go for the bow! Fewer guns and fewer emitters!"

"*Will do!*" Loki replied. "*Thanks!*"

"Good luck, guys," Robert added. "Strikers, Leader. Follow me in, single column, left right, high low peel off. We'll get pounded, but it'll be like dangling a piece of meat in front of an angry tiger!"

"At least we'll only have to make one pass," Sasha commented.

"Here we go!" Robert declared as he pressed his jump button. A split second later, his forward windows were filled with the black and crimson battleship. He pressed the firing button on his flight control stick, sending wave after wave of plasma torpedoes into the enemy warship's shields, causing them to flash brilliantly with each impact. A mere second after his first round of torpedoes had left their tubes, the battleship opened fire, as well, sending more than twenty streams of plasma bolts into the gunship's forward shields.

"Shields down to fifty percent!" Sasha warned as the gunship rocked from the impacts.

"Just a few more seconds," Robert mumbled to himself.

"Thirty percent!"

Robert held his course, firing away as the gunship shook violently from the incoming energy weapons fire.

"Ten percent!"

"Jumping!" Robert announced, taking his finger off the firing button, pitching up, and pressing the jump button.

Vladimir gave a mighty battle cry as he swung the heavy pry bar with all his might, striking a Dusahn soldier in the face as he came through the blasted-open hatch. The soldier directly behind the first fired his weapon, sending an energy bolt through the first guard before he fell. The energy bolt struck the pry bar, instantly superheating the metal, causing Vladimir to drop it. The burly engineer lunged at the second soldier, throwing all his body weight into the man and knocking him over.

The two men fell to the deck, rolling over, as each struggled to get the upper hand on the other. Vladimir found himself on the bottom, with the Dusahn soldier's hands on his neck. Vladimir grabbed the man's left arm with both hands, trying to wrench it from his neck. The soldier raised his right hand and punched Vladimir repeatedly in the face; once, twice, three times, before Vladimir managed to knock the enemy soldier's left hand from his neck. He twisted as the soldier lost his balance and fell forward, managing to roll over on top of the

Dusahn intruder's back, reaching around his neck to put him in a choke hold and pulling back hard.

Two more soldiers charged into the compartment, bringing their weapons to bear on the man attacking their comrade, but were cut down by energy weapons fire coming from behind.

Vladimir squeezed with all his might as weapons fire sounded from the corridor. He grunted while he pulled back on the enemy soldier's neck. The Dusahn soldier's face began to turn red as he tried to break Vladimir's hold on him. Feeling like he was slipping away, the soldier started flailing his arms about, attempting to reach Vladimir's face, his eyes, his mouth, anything he could to disrupt the attack and save himself.

But Vladimir held firm, even biting off the man's finger when he found the engineer's mouth and tried to rip open his cheek. The man tried to cry out in pain but had insufficient breath to do anything but whimper.

Four Ghatazhak charged into the compartment, ready to mow down any enemy troops inside, but all they found was the Aurora's chief engineer, choking the life out of a Dusahn soldier.

Specialist Vallo instinctively raised his weapon to end the doomed soldier's life, but Sergeant Estabol pushed the specialist's weapon down.

Vladimir let out one last cry of anger as he ended the life of his attacker. "NOT IN MY SHIP!" he yelled. The Dusahn soldier finally went limp, and Vladimir gave one last twist, snapping the man's neck, just to be sure. Finally, he pushed the limp body aside and fell back on the floor, trying to catch his breath.

"Cheng's a fucking badass," Corporal DaPra declared.

"*Bridge is secure,*" Sergeant Rossi reported over comms. "*Nash and Scott are alive.*"

"Engineering is secure," Sergeant Estabol replied, smiling as he walked over to Vladimir and offered him a hand up. "Commander."

Vladimir opened his eyes and looked at the grinning sergeant. "What are you smiling about?"

"I didn't realize you were a killer," the sergeant said.

"I used to be," Vladimir replied as he took the sergeant's hand and climbed to his feet.

"*Vlad! You still with us?*" Nathan called over Vladimir's comm-set, lying on the deck next to him. "*I need some kind of forward propulsion!*"

"*Chort!*" Vladimir cursed as he reached for his comm-set. "He's so demanding!"

The Sugali fighter jerked violently, like it had backed into something solid at a high speed. At that moment, their engines shut down, all their systems went dark, and the emergency lights in the overhead switched on.

"I guess we're in," Josh decided as he immediately activated the reactor restart cycle. "How long do we have before we collide with them?"

"Their forward shields stand about fifty meters out, and our closure rate was fifty meters per minute, so..."

"Not long, then..." Josh said. "Reactor is spinning up. Engine restart in ten."

"Weapons held their charge," Loki reported. "That's surprising."

"I'll take it." Josh checked his flight dynamics

display as it came back to life. "Reactor at ten percent. Restarting propulsion and maneuvering."

"Thirty seconds," Loki warned. "Sensors and weapons are coming back online."

"Propulsion and maneuvering are almost up."

"Fifteen seconds," Loki announced.

The window screens started flickering, coming to life a few seconds later. Josh looked back over his shoulder, spotting the massive Dusahn battleship looming behind them, twenty meters away and closing much too quickly for his taste. "Come on, baby..." Finally, his ship came back to life, and he fired his aft thrusters just enough to suspend their approach and avoid a collision. "We're in business, Lok!" he declared as he twisted his flight control stick, spinning the tiny fighter around one hundred and eighty degrees.

"Targeting all forward shield emitters!" Loki reported.

Small red squares began popping up on the window screens all around him. Josh twisted his flight control stick again, pitching slightly up, in line with the nearest target. The red square near the upper middle of his forward window screen turned green, and he pressed and released the firing button on his control stick, sending a single bolt of energy from both his left and right wingtip cannons. The bolts of plasma slammed into the unprotected emitter only ten meters away, blowing it apart. "That's one!" Josh bragged.

Loki kept his eyes on his sensor display, watching for any sign that the Dusahn battleship just outside was locking weapons onto them.

"That's two!" Josh declared as the next emitter to their left blew apart. Another emitter exploded a second later. "This is easier than Jelladar!" he giggled as he blew up another emitter.

"I used to *love* that game," Loki said, remembering the hours they used to spend on that game console back on Haven.

"How many emitters do we need to kill to take down their forward shields?" Josh wondered as he adjusted his fighter's angle and fired at the next emitter.

"At least ten, I would think," Loki replied, still watching his sensor display. "Man, they're really taking a pounding out there," he commented as he watched the Strikers and Gunyoki attack the port midship area of the enemy warship.

"That's six!" Josh exclaimed, sounding like he was having the time of his life.

"Uh-oh," Loki declared as the threat alert on his console lit up.

"No uh-ohs!" Josh barked as he shot another emitter.

"We're being targeted!" Loki warned. "From the right! Translate left! NOW, NOW, NOW!"

Josh immediately shifted the base of his flight control stick hard to the left, causing the translation thrusters on the Sugali fighter's starboard side to fire at maximum power. The fighter jerked hard to port, causing both of them to jerk to the right. Another red square turned green, and he fired, blowing it apart. "That's nine!"

"Another turret is painting us!" Loki exclaimed. "We gotta go!"

"Where?" Josh demanded as he fired at another emitter.

He never saw the tenth emitter explode.

"I've got the threat board back up!" Jessica exclaimed. "They're still out there!"

"The battleship?" Nathan asked.

"Who the fuck else?" she replied. "Oh, my God! The Sugali fighter!"

"Josh and Loki?"

"They just took a direct hit, from only thirty meters away!"

"How the hell did they get inside their shields?"

"What shields?" Jessica exclaimed gleefully. "Their forward shields are down!"

"Then, fire!" Nathan ordered.

"We're no longer pointed at them!" she replied.

"How far off are we?"

"At least ten degrees."

"Vlad! I need maneuvering now!"

"They're targeting us," Jessica warned. "Big guns! Coming around!"

"Fuck!" Josh cursed. "I've got nothing!"

"Reactor has scrammed!" Loki reported. "The core has ejected!"

"We're going down!" Josh announced. "Jesus! Twice in two days! What are the chances?"

"They blew off our entire port side!" Loki realized. "Do you have flight dynamics?"

"Yeah, but I don't know how accurate they are!" Josh replied as the window screens went black all at once. "Oh, great, and we can't even punch out!"

"I TOLD YOU WE NEEDED FLIGHT SUITS!" Loki yelled.

"Really, Lok? You enjoying being right?"

"How fast?" Loki asked.

"How fast what?" Josh replied. "How fast are we going to die? Pretty damned fast, I'd say."

"No! How fast are we losing altitude!"

Josh glanced at his flickering flight dynamics display. "Five hundred meters per second!"

"That's good!" Loki exclaimed.

"In what universe is that good?" Josh asked.

"This ship can handle that, and probably much more!"

"How would you know?" Josh demanded. "You read the fucking manual, or something?"

"Shut the fuck up, Josh!" Loki barked. "As soon as we get into thicker atmosphere, you can get us under control!"

"Nothing is working!" Josh reminded him as he moved the flight control stick around, getting no response as expected.

"This ship has direct cable backup to the aerodynamic control surfaces!" Loki explained.

"This thing has aerodynamic control surfaces?"

"No! I just made that shit up!"

"So, I can fly it, then!"

"That's what I'm trying to tell you!"

"But what good is that going to do?" Josh wondered as they continued to plummet toward Rakuen. "I'm not going to be able to land it!"

"We can eject once we get low enough, dumbass!"

"Oh, yeah!"

"That's assuming we don't burn up on the way down," Loki added.

"You had to go and ruin it for me, didn't you!" Josh exclaimed.

The ship began to shake violently.

"We've hit the atmosphere!" Loki announced.

"No shit!"

"We're heating up," Loki warned. "Eight hundred Kelvin and rising fast."

"I'm really starting to feel like I need to find a new line of work," Josh declared.

"*Now*, you come to that realization," Loki laughed. "Twenty-five hundred Kelvin. Three thousand. Thirty-five hundred. Four thou..."

Josh was already dripping with sweat and was having a hard time breathing. "Thanks......for always......being there......Loki."

"It's been......a wild......ride......Josh."

"They did it!" Ensign Weston reported urgently. "The battleship's forward shields are down!"

"TAC-COM to all Alliance forces! The target's forward shields are down! Pound them!"

"The battleship is targeting the Aurora!" the ensign added.

"Oh, my God," Cameron gasped.

"The battleship is targeting the Aurora!" the Morsiko-Tavi's sensor operator exclaimed. "They're bringing one of their big forward guns around!"

"Which one!" Captain Tobas demanded.

"The starboard gun!"

"Geo! Can you put us between the Aurora and that gun?"

"What?"

"Can you do it?" the captain demanded.

"Yes, but..."

"Do it!"

"Yes, sir," the pilot replied, still in disbelief.

Captain Tobas tapped his comm-set. "Tavi to all flatbeds! We're the biggest ships available right now! We need to jump in and block their line of fire on the Aurora!"

"That's suicide!" the Morsiko-Tavi's XO argued.

"If the Aurora dies, we all die!" the captain barked. "It's only a matter of when!" He turned to face the forward windows. "If we are to die, better to die heroes."

"Better not to die at all!" the XO argued, stepping forward to challenge his captain.

Captain Tobas swung his right arm out, backhanding the younger man with all his might, knocking him to the deck. "I'm going to pretend I didn't hear that, Quarren!" he barked, shaking a finger at the man.

"Jump plotted," the pilot reported somberly.

"Execute," Captain Tobas ordered without hesitation.

A second later, the forward windows were filled with the Dusahn battleship. Captain Tobas could see the battleship's massive starboard main cannon as it came around to point directly at them.

"Fire all guns," the captain instructed quietly.

"Firing all turrets," the weapons officer replied.

"All flatbeds have jumped in, as well," the sensor operator reported in somber tone.

"Who would ever believe that four flatbed pod haulers would save the mighty Aurora," Captain Tobas declared proudly as the battleship's massive cannon fired its first shot.

"Holy shit!" Jessica exclaimed. "Four flatbed gunships just jumped in between us and that battleship! They just blew the Tavi away!"

"VLAD!" Nathan yelled into his comm-set.

"*YOU HAVE DOCKING THRUSTERS!*" Vladimir yelled over comm-sets.

"I need more than that!" Nathan replied, jumping back into the helmsman's chair and grabbing the flight control stick.

"They just blew the Baltus away!"

"*I'm working on it!*" Vladimir replied.

"Port or starboard?" he asked Jessica.

"To starboard! To starboard!"

Nathan switched the flight control stick to docking mode, twisting to the right as hard as he could and holding it there. "COME ON!"

Sergeant Rossi came back onto the bridge, stepping up to the right of the tactical station.

"They're firing again!" Jessica announced. "The Lorino is destroyed! The Gannimay is the only one left!"

"How much further!" Nathan barked.

"Six more degrees until I can fire!" Jessica replied.

"MANEUVERING IS UP!" Vladimir reported over comm-sets. "BUT ONLY AT TEN PERCENT!"

"That'll work!" Nathan replied, hope suddenly returning to his voice.

Nathan released his hold on the flight control stick and switched it back to maneuvering mode. He gave it another twist to the right, but released it immediately, knowing that even at only ten percent power, it would be enough. "FIRE AT WILL!"

"Nathan," Vladimir called in far more subdued tones. "I can blow the ship on your command."

"Stand by," Nathan replied as he pushed the

base of the flight control stick forward and held it. The ship's aft thrusters began to burn, also at ten percent power, and the Aurora began to accelerate slowly toward the enemy warship that was about to destroy them with a single shot.

Jessica kept her eyes on her tactical display. "We're closing on them," she reported. "Four more degrees. They're charging their main starboard gun again. Two degrees......one..."

The Aurora slid slowly toward the backwards-flying Dusahn battleship, closing the gap between them. Suddenly, four plasma torpedoes leapt from the Aurora's ventral forward tubes and streaked toward the approaching battleship. The base of the great battleship's forward starboard cannon began to glow red as its plasma cell neared firing charge, but it would never complete its task. Only two seconds after they were launched, all four red-orange plasma torpedoes slammed into the black and crimson battleship's unprotected bow, tearing deep into her hull, setting off numerous secondary explosions that tore the ship apart. A brilliant, blinding flash followed as the pride of the Dusahn fleet blew completely apart, sending debris in all directions, clearing a path through which the Aurora could safely pass.

"YES!" Jessica yelled at her tactical display as the icon representing the Dusahn battleship turned into a collection of red dots spreading apart. "FUCK YOU!"

Nathan slumped back in his chair. "I need a few days off."

* * *

Two men stared out the side windows of the Rakuen hovercraft as it raced along less than twenty meters above the ocean's surface, while the third man kept his eyes glued to the sensor screen before him.

"I've got something," the man staring at the sensor screen reported. "Fifteen degrees to starboard, half a kilometer."

"I see it," the man staring out the right window announced.

"Damn, this water is warmer than you would think," Josh said as he bounced up and down, riding the rolling ocean on his seat cushion.

The sound of turbines became audible in the distance, and Loki turned his head so quickly, he almost fell off his own cushion-float. "There!" he shouted, pointing in the direction of the approaching airship.

"See, I told you they'd find us before anything big and scary ate us," Josh said, smiling.

"Yes, you did," Loki agreed. "But, can I ask you a favor?"

"You name it, buddy," Josh replied.

"When we get back, please don't tell my wife what we did."

Josh didn't reply, he just laughed.

CHAPTER TWELVE

Lord Mahtize climbed the winding staircase, his third drink of the evening in hand. The hour was late, and his family was at their country estate by the lake, for security reasons. They had begged him to join them, but he had refused. With all the recent changes in the structure of the noble houses of Takara, his attention was required here, monitoring the markets and taking advantage of every new opportunity to increase his house's wealth and status while others fell.

The disappearance of Terig Espan and his wife more than a week ago, and the sudden decrease in the number of Dusahn ships in the Takar system, had raised more questions in his mind than he could find answers. It was those unanswered questions that made sleep difficult for him these nights.

Mahtize reached the top of the stairs and headed down the lavishly decorated hallway toward the master suite. As he approached the massive double doors, he took one last sip to finish his drink, and then left it on the hallway table for one of the servants to collect. Once he passed through those doors, he expected not to be bothered. He only wished to fall into his bed and become unconscious, even if only for a few hours.

Lord Mahtize stepped into his suite, closing the door behind him, and headed for the bathroom, tossing his suit jacket on a nearby sitting chair.

"*You really should hang that up,*" a man's voice sounded from behind.

The voice was familiar, and it sent a chill down Mahtize's spine.

"Out of respect for the fabric. Garamond wrinkles quite easily."

Lord Mahtize turned around slowly, trying his best not to appear startled or intimidated in any way. As he turned, his unannounced visitor turned on the light beside him. It was the man he had suspected, sitting there in stylish Takaran business attire, looking every bit as noble as Mahtize himself, if not more so. "I suppose you've come to kill me, as well."

"If I had, I would have already done so. Besides, I have killed no one," General Telles corrected. "At least not *directly*."

"Is that supposed to comfort me, General?"

"Please, Yassey, call me Lucius."

Again, Lord Mahtize had to fight to control his reaction. The last thing he wanted was for his enemy to sense his fear.

"Do you ever make appointments?" Lord Mahtize wondered as he picked up his suit jacket and walked over to the closet.

"As I said at our last meeting, I prefer no record of my visits," the general replied. "Besides, I think this method has more impact, wouldn't you agree?"

Lord Mahtize opened his closet door and stepped inside to hang up his jacket.

"Do not bother looking for your weapon," General Telles said. "I have it."

"You are thorough."

"It is the nature of my training," the general replied. "We need to talk, Yassey."

"You framed them all, did you not?" Mahtize accused as he came back into the bedroom and walked over to the chair next to General Telles.

"I did what was necessary for the protection of Takara," the general explained. "I told no lies, I breached no laws. I simply made the Dusahn aware of *all* the dealings of certain nobles. Distasteful though it was, it was *necessary* for the protection of Takara."

"The protection of Takara? Takara is better off now than it was before the Dusahn arrived."

"Is it better off than it was under the leadership of Casimir?" General Telles wondered.

"So, *that* is what this is about. You seek vengeance."

"Vengeance is for the weak. I seek *justice*. Nothing more; nothing less."

"Justice is subjective, my friend," Mahtize said, taking his seat.

"Not if you follow the letter of Takaran law," General Telles corrected.

Lord Mahtize smiled. "Many would consider *that* to be open to interpretation, as well."

"I am not one of them."

Lord Mahtize sighed. "What is it you wish to speak with me about, Lucius?"

"The time has come for you to make a choice, Yassey. Or do you prefer Mikal?"

"If you insist on familiarity, my *name* is Alejandro."

"Very well, Alejandro," the general agreed.

"What is this choice that I must make?" Alejandro wondered.

General Telles took a deep breath. "As I see it, you have two options."

"And they are?"

"Option number one, you serve the Karuzari as an intelligence asset on Takara. Not only will this help the people of Takara, but it will allow your house to become wealthy beyond imagination."

"I have a pretty big imagination," Alejandro chuckled. "And my second option?"

"I turn over everything I have on you. Your personal

files, your association with Suvan Navarro and his attempt to steal the Teyentah, Aronis Burklund, the hotel Entorio in Siskeena...everything. I am certain the Dusahn will find it all quite interesting."

"I understand that you despise me for my support of the assassination of Casimir Ta'Akar, but are you willing to condemn my wife, my children, my grandchildren..."

"It is not I who placed them in jeopardy," General Telles stated.

"Yet, you would throw them to the wolves?"

"If you mean, would I condemn them to a life of having to work like everyone else in order to survive, then yes, and without compunction."

Lord Mahtize leaned back in his chair, deep in thought. "Why me?"

"Of all the nobles who supported Casimir's assassination, you are the one best suited for the task," General Telles explained. "Your corporate holdings are the most diversified, and therefore offer the greatest number of intelligence sources. Also, due to recent executions, your house has become considerably wealthier *and* more powerful."

"So, I have more to lose."

"Precisely."

"Then, should that not be a reason to refuse your offer and tell the Dusahn of your visit? Who knows, I might even be able to convince them that I was attempting to use young mister Espan as a source of intelligence to *help* them."

"You're right; you do have a big imagination."

"I am also the *last* of them, aren't I?"

"As of today's execution, yes," General Telles confirmed.

"Why all this subterfuge?" Lord Mahtize wondered.

"I thought the Ghatazhak were trained killers, yet you have gone to great lengths to *avoid* killing."

"A promise to a friend," the general replied. "Believe me, I would have preferred dispatching them directly."

"How do I know that you will not kill *me*, directly *or* indirectly, once I am no longer of use to you?"

"There are times when the taking of life is needed, and there are times when choosing *not* to take a life, even though the individual deserves to have it taken from them, is the wiser course of action. Ensure that yours is always the latter, and you will have nothing to fear from me."

Lord Mahtize looked at the general. "Did you make the same offer to Weller? To Mendoza? To Constorta?"

"You are the only conspirator in the assassination of Casimir who has been offered this dispensation," the general replied. "If you do not agree, your family will come home to the gruesome suicide of their patriarch."

"I thought you made a promise to a friend not to kill," Lord Mahtize reminded him.

"I believe he would forgive me in this instance."

"And what if I agree to this now, and then betray you later?" Lord Mahtize asked.

"That, too, would be unwise," General Telles warned with steely eyes. "Your security forces cannot protect you, and neither can the Dusahn," he added as he rose from his seat and headed for the door. Upon reaching it, he turned to face Lord Mahtize. "You cannot outthink me, and you certainly cannot outfight me, for I am Ghatazhak. More importantly, I am Karuzari; therefore, I *am* justice."

Thank you for reading this story.
(*A review would be greatly appreciated!*)

COMING SOON

Episode 10
of
The Frontiers Saga:
Rogue Castes

Visit us online at
frontierssaga.com
or on Facebook

Want to be notified when
new episodes are published?
Want access to additional scenes and more?
Join our mailing list!

frontierssaga.com/mailinglist/

Made in the USA
Columbia, SC
11 December 2021

50969506R00250